A Corfu Love Affair

Matt Wells

Introduction.

It was one of those typically British mornings, cold, damp, dreary and uninspiring. And as I looked out through my living room window and across the soggy village green, nothing made any sense to me any more and I kept thinking to myself, how did it all go so wrong?

"Oh, by the way, I'm Max and I share my entire life with my childhood sweetheart, the love of my life and my true soulmate of fifteen years and her name is Kathy, or Kat if you get to know her well enough."

Let me explain…

(Contains occasional and mildly strong language, some sexual references and topics which some readers may find sensitive or upsetting. This edition is the author's edit and

A Corfu Love Affair by Matt Wells ~ May 2025.

Chapter 1 ~ In The Beginning, There Was Adam And Eve.

Max had everything he ever wanted from life. A house he owned in a quiet village, purchased with a little help from some family inheritance. The girl of his dreams living under the same roof, his childhood sweetheart: that's Kathy by the way. Having done his fair share of the stressful graft over the years, he was now happy to live a simple and stress free life, where free time and exciting travel were the main priorities of being alive. Max now worked part time as a delivery driver, only twenty hours per week but even that was too much for Max sometimes, okay, all of the time. He was done with work and loved traveling and exploring, more so than any job which could deliver similar rewards or satisfaction.

Kathy, or Kat as she was known to the inner circle, loved Max with all her heart and that love grew from what was nothing more than a childhood friendship, when they were both in their early teens. The two of them, falling in and out of love almost every other day, as young teens do. Promising each other to never fall in love with anyone else ever again but falling again the day after the promise was made. Kat worked in advertising and still had a point to prove. She was ambitious and wanted to be the best in her field and she was also what a builder would describe as a stunner. Tall, slim, elegant and that annoying person who could look amazing in a potato sack and welly boots.

Max and Kat officially became an item when they had both just turned fifteen and so far, their fifteen year journey together was almost script perfect. They would kiss and cuddle behind people's backs but before too long, they would display their love for each other like mating peacocks. Together, they were sweet harmony in motion, solid and reliable and together, offering a glimmer of hope and positivity amidst a world of chaos, conflict and uncertainty. Max would often quote philosophically, "If only everyone was like us Kat, the world would be a beautiful place to live," and Kat would engage and respond by comparing them to Adam and Eve. Kat was also quick to remind Max that not everyone was like them and most people never would be just like them.

Max had just celebrated his thirtieth birthday, if you can call a Max style celebration anything which remotely resembles some sort of celebration and Kat would celebrate the same milestone in a couple of months time. Max had a strong opinion on birthday celebrations, stating, "Why would anybody choose to celebrate getting older? It makes no sense!" And I guess he was right to a degree but many would choose to challenge him on his philosophy on life and death. Max thought that people should be celebrated for becoming wiser as they got older and not just for getting one year nearer to the big ending and as most of the people who Max knew failed to get any wiser as they got older, he stood his ground and would wear his opinion like a badge of honor.

Kathy's thirtieth birthday celebration was, however, a whole different kettle of fish. Friends, family and work colleagues all descended on one of York's finest restaurants. The sort of place where the price of a starter, main course, desert and a bottle of wine could instead and easily buy return flights from the UK to somewhere warm, sunny and interesting, and back with change to spare. Kathy's work colleagues were mostly from Leeds and York but a couple had travelled up from London, which is where the advertising agency which Kathy worked for had their Flagship Office, a swanky looking premises just off Paternoster Square, all glass and immaculately polished chrome. Regardless of where her colleagues hung out, they all appeared to be cut from the same piece of cloth. A very expensive piece of cloth with perfectly ironed creases and immaculately stitched seams.

As hangovers go, the hangovers which both Max and Kat nursed the morning after her birthday celebrations were both pretty historic. Too much wine, not enough food to soak up the wine and too many smart people trying to impress the crowd by constantly getting the drinks in. Max was never one to turn down a free glass or bottle of wine but was equally happy with a few drinks at home in front of the fire. Max was literally hanging that morning but he genuinely thought that Kat still managed to look beautiful, despite the celebratory war wounds. Still in bed, Kat whispered to Max, "Maxi, look at the state of us, do you still love me and fancy me, even when I look tired and worse for wear?"
"Of course I do!" Max replied, "I always will, we're Adam and Eve, right?"

Another Monday morning very quickly arrived and as Max figured out how to constructively use his free time, Kat was

4

busy digesting her tiny breakfast and an email from Fabio. That's her boss and he spends most of his time at the London office. Fabio wanted Kat to base herself from there two or three times a week. They had just signed up a new client, a Property Developer called Grant Fisher, who had big plans for London and all the abandoned and empty buildings. He had a vision to provide affordable housing for the masses without building any new homes. Instead, he would convert old Victorian buildings into smart and trendy but also affordable dwellings for those who earned 200k plus a year and wanted to create a future for themselves in the capital city. He was clearly a visionary but clearly needed a wingman or a strong and ambitious advertising executive to help him create and then sell his dream. Max spent his day sorting out stuff which didn't really need sorting out and then planned another adventure overseas. Kat spent her day charming business owners and decision makers out of money they couldn't afford to spend and a signature on a dotted line which would cost them dearly if the advertising agenda they were sold fell flat on its face. The advertising agency neither offered nor promised any guarantees of success but those who signed away their last penny were usually desperate for a quick fix and were going to hit the wall of doom anyway. The advertising agency was all about making money and far removed from guaranteeing the success of every client they serviced but maybe, just maybe, Grant Fisher could be the client who delivered both profit for the agency along with a solution to London's evident and ever worsening housing crisis.

Fabio moved from Italy to London with his Parents about twenty years ago. Fabio's Father had a dream of opening a small Italian Restaurant in Hampstead and he did exactly that. The restaurant was called Lucia's, named after Fabio's Mother, and Lucia worked the kitchen while Marco, that's Fabio's Father, worked front of house. Fabio was expected to do whatever else needed doing, along with waiting tables and washing dishes. This was not for Fabio, so he came up with a plan to expand Lucia's and create a chain of restaurants, all located in the most desirable parts of London and he presented his plan to his father. This was not for Marco and this event very quickly divided the father and son relationship. Amicably, Fabio left the family business and charmed his way into the world of advertising. Fabio was an overnight success at a small advertising agency called No.1 Promote, attracting many new clients and helping them kick start their new business ventures or helping successful businesses become even more successful. Fabio was a natural presenter and could close the most stubborn of prospect but he was on the payroll with commission and was very aware that he was making No.1 Promote an awful lot of money. After a couple of years, Fabio decided to go it alone and he launched Fab Success. Fab Success was an instant success and more than likely contributed to the collapse of No. 1 Promote, the fact that Fabio took most of their clients with him could be used as evidence to back this theory up. But Fabio now needed a team around him to keep his growing advertising empire growing and this was the open door for Kathy to walk through.

Kat's phone had been ringing all morning but she was choosing to ignore it for some reason. That was very unlike Kat, especially when work was involved and the prospect of another signature from a another desperate new client meant more commission for Kat. Kat brought home decent money, which when added to Max's contributions, allowed them to do pretty much what they wanted, when they wanted. Max had no work obligations as a contractor and Kat could work remotely for Fab Success, as long as she continued to deliver signatures and profit. "Kat!", Max yelled, "Will you please answer your phone or turn the damn thing off!" Max had no problem with what his sweetheart did for money but he hated ringing mobiles being left unanswered when turned on, they're on for a reason he would state, "So answer it or please turn it off!"

Kat eventually answered her phone, it was Fabio. "Kat, my darling, my number one. I know it's a big decision but I need an answer from you by 5pm tomorrow, end of!" Fabio wanted Kat to make a decision on whether working in London with Grant Fisher was a yes or a no. Making the decision was not the hard part for Kat, she really wanted to do it but didn't know how to address the subject with Max. Max had always felt that he was punching above his weight with Kat but whilst the two of them were always within touching distance, just like Adam and Eve, Max found reassurance that he would never lose his Kathy to another man nor lifestyle beyond what they had created. Their perfect life together, just the two of them, travelling and exploring the world, falling in love with exciting new places and falling in love with each other, again and again and again. But the perfect storm was brewing and it was about to start raining like it's never rained before and the storm was heading their way.

During her commute back from Harrogate, this was where Fabio also had an office which serviced the Northern Territory of his advertising empire, she recited to herself again and again, "It's going to be fine, Max will understand

and support me. It's going to be fine, everything is going to be fine" Kat made a point of getting home early to spend some extra time with Max. They had a meal which Max had prepared earlier, a few glasses of wine and they talked about their individual days. Max bought Kat up to speed on the next overseas adventure he'd been planning: a four week explore of Corfu. Corfu was a place which Max had visited with his parents as a child and always had fond memories of the place and the people and he was keen to return. He'd put together an itinerary which would see the two of them explore pretty much the entire island and he was buzzing at the thought.

The thought of visiting one of his favorite places, although the childhood memories where slightly vague, with the love of his life led Max to a new level of excitement and he was keen to start cementing his plans and getting things booked, like flights and accommodation. But before Max could proceed to, "Shall we fly on a Monday or a Saturday, there are pros and cons?" he was stopped in his tracks by Kat. "Maxi, I have something to tell you or discuss with you," Kat interrupted with a nervous smile. She knew her mind was already made up and she was heading for London to meet and work with Grant Fisher but she wanted to appear as if her future plans were still open to discussion. Max was soon on the receiving end of a very hard punch from a beautiful and elegant version of Tyson Fury!

"Max, Max!, please will you at least listen to me and see my side of the deal. I know this is not what we do, this is not how we roll and it ain't Adam and fucking Eve but we can't be Adam and Eve forever!" Max was rubbish at dealing with things which made no sense to him and he couldn't understand why Kat needed to move to London to find

8

another version of happiness nor to make more money, more money was the last thing they needed. They already had enough money between them and they had each other. Surely that was the sweet spot and Max was going to take some serious convincing to conclude for himself that anything other than what they already had was a better deal. Max finally broke his silence, "What about Corfu, what about Corfu Kat? Have you already forgotten about that, now that fucking London is calling!"

"Now you're just being petty and ridiculous Max! What makes you think I'll have to cancel Corfu on you?"

"Well I don't know and I don't really know what I know anymore. I'm really confused Kat."

To hear Max and Kat swear was very unusual indeed. Both had the capacity to swear like troopers but both had the grace and integrity to reserve their foul mouths for only the finest moments or essential scenarios. Max would swear when he was frustrated by people's stupidity and Kat would swear at people when she'd had a drink and had mustered up the courage to shoot from one of her perfectly toned hips. But to hear Max and Kat swear at each other was not a good sign at all. In fact, it should have been recognised as a warning sign by both Max and Kat that the perfect storm which was heading their way was about to reach shore and unless they both took some responsibility for preventing a relationship disaster, a catastrophic relationship disaster was inevitable.

It took three or four days to pass before there were any signs of relationship normality between Max and Kat, but there was no more swearing at each other. Max had started to talk briefly about Corfu again and Kat tried to gently shoehorn her London plans into the conversation without starting another war. "I'm only go to be in London on a Monday, Tuesday and Wednesday Max and I'll be home Wednesday evening, just in time for a glass of wine with my Maxi." Max sensed that Kat was extending an olive branch and the last thing she wanted was to wreck their beautiful relationship, so he seized the opportunity to reopen the Corfu book of plans. "Okay Kat," Max said affirmatively. "I think it's best that we fly to Corfu on the Saturday, the flight lands at 6:30pm Greek time and that means we can travel to our first accommodation, get checked in, freshened up and still be in one of those fabulous Greek Tavernas by 9:30pm. What do you say?" Kat's reply was exactly what Max wanted to hear. "Maxi my love, it sounds absolutely perfect!"

Chapter 2 ~ Welcome To London Baby.

It was now just three months, two weeks and four days until Max and Kat flew to Corfu. Max was busy arranging accommodation and making tweaks to their itinerary. He had also been busy going through his old childhood photographs, looking for photos which were taken when he visited Corfu with his parents and his older brother. Max's older brother died shortly after his twentieth birthday, suddenly and very unexpectedly after a short but incurable illness. It was this tragic event which made Max realise that life can be incredibly short, bitterly cruel and tomorrow offers no man nor women a money back guarantee if it never arrives.

From that day on, Max made a pledge to himself and his late brother that he would always live life to the full, travel often and be kind. After spending a good couple of hours sat on the floor going through his old photographs, Max found a photo of himself and Spike. Max's brother had always been called Spike because of his spikey hair. Spike's hair was a tribute to some angry young man who was in a band and sang songs about bringing down the establishment. However, the photo which Max had found of him and his brother was taken at one of those fabulous greek tavernas and not at an anti government protest. The taverna was called Bacchus on The Beach and it was, funny enough, located on the beach, just South of the Messonghi River, which separated Moraitika and Messonghi. The river was often mosquito infested but always home to Captain Homer's boat, which ran daily pleasure trips from the South Bank of the river down to Notos Beach.

Whilst Max was keeping himself busy with Project Corfu, Kat was busy trying to figure out how best to take a perfectly formed life, cut it in half and end up with two perfectly formed lives, one with Max in Yorkshire and one in London. It was turning out to be a bit of a challenge, simply because Kat had known no other way of living life for the past fifteen years. It was just her and Max, the cottage overlooking the soggy village green, Max's philosophy on life and all things which mattered, bottles of wine most nights of the week and work responsibilities until it was time to fly off again on another fabulous adventure. Kat's move to London was being made slightly easier by the fact that Grant Fisher owned several properties in London and he'd promised free accommodation in

London for Kat as part of the deal. Kat would live free of charge in an apartment, which formed part of an old converted warehouse. It was this successful residential conversion project which gave Grant the stimulus to expand his property empire and expand in a very specific way. After all, the young and the wealthy love a knackered old building to call home and the exposed brickwork and old beams added charm and character, along with another 20k to the asking price.

It was Monday morning 4:30am, and Kat slipped out of bed trying not to wake Max. Kat was always up and about before Max and Max would always stir but to Max, this was still the middle of the night. Kat was heading for London for the first time, initially to check in at the glass and chrome temple of advertising, then to meet Grant for the first time, have a business lunch with Grant and Fabio and then settle down for her first night alone in London. "Max, Maxi my darling, I've got to go now." Kat whispered in her pure but slightly nervous and still tired voice. Max tried his best to reply but it was still 5:30am and Max was still at least three hours away from resembling anything like a human, let alone being a three hour drive away from London. But he still managed to muster up the words Kat wanted to hear that morning. "Safe travels my love, keep in touch and let me know when you arrive safely in London. Oh, by the way, I'm super proud of you and there's nobody out there who's better for this job. And finally, don't go falling in love with London or anything nor anyone else for that matter, I'll be waiting for you Kathy!" Max just about finished what he wanted to say before the thought of three hours more sleep got the better of him. Kat kissed her Man on the cheek, took a deep breath and made her way downstairs.

The drive from Yorkshire to London was decidedly boring, whichever way you looked at it and the most important decisions you would have to make were whether you took the A1 or the M1 and, if you needed to stop, whether you could stomach a McDonalds or a KFC. Neither were particularly appealing, both were fattening and full of food additives and both options guaranteed you at least a week of food guilt and horrible aftertastes. Kat did stop for some food but opted for an M&S Pasta Salad in a plastic box, only £6.95, but it did come with a free wooden fork. Kat, feeling refreshed and not far from central London now, called Max and updated him on her journey so far. She was bored of driving now and was already missing Max but something inside her was driving her on and by now, it was too late to ditch the deal and head straight back to Yorkshire and her Maxi. Kat had finally arrived at Fab Success HQ and her first words were, "Oh my fucking God, this place is like a space station!"

"Welcome to London baby!" Kat was very quickly met by Fabio at reception and was soon on a personal VIP tour of Fabio's palace. Fabio gave Kat a detailed running commentary whilst showing her around Fab HQ. "Kathy my flower, you need to take this all in and very quickly get used to how things work here. This department here, called New Business Prospecting, is responsible for identifying businesses which are either failing already or struggling to expand. These guys here, sat in pods and with headsets on, make first contact with the target. They gain permission from the dying or the struggling to escalate things further and then hand the prospects over to the team of Advertising

Executives. Kathy, that's you by the way but you have been spared the process of being nice to people and you my love are heading straight for the finish line, well almost!"

Fabio's personal tour ended in what could be described as a rectangular fish tank. It was however the boardroom and sat at the end of the long meeting table, where business strategies would be discussed and new recruits were interrogated to within an inch of their lives, sat a tall and tanned gentleman, immaculately dressed and as well polished as the tabletop itself. This was Grant Fisher, the property developer with big plans for London's derelict Victorian buildings and a housing crisis solution which was as exciting to him as a new bike for Christmas would be to a young child. Grant gently pushed his chair back, stood up and then walked confidently towards Kathy. "Kathy or is it Kat? Let's at least start on correct first name terms shall we?" Kathy replied, slightly nervously, "Let's start with Kathy shall we and you must be Grant?" Fabio stepped in and in his usually flamboyant manner called lunch. "People, beautiful people, let's do lunch, our carriage awaits!" A black Mercedes with blacked out windows was waiting outside Fab HQ and ready to drive Fabio, Grant and Kathy to their lunch destination. Lunch was being taken at a restaurant called No. 9 and unless you knew it was a restaurant, you would walk straight past the black door which was the entrance to No.9, one of London's finest restaurants and known only to those who knew or those lucky enough to know someone who knew. Fabio was one of those who knew and was welcome anytime at No.9, even without a reservation.

Lunch consisted of small dishes with fancy names, none of which Kat recognised nor enjoyed and it certainly wasn't a meal prepared by Max. The lunchtime conversation was very much controlled by Fabio, occasionally inviting Grant to agree with what he thought was the best strategy moving forward and Kathy felt obliged to nod politely at what was being set out and established as a formula for success. Lunch was wrapped up and washed down with a bottle of Champagne, glasses were raised, glass met glass and a toast was made to success and prosperity. However, Kat felt sad, alone and isolated, in a world she was unfamiliar with, where the two new men in her life were only interested in making money and more money. Fabio and Grant took the Mercedes back to Fab HQ and Kat was put in a taxi which would take her to her provided accommodation. From the outside, the old Victorian warehouse looked just like an old Victorian warehouse, run down and in need of demolition or a proper good makeover. This particular warehouse had been exposed to the latter, and although looking tired and past its best from the outside, once inside, you couldn't think of anything else to say but wow. The warehouse had been converted into thirty luxury apartments, with all mod cons, AC and a Smart TV in every room and LED control panels everywhere. Exposed brickwork and steel beams, chunky light switches and old Victorian features, which your Grandmother would consider a basic essential and certainly not a luxury. Kat instantly loved her apartment, but it wasn't the cottage overlooking the soggy village green, which was her home with Max. Kat thought to herself, "Kathy, this'll do. Let's get on with the job in hand. Let's get the job done, make some decent money, make a name for myself and then let's go home."

Back in Yorkshire, Max had even more spare time on his hands. Kat was quite possibly the most untidiest and chaotic person you could ever meet. It wasn't intentional but it was how she rolled. Max could easily spend two hours a day just tidying up after Kat and putting back everything which was living quite happily where it was, even though Kat thought that books lived on the floor and not on a bookshelf and clothes were scared of wardrobes. Max was obviously missing Kat and without even thinking, he'd prepared dinner for two for a Monday night. Max loved to cook and create: he'd take culinary ideas from their travels around the world, add his own twist and, most of the time, cook up something delicious. Kat was obviously the crash test dummy and most of the time, loved Max's creations. Kat would often say, "Max, why don't you make your love of cooking a career, you're fantastic and your food always tastes and looks so good!" But Max had no desire whatsoever to become a chef. In fact, the thought of being a slave in someone else's kitchen and serving up food for the masses or the richest, turned him inside out and that thought was never going to change. Whilst Kat spent her first night in London alone, Max was doing what he loved to do. He'd eaten, he was on his second bottle of wine, the fire was on and although he was sleepy from food and mostly wine consumption, he still managed to stay awake for a few more hours to do some travel research and do some further itinerary planning for the Corfu adventure.

It was Tuesday morning and Kat was taking the underground to work. Today was her first full day working at Fab HQ and this meant that it was time to get down to some serious business. Between surfacing from the tube station and entering advertising central, she called Max. Max was still in bed, still sleepy and feeling slightly fuzzy from the night before; he'd had a few glasses of wine too many and had fallen asleep on the sofa. Kat's incoming phone call startled him but he was quick and obviously delighted to take that call. "Max, how are you my love?" Max replied, "I'm okay but I miss you terribly and it's only been two days! Please tell me you're coming home tomorrow." Kat confirmed that she was coming home tomorrow and hoped to be back in Yorkshire by 6:30pm. They spoke for a few minutes more about stuff in general, Max told Kat that the Corfu trip was shaping up nicely and she was going to love every minute of it. Kat gave Max a brief overview of her new London home and how things were going but it was early days and it didn't take long for Kat to run out of things to say about her London experience so far. They told each other how much they loved each other and ended the call. Kat put on an invisible cloak of confidence and entered Fab HQ and Max went back to sleep to dream of Kat and all the exciting plans they had ahead of them.

It was 1pm before Max surfaced. He decided to sack the day off and do nothing remotely resembling driving his van and delivering small packages for a big organisation. However, in London, Kat had spent the morning with Fabio and Grant. They had been brainstorming ideas on how best to attract new investors and purchasers for the first phase release of Grant's latest Victorian warehouse conversions. Grant had committed to a very large advertising budget with Fab Success and was keen to move things along very quickly and without any delay. A lot of ground was covered that Tuesday morning and lunchtime came just at the right time. Kat was already exhausted and needed a break from Fabio. She loved Fabio as her Boss but she was convinced that Fabio was some kind of robot that knew only two speeds - stop and full speed ahead. Kat took a short stroll along the banks of The River Thames, grabbed a coffee and a pastry and enjoyed what little silence there was to be found in London. The afternoon at Fab HQ was entirely identical to the morning, spent in the boardroom with Fabio and Grant. By the end of the day, ideas had been cemented, lots of money had been committed and lots of coffee and fancy snacks had been consumed. Fabio stood up and in his usual manner, concluded that the day was over. "Darlings, I think today is officially what we call a wrap! Grant, Kathy my love, what say you? Let's hit the town and celebrate another successful day!" Hitting the town was the last thing Kat wanted to do, all she wanted to do was curl up on the sofa with Max and talk crap, whilst sharing a bottle of their favourite wine. Kat found the strength from somewhere to decline Fabio's invitation and left the town hitting in the capable hands of Fabio and Grant, who were very quickly out the door like a pair of children who both hated school.

Chapter 3 ~ This City Will Either Make Or Break You.

Kat's first three days alone in London, without Max by her side and working at Fab HQ was now just one day away from also being a wrap. Today however offered a different, and what Kat was hoping would be a less frantic, agenda. Grant was in charge today as Fabio had decided to take the day off. Kat assumed that Fabio's absence had something to do with hitting the town with Grant yesterday at 4:30pm, but Grant looked as fresh as a daisy and raring to go. Grant set out an agenda for the day which would conclude at 2pm. He was aware that Kat had a three hour drive back to her second home and Kat genuinely appreciated his kind consideration. "Okay Kathy, let's get going, I want to show you the latest development, it's still work in progress but completion is not far off now. Please bare that in mind but it's really important you get a hands on feel for what you are very soon going to be selling on my behalf." Grant was always to the point and polite but he also had a subtle way of letting Kat know that she was working for him and she was on the payroll.

Grant and Kat took a black cab across town and over the murky River Thames to South Bank, where the latest development was taking place. "Kathy," Grant chipped in out of the blue. "This city will make or break you, I need to make you aware of that." Kat wasn't quite sure how to respond to Grant's statement so replied with, "Well let's hope it doesn't break me Grant. I'm not here to be broken. I'm here to further my career, make some extra and now promised money and then return to Yorkshire to be with Max again. We have made some exciting travel plans for the year ahead, including a four week explore of Corfu and I reckon that after my time in London is done, I'm going to need that time to recover and find myself again." To avoid any awkward silences after her reply, Kat asked Grant if he also explored and travelled the world. Surely with him having access to what appeared to be a flourishing money tree, he would be jetting off somewhere beautiful and exciting all the time. "No Kathy, I don't and I honestly can't remember the last time I did! My life is here in London. This is where I live and this is where I make money." Kat was also in London to make money but only temporarily. For Grant, this existence was clearly his whole life, nothing but the hustle and bustle of a city which quite clearly breaks an awful lot of people and a city full of old buildings just waiting to be converted into piles of money.

At the end of a trendy looking street, not exactly tree lined but instead, BMW, Audi and Porsche lined, were the security boards which kept the nosey time wasters and opportunistic thieves at bay. Behind the boards was an old Victorian building and, according to Grant, it used to be a factory which made some of the best shoes in the world. So good were the shoes that even the King of England used to wear them. Along with a passion for converting old buildings into homes and profit, Grant enjoyed researching the history of the buildings he was developing. Kathy remembered seeing old photographs in the reception area of the converted building which her London home formed part of and now that made sence to her. The history of the building is all part of the buy in process and more than likely adds another 5k to the asking price. She could imagine the topic of conversation being had amongst those who owned, or aspired to own, one of these homes. "Yah, that's right, we own an apartment in the old factory which used to make shoes for the King. Every morning we wake up and feel that we are walking in the King's footsteps, it's totally amazing!"

"OMG, I'd love to live there but we just can't justify the spend at the moment." That was the discreet way of saying, we just can't afford the spend at the moment.

"Good morning Mr Fisher and guest, I'm sure I don't need to remind you of the site rules but just in case and to save my backside if someone does get hurt, hard hats and hi viz jackets are to be worn at all times!" That came from Colin, the Site Manager and a trusted worker from Grant's vast team of site workers. Grant employed his management team and skilled trades, which meant that they were his property and would be ready to work for him whenever he required them to do so, which at the moment, was most of the time. Those who didn't know the difference between a hammer and a saw were contractors and could be removed from site at the drop of a bucket, quite literally, at the drop of bucket. Grant and Kathy put on their hard hats and hi viz jackets and proceeded to explore and inspect the site. "Colin!" Grant shouted. "Who's that asleep behind the timber store? Unless he's been awake all night because his partner has just given birth, get rid of him please!" Colin wasn't entirely sure who he was nor whether his partner had just given birth, but he woke him up all the same and escorted him off site.

"Time is money on site Kathy and wasted money means less profit. I provide people with good opportunities here but I'm not a charity." Again, Grant was very clear and precise with what he said and although Kat felt slightly intimidated by Grant, she also knew exactly where he was coming from and how things were going to work between the two of them. Grant was spending the money, taking the risks and in return, he expected results from those who were happy to take his money and avoid the risk taking. Grant asked Kat, "So Kathy, what do you think? Do you think you can help me sell every unit for the maximum price or will London break you?" Kat sensed that Grant was purposely provoking her, dangling a carrot for her to chase but as Kat explained earlier in the taxi, she was not in London to be broken and then sent back to Yorkshire with her tail between her legs. She was in London on a mission, a mission to be completed and then boxed away like your School or University qualification certificates. Once boxed away, her life would resume as normal with Max in Yorkshire or wherever they decided to take themselves next. Corfu was on Kat's mind right now, not development sites and she was ready to leave London and head for home.

Before leaving the site, Kat answered Grant's question, "If these apartments are anything like the one I have, I'll sell them all day long and for the very best price, trust me on that Grant."

Grant replied with a wry smile, "These apartments are going to be even better than the one I'm lending you Kathy, remember that, so top Dollar should be a given then." The tour of the site concluded, another taxi was waiting. Colin collected the hard hats and hi viz jackets and they said their goodbyes. The taxi weaved its way through the busy streets of London and in the direction of Kat's parked car. On route, Grant took the opportunity to point out other buildings which were ripe for development. They were on every corner of every street and sat in the middle of every open space which had been fenced off from the public. "There's money to be made everywhere you look in London, opportunities to get rich and live a fantastic life, yet so many people choose to do nothing about it." Was Grant quoting facts or was he appealing for some kind of approval or agreement from Kat which would confirm that the two of them were singing from the same hymn sheet? Kat could never agree with Grant's philosophy but politely nodded as a gesture and then informed the taxi driver that her car was parked somewhere over there, in one of those tatty car parks which charged a fortune.

It was now exactly 2pm and although Kat disagreed with Grant's philosophy on life, love and happiness, he had at least proved to Kat that he was reliable. He said that Kat would be done for the day and on her way home by 2pm and that was delivered. He even picked up the tab for three days parking, which came in at a cool £225.00. Kat thanked Grant for that and everything. She told him that today had genuinely been interesting and confirmed that business would resume next Monday at Fab HQ. Grant thanked and congratulated Kat for surviving three days in the City of Dreams or Tears. He wished her a safe journey home and told her that he was really looking forward to next Monday. He didn't say why but Kat guessed that it had something to do with selling apartments and making money.

Kat made herself comfortable in her car and immediately called Max. "Max, Max, Max, I've survived three days in London! Everything is okay and I'm on my way home, home to you my darling!" Max was expecting this call but wasn't prepared nor rehearsed for any sort of homecoming announcement. "Kat my love. I've missed you so much and as promised, I'm here and waiting for you. So please drive carefully and let me know if you're going to be later than planned." Kat obviously agreed to do exactly that. She started her car and started the long journey home. Kat was only an hour into her journey and was already sitting in a long queue of traffic and all she could see around her was red lights and miserable faces behind glass. She hadn't even made it out of London yet and was already pulling her hair out. She wanted out of London and wanted to be at home now! Eventually she reached the M25, then the M1 and then she started to see signs for Leeds and York. All being well, she would be on the sofa, in front of the fire with Max in little over an hour. That thought brought a smile to her tired looking face. That pretty face, which Max would always consider to be the prettiest face on Earth. It was dark when Kat arrived back home in Yorkshire. She very briefly looked up at the stars in the clear night sky and immediately knew that Max had lit the fire, which would also suggest that Max had already opened a bottle of wine or two.

"Max, I'm home darling, where the fuck are you? I need to see you now!" Kat was ready to fall into the arms of her lover and be held tight and reassured that nothing had changed whilst she was away. Max came running down the stairs, missing the last three stairs and launched himself at Kat. The two sweethearts became one and if they were wearing matching outfits, it would have been impossible to tell which limb belonged to who. Max and Kat kissed each other like teenagers on a first date and still joined together, they fell, as if drunk, on to the sofa. Max pulled away, grabbed a glass and filled it to the brim with Sauvignon Blanc. He put it in Kat's hand and without any attempt to raise a glass with Max, Kat started swigging from the glass as if she'd just completed dry January. "Welcome home you gorgeous human, tell me about London and I'll tell you about Corfu!" Max demanded.

"Well Max, London is busy and noisy. Nobody appears to be genuinely happy and everything seems to pivot on making money!"

Max replied and pushed further, "How's Fabio and his advertising empire? What's Grant Fisher like?"

It was very easy for Kat to describe to Max how Fabio was and how his empire was doing. "Well, Fabio is still Fabio. He still functions at a thousand miles an hour and his empire is continuing to grow." It was however more difficult for Kat to describe Grant Fisher to him. There was that same sort of awkwardness you feel when your current lover asks you to describe an ex lover. "Grant is a business man Max, well groomed and always dressed to impress. He calls the shots and appears to be in control of everything which matters to him and he is in love with making money! He does nothing other than do deals and make money. He doesn't even travel! Can you imagine that Max, a life without travelling?"

Max was quick to respond and maybe subconsciously and hypothetically took a precautionary swing at Grant, just to let Grant know that his girl was off limits. "He sounds like a boring fucker to me, if I'm being honest!"

After a short pause, Kat replied, "I wouldn't call him boring Max but he's certainly not you nor your type of guy but I wouldn't have it any other way." It seemed to be a good time to move on from talking about London and Grant Fisher, so Kat asked Max to tell her where they were with their upcoming trip to Corfu. Max explained how they would grab a taxi from the airport and head for Kavos. Kavos used to be the 18 to 30 hot spot a few years ago but now that the young and promiscuous had moved on, it had returned to being a really nice place to visit and had a fantastic golden beach. From Kavos, the plan was to head North and pick off all the places of interest, including Lefkimmi, Petriti, Messonghi and Moraitika. Max was keen to join Captain Homer again on his old boat and take that memorable trip down the East coast to Notos. According to Facebook, Yiani, who was the original Captain Homer, had semi-retired and his son was now part time Captain Homer. To be honest, Max didn't really care who the latest version of Captain Homer was as long as the experience was almost the same as he remembered and he was experiencing that trip with Kat. Max was also keen to wine and dine with his childhood sweetheart at Bacchus on the Beach. The last time Max was at Bacchus was when his brother Spike was still alive. It was now clear to Max that his love for this beautiful island started whilst on that family holiday with his parents and Spike and it was now time to rekindle that love and share it with the person who meant everything to him, and that was his Kathy.

Max was on a roll now whilst Kat was flagging. The long drive back from London was finally taking its toll on Kat but Max kept going. "From Messonghi and Moraitika we could head across to the West coast and enjoy the rugged coastline and hidden beaches. There's also an old Byzantine Fortress to explore whilst on our way to Agios Georgios. I can still remember playing there with Spike. Spike was the attacker and I was the defender. Kat, Kat, are you still awake or have I bored you to sleep with my Corfu agenda?" Kat stirred and managed a few soft words before nodding off again. "No Max, you didn't bore me to sleep with your Corfu agenda. I'm just shattered but I'm really looking forward to the boat trip with Captain Homer and the old fortress sounds really interesting."

Chapter 4 ~ A New Kind Of Normal.

It was Thursday morning and for once, Max was up and on it before Kat. Fabio had told Kat to work from home but also to get some deals done and finalise the advertising schedule and week 1 costs with Grant. Max had prepared breakfast and had coffee ready to go as soon as Kat joined him downstairs. After Max had spent about an hour looking at maps of Corfu, Kat appeared looking refreshed and damn sexy in one of Max's old T Shirts. She sat down at the small kitchen table opposite Max, poured some coffee and looked lovingly at her man. "I don't know what I'd do without you Max?", she said with her sultry brown eyes fixed on their target. "Well Kat, my love, you're going to have to do without me today because this delivery driver has some deliveries and money to make!" Kat had never seen Max so enthusiastic about going to work. Maybe he was taking a leaf out of Grant Fisher's book and trying to prove to his girl that he could also be a responsible money making machine, just one from the lower echelons of the business pyramid. But Max very quickly put Kat's thoughts back in their box and revealed the real reason why he was up and on it today. "It's just over three months now Kat until we fly to Corfu and I need to make some serious Euros. We are going to have the time of our lives and this guy right here, is paying for more than his fair share of the fun!" With that statement delivered, Max picked up his van keys and a large bag of Haribo Super Mix, kissed his girl bang on the lips, and somewhere else, and was out the door and gone, loudly calling back, "Back by 5pm at the latest and make sure you've still got that T Shirt on!"

Kat took her coffee and toast to the sofa, along with her laptop and her phone and contemplated starting her day. Upon checking her emails at 10:30am, Kat read an email from Fabio. He was already checking in on Kat and asked how her day was going so far. Kat thought to herself, bloody marvellous so far, but that thought had nothing to do with what Fabio was asking nor wanted to hear. Kat knew that she was one phone call away from signing up another client, a failing estate agency which was rapidly running out of homes to sell and had only just realised that that was eventually going to be a problem. Kat made the call to the Finance Director of Bailey, Harris, Roberts and Partners, promising them a truly awesome advertising campaign which would bring new customers flocking to their doors and she quickly closed the deal. She then replied to Fabio with the good news he wanted to hear. "Dear Fabio, Another 45k income guaranteed for next month! Best Wishes, Kathy." This was pretty much how Kat's day at home without Max played out, until she had to update Grant on the final advertising schedule and cost burn for the first week. This was to be done over the phone and not by email and she was strangely looking forward to making that call to Grant.

Max was out and about around the North East of England somewhere, earning his Euros. Occasionally he'd stop and take a picture of something he'd seen and he would send it to Kat. Sometimes he'd be by the sea and he would send Kat a moody picture from Redcar Beach, showing the murky grey water of the North Sea in the background. He'd caption it with something like, "It certainly ain't the Caribbean is it Kat?" Kat would usually reply with a smiley face Emoji and a comment along the lines of, "No but only a few more weeks before we will be swimming in crystal clear waters again!" This kept Max going on a daily basis and kept him doing what he did for a living. He didn't do it for himself nor the job satisfaction. He did it because it allowed him be with and travel the world with Kat, it was as simple as that. For some reason known only to Kat, she wanted to make the call to Grant before Max got home and Max had just sent her a message saying that he was done for the day and would be about an hour, that meant that Max should be home by 4:30pm. So she picked up her phone and made the all important phone call.

Grant answered his phone after only two rings, which caught Kat slightly of guard. "Kathy, how's it going, is it nearly showtime?"

"Yes!" she replied. "Do you want the good news or the bad news first?" Grant wanted to hear the good news first because he knew that the bad news was going to be all about how much the good news was going to cost him. "Okay Grant, I'll send this to you in an email later but this is a run through of the advertising campaign for week 1 and this will repeat until week 4, unless things are not going according to plan and the off plan sale enquiries are not flooding in. So, expect to see your latest development being advertised on every London bus which covers that area. I've seen the CGI Images and they look fantastic. In fact, I might even make an enquiry myself! 50% of the black cab owners which we have approached are happy with what we are offering them and I'm expecting another 25% take up, at least! Local newspaper adverts are ready to go and I've secured you a centre spread for at least four weeks and four local lifestyle magazines have agreed to a 50% discount, as long as we keep spending regularly with them for at least three months. If this campaign doesn't sell every unit for the best price, I'll be amazed Grant! So make sure that your sales team are ready for a sudden influx of enquiries, week commencing the 1st of April, and that's no joke! Now the bad news…"

Grant interrupted, "Kathy, spare me the bad news and have your accounts people send my accounts people the bill. If this campaign turns out to be as good as you're making it sound, the cost will be worth every penny! See you in London on Monday I hope?"

"Absolutely Grant and raring to go!"

Kat was feeling pleased with herself and was surprised at how easy it was to push the start button on Grant's advertising campaign. Maybe she was underestimating herself and her ability within the world of advertising to run big and expensive campaigns. Maybe Grant was going easy on his new asset or maybe Grant had faith in Fabio to not employ morons. Either way, the first phase of the job was a wrap. Fabio would be bouncing off the walls that there was no resistance nor kick back from Grant and based on what Grant had just spent, Fabio and Kat were now, but not necessarily equally, far better off financially. This called for a celebration and that evening would comprise of a few bottles of their favourite wine, a takeaway meal, so that Max didn't have to cook that evening and as long as Kat didn't have too much to drink, Max might even get his T Shirt handed back to him on a silver tray.

Kat's life in Yorkshire with Max, her second life in London with Fabio and Grant and a few extra K's on their way at the end of the month, was already starting to feel like a new kind of normal. The incoming storm which was threatening to destroy their perfect relationship only a few weeks earlier had either blown itself out or had been subconsciously dealt with by both Max and Kat and for now, in that very moment, everything was pucker and Kat felt that things couldn't get any better. But they just did, Max was now home. That beautiful Thursday evening went according to plan. The food arrived on time, the wine flowed like a mountain stream in Spring and Max did get his T Shirt back. But before our two lovers fell into each others arms and then into bed, the conversation they shared that evening was on point and mostly covered Corfu, Yorkshire and London.

Another weekend in Yorkshire had declared itself open for business and Max was meeting an old friend for a few drinks and a curry. Kat was heading into York to catch up with her friends from the world of advertising and would no doubt be telling them about her recent successes in London. Kat was never one to brag about what she did but she had found a new level of confidence and was incredibly proud of what she had just achieved. The deal she had just closed with Grant Fisher was a big deal as far as property development accounts were concerned and the rumours of the possible spend were already bouncing around the various agencies. Unlike Kat, Max had a very small circle of friends. In fact, his circle of friends would be better described as a very short queue of just two friends, who he would occasionally meet up with when there was some kind of crisis on the horizon. This evening, Max was meeting up with Charlie who was Christened, Charles Henry James Smyth-Buchanan. Charlie was from good stock. His father worked in banking and his mother was a reputable lawyer based in Harrogate. Charlie was the first in their small gang to get a half decent computer and taught himself how to program it. However, this skill meant that Charlie had very few friends and even fewer girlfriends. But he was a good lad with a dark and to the point sense of humour and Max liked that. The two scally wags had known each other for as long as Max had known Kat and during that time, they'd only fallen out once and that was when Charlie told Max that Kathy wasn't the right one for him. It turned out that Charlie also had eyes on Kat and was trying to get to the front of the queue of boys who wanted to date her. That little tiff soon passed with a little help from Kathy, who eventually told Charlie that she didn't fancy him and never would. Now the two grown up lads just laugh about, and occasionally play out, how things could or would have been if Kathy ended up with Charlie.

Max and Charlie were meeting in an old drinking haunt called Ted the Grass, alternatively known by its original name of Edward the Confessor. It was a drinkers pub - it had a juke box which played Pink Floyd and The Smiths, it sold Bacon Fries and served a decent pint. It was also just around the corner from their favourite curry house, the originally named, Taj Mahal. Max had arrived about half an hour before Charlie and was already half way through his first pint and a pack of bacon snacks. Charlie soon arrived with what appeared to be a rain cloud above his head, like that character from Snoopy. Max greeted Charlie with, "Fuck me mate, what's going on?" Both now armed with full pints and more bacon snacks, Charlie explained. "Max my friend, it's all about to fall apart at the seams!"
"What do you mean Charlie, what is?"
"I'm on borrowed time Max and I don't know what to do!"

Max was quick to reply, "For fucks sake Charlie, if you're ill or you think you might be dying, then go and see your doctor. If you're not ill, then tell me what the problem is because at the moment, trying to read you is like trying to read one of those computer programs you write!"

Charlie proceeded to tell Max that things between him and Laura, Charlie's wife and mother to their two children, had hit what he described as rock bottom. Apparently, Laura quit work because she wasn't coping with being a mother and an accountant and would often lose her shit and lock herself in the bathroom for hours on end. Charlie had promised Laura that everything was going to be okay and he would sort everything out. Perhaps he was thinking that he could write a computer program or create a new algorithm that would fix their shit, but there was no chance of that. This episode of The Sims was well and truly screwed and the program it ran on was about to crash for the very last time. Charlie had been hiding the financial shit storm from Laura, she preferred it that way, and Charlie was now four months behind on the mortgage and the credit cards hadn't seen a minimum payment for at least six months. The letters and phones calls were now flying in thick and fast and it was only a matter of time before those very nice gentlemen in stab proof vests and steel toe capped boots turned up.

Max got another round in, loaded the juke box with all the change he had in his pocket, selected a track by The Smiths, Heaven Knows I'm Miserable Now and another by Pink Floyd, Wish You Were. Both tracks were very poignant, one fitting the mood in The Ted that night perfectly and the other being one of Max's favorite songs. He would always play the latter whenever Kat was away, which up until recently, was when she used to visit her parents in Ireland. Max put the drinks and snacks on the now sticky table and proceeded to set out a plan of action. "Right Charlie, you need to contact one of those debt management organisations straight away mate. They can get the mortgage and credit card payments frozen immediately and then they'll help you set up some sort of repayment plan."

Charlie glumly replied, "That's all well and good Max but can they stop me losing my job in two months time?"

Max didn't know what to say so instead, he got another round in. "Tonight's on me Charlie, don't you worry about that mate."

Charlie currently worked for a large computer software company. They specialised in writing computer programs which taught computers to do pretty much anything the computer thought was the right or smart thing to do. The machines which Charlie was working on were often more alive, more awake and far more intelligent than the tech geeks who were teaching them. But Charlie, nor none of his department, were awake nor intelligent enough to realise that they were all busy coding and programming themselves out of their jobs and not even Ctrl, Alt, Del could stop this technological advancement. Charlie and his department were being replaced by a robot, a chip and an algorithm. Another new kind of normal. Max tried his best to reassure Charlie that everything was going to be okay, even though he had no idea how to make things okay for Charlie. Charlie was in big trouble and there was very little he nor Max could do to stop a further wave of shit breaking on Charlie's shore. Max prompted Charlie to drink up, "Come on mate, let's go for that curry and talk about the good old days but please don't tell me that story again about how close you were to bagging my Kat." For a moment, Charlie forgot about his problems and he thanked Max for always being there for him. The two old friends staggered off down the road in the direction of the Taj Mahal, telling each other how much they loved each other and how they were each other's best mate. Max jokingly reminded Charlie, "Charles you twat, I'm your only fucking mate!"

Chapter 5 ~ Meanwhile In York And The Taj Mahal.

Meanwhile in York, and whilst Max and Charlie were busy consuming vast quantities of bright red spicy food, washed down with ice cold bottles of beer, Kat was enjoying cocktails and olives with her group of glamorous friends at the Water Lily. The Water Lily was a Thai restaurant which also had a cocktail lounge and you could book a private booth there if your party consisted of more than six people. It was never a problem for Kat to find six people or more to drink cocktails and eat olives with. She had lots of female friends and knew almost as many guys, most of whom were keen to get her into their bed for the night. Although Kat had a large male fan base, she never led the guys on and was crystal clear with all who approached her that she was never going to be anything more than a friend to them and if they overstepped the mark or pushed to hard, they wouldn't even be her friend, let alone her lover. Kat had eyes only for Max and that was how things were and how things were going to stay.

Kat's best friend was a blonde bombshell called Lucy. Lucy also worked in advertising but was nothing like Kat. Lucy was proud of the fact that she kept herself looking young, free and very single. Some would say that Lucy had a bit of reputation around town but Lucy would counter that accusation by claiming that they were only jealous. Even if the claims surrounding Lucy's reputation were true, you would be hard pushed not to be impressed by Lucy's long list of male acquaintances, which read like a celebrity whose who. Lucy would use LinkedIn to find rich and attractive men to date, like a forty year old virgin would use Tinder to try and get laid for the first time. Company Directors, global CEO's, TV celebrities and even professional footballers could be found on Lucy's list of men worth dating. But how many of these men Lucy had actually slept with was a closely guarded secret and known only to Lucy and Kat. Kat loved Lucy like a sister she never had and never once judged her for the way she chose to live her life. Occasionally, Kat would feel slightly jealous of Lucy and the glamorous life she had created for herself. Every birthday, Christmas and Valentines Day, Lucy would receive a shower of expensive gifts from men she'd only just met, men she met months or years ago and some who she hadn't even met yet. Lucy had created for herself a very unique business model, where she was taken seriously because of her job, and she was good at her job, but very rarely had to pay for anything which cost more than £200 and wasn't regarded by the masses as an essential item required to live a normal everyday life.

"So Kat, tell me all about London, should I come and join you?" Lucy asked of Kat in her usual sassy way.

"Well my love. First, I think you're doing just fine here and I've also been told that London will either make or break you. Do you fancy being broken and then sent packing? It's not really your style is it Lucy?"

Lucy quickly responded with a cheeky smile, "And what about Grant, Mr Fisher? Is he as handsome and as god damn sexy in real life?" Kat took a second or two to process what Lucy had just said and then came to the conclusion that Lucy had already checked Grant out on LinkedIn and wanted some sort of verification from her that Grant was genuinely hot and worth a punt, or whether he was in fact, like most of the men on Tinder, nothing like his picture and 'entrepreneur' meant self employed window cleaner. Kat avoided the question. "Putting Grant to one side, London is not exactly my cup of tea. It's noisy and busy. Nobody looks happy nor genuinely content with their lives but maybe that's the London deal Lucy. They're all there to try and make a better or even a perfect life for themselves. Dick Whittington went to London because he was told that the streets were paved with gold. Maybe that big fat lie is still being believed today?"

More cocktails and little bowls of olives and Thai snacks had just arrived and the conversation regarding London and Grant Fisher was gathering pace, very much fulled by Lucy. Lucy raised her cocktail glass and unashamedly announced to the group of ladies, "Well my lovelies, if Kat doesn't want to take advantage of Grant's good looks and healthy bank accounts, I might just have to take another one for the team." Those in the private booth who didn't know Lucy as well as Kat did, winced slightly and crossed their legs.

However, Kat knew where Lucy was coming from and her provocative statement didn't necessarily mean that she was about to jump into bed with another man. Lucy was simply keeping her side hustle going and well fed by lining up another handsome and wealthy subscriber.

Cocktails finished, Kat pulled Lucy to one side. "You're serious aren't you, about Grant and if someone has to do it, then I'm the girl to do it?" Lucy looked at Kat, feeling slightly sorry for her best female friend whilst sensing a tiny bit of jealousy towards her and replied, "You've become comfortable Kat. Comfortable with Max and the life you share with him. Comfortable with what you do every day of the week. Comfortable with working for Fabio and his clients. Comfortable in every aspect of your life Kat. You've become comfortable. Now if that makes you happy, then crack on my beauty, but please don't question me on my life choices and how I choose to make my life exciting, very interesting and far from comfortable." Kat knew that Lucy was right, but she couldn't shake the faint wriggle of jealousy she was feeling. Shaking it off with a small laugh, she gave Lucy a hug. Lucy reached down and pinched Kat's backside whilst commenting, "You've still got a firmer arse than me, you lucky bitch!" They laughed at each other like silly schoolgirls who had just seen the male anatomy for the first time and then gracefully returned to the group as if nothing had happened.

Max and Charlie had finished their Indian banquet and just about managed to stagger back to Max's place for a night cap. Before Max left his house to meet Charlie, he'd been studying more maps and guide books on Corfu, these were still spread out on the kitchen table in an orderly fashion.

"What's all this then Max, you and Kat off on your glamorous travels again? You lucky buggers!" Charlie drunkenly slurred at Max whilst being genuinely interested in what the plan was. Charlie hadn't been anywhere other than his desk and the bottom of another wine bottle for many years now. He simply couldn't afford it and the thought of dragging his family halfway across the world, only for his wife to lose her shit again and then lock herself in a hotel bathroom for the day, was not exactly Charlie's idea of a vacation. Max sat Charlie down before he fell down, put a large whiskey and coke in his hand and proceeded to satisfy Charlie's curiosity. "Just three months now Charlie until Kat and I head for Corfu. You know, that lovely island which is always green and lush, just off the coast of the Greek mainland and Albania." Charlie looked at Max with a vague expression on his face and Max couldn't decide whether Charlie genuinely didn't know where Corfu was or whether Charlie had fallen asleep with his eyes open. Max went again, "Come on Charlie, you must remember this? We invited you to join us when I went to Corfu with my parents and Spike but your strict parents said no because you had too much school work to do, even though it was during the long summer holidays!" Charlie eventually found his second wind and replied to Max. "Yes Max, I remember now and I also remember hating my parents for weeks after they stopped me joining you. You must have great memories of that holiday Max, especially with Spike being there?"

Max sighed. "Yes indeed mate and it was not long after we returned home that Spike got the bad news from the doctor. His illness was terminal and there was nothing they could do to help him." Charlie charged their glasses with more whiskey and coke and they raised a glass to dear Spike. "To Spike, one of a kind and one of the true rebels!"

Kat and her beautiful girls were finishing their last round of cocktails in the Water Lily. It had been a great night, very different to how Max and Charlie had spent their evening but that was usually the case with Max and Kat when they went out separately. Lucy looked across at Kat and gave her one of her warm smiles, which usually meant that Lucy was genuinely happy for Kat and everything she had in her life. It also meant, more often than not, that Lucy thought that Kat could do so much better for herself and her life with Max had now become an addiction which she wanted to kick into touch but didn't know where nor when to start kicking. Lucy had arranged for the girls to all get home safely and as no men were involved this evening, it involved a luxury 16 seater with complimentary Champagne on board. Lucy had standards to uphold, even when it came to taking a taxi home. The task of arranging this mode of transport was made slightly easier by the fact that Lucy had been out on a couple of dates with the guy who owned the company. His name was Chris and he'd built up a very successful and profitable business from scratch. Just three years ago, Chris was driving someone else's taxi for a living, now he owned a fleet of 25 luxury coaches which quite often carried famous bands and political parties around the country. However, Chris could never speak about who he had in his taxi last week because he'd signed a number of agreements which meant, what happens on Chris's coach, stays on Chris's coach.

It was now almost midnight and the small luxury coach was due in half an hour, so the girls ordered one last round of drinks. Fancy little shot glasses soon arrived and they raised a toast to life, love and happiness. Kat was convinced that she heard Lucy say handsome men instead of happiness but it was late and many cocktails and shots had now been consumed. After the toast was made, Lucy lent towards Kat and whispered in her ear, "It's a shame that you're stuck with Max because I think that you and Grant Fisher would look simply devine together."

Kat was quick to respond, "Lucy, I'm not stuck with Max, it's my choice and if you keep going on about Grant Fisher, I'm going to tell everyone I know exactly how many men you have slept with!"

Lucy grinned at Kat, "Kat, that's our secret and if you do, I'll never speak to you again, got that!" She winked at Kat knowing all too well that her BFF would never do something like that.

Kat's stop was next and she was feeling relieved to be almost home. She was ready to fall into bed with Max and she knew that Max would want nothing more that night than a good night's sleep. She knew that when Max and Charlie got together they got stupidly drunk and in all fairness to Max and Charlie, Kat wasn't far behind them on the drunkenness scale. Kat arrived home shortly after 1:30am to find Max and Charlie both asleep on a sofa each, the two of them were both snoring and the fire had almost gone out. She gently nudged Max until he was awake enough to recognise that it was Kat who was standing over him and she was pointing in the general direction of the stairs. They left Charlie on the sofa to sleep off his night out and quietly made their way upstairs to bed. Max was the first to rise the following day and made his way downstairs to put the kettle on and make coffee for everyone. But he was surprised to see that Charlie was also awake and busy perusing Max's collection of maps and guide books on Corfu. Charlie was quick to comment when he saw Max that morning, "Looks like one hell of a trip you've planned here mate. I wish I was coming with you and the way things are going right now, I won't have anyone to stop me this time. When do you fly out?"

Max smiled, "I totally get that mate but this time it's just Kat and I, I'm sorry Charlie! It's a big fat no I'm afraid and we fly out to Corfu on Saturday the 5th of July." Max joined Charlie at the table with a black coffee for each of them and gently quizzed his mate on what his plan of action was. "So Charlie, what are you going to do? You're going to have to come clean with Laura at some point and from what you told me last night, a really bad outcome is inevitable. But she deserves to know about the mountain of debt and your pending redundancy!"

Charlie looked up from his coffee, "Yes Max you're right. I've got to tell Laura and the sooner I do, the sooner I'll know how she's going to respond. But it ain't gonna be pretty Max and I'll bet my last dollar that she'll leave me and take the children with her. She'll go back to her parents and they'll look after her and the kids, while I'm left alone to deal with the fallout!"

Laura's parents never liked Charlie and were constantly warning their daughter that life with Charlie was going to end in tears. Laura's life with Charlie though was not only going to end in tears but it was a constant life of tears. Tears and emotional tantrums from Laura when even the smallest of wave rocked the family boat. Charlie being late home from work one evening, because the latest phase of programming was behind schedule, would end in a kitchen destroying fight, Charlie battered and bruised and Laura sobbing uncontrollably in the bathroom. Deep down, Charlie knew that his life with Laura was almost over. Max recognised it and Charlie was about to become a real man for once and deal with it.

Chapter 6 ~ Times They Are A Changin', Part 1.

For Max and Kat, Fabio and Grant, Charlie and Laura, the next two to three months were going to be life changing and in many different ways. For Max, life with Kat was back to normal, getting better by the day and with every day which passed, he found himself one day nearer to his big Corfu adventure with Kat. Kat was on the brink of proving to herself and the world of advertising that she was the golden girl and if everything went according to plan, she would be the talk of the town and target number one for every advertising agency in London. As a result of Kat's hard work and success, Fabio and Grant would instantly become richer and happier over night and their individual business empires would continue to grow. For Charlie and Laura, the life they knew and everything they had was about to fall off the edge of a cliff. Poor Charlie was just one admission away from bringing their whole pack of cards tumbling down.

It was Monday the 1st of April and Kat was on her way to London again. Today was the big day, the day upon which the advertising campaign she'd been working hard on went live. Kat had left extra early this morning, leaving Max fast asleep and blissfully unaware that she'd gone. She left a note for Max on the table, propped up against his coffee cup, which said I Love You Max! As she drove across London, with the streets quieter than she remembered, she was suddenly hit by a surprise feeling of mixed emotion. Excitement meets anxiousness, would be a good way to describe that feeling. Kat was excited to be back in London and hopefully see her work in all its glory but she was also nervous. What if the campaign fell flat on its face and she was sent packing back to Yorkshire with her tail between her legs, another London casualty. Kat was almost at work but currently tucked in behind a red London bus. Kat read out load to herself what she'd just seen plastered across the back of the bus, "Fisher Developments proudly present a unique collection of luxury apartments, located in South Bank, London. Individual in every way, beautifully appointed throughout and selling now! With prices starting from just £495,000, you too can live your best life in London!" Oh my god, Kat thought to herself, it's real, it really is happening!

Kat was now at work and sat in the boardroom with Fabio and Grant. Fabio was unusually quiet for Fabio and Grant had his head buried in his laptop. Kat asked Fabio if everything was okay and waited for his response. "Kat, I've got a hangover and I wasn't even celebrating anything last night."

Kat knew Fabio well enough to advise him, "Perhaps you should wind your drinking in a bit then, try and have a few dry days each week?"

Fabio replied, "You're right Kat, I should and I'll start next week because hopefully we've got some celebrating to do

44

this week." Grant then looked up from his laptop and spoke to Kat for the first time that morning. "Good morning Kathy, how are you and how was your weekend in Yorkshire." Kat briefly told Grant what she'd been up to, Grant acknowledged Kat with a gentle nod of his head and got back to whatever he was doing on his laptop. Without notice, Grant then span his laptop around so that Fabio and Kat could finally see what he'd been looking at. On the screen was some kind of dashboard which was displaying graphs and data. Grant explained, "What you can see here is an overview of what is going on out there. This dashboard is showing us the number of phone calls and text messages we're receiving. The number of emails we're receiving and how many QR Codes are being scanned, as a result of the advertising going live today. The system was woken up at 4:30am this morning and in full swing by 5:30am and according to the data, we've already taken over two hundred enquiries for the apartments in South Bank. That doesn't mean that everyone is buying but even if only 25% are genuinely serious, that means we've sold out already. Let's go and get some coffee and some breakfast. Kathy, you must be hungry and in need of a coffee after that long drive?"

Fabio declined Grant's offer of a free breakfast and instead, decided to hide in his private office until he was feeling better about his life. Grant and Kat headed in the direction of Paternoster Square, where Grant knew of a great little bistro. They ordered coffee, freshly squeezed orange juice and a vegetarian breakfast each. It wasn't your typical all day English Breakfast kind of place and the name above the door, The Healthy Food Hut, should make it very clear to every scaffolder in London that fatty sausages and black pudding were not on the menu. "I hope you don't mind me asking you this Kathy, Fabio tells me that you have a partner back in Yorkshire called Max. What's the deal with Max, are you engaged, married or just together?" Kat knew that Fabio wouldn't just tell anyone what her relationship status was for the sake nor fun of it, so guessed that Grant must have asked Fabio, probably when Fabio was two bottles of wine in and happy to chat about anything, quite literally anything. Kat confidently and proudly answered Grant, "I've been with Max since I was fifteen and we live together. We're not engaged nor married (Kat presented Grant with her hands) and we haven't even spoken about that. Weddings cost time and money Grant and Max and I would rather spend the free time and spare money we have between the two us on traveling. We've already visited twenty five different countries and have plans to visit many, many more. In fact, in less than three months now, Max and I are going to Corfu for four weeks, to explore the entire island. Do you remember me telling you that Grant, whilst we were visiting the South Bank development. Anyway, why do you ask?"

After finishing the last of his healthy breakfast and second coffee of the morning, Grant replied, "I'm just being nosy, no, I mean I'm genuinely interested Kathy, what's Max like?" Kat got the feeling that Grant was sizing up the competition, checking out whether or not he stood a chance with the absolute stunner who was currently sat opposite him. Most of the people in The Healthy Food Hut would have more than likely assumed that Grant and Kathy were actually a couple and not just recently introduced work partners. "Well Grant, where do I start? My Max is one of a kind. He owns two T Shirts, one to wear and one in the wash. He loves alternative music, bands which most people haven't heard of. He has only two friends, but he's happy with that. He loves to cook and loves to travel even more. He cannot tolerate stupidity and all the woke shit that exists today and he specialises in doing as little work as possible. He's also very philosophical and for a lad who left school with barely enough qualifications to catch a bus, he sometimes leaves even the most well educated individuals speechless with his quotes on love and life in general and geopolitical topics. And finally, he's back in Yorkshire, probably still in bed, but waiting for me to return home on Wednesday."

For once, Grant was left almost speechless but still managed to muster up a reply, "It sounds to me Kathy that your Max is a kept man and taking you for every dime you earn, please tell me you're pulling my leg and Max actually works in recruitment or something. Grant paused for a second or two, You're not pulling my leg are you, you're serious aren't you? The person you just described is your Max?" Initially Kat was fuming at Grant's response but found enough restraint to not swipe back at him in anger. After all, Kat was on Fabio's payroll and Grant was currently picking up the tab. The conversation went quiet for a few awkward minutes but was soon reignited by Kat, "He's a good guy Grant, you wouldn't get him and he'd hate you but that can't get in the way of why you and I are both sat here now. We're here because there's work to do and money to be made. So let's get on with what we are here to do and focus a little less on my love life, is that okay with you?" Strangely, Kat enjoyed being quizzed by Grant on her love life, it made her feel exposed but also in control. Every answer she gave, be it true or slightly exaggerated to create a response or a reaction from Grant, empowered her. A new version of Kathy was being born in London and she was slowly but surely growing into a force to be reckoned with.

Grant suggested that they should now make their way back to Fab HQ, they needed to check in with Fabio and check the latest data. On the way there, Grant explained to Kat how the numbers worked and what exactly he was looking for before moving on to the next development. He had recently purchased a few more old buildings and was ready to green light both of them. Grant was already confident that all of the South Bank apartments would sell and was expecting to see that hefty deposits had now been received, in order to reserve the apartment of choice. The data was looking good, Fabio was feeling better and back in the game and the general mood at Fab HQ was positive and vibrant. Fabio, Grant and Kat met in the boardroom for an update on South Bank and Fabio kicked things off, "So Grant, how's the dashboard looking, have we delivered a thumbs up or a thumbs down so far." Grant replied confidently, "It's a big thumbs up so far guys and we are already holding non-refundable deposits on 25% of the units. That generally means that the prospective purchases are 99% guaranteed of being able to raise the full funds which are due upon completion of the development, which is still ahead of schedule and aiming to be the 30th of June. So, off the back of this data, we should now crack on with the advertising campaigns for the Bow Road and Thames Side developments."

Celebrations were due but Fabio had taken Kat's advice seriously and decided to abstain from drinking for at least one night. Grant genuinely wanted to thank Kat for the initial successes and also felt he owed her an apology for his comments aimed at Max. "What are you doing tonight Kathy?" Grant asked, knowing full well that Kat wouldn't be doing anything other than spending the evening on her own and occasionally catching up with Max. Kat cautiously replied, "Nothing, other than checking in with Max and getting a good nights sleep. Why do you ask?"

"We should celebrate Kathy and I owe you an apology for what I said about Max. I was out of order and I want to prove to you that I'm not a complete arsehole. Let's do dinner and a few drinks, nothing more than that, I promise!" Kat was caught off guard but the thought of a night out in London with Grant was genuinely more appealing than an evening alone in an apartment owned by Grant. So she said yes and told him that she would be ready by 7:30pm. Grant smiled and confirmed the appointment or date with, "Perfect."

Whilst Kat was getting ready, she phoned Max and told him that the initial campaign was going well so far and that Grant was happy to move things forward and in the direction of the next two developments. To Kat, this looked and felt like success but to Max, it meant that Kat's life would continue to be split between him in Yorkshire and Fabio and Grant in London. Max, forever being in love and proud of his girl, congratulated Kat on her achievements and promised to call her before he went to bed. Before ending their call, Kat told Max that she loved him and how much she was looking forward to seeing him tomorrow evening and then continued getting ready for her evening out with Grant. The reality of what Kat was doing very quickly caught up with her and for a moment, she started panicking. She thought to herself, "Kat, what are you doing? You're getting dressed up to go out for dinner with a guy you hardly know and Max knows nothing about it. It really doesn't matter what you're doing, Max doesn't know and it's never been like that, ever! How would Max feel if he did know and how would I feel if the same thing was happening back in Yorkshire? For fucks sake Kat, what are you doing?" Kat had no more time left to ponder on what may be a huge mistake, because Grant had arrived and it was time to go. "Kathy, you look fantastic and thank you for tonight. Without you this evening, I'd be stuck with Fabio or celebrating on my own and both of those options suck compared to this." Kat wasn't quite sure where she stood after that statement. Was Grant genuinely thankful and apologetic but simply said the wrong thing? Was she just filling in some blanks in Grant's life tonight or had Grant got no idea whatsoever how to make a lady feel appreciated and valued? Kat was confused, she felt emotional and already, she wanted her night out with Grant to be over before it had even begun. But there was no turning back now and she hoped that Grant was just out of practice when it came to spending recreational time with females.

Grant had hired a private driver and a car for the evening so that the two of them could have a couple of drinks each and then get home safely and in style. The white BMW quickly took off around the streets of London and in the direction of the restaurant which Grant had chosen. It came as no surprise to Kat that the chosen bar and restaurant was a fancy one and not a Whetherspoons or something similar. Although it was just a normal Tuesday evening in London, the streets were busy and the place was alive. Kat could see and feel the heartbeat of the city through the tinted windows, she was captivated by the bright lights and felt hypnotised by what she saw. She was like a child looking in through the window of a toy shop at Christmas. Grant snapped Kat out of her trance with, "You're starting to like London, aren't you Kathy? It's early days for you and you're still in the honeymoon period but I've seen that look before. You could easily get used to this, tell me what you're thinking Kathy." Kathy was warming to London and it was starting to feel more like home, or at least an acceptable place to call a second home. "You might be right Grant, who knows. But at the moment, I'm just living in the here and now and taking one day at a time and if each day I spend in London gets better, then surely that's a good thing, right or wrong?"

After Max lost his Brother, he immediately started living his life in the here and now and would try never to delay doing something or anything which could be done immediately. He'd learnt from Spike's death that tomorrow was not a given and that the only time which mattered was that moment in time when you could physically act on doing things, the here and now. Max often reminded Kat of that when she would put off doing things which could easily be done straight away and if Max was in that car with Kat and Grant, he would probably say something like, "I told you that Kat, tomorrow offers no guarantees!"

Grant had no time to reply to Kat on whether her philosophy (borrowed from Max) was right or wrong because they'd arrived at the restaurant and within seconds of the car pulling up outside, Kat's door was being opened by the driver. Grant let himself out and waited for Kat on the pavement with an extended arm. Kat thought to herself, "Okay, that's better, he's learning." She was starting to feel better about her evening out with Grant and kept reminding herself that it was all part of the process, wining and dining with business associates was either a perk of the job or something you occasionally had to tolerate. However, she felt guilty for not telling Max but also thought that telling the truth may stir up unnecessary tensions again. Outside the restaurant, a doorman was waiting to open the glass door and welcome them in. "Good evening Mr Fisher, great to see you again and how may I welcome your guest this evening?"

"This is Kathy or Kat, it depends on how well you know her."

Chapter 7 ~ Times They Are A Changin', Part 2.

Whilst Grant and Kat were enjoying their evening meal at The Basement Restaurant, Max had company back in Yorkshire. Charlie had finally told Laura about the mountain of debt he was struggling to manage and his pending redundancy. Needless to say, it had all kicked off and Laura had kicked Charlie out, telling him not to come home until he had figured something out. But there was nothing left for Charlie to figure out, it was now down to the banks to figure out how best and how fast they could recover some of their losses. Charlie reckoned that they could remain in the house for two to three months longer and then it would be repossessed. Charlie had succumbed to the inevitable. All was lost: his wife, his children, the house and his job and no amount of figuring out was going to change that. The only thing which Charlie had or hoped to figure out was how to convince Laura to let him come home. After all, he couldn't stay at Max's place for more than one night because Kat was due home tomorrow and as much as Kat liked Charlie, three would be a crowd in their little cottage.

"Come gather 'round people, wherever you roam and admit that the waters around you have grown and accept it that soon you'll be drenched to the bone. If your time to you is worth savin' then you better start swimmin' or you'll sink like a stone, for the times they are a-changin'." Max and Charlie were listening to Bob Dylan. Max thought strongly that the world needed more people like Bob, first generation versions of Spike. Happy and confident to preach or sing about how the world was being destroyed by the political elite. Charlie then hit Max with his best Bob Dylan impression. "Once upon a time you dressed so fine, you threw the bums a dime in your prime, didn't you." This caused Max to choke on his wine and then spit what was left in his mouth in the direction of his mate. "Charlie, you know what, I've never seen you looking so relaxed." Charlie topped up Max's glass and replied, "Well Max, when you've got nothing left, you've also got nothing left to lose and let's face it, we only get upset or sad when we lose stuff. So, off the back of that statement and once I've finally lost everything, I should never feel upset or sad again."

"Christ on a bike Charlie, where'd that come from? You're sounding more like me every day. Charlie, hold that thought, I need to call Kat." Max picked up his old mobile phone and selected Kat's number from his call list of just four numbers. Numbers for Angus, Charlie, Kat and Spike were the only numbers you would find on Max's phone. Max's call went straight to voicemail, suggesting that Kat had either turned her phone off, which was highly unlikely, or she had no signal where she was. "That's strange, thought Max. Oh well, I'll try again later."

Charlie commented, "Everything okay Max?" Max thought for a minute about whether or not everything was okay and then replied to Charlie, "I guess so mate, but it's very unlike Kat to turn her phone off and the apartment she's staying in gets a good signal and has excellent WiFi. Maybe she's had a busy day, her battery has died and she hasn't realised it yet. I'll try again when you've finally done one for night and before I go to bed."

"Do you ever worry about Kat when she's away Max?"

"Of course I do Charlie, I worry all the time about Kat and her safety."

"Let me rephrase that, I mean worry about her meeting someone else or finding herself wanting to be somewhere else other than Yorkshire. After all, it's pretty grim up here most of the time and even when the sun finally does come out, it brings with it all the worst people you can possibly imagine. You know, the sun's out, guns out brigade, all dressed in their piss stained tracky bottoms, T Shirts tucked into their waistband, a can of Stella in one hand and a buggy handle in the other." Max didn't really want to engage in Charlie's conversation about whether or not Kat would be playing away from home, so he quickly switched the subject back to music and asked Charlie whether he preferred The Stone Roses or Shed Seven.

Back in London, Kat was now genuinely enjoying her evening out with Grant. He'd learnt a few more lessons on how to socialise with the opposite sex, he wasn't talking about development projects and he was almost the perfect male companion who wanted nothing more than some intelligent and interesting companionship from an attractive female. Kat checked her phone to check the time. It was now 11:30pm and she was surprised that Max hadn't tried calling. What she would have done if he had, was another matter. But she then noticed that she had no signal. The name of the restaurant should have offered some inclination that phone signals may be a problem and the last thing she was thinking about, whilst being seated at a table for two in a quiet corner, was obtaining a WiFi code. Kat knew that Max would have tried calling her a few times and she knew that Max would now be wondering where she was. This could turn out to be a slight problem for Kat, so she had to come up with an explanation which would satisfy Max's curiosity on her whereabouts.

Max and Charlie were now four bottles of wine into their evening, Bob Dylan was still putting the world to rights and Max still hadn't managed to get hold of Kat. Max told Charlie that he could stay the night but he needed to be gone by lunchtime because Kat was due home and he needed to get everything squared up before she did. Charlie thanked Max for being so understanding and for letting him stay and he told Max to try and call Kat one last time. Max did exactly that and was instantly met by her voicemail. Max spoke out loud, "Oh fuck it Charlie, I'm going to bed! I'm sure there's an obvious or genuine reason why I can't get hold of her and I'll deal with that in the morning. Night mate and if I'm not up by lunchtime, please make sure that you are and you're out of my house!" Charlie reassured Max that everything was going to be okay, he poured himself another glass of wine and settled down for another night on Max's sofa.

It was now midnight and Grant and Kat's evening was also drawing to a close. Grant pushed his shirt cuff up, tapped his expensive looking watch and suggested to Kat that they should start making a move. Kat agreed, thanked Grant for a wonderful evening and then asked him what the plan was for tomorrow. Grant already had plans for tomorrow. "I know it's early, after a late one tonight, but I'll pick you up at 8:30am and I'll show you the Bow Road and Thames Side sites. These are both going to be different to South Bank and both will need more specific advertising campaigns, especially Bow Road. Here we will be appealing to the Crafty Cockneys and wanna be Kray Twins. Kat, these guys have money and lots of it, it's just best not to ask where it came from and if you dredged the canal which these apartments will overlook, you'll probably find a few people who didn't pay up on time. As for Thames Side, this is sailing in uncharted waters for me but I'll explain and show you more tomorrow. This development is a big deal Kat and we need the profits from both South Bank and Bow Road to make this one work, this one is make or break for me! After we've visited the sites, I'll take you to my offices and you can meet the team. They're a great bunch and they're really looking forward to meeting you. As promised and delivered last week, you'll be on your way home by 2pm, does that all sound okay?" Kat replied with a positive yes and was already looking forward to tomorrow.

The white BMW and its driver had arrived to take them home and Kat was the first to be dropped off. The London streets were slowly emptying, making the journey back to her apartment quicker and she would very soon be home, but it was now 1am in the morning and too late to call Max. Kat thanked Grant again for a great evening, said goodbye with her warm smile and made her way up to her apartment. She checked her phone one last time to see if Max had tried calling or sent her a message, but he hadn't, so she climbed into bed and settled down for the night. Before falling asleep, she thought briefly about what Grant had said to her, about warming to London and getting used to a very different way of life, a life which she was now starting to enjoy. With tomorrow came some new challenges. Kat had to explain to Max why she was unavailable all evening, but she'd already got that covered. She was off visiting some of the less glamorous parts of London with Grant. She was meeting new people from Grant's offices and then she'd got the long journey home to Yorkshire again, which she was now hating with a passion. Kat picked up her phone, downed a mouthful of coffee and called Max, after ringing for what felt like an eternity, Max answered. "Kat, where have you been? I was getting worried about you." Max was obviously still in bed, slightly hungover but delighted to hear from Kat. "I'm so sorry Max but I was asked by Fabio to join him and Grant for dinner at this restaurant which was in a converted World War 2 bomb shelter. Needless to say, there was no signal down there and it wasn't the sort of place where you could ask the waiter for a WiFi code and anyway, I lost track of time and then it was late and I would have been calling you at 1am in the morning and I knew that you would of been asleep, so here I am and again, I'm sorry Max!"

"Kat, it's fine and as long as your okay and there's no problems, then that's fine. Like I said Kat, I was just getting worried. Anyway, you're home tonight and you can tell me all about the bomb shelter restaurant and what you've been up to then and I'll tell you what's going on with Charlie and by the way, he's asleep on the sofa downstairs, so I think you can guess. Don't worry though, I've told him that he's got to be gone by lunchtime today and on that note, I'm going to wake him up now and then get some coffee on. Have a great day and call me when you're leaving London." Throwing Fabio into the mix meant that Kat didn't have to explain why she was out with Grant last night, just the two of them, and her reason for not not being available, the bomb shelter restaurant, was 100% genuine. But she couldn't help feel that now, she was not only hiding things from Max but she was also lying to him. Under her breath, she thanked Fabio for getting her out of jail without even a scratch and thought to herself, "That could have been a whole lot worse!" Grant had now arrived and was waiting outside in his Range Rover, it was time to hit the road and get back to work. It would take about an hour to reach the East End of London and Grant was making sure that there was plenty to talk about on the way by pointing out famous landmarks and buildings. Kat was impressed with his knowledge of London and it appeared that Grant knew as much about London as Max now knew about Corfu. Max was currently obsessed with the island and Kat knew that when she got home and brought Max up to speed on her second life in London, he would want to talk endlessly about Corfu. After all, the trip he was busy planning was now less than three months away and Max was getting more excited about it as each day passed.

Occasionally though, Kat would now find herself forgetting that she was about to jet off on another journey of beautiful discovery and exploration. Had that way of life with Max finally become another normal or was she being distracted or enticed by the bright lights, endless excitement and according to Grant, limitless opportunities which London had to offer? She needed to figure that out for herself and pretty quick because she was definitely feeling a shift within her, a feeling that she'd never felt before and one which she had no control over. Grant pulled up alongside the towpath which ran along the banks of the Victoria Canal and gave Kat an update, "You see that three story building over there, the one with the Sold STC board on it, that's mine. Many years ago, they made paint brushes there. For years they were exported all around the world. Wooden handles, genuine horse hair bristles and guaranteed to last a lifetime. Then the Chinese invented a much cheaper alternative with a plastic handle, synthetic bristles and guaranteed to last less than a month. The rest was history as they say. The building had been empty and derelict for years, I got it for a steal and now it's worth millions. We'll take a walk down the towpath and over the bridge. It's a nice walk along here and this toe path runs all the way into the Hertfordshire countryside. We should walk some of it one day Kathy, you'd love it."

Grant explained how the old paint brush factory was going to be converted into twenty luxury apartments, with prices starting from £750,000 each. This development was set to profit him a cool five million pounds but some of that profit would be passed on in order to kickstart the next development. That was Thames Side and if all went according to plan, he'd net a whopping fifteen million from that one. Grant had his financial future all mapped out but he also explained to Kat that once you'd started in this game, it was very difficult to stop or walk away, because your money was always tied up or invested in another old building somewhere. Work on Bow Road was due to start in eight weeks time, so there was nothing more to see here than an old knackered paint brush factory. They walked back along the toe path, jumped in the Range Rover and headed for Thames Side. On the way, Grant told Kat that the Thames Side development was something else and not only was it going the create some amazing homes, it was going to be the start of a whole new neighbourhood.

After a thirty minute drive through some pretty rough parts of the East End, Grant indicated to turn left and headed off down a bumpy old gravel track which went in the general direction of the river. He pulled over, quickly got out and invited Kat to do the same. He pointed at what must have been fifteen or twenty old buildings. All sat there, looking sorry for themselves, directly on the North Bank of the River Thames. Kat asked him, "So which one are you developing Grant?" He replied, "What do you mean, which one? I'm developing all of them Kathy. Remember, I told you in the car that Thames Side was going to be something else. There's going to be apartments for the young singles, houses and maisonettes for families, bungalows and easy access accommodation for the elderly. There'll be a new school, a doctors surgery, shops and a gym. Parks and open spaces for the residents to enjoy. Thames Side will be the East End of London reborn and like I said yesterday evening, it will either make or break me Kathy."

It was now lunchtime and although Kat was fascinated by
Grant's vision for the deprived and rundown parts of the
East End and genuinely wanted to hear more, she was
getting hungry and really couldn't be late setting off on her
journey home, especially after last nights narrow escape. So
she confidently took control of the agenda and told Grant
that it was time to head towards his offices and then grab
some lunch. Grant's offices were also located in the East
End, they were in an old converted church which
overlooked Victoria Park. Prior to him going big on
converting old industrial buildings into homes, Grant had
made some decent money from chopping up Victorian
terraces into small flats. The church which overlooked the
park was up for sale, planning to turn it into homes had
already been declined but he was happy to take a punt on it.
Grant's planning application also got declined and for a
short while, he was stuck with it. But he was allowed to
turn it into offices and that's what he did, his offices. He
knew eventually he would need a home for his expanding
business and team of property professionals and this ended
up being the perfect solution. Converting the church was
easy and gave him the idea and thirst to convert more old
buildings. They pulled into a small car park next to the
church, Grant parked in a bay marked GF and then told Kat,
"This is my church, this is where miracles happen!"

Chapter 8 ~ In God We Trust. In Church, We Make Money.

Kat strolled around the small car park for a minute or two taking in yet more new surroundings. To the left of the church was a florist and then a coffee shop. To the right, she spotted a lovely looking shop which sold ladies clothing, all designer brands and unique labels. Then there was an Italian restaurant and a shop which sold beautiful paintings and sculptures. Opposite the church was Victoria Park, a vast open space with duck ponds, walk and cycle ways, a bandstand and what appeared to be hundreds of joggers. Kat felt an immediate feeling of love towards this place and it was nothing like the East End of London which she had experienced earlier in the day. She was in her own little micro daydream when Grant called out to her, "Kathy, come on, it's time to go to church!"

"Sorry Grant, I was miles away. But this place, it's like a little village within London, it's absolutely gorgeous!"

Grant pointed Kathy in the direction of the original church door and then stepped in front of her to open it. She walked through the large wooden door and was immediately met by an attractive receptionist, this was Anne, 45 going on 25 but pulling it off immaculately. Anne stood up from behind her desk and was very quickly in the right place to take Grant's jacket and then welcome him and his guest. "Grant, welcome back, we were starting to wonder where you were or whether you were even coming back. And this must be Kathy? We've heard a lot about you Kathy. Welcome, please let me take your coat."

Whilst Anne was neatly hanging up their garments, Grant replied, "Come on Anne, you know I only get in the way when I'm here and anyhow, I'm better suited out there, sniffing out new opportunities. Anyway, you keep everything tight here and running like clockwork and I guess that's how things are today, running like clockwork?"

Anne was not only the receptionist but also the glue which held Grant's office based team together. They were a mixed bunch from all walks of life and Anne was clearly Mother Hen, picking them up when they were down and telling them to real things in when overstepping the mark and Kat was about to meet them.

Grant asked Anne if she'd remembered to order in lunch for everyone today and was met with, "What do you think Grant? The buffet arrived about 20 minutes before you did and it's in the kitchen for when everyone is ready." Grant led the way, whilst confirming with Kat that that was Anne. They walked up what used to be the aisle of the church and in the direction of what used to be the alter. The alter was now an office and this office was home to Grant's architect and planning manager. These two guys basically dealt with all the technical stuff and in a nutshell, reported back to Grant on whether or not an old building he'd spotted could be renovated or converted into homes and profit. Grant introduced Kat to William and Nigel, William was the architect and Nigel was the planning guy. The two of them looked over the top of their monitors like meerkats, nodding at Grant in a way which suggested that everything was going according to plan and then said hello to Kat, before disappearing behind their screens again. Grant was about to enter another office, this was accounts, but before he walked through the door, he gave Kat a heads up. "Kathy, these guys do numbers, not conversation. Please be aware of that and don't take the lack of interest in your presence personally." Kathy was introduced to Muriel, a drab and boring looking lady who was responsible for keeping as much of Grant's money in his bank account as possible, and Duncan, who was a trainee accountant and trying his hardest to be a male version of Muriel. Once out of the office, Grant explained, "Muriel has saved my financial arse on many occasion. She may look like a washed up middle aged women who's given up on life, but she eats, sleeps and breathes numbers and is probably the only person I know who could genuinely fix the UK's broken economy."

Grant led Kathy upstairs and then entered the sales office. "Kathy, please meet Stu, Abi and Megan. These relentless little termites are responsible for selling or letting anything and everything we have renovated or converted into a home. Stu is new and already addicted to RedBull and Haribo. Abi has been here for just over two years now and has sold or let hundreds of units and Megan is the boss of this department. By hook or by crook, she makes one hundred percent sure that the monthly income targets are not only met but smashed!" Kat had just learnt, very quickly, that there was an awful lot more going on inside of Grant's property business than initially met the eye. She had assumed that he was just some flash guy who had rocked up in London, with a load of money and decided to convert factories and warehouses. Kat was so wrong, Grant had small scale projects going on all over London, as small as a basement, loft or even garage conversion. Grant later informed Kat that these small projects were now the bread and butter of his business and simply covered his costs and payroll. The big money was to be made in the big projects, those which required big commitment and even bigger investment.

Grant and Kathy made their way downstairs and back to Anne at reception. He asked Anne to send an email to all staff, informing them that lunch was now available in the meeting room and everyone was expected to attend. Grant made his way to the meeting room, closely followed by Anne and Kathy and they were soon joined by the entire team. With everyone present and with either a smoked salmon bagel or a chicken, bacon and brie wrap in hand, Grant systematically asked each department for a quick but accurate update on current business matters. His team were obviously well rehearsed for Grant's interpretation of a service at his church and provided Rev Fisher with what he wanted to hear, facts and nothing but the facts. Grant concluded the brief meeting by inviting anyone who needed to discuss anything in private to meet him in his office, after lunch had finished. The mood in the room suggested that that wasn't going to be necessary and everyone got on with enjoying their free lunch. Kat found herself standing there, taking it all in and one by one she observed the individuals. Muriel and Duncan cut their bagels into precise quarters before eating them with a knife and fork. The architect and planning guys were busy trying to express size and shape with their hands, whilst holding a bagel and a wrap at the same time. Stu and Abi were just happy to be stuffing their faces with free food and Anne kept a close eye on all of them, whilst making sure the food supply didn't run out. Grant had disappeared somewhere and Megan had gone outside for a quick smoke.

Anne approached Kat and asked her, "Is everything okay Kathy, you appear to be a million miles away?" Kat was in fact a million miles away. A million miles away from everything she knew, everything she believed in and everything which her life with Max had become. However, her life with Max was less than three hundred miles away but she was feeling comfortable and content with being a million miles away from that life. Grant came back into the room and proceeded to touch base with and thank everyone for their efforts. He caught up with Kat and reminded her of the time, it was now almost 2pm. He made sure that Anne was still at the helm and then briefly surveyed the room for Megan. Kat knew where Megan was and informed Grant accordingly, "She's outside having a smoke, if you're looking for Megan?" Grant replied, "Thanks Kathy and yes I was looking for Megan. She could sell ice to an Eskimo that one but I have to keep an eye on her. She's great at what she does here but she has a troubled past and one which occasionally follows her around." Kat knew that Grant couldn't give too much away but she also knew that if she asked, she would most likely get some answers. "What do you mean by troubled past Grant?" Grant pulled Kat away from the rest of the group and explained, "Her Dad used to knock her and her mother about quite a bit, usually after he'd been drinking. Eventually, Megan, her brother and their mother ran away and found shelter and safety at a hostel, which was around the same time as I was trying to put together a formidable sales team. I was going down the usual channels of recruitment with little success when I received an application from Megan. You couldn't even call it an application really, it was no more than an email which read: "Please can I have more information on the salary and if you give me a chance, I promise I won't let you down." Kat, I invited Megan in for an interview and it ended up with her interviewing me. I remember closing the interview with, "Please don't let me down Megan and make me regret my decision!"

Kat was starting to see a very different side to Grant. He was clearly capable of calling the shots and controlling every situation which involved his money but he was also very kind and considerate towards those who were helping him build his empire. Kat thought to herself, "Maybe I'm the latest version of Megan or even Anne for that matter. I know nothing about Anne's background yet. Does Grant see another Megan or Anne in me, but without the beatings or whatever. Does he look at me and think, I can see you're not entirely happy nor are you getting from life what you genuinely want but it's okay, because I'm here and here to help."

Megan had now returned to the room and obviously put a stop to the conversation which Grant and Kat were having, she grabbed herself a bagel and made her way over to Grant and Kat and started a new conversation with, "Bloody men, or should I say boys? Can you believe it? I just called my fella and suggested that we went to Brighton for the weekend, do you wanna know what he said? I'll tell you what he said, Spurs are playing The Gunners at home this weekend and I'd rather go to the match! Honestly, the guys I meet either love football more than me or they fancy themselves as the new Frank Bruno! Oh well, at least this one doesn't use me like a punch bag!" Grant had heard all this before from Megan and didn't even bat an eyelid but made sure that she was okay and coping with her life. Kat however was taken back by Megan's openness towards her bad choices in men and wasn't quite sure what to say but she found herself instantly liking Megan and did her best to comfort her. "No one gets love right first time Megan, that's the rule. You have to shed some tears in order to find your Prince Charming. It's how it was for me before I met and finally fell in love with Max and we've now been together for just over fifteen years." This was the first time Kat had thought about Max for a good few hours now and it reminded her that she should get going very soon or she'll get stuck in traffic and be late home again. But Megan wasn't quite finished with Kat just yet, "What you doing next week Kat? It's my birthday and I'm heading up town with Abi and a couple of my other girlfriends, do you wanna come? I'm telling you now, it'll be a great night out." It took Kat no time at all to reply with, "Megan, that's really kind of you to invite me and I'd love that, what day next week?"

"Saturday!" Megan replied…

Kat realised instantly what she had just committed to and knew that she had made that decision without even thinking about her other life in Yorkshire with Max. She would have to work her magic on Max again and hope that he would understand and accept it as a one off. Grant prompted Kat to bid farewell to his team and hit the road back home before the city traffic started building up. She quickly mingled through the room and thanked everyone for making her feel welcome, she said her goodbyes, swapped phone numbers with Megan and made her way to reception. Anne was waiting there with her coat. She put it on Kat's shoulders and gave her a gentle hug before wishing her a safe journey. Grant then drove Kat back to her car and he made sure that she was okay. They quickly wrapped up all the business matters and just like that, her life in London would come to an end for another week. But Grant sensed a feeling of sadness or disappointment from Kat and wanted to know more. "Is everything okay Kathy? You look like you've suddenly lost your sparkle, normally you're buzzing at the thought of getting out of here and back home to Max. What's up?"

"I am looking forward to getting back home to Max but this place is also starting to feel like home to me. It started out as a compromise but now, if I had to choose between Yorkshire or London, I'd choose London." Grant wasn't really surprised by what Kat had said and could see where this was all potentially going. But he reminded Kat that Max was the guy in her life, he was in Yorkshire and that's where she needed to be for now. Grant added, "Anyway, as soon as you get home this evening, your life in Yorkshire with Max will soon be your preferred choice again. You'll soon drop back into your routine together and everything will be fine. And don't forget Kathy, you've got that trip of a lifetime to look forward to. It's Corfu isn't it, when are you going again and how long for?"

Over her weeks spent in London, Kathy had noticed that Grant could be very forgetful when it came to remembering things which weren't entirely related to business, so she reminded him again in a way which was born out of her new found confidence, "Come on Grant, I must have told you this a dozen times already! Yes, Max and I are going to Corfu. We're going for four weeks, that's almost the entire month and we fly on Saturday the 5th of July. Can you remember all that or do I need to write it down on sticky notes and put them on you dashboard?" Grant looked across at Kat and then laughed out load in a way she had never seen before. Grant wasted no time in responding to Kat's slightly sarcastic put down, "Well you've come a long way in a short space of time, haven't you? I've witnessed London change many people but for most, it takes at least six months. You Kathy, have embraced and become part of this unique environment in less than six weeks, that's pretty impressive and I now understand why you like it here, you're not intimidated by it, are you?"

"No Grant, I'm not and the problem is this, the more time I spend in London, the more I love it and the more I find myself questioning why I have to stay in Yorkshire." They were almost at the car park but Grant wasn't finished, "What's stopping you leaving Yorkshire? Is it fear? Is it because you've never thought about it before or is it Max? Would Max move to London?" Grant's questions had Kat thinking seriously about the reason why she'd become comfortable in Yorkshire with Max and why she had never broadened her horizons. She had less than five minutes to reply to Grant, so she shot from the hip, "Fuck knows Grant, fuck knows why and I'm so glad you grilled me on that, because I'm going to spend the next three or four hours, alone in my car, trying to figure all that out!"

Grant had now delivered Kat safely back to her car again, albeit an hour late, and it was that time again. But before they said goodbye for another week, Kat satisfied Grant's curiosity on whether or not Max would move to London. "Oh Grant, would Max move to London? Absolutely not, he hates the place! He says it's too busy, too noisy, too expensive and there's too many rats. There's only one place Max would rather be right now, and that's Corfu!"

Chapter 9 ~ If You Want Something You've Never Had,

You Have To Something You've Never Done.

Kat arrived home shortly after 7pm to find Max and Charlie in front of the TV, with a large glass of wine each and watching old episodes of The Fast Show on YouTube. Max hit pause, put his glass on the table and quickly jumped up to meet his girl. They embraced and Max started to explain that Charlie had dropped by earlier that evening for a quick chat and that he thought he needed cheering up. Max hadn't planned his evening with both Charlie and Kat in mind so he prompted Charlie to drink up and make tracks but Kat was already on a mission to get herself in Max's good books and stepped in with an alternative plan. "No Charlie, you don't need to go just yet, stay and have another drink. Max, grab another bottle of wine and a glass for me please, one of the big glasses." Max and Charlie looked at each other in a WTF kind of way but both were delighted with what Kat had just said.

Max had already told Kat that Charlie's life was about to hit the wall but she wanted to hear the latest episode, "So Charlie, what's the crack with you and Laura right now and how long have you got before you lose the house and your job?" Both Max and Charlie were slightly taken aback by Kat's direct approach, neither of them had heard nor seen that side of her character before and again, they both looked at each other in a way which was questioning whether or not it was actually Kat in the room or an imposter. Charlie took a big gulp of wine from his glass and proceeded to bring Kat up to speed. "Well Kat, Laura has let me back in the house but we're in separate bedrooms and that's not going to change anytime soon, if at all. She refuses to go back to work, even part time and that ain't going to change, ever. She's given me until the end of May to come up with a plan to save everything, that's only five weeks, so that ain't happening either and as for the house, the bank want their money or the house by the end of June. So they'll be getting the house, because I can't raise the money on my own. On a brighter note though, I'll soon be on the Government Payroll."

"You've found a new job?" Kat asked of Charlie, "That's great news!"

"No Kat, I haven't found a new job! I'm still being made redundant and what I mean is that I'll soon be on the dole! Nobody is hiring programmers at the moment, so at this rate, I'll be on the dole or flipping burgers at Happy Burger!"

Max chipped in, "There's nothing wrong with being a grill chef Charlie, people are addicted to crap food. So let their addiction provide you with job security, some honest income and a fresh start." Charlie was trying hard to find the positive within what Max had just said, but was failing miserably. "Are you fucking serious Max! I'm a programmer on £250k a year and you're trying to sell me the dream of becoming a burger technician who earns £250.00 a week, plus one free meal per day, which is guaranteed to destroy your body from the inside out!" Max was quick to respond to Charlie's outburst. "Charlie, you were a programmer on £250k a year, have you forgotten something mate? You're being made redundant and nobody wants to employ you. I'm sorry Charlie if that hits hard but you have to accept the fact that your life is about to play out on completely different terms and if I didn't remind you of that, what sort of a friend would I be to you?" Charlie downed his drink and stood up as if he was going to walk out on Max but instead, he invited Max and Kat in for a group hug. "I fucking love you guys and I honestly don't know where I'd be right now without you."

Kat broke away from the group, grabbed a half empty bottle of wine and topped up the glasses. She raised her glass high in the air and made a toast to new beginnings. The Three Musketeers, all dealing with the complexities of life but in different ways, chanted, "All for one and one for all." The feeling of solidarity was strong that evening in the cottage overlooking the village green, and the topic of conversation was very much focused on the positive future and not the troubled past. Max was in one of his philosophical moods and quoted something he'd heard and then plagiarised into one of his motivational quotes, "If you want something you've never had, you have to do something you've never done." "Charlie, that's for you my friend. If you want to create a new life for yourself after the current one has shut up shop, you're going to have to start thinking and doing things differently." Max's 'not so original quote' got Kat thinking about life in London and, quite possibly, life without Max, "If I want something I've never had, a life in London. I have to do something I've never done, live my life without Max, period." This thought took the edge off Kat's banter for a short while but she soon bounced back with, "Maxi, what's for dinner tonight? I'm starving and Charlie looks like he hasn't eaten anything other than ready meals for weeks now." Max had started preparing dinner for two when Charlie rocked up and that was as far as dinner for two got. A bit of prep but nothing to eat. Kat decided that a takeaway was in order and asked the guys if they preferred Indian or Chinese. She also reminded Charlie that he was in no fit state to drive home and he could crash on the sofa again. The last thing Charlie needed now was to get stopped by the police, breathalysed and as a result, lose his license.

Whilst waiting for the Indian takeaway to arrive, they opened and consumed a few more bottles of wine and picked a film from Max's vast collection of DVDs. They all agreed on watching a film about a group of elderly people who chose to leave the UK and spend their golden years in India. In the film, the elders had all financially committed to a spiritual retirement at a hotel which wasn't quite finished and was due to be sold to developers. Needless to say, the run down hotel in India never got sold and the elderly guests, minus one who died and one who returned to England, lived happily ever after. As far as nights in on a Wednesday go, this was up there with the best of them and it could have easily been a Friday or Saturday night, when most people celebrate surviving another week in the hamster wheel. Max referred to this way of life as the Matrix. A way of life he had left a few years ago and vowed never to return to. A way of life where having no free time for your friends, family and loved ones was persistently sold to you as a job promotion or career move of a lifetime. Charlie was a victim of the Matrix but amidst all the current chaos and calamity in his life right now, unbeknown to him, blue skies were on their way. He was very soon going to be set free and he would be free to fly again like a caged bird who had just been released back into the wild. Even if it meant flipping burgers at Happy Burger, he would be free again to choose for himself exactly where he wanted his life to go. Max knew that his Kat was becoming part of the hamster wheel workforce and her recent promotion in London had already driven a wedge between the two of them and taken away some of their time together. Living proof that on paper, promotion and more money sounds great but in reality, it means more work and less free time.

Charlie had by now fallen asleep on the sofa with his glass still half full and still in his hand, clinging on to it like a child clutches their favourite toy. Max gently prized the glass out of his hand and quietly placed it on the table next to him. It was getting late and although Max and Kat were both starting to feel the effects of a great evening in, they both had just about enough left in reserve to enjoy some quiet conversation time together, occasionally interrupted by Charlie's snoring. Kat told Max all about London and Grant's big plans for the East End, the people she had met and her new friend Megan. She also described to him the beautiful little village she'd fallen in love with, located within the busyness and grubbiness of the real East End. "You'd love it Max, right up your street it is. Independant shops and cafes, I even spotted a cool little shop which sold old vinyl records, DVDs, band T Shirts and movie memorabilia. I reckon you'd spend your entire life in that shop and I'd never see you!" Max was quick to reply, "It does sound lovely Kat but you know my thoughts on London and further more, our current salaries wouldn't get us very far in London. I'd have to get a proper job again and that move, combined with having less free money at the end of each month, would soon put a stop to our travel plans. It's a novel idea but it's not for me Kat. I'm sorry if that's where you were going with that." Kat was loosely testing the water and wasn't at all surprised by Max's response but his response hadn't dampened her feelings towards a life outside of Yorkshire and at least she now knew that for her, a life in London would definitely be a life without Max.

Keen to avoid an awkward silence, Max immediately started telling Kat about the old abandoned village in Corfu he'd been researching, "It's called Old Perithia but people refer to it as the Ghost Village. It used to be a vibrant and prosperous community. It's located on the northern slopes of Mount Pantokrator, but now only a handful of people live there, including a couple who run a boutique bed and breakfast. I've penciled a visit there into our schedule and if we're doing okay for money, we could spend a night at The Merchant's House, that's the name of the B&B. It's not cheap mind you but people say a night in Old Perithia is like nothing else. Here, take a look at these photos of Old Perithia and all the abandoned buildings, that one there used to be the school. I've also found out that many of the old buildings are up for sale, if you're really looking for a change of scenery and a project to keep us busy?" Kat perused the photos with genuine interest and was half tempted to comment and compare the old buildings in Old Perithia with the old buildings which Grant buys up in London and then renovates into homes. But she was cute enough to know that Project Corfu was Max's baby and Grant should be left well and truly out of this conversation. She kept the conversation going, "I wouldn't know where to start Max, that one there hasn't even got a roof on it and that one looks like it's about to fall down!"

"I know what your saying Kat and apparently it's not easy to get started on the works required, even after you officially own the building. The village is now a place of architectural and historical interest and anything to do with renovating the buildings has to be approved first and then signed off by the local authorities, it could be an absolute nightmare. But the thought of living somewhere like that or even another village somewhere on the island is very appealing to me. What about you Kat? I know it's not the village in London you described but property on Corfu can be incredibly cheap and we could easily afford to buy something which we could move straight into and then fix up and make it our own over time?"

"It sounds lovely Max and you know how much I love Greece and the sunshine but I haven't even been to Corfu yet, so let's park that idea up for now, shall we?"

Kat wasn't quite sure how the conversation had ended up with her proposing that the two of them could live in London and with Max suggesting that they could move to Corfu. He'd never even spoken about leaving Yorkshire, let alone the UK. Perhaps it was Kat opening up about wanting to live in London which made Max feel that he could also have an opinion on where he'd prefer to live. However it happened, a couple of new truths had been established in their relationship that evening. Kat fancied a new life in London and Max fancied a new life in Corfu. Kat's decision to work in London three days a week had caused a little bit of fallout but it was never going to be a killer blow to their relationship and the new arrangement had very quickly become part of the weekly routine. But this time, the two of them had openly declared to each other where they would prefer to live and at the moment, neither of them appeared to be willing to budge on their decisions. But maybe, just maybe, Max will eventually get bored of travelling around the world and warm to the idea of a life with Kat in London. Perhaps Kat will fall in love with Corfu and eventually share Max's dream of owning an old house in a quiet village in the mountains. But for now, life will carry on as normal and only time will tell where they end up in the future. It was however, now time for them both to sleep on their thoughts and let Charlie sleep in peace and without their background conversation. Kat reached out and grabbed Max's hand, "Come on Maxi, it's time for bed, are you coming with me or breaking my heart this evening?" Max needed no time to consider his options, "I'm coming with you, come on, let's go!"

Chapter 10 ~ How Did It All Go So Wrong.

It was the morning after the great night in and the night of new truths and revelations. Charlie was off to work and had a whole day ahead of him which would involve programming more nails into his professional coffin. Kat was off to Harrogate to catch up with some existing and new clients and Max would spend the first two or three hours of his day tidying up after the night before. Max gave very little consideration towards how he dressed and looked but he liked the cottage he shared with Kat to be clean and tidy and looking show home ready at all times. It was just his thing and nobody was ever going to change that thing, not even Kat. He would put his favourite music on, do all the essential cleaning and tidying up first and then systematically work his way through the cottage making sure that every room was exactly how he wanted it. Mood pieces and candles would be moved from one end of the table to the other. Pictures and cushions were never exempt from Max's routine and plants and flowers would never find the time to settle and flourish in just one place. Once Max had finished his morning ritual of organizing and pimping, he'd wrap things up by checking each room one last time and apply any minor adjustments which he thought were required to achieve perfection. Whilst in the process of making the cottage perfect, Max would often talk out loud to himself, "Honestly dude, with the way you live your life right now, you wouldn't have time for a full time job. You struggle to fit in four hours of work each day, let alone eight." But he had no regrets surrounding his way of life and was quite proud of the fact that he could tell people that he was now either 'only working part time' or he was 'semi retired at thirty'. His choice of admission would depend on who he was pitching to and whether he was trying to convince someone that there was more to life than work, work, work and money, money, money or avoid a punch in the face from someone who may perceive him to be a jumped up and privileged little prick.

Max was also very aware of the fact and never forgot that it was his late brother's inheritance which allowed him to buy the cottage. Although Spike was anti establishment and wanted to see the downfall of Capitalism, he was far from stupid and well aware of how the system worked. Spike had made some small investments in a couple of startups which turned out to be great investments. He then invested those returns into a couple of larger safe bets and within two years, Spike was what some people would describe as minted. When Spike died, he left everything he owned to Max, apart from a couple of guitars he'd never learnt to play. He left those to a local band who had a guitarist but no guitars and he left his record collection to a local and independent record dealer, who may very well still have every record he inherited. The fact that Max had no mortgage nor rent to pay each month meant that him and Kat lived a very privileged and unique way of life. Both thirty years old and apart from a couple of very small credit card payments each month, they lived debt free. This in turn allowed them to travel all the time and not watch the pennies like most other thirty year olds had to.

Max had finally finished getting the cottage straight and took a few minutes out to check in on his friend and then his sweetheart, "Charlie, it's Max, you okay?"

"Yes Max, I'm fine, thanks for calling and thanks for a fab evening. What time did I fall asleep last night?"

"It must have been around midnight. Kat and I chatted for about an hour before hitting the sack and that was around 1pm."

"Okay, what we're you talking about that was so important that it couldn't wait until the morning?"

"It's a long story Charlie but I'll try and condense it into a few minutes. Kat was telling me about London and this place she'd been to, like a little village within the city. She said it was lovely and I'd love it, but you know my thoughts on London Charlie? I fucking hate the place and even if I didn't hate the place, I'm not risking everything I own and potentially getting into debt to move from one end of the UK to the other. If Kat and I were going to move and take a risk, put everything we have on black or red, then let's go big. Let's get out of here and move to one of the places we've visited and fallen in love with and not a dirty and overpriced city down south."

"I hear you Max, I hear you and I hope you fought back with a good reply?"

"I did Charlie. I offered Corfu as an alternative to London. A pretty good and valid alternative I thought, if Kat was genuinely looking for a change of scenery."

"And?"

"I'm not entirely sure Charlie but the conversation didn't end in tears. So surely that's a good thing?"

"Maybe for now it's a good thing but you need to keep a close eye on this Max. You guys are clearly divided on where you want your future to be and that could end in tears."

"Charlie, that's a bit rich coming from you but I think this little ripple will soon smooth itself out. Anyway, what are you doing this Saturday? Kat has invited Lucy over for dinner and that means I'm cooking for three and then listening to girl talk all night."

"Are you talking about Lucy Palmer, the fit looking one with long blonde hair? If so, I think I should join you and let's make it dinner for four."

"Yes I am and she would eat you alive Charlie, I couldn't do that to you. So let's leave the girls to it and we'll do the Ted and the Taj again."

"Okay Max, what time is Lucy getting to yours?"

"I think Kat said six o'clock."

"Cool, I'll be with you just after six then."

Over the last few weeks, Max had seen the lives of two people who were very close to him change. Kat's life was changing because of the work decisions she'd made. Those decisions were seeing her working and hanging out in new places and as a result, bringing new people into her life.

With that came a new way of living, living with and without Max. Charlie's life was also changing but not as a result of recent decisions he'd made. His life was changing because of decisions he'd made years ago. Deciding to buy a big house he could only just about afford. Constantly upgrading his car each year and doing the same for Laura. Choosing private schools over state schools for the children and pretending that he could pick up the tab for all this expense on his own when Laura gave up on multitasking. Max's life was changing but he wasn't in control nor paying a high price for some bad historical decisions. His life was being changed by those around him and it was finally starting to freak him out. What if Kat is hell bent on living in London and eventually drops an ultimatum, London with Kat or it's over? And as much as Max loved Charlie and would do anything for him, the thought of having Charlie in his life full time was frightening. Charlie had finally come to terms with the fact that his life with Laura and the children was over and was already fancying his chances with Lucy Palmer. Max could already imagine what Charlie's idea of a great Saturday night out would soon look like and it certainly wasn't the Ted and the Taj. Max was happy with his life and although living in an old stone cottage on Corfu somewhere would make him happier, for as long as Kat was there most of the time and Charlie was there when it suited him, things were just fine and no further change was required.

Max had some work booked for that afternoon and needed to be at the pickup station in just under an hour. So he grabbed his keys, jumped in his van and made his way to the depot whilst catching up with Kat, "Maxi my love, how was your morning, need I ask what you've been doing?"

82

"Very funny Kat and I'm getting bored of saying this now but if I didn't do all the housework, it would never get done!"

"I love you Max and I appreciate everything you do, you know that."

"Yes I know that Kat and that's why it works so perfectly for us. Anyway how's your morning been?"

"It's been okay but working in the Harrogate office is so boring compared to working in London. The clients are either struggling farmers, failing estate agents or boring startups who used to be farmers or estate agents. We dont create success at Harrogate Max, we charge a small fortune for putting a Band Aid on a broken leg and Fabio knows that. That's why he hardly ever visits the Harrogate office and prefers to spend his time in London."

"That sounds to me like you'd quite happily spend all week in London then, right or wrong?"

"As far as work goes Max, yes I would but we now know where we stand as far as London is concerned, don't we?"

"Exactly Kat, not where I stand nor where you stand but where we stand. It has to be right for both of us and at the moment, London is not right for me. In the same way you're not ready for a life on Corfu yet. Do you get what I'm saying?"

"I get what you're saying Max but don't forget, you asked the question and now you're getting arsy with me because I've given you an honest answer. Would you prefer it if I lied to you?"

"Crying out load Kat, I only called to see how your day was going and now listen to us. Anyway, I'm sure you're busy and you've got money to make, so you better get going. By the way, Charlie and I are going out on Saturday, so you and Lucy can sort yourselves out as far as dinner is concerned and then spend the evening bitching on about how unreasonable men are these days!"

Kat was just about to respond and play her part in trying to cool things down when Max entered the Tyne Tunnel. "Max, we need to get a handle on this, it's becoming a problem and that's not what I want. Max, are you there, are you ignoring me? Max, Max, you better not have hung up on me!" Kat looked at her phone, noticed the time and it suddenly dawned on her that she was now ten minutes late for a meeting with a new client. She quickly made her way to the meeting room, put her phone on silent and tried her best to come up with a valid excuse for being late. Max exited the tunnel on the North Bank of the River Tyne, a place called Wallsend, where more of the houses were boarded up instead of lived in. He often wondered how on earth there could be a housing crisis or shortage of homes when there was row upon row of boarded up terraces everywhere. Now clear of the tunnel, Max called Kat back but after a couple of rings, he was put through to voicemail. He tried a few more times before giving up and then muttering to himself, "Well Maxi boy, that ended well didn't it?"

Max hated the Tyne Tunnel for a number of reasons and he now had another reason to add to his list. Him using the tunnel lost him his call to Kat and now Kat's not answering her phone. Kat hated being late, especially for meetings with new clients and her unexpected tiff with Max made her late for her meeting and may have cost her a new client, who wasn't impressed with her turning up late. All in all, things today were not going according to plan for Max and Kat nor were they running like clockwork, which is how things usually run. Nothing major had happened today, neither had confessed to having an affair or a secret addiction but somehow, voices were raised and they ended up falling out big time. Max was struggling to get his head around how only the night before they were raising glasses to a positive future and now they weren't even talking to each other. Perhaps Kat had been secretly raising a glass to her own positive future whilst leaving Max and Charlie to figure theirs out for themselves. After all, Kat was the only one out of the three of them who was actually in control of the future. Charlie was simply having to deal with whatever his life had to throw at him, which was quite often the contents of his wardrobe and occasionally some very expensive plates, and hope that his future was going to be better than his present. For Max, it was now looking like he would inherit whatever Kat was happy to walk away from or leave behind and a Charlie who wants to go out on the pull every Friday and Saturday night.

Max had just finished his last delivery when his phoned pinged. Kat had sent him a message, "Max, I'm not sure what happened earlier but if it was me, I'm sorry. Things are not right between us at the moment and I don't know why, we have to figure this out Max or we could soon end up really losing it, losing everything we have together. I'm probably going to make things worse now, but Lucy messaged me earlier and asked if I fancied a couple of drinks after work and to be honest with you Max, I do fancy a couple of drinks after work. I won't be late, Love K x." Max sat in his van and thought to himself, "How did it all go so wrong?" He wasn't quite sure what to do now. Should he call Kat and try and figure things out over the phone? Should he reply to her message and then get caught up in a series of messages, most of which will be misinterpreted or should he just leave it there? Kat wasn't asking him if he minded her going for drinks with Lucy, she was telling him that she was going for drinks. Max thought about his plan of action and decided on Plan C, which was, "No questions asked, no reply required." Kat had told him what she was doing and that she wouldn't be late, therefore she was coming home that evening and Max would be waiting for her, as always. Where things go and end up from there could be anyone's guess now but Max was now heading home, taking the long route and avoiding the Tyne Tunnel.

Chapter 11 ~ Truth Bombs And More Revelations.

It took Max an extra hour to get home because he chose to boycott the Tyne Tunnel. That decision saved him £2.50 but he then got hit with a £12.50 ULEZ charge because he'd entered central Newcastle. Max had to cover that cost, along with his diesel costs for the day with what he'd been paid for delivering groceries around boarded up Wallsend, which meant he'd take home less than £50.00. He started thinking to himself, "I bet delivery drivers on Corfu don't have to deal with this crap? £2.50 to use a tunnel. £12.50 just to drive around a part of town where most people live. Constantly watching your back and your van and I bet they're not driving around in the pissing rain and freezing cold. What the fuck am I doing this for?" Max couldn't wait to get home now and pick up from where he'd left off with Project Corfu. He was keen to research Kassiopi and another old fortress he'd read about, along with Kalami Bay, which featured in The Durrells. Max absolutely loved The Durrells and he'd made his mind up on how his evening without Kat was going to be spent. A couple of bottles of wine, some leftover Indian takeaway, no Charlie and a binge watch of The Durrells.

There were many reasons why Max loved The Durrells but his favourite reason was how this beautiful series, set on Corfu in the late 1930's, captured not only the laid back manner of those who lived on the island but also their resilience during challenging times. In the series, Louisa Durrell and her four slightly odd children have to deal with some challenging times of their own. Initially after Mr Durrell unexpectedly and inconveniently passed away and then when Louisa decided to up sticks and move the family to Corfu to start a new life. Max also loved trying to identify where each scene was shot and he was proud of the fact that he'd managed to geolocate the actual house which was the Durrells rented home in the series. The house is located on the East coast of the island, just South of Kontokali Bay and Max had already scheduled a visit there in his itinerary for their upcoming trip. He hadn't yet told Kat about this plan because he knew she wouldn't share his fascination of nor desire to visit some random old house on Corfu. But for Max, this beautiful and almost perfectly square house wasn't just any old house, this was where life for the Durrells was reborn and then flourished into something special and then spectacular. With of course, a little help from Spyro, Theo and Lugaretza.

Whilst Max was at home enjoying his wine and his left over takeaway, watching The Durrells and fantasizing about a peaceful and laidback way of life on Corfu, Kat was in a trendy little wine bar in Harrogate with Lucy. Kat got the first round of drinks in and then proceeded to tell Lucy how her day had been an absolute disaster. "Everything was going fine, then Max called, then we started arguing, then he hung up on me and then I was late for my meeting. I was meeting a potential new client for the first time and he was really pissed off that I'd kept him waiting for ten minutes. I needed this client to sign up in order for me to hit my target and get my monthly bonus. Anyway, he said he'd consider his options and get back to me next month, as if he knew that his decision would scupper my bonus for this month. He was a bit of a twat anyway and would have more than likely been a nightmare from day one." Lucy looked at Kat with a confused look on her face and then replied, "Kat, why are you making such a big deal out of some minor issues which to be honest, happen to most people all the time. All couples argue occasionally and as good as you are at your job, you're not perfect, nobody is. And like you said, if he couldn't wait ten minutes for the best in the business to turn up, he probably just wanted to eye you up and was more than likely going to go elsewhere anyway."

"I know Lucy, you're right and it's not the end of the world but every part of my life feels uncomfortable at the moment, I feel like everything is being stretched and twisted."

"I've said this before my beauty, you got comfortable and now your life is finally starting to change for the first time, you're feeling the discomfort which comes with change. That's what you're feeling Kat but don't worry, that feeling won't last forever but also, it won't disappear if you don't embrace the changes which are taking place in your life right now. You've got to make some tough decisions over the next few weeks, how serious are you about London?"

"I'm going to sound like a right bitch now and this will sound like it's all Max's fault, but if it wasn't for him, I'd probably be at home right now packing my stuff up and then leaving for London. I haven't even told him yet that I'm leaving for London next week on Friday and not the following Monday as usual, that's almost a whole week away from Max. I've accepted an invitation to a birthday bash which is on the Saturday and I really want to go, I'm really looking forward to it."

"Promise me one thing Kat."

"What's that?"

"This may not initially make sense, but please don't let Max down gently. He won't get it, he won't read the signs and he won't cope with the two of you gently slipping away from each other. Once you've decided what you want and where you would rather be, you have to let Max know, it's only fair. He's a good guy and he deserves that from you."

"Christ Lucy, that thought terrifies me!"

"It will do but if you don't follow your instincts, you'll forever live to regret the choices you made. Use your extended time away in London to think things through but be sure to come back knowing exactly how you want your life to look and feel."

Lucy went to the bar to order a couple of mocktails, they were both driving home and both had early starts the following day. Month end in advertising was always busy for them as they pulled out all the stops to hit targets which meant bonuses. The month of May was no different and they'd only got a handful of days left now to bring home the goods. Whilst Lucy was at the bar, Kat stared into the bottom of her empty wine glass and thought long and hard about where her life was parked right now. She loved Max dearly and found it incredibly hard to imagine life without him, in the same way she found it almost impossible to imagine her life with another man. Max was the only guy she'd slept with and therefore the only guy to ever see her naked. The thought of standing naked in front of another man made her shiver and the thought of sleeping with another man slightly repulsed her. But her current dilemma had nothing to do with another man, Kat had simply reached a point in her life where she wanted more and London appeared to be open for business.

Lucy arrived back at the table with a couple of fancy looking drinks. She sat down next to Kat and held her hand, "It's going to be okay, trust me and it's going to be difficult whatever you choose to do. Staying here with Max means you'll have to completely let go of the London dream and find a way of being content again with what you've got together. If Max is adamant about not moving to London and you're absolutely sure that's what you want, then you're going to have to deal with that and end things with Max. You in London and Max in Yorkshire, that type of relationship won't work for either of you but sometimes you have to break everything down before you can start building things back up again."

"I'm scared Lucy, really scared! I've never had to make life changing decisions before and as far as I know, I've never broken anyone's heart before? Max will be heartbroken!"

"You know me better than anyone Kat but do you really know why I don't allow myself to get too close to any one guy? It's because true love always ends in tears, someone either leaves or someone dies and I couldn't cope with that. So I guard my heart like the Crown Jewels and do my best to make sure that someone is always there to make me feel good, it's selfish, I know."

"But you always come across as being so strong and in control of your life?"

"I'm weak Kat, insecure and weak and as much as I genuinely want to meet Mr Right and settle down, I'm terrified of having my heart broken because I know I wouldn't cope, it would literally destroy me. You're the tough one Kat, not me, you just haven't realised it yet."

Max was now well fed, slightly pissed and well into Series 1 of The Durrells. Gerry was busy turning his bedroom into a Centre for Scientific Learning. Leslie had just been accused of armed robbery and Margo was falling in love again. "You couldn't make it up." Max thought to himself, "And I thought my life was all going a bit Pete Tong." Max found comfort in what he was watching. It took him away to a place he loved and was excited to be visiting again. It also reminded him of the fact that you can't run away from your problems and just because Louisa Durrell and her children left England for Corfu, it certainly didn't mean that they'd left all their problems behind, never to be seen again. In fact, Corfu was now creating its own fair share of problems for the Durrells, especially as far as Spyro was concerned. Max was hoping that Kat would soon be home and together they could start to figure out how to fix the minor ripples in their relationship. So he picked up his phone and sent Kat a short message or four, "Hey, the fire's on, the candles are lit and there's wine in the fridge. What time do you think you'll be home?"

"By the way, sorry about earlier! I had to go to Wallsend and you know what Wallsend does to me, it stresses me out and don't even mention that tunnel, bloody thing!"

"Love you!"

"Max."

Kat and Lucy were winding things up in Harrogate and both were ready to head home. Kat was heading home to Max and the cottage on the green and Lucy was heading home to entertain a guy she'd already seen a couple of times. Lucy had no intention of making her night a late one but she had a birthday coming up soon and she thought that it would be rude not to take advantage of her special day. Kat checked her phone and noticed that Max had messaged her. She used that as a prompt to find some privacy in her car and said goodbye to Lucy. "Thank you for tonight. I wasn't expecting to be told some home truths but I appreciate your honesty and I'll do my best to deal with things, I promise. As for you, don't be late tonight, there's money to be made tomorrow and I'll see you on Saturday." Kat put a few miles between her brief evening spent with Lucy in Harrogate and her life with Max before responding to his message. She'd decided to call Max and reassure him that she was on her way, "Max, I'm on my way home and I should be back in just over an hour, are you okay."

"Cool, yeh I'm good. Just hanging out and watching The Durrells, again."

"Okay, you enjoy The Durrells and I'll see you soon."

"See you soon and please get home safely!"

Kat arrived home and soon found herself sitting on the sofa next to Max. Max put The Durrells on pause, he poured Kat a large glass of wine and topped his own glass up to the brim. They both took a drink and then Kat started the process of breaking the ice. "Oh Maxi, what a day! You didn't hang up on me did you?"

"Of course I didn't, you can blame the Tyne Tunnel for that, not me."

"I'm not looking to blame anyone Max, I just need to be reassured that we haven't reached that point in our relationship. I hope you agree with me, but I think we've got a few things to sort out and we have to be able to talk to each other like adults and not behave like children."

"Of course Kat, I totally agree with you. So what are you saying?"

"Well, I'm going to be completely honest with you Max and tell you exactly where my head is right now. As much as I love you and I'm still in love with you, if you need clarity as to what I mean by the word love, but I feel trapped here. Not trapped by you, let me also make that clear. When I'm in London, I feel alive. I'm visiting new places and I'm meeting new people, learning new things and I feel like I belong. This place is suffocating me Max and I can't see myself getting out of here alive, something has to change."

"So what are you proposing Kat? This is already starting to sound like a break up song. Is that what's happening, are we breaking up?"

"Max, we need a break, some time to clear our heads and get our thoughts together."

"You mean you need a break or a trial run at life without me. That's what you really mean Kat and if things go well for you and you cope in London for more than a few days, then we're finished. I should have seen this coming, I'm a fucking idiot for thinking otherwise! Has Grant got anything to do with this, anything else I should know?"

"This has nothing to do with Grant, whatever makes you think that and what makes you think he's even my type?"

"Ooh, where do I begin? He's rich, he's handsome, he drives a Range Rover, he's successful and he's single-handedly making the capital a better place for people to live. Oh yes, and he just so happens to live in London!"

"So much for behaving like adults! Max, please listen to me! This has nothing to do with Grant, got that!"

"Well, whatever! It still doesn't change the story does it, so when are you leaving?"

Kat now had to tell Max that she was leaving for London a week on Friday and she would be home as normal the following Wednesday evening. Her extended time away was smelling very much like Max's suggestion that she wanted a trial run before jumping full on into a life without him. Three days away would soon become five. Five days would soon become a week and without even noticing, a week would become a month and they'd slowly slipped away from each other. Until this evening, Kat hadn't thought seriously about leaving and never coming back but now, she'd practically told Max that they were finished, she was about to tell him that she would be leaving for London next week earlier than normal but not to worry, because she would be coming back on Wednesday evening, just as normal. What's normal about that little setup and if Max accepted that as normal, then his love for Kat obviously ran far deeper than anyone knew.

"I'm leaving for London next week on Friday and not the Monday after, that's five nights but I'll be back on

Wednesday as usual. Megan has invited me to join her and some friends for her birthday celebration on the Saturday, I told you about Megan didn't I? She works for Grant at his office in Bow Village, she's nice and I'm looking forward to going."

"Why are you coming back on Wednesday?"

"Because that was always the plan Max, I just hadn't got round to telling you before all this came out."

"Okay, and you expect me to sit tight up here while you crash test your new life in London? I don't think so Kat and from what you've just told me, I'm guessing the next time you leave for London, you'll be leaving for good. So when you leave next Friday, please take as much of your stuff with you. But if you come back on the Wednesday as planned, please only come back if you intend to stay and by that, I mean forever. If you don't come back, I'll have whatever you've left behind sent down to you in a van. I'll just need an address for the courier, you can message me!"

Chapter 12 ~ Is Breaking Up Really That Hard To Do.

To say that Kat was surprised by Max's reaction to her trial breakup proposal was the understatement of the year. She knew him well enough to know that he wouldn't run off crying and lock himself in the bathroom until she promised to stay and never, ever leave. But he didn't even fight back nor ask her to reconsider her plans, it was if he knew this day would eventually come and by now, he'd had fifteen years to prepare for it. However, his reaction did make

Kat's life slightly easier and also, her new life in London feel very real. Had Max fought for his girl instead of accepting defeat, Kat would have felt guilty and she would have ended up going down the path which she'd promised Lucy she wouldn't go down, separation by a thousand cuts. Max had always lived his life in a way where decisions were made and situations dealt with based on facts, not ifs, buts or maybes and the situation he was being presented with right now was pretty simple. Kat still loved him but she now wanted to live in London. Max still loved Kat but he hated London and refused to go with her. Max's philosophical way of looking at things would have meant that he'd calculated that this breakup was not entirely Kat's fault and the breakup could be prevented if the two of them moved to London. But the two of them weren't moving to London, therefore they were breaking up and eventually they would both get over it and move on with their separate lives. Although Kat was relieved that there was no screaming and shouting, plate smashing and clothes throwing that evening, she still offered Max the chance to kick all that off. "Max, do you have anything to say, anything else you want to know or discuss?"

"Not really, it's all pretty much cut and dried, isn't it?"

"If you say so Max but I thought we could at least explore whether or not we could make things work with me being in London and you…"

"Stop right there Kat! You living in London, I'm living in Yorkshire and we're still together. That's never going to work nor is it the relationship I want. Not with you, not with anyone. I'd rather be on my own and avoid all the potential misunderstandings, pointless curiosity and unnecessary jealousy. Absolutely no way!"

"Okay, anything else?"

"Well, if you're finally finished with trashing everything we have, or had, I'd quite like to get back to watching The Durrells. Sven has just proposed to Louisa. Nancy has arrived and can't keep her hands of Larry and Margo is about to find out that being in love sucks!"

Kat hadn't eaten that evening neither was she hungry, for some reason she'd lost her appetite. Her stomach felt like it was in knots and she was even struggling to keep her wine down, which was very unlike Kat. All she wanted to do was go to bed, fall asleep and wake up to find that all the drama was over and two new lives were smoothly up and running. In reality, it would never be that simple and she knew that, but the next few days, before she left for London and potentially never come back, could quite easily be Hell on Earth. Surely Max was eventually going to kick off, surely there'd be screaming and shouting at some point and surely they would call each other all the worst names they could possibly think of. That's what happens when couples break up, right or wrong? But when couples usually break up, it's because one side has decided to check out the greener grass, fucked around and got found out. Then follows all the apologies and classic clichés, "I'm so sorry but I was confused and feeling unloved. It won't happen again, I promise. But we haven't, you know, for months now and I couldn't help myself. And finally, the best one of all, how is this even my fault." But none of these applied to Max and Kat's breakup. Neither had shopped elsewhere and they still loved each other, surely that's the recipe for the perfect breakup. Mutual understanding, minimal tears and a shared realisation that it was time to move on. For a brief moment, Kat thought that breaking up was actually easier than trying to make a relationship last forever. But she needed to go to bed and would usually ask Max if he was joining her. Sometimes she would summon Max to the bedroom whilst showing him a bit of extra leg. Sometimes the two of them would connect without even speaking to each other and agree that bed was the best place to be and whatever happened from there, happened for a reason.

"Max, I need to go to bed. What are you doing?"

"I'm watching The Durrells."

"I know you're watching The Durrells but are you coming to bed? Are you going to be long or are you going to watch The Durrells until the sun comes up?"

"I haven't decided yet but for now, I'm watching The Durrells. You go to bed."

"Okay, I'll see you soon or whenever?"

Was this night the start of Kat's new life without Max? Alone in bed, alone with her thoughts and not really knowing what Max was doing next. Although there was no chaos or conflict, this part of the breakup was not as easy as Kat had initially thought. Downstairs, Max was still drinking and powering on through his favourite series and he was at the part where Sven was being interrogated by the junior Durrells and although he passed with flying colours, Louisa Durrell was soon to find out that Sven, her soon to be husband, was not entirely the man he appeared to be. Max woke up at 5am and found himself still on the sofa. Kat had obviously come down at some point during the night to turn the television off and remove a wine glass from Max's hand but she either chose not to wake him or couldn't wake him. He slowly and quietly made his way to the kitchen to make some coffee, on the side were four empty wine bottles and he thought to himself, "Bloody good effort kid, even if she did help you out with a glass or two." Upstairs he could hear Kat wandering around and getting ready for work. She was up earlier than normal but today was the last day of May and although Max didn't know too much about how things worked in the world of advertising, he knew enough to know that it was mostly about doing deals and making money. Kat would be looking to sign up anything which moved today and she was obviously starting early. Max had refrained from being childish this time and made enough coffee for the two of them and dropped a couple of slices of Kat's healthy bread into the toaster. The smell of fresh coffee and toasted bread had obviously reached upstairs and Kat soon joined Max in the kitchen. On the table were a couple of books and a map of Corfu, the subject of Corfu would need discussing at some point and Max thought that there was no time better than the present. "So what about Corfu? It's just over four weeks away now."

"I can't Max, I can't go and pretend that everything is okay or back to normal. I've got to do this, I'm sorry. If I live to regret it, well, I'll just have to deal with it."

"I thought you were going to say that but I wanted to do the right thing and ask you anyway."

"Thanks Max and you should still go. After all, it's your baby."

"It was my idea but it was our baby, I'll give your suggestion some thought."

"You do that, you deserve a break Max and you'll be letting Spike down if you don't go. I hope you don't mind me saying that?"

"You're absolutely right Kat, last chance to change your mind."

Kat looked across the table at Max and shook her head. She finished her toast, stood up, put one hand on Max's shoulder and told him that she was now off to work. The parts of the perfect break up were slowly falling into place and Max was now starting to imagine for the first time what life without Kat was going to look and feel like. He thought the best way to get through his first day was to keep himself busy. He quickly checked his delivery app and managed to book enough work for the day ahead and which would see him out until just after 5pm and earn him just over £120.00. "That'll do." He thought to himself, "Onwards and upwards Maxi boy, onwards and upwards. You've just got to get through the next few weeks and then you'll soon be on a plane out of here!" He made his way to the pick up station, loaded his van and set off on his first route. As he drove around Middlesbrough and Stockton making his deliveries, all sorts of thoughts were running through his head. He kept thinking back to when he first met Kat, she was still Kathy back then, and the first proper date that they went on. He thought about their first kiss and everything which slowly followed. He thought about their first overseas holiday together and how they then became obsessed with travelling and exploring the world. He thought about how beautiful she always looked and how lucky he was to have her by his side for all this time. But he knew that that chapter of his life was coming to an end, if it hadn't already ended. He tried his best to look towards the future and he tried his best to imagine a life which would be just as good but without this amazing lady in it. He was struggling big time and eventually found himself fighting back his tears. The emotional floodgates had finally opened and the process of healing a broken heart had just begun.

Kat had taken a short break from the usual last day of the month shenanigans to call Lucy. "Kat, you okay, what's up my love? Something must be up because you wouldn't waste a phone call on me, not on the last day of the month, so what's up?"

"Max and I, that's what's up, it's all over. This time next week I'll be driving to London to start a new life without him."

"Crikey Kat! I know I asked you not to keep him hanging but did you even put him on notice?"

"No, not really. I got in, we started talking and I was going in the direction of us taking a break and then Max thought that I was leaving him for Grant but letting him down gently. I told him it had nothing to do with Grant and then we kind of came to a joint conclusion that we were finished. I went to bed, Max got drunk, this morning he made me breakfast and that was that."

"Oh, I see and how are you feeling about everything?"

"I'm okay I think but it may just be that it hasn't all sunk in yet."

"And Max, is he okay?"

"I'm not really sure and I have no idea what he's doing today. I do know that he's going to Corfu on his own though."

"Have you thought about where you're going to live? I know you've got the apartment which comes with your work in London but is that available all week and potentially for the foreseeable?"

"I've no idea but I'll speak to Grant later and find out, it makes obvious sense for now."

"Make sure you do and let's talk more tomorrow. Ill be with you at 6pm."

"Absolutely and bring some pizzas and some wine because Max is going out with Charlie. Also, if you want to stay the night, bring your PJs."

Max was now halfway through his day and there was only one person who he could confide with and that was Charlie. "Charlie, yesterday was the day."

"I'm fine thanks Max, thanks for asking and how are you?"

"Sorry mate but it's my turn."

"What the fuck are you going on about, are you out daytime drinking?"

"No Charlie, I'm actually driving at the moment but yesterday was the day that my luck with Kat finally ran out."

"Oh, what's happened mate?"

"Kat's leaving me for a new life in London."

"You mean she's leaving you for Grant Fisher?"

"Apparently not but I reckon he may have something to do with it. Anyway, this time next week, unless anything changes, I'll be joining your club Charlie, thirty something and looking for love again."

"Oh bollocks mate, I'm really sorry to hear that."

"Yeh, it's all a bit surreal at the moment but I kind of saw it coming, I just didn't want to see it for real, that's all."

"Alright mate, get through today and tonight and we'll hit the town tomorrow. Two deflated and washed up lilos, both stranded on the beach and waiting to be treasured again."

"Very poetic Charlie but don't give up your day job, while you've still got one to give up."

"Max, you're a dick and yes, I'll see you tomorrow, just after 6pm."

Kat had almost given up on earning her monthly bonus when her phone rang. It was the guy who wasn't impressed by her ten minute late arrival, the one who she also thought was going to be a nightmare from day one. But on the last day of the month and when it boiled down to hitting target or not, his money could be as good as anyone's, he just needed to be calling with some good news, "Mr Metcalf, nice to hear from you and how are you sir?"

"Kathy, I haven't forgotten just how bad your timekeeping is but my business is on borrowed time and it needs the best advertising agency out there. I've tried my best to avoid you but every other avenue I explore, I see a sign which tells me to do a U turn and head straight back to Fab Success. So, apart from my money and a signature, what else do you need from me?" She needed nothing more than a monthly spend agreement and a signature and both were handed to her on a plate. Mr Metcalf's initial monthly spend was enough to ensure that Kat hit her target for May and she would earn her monthly bonus. Although she really disliked Mr Metcalf, Kat loved him for the extra money she was about to be paid, money she was really going to need soon. And if life in London went according to her plans, she would probably never see his bloated and blotchy red face again. That reminded Kat that she needed to update Fabio and hope that he needed her in London for more than three days a week and she needed to speak to Grant about her accommodation requirements, Kat had very quickly found herself with another task list to manage. She was no longer just managing appointment schedules and advertising budgets, she was now managing her day to day life, something she would very quickly have to get used to once Max was no longer around.

Max generally dealt with 'the stuff', all the mundane and boring stuff which made life for the two of them work. He had the time to do the shopping, the cleaning and the cooking. He also had time to make sure that everything was sorted before Kat came home from another busy and stressful day at work. The washing up would be dried and put away. The washing folded and put away. The wine was always chilling in the fridge and the candles and fire were always lit before Kat got home. It was how it was and how it worked. And as usual, on the day after the breakup became official, Max was home before Kat and busy making sure that everything was squared up around the cottage. Kat was now on her way back from Harrogate and used her driving time to call Fabio and Grant. She needed a small favour from Fabio, so she called him first, "Fabio, good news! Targets hit for another month and I think you'll be impressed when you see the final numbers."

"That's great news Kat, well done and how are you?"

"I'm okay but I need a small favour from you. I need to stay around here on Monday, Tuesday and Wednesday of next week but I'll be back in London on the Friday. Can we make that work?"

"Sure babe, no problem. Are you and Max doing anything nice, it sounds like a very long weekend of lust and love to me?"

"Not exactly, Max and I are going our separate ways and I need this weekend and early next week to pack up my life."

"That comes as a bit of a shock to me Kat, so please take your time and get yourself sorted. Keep me posted and I'll catch up with you when you arrive in London on Friday and don't forget to brief Grant but trust me, he'll be fine."

"Thanks Fabio, you're an absolute treasure and I'll phone Grant straight away."

Chapter 13 ~ Is He Prince Charming Or Diablo.

As far as breakups were concerned, this one was going as smoothly as a well rehearsed Sunday Dinner. There was no arguing or squabbling, everyone appeared to be playing their part and everyone was either understanding or helping out in equal measures, so far. It was just a terrible shame that all the pleasantries and niceties would not end with a large gathering of friends and lovers, all sat at the same table, feasting on the fruits of their hard work. This pending ending of what was, and could still be, a beautiful relationship was far from being that romantic fantasy. It was in reality, another relationship hitting a very hard and very high wall.

Kat now had to call Grant and inform him of the slight change to their usual plans. In fact, it was a big change to their usual plans and Grant was expecting Kat to be in London on Monday, bright and early and ready for a busy three days. The South Bank development was pretty much sold through now and apart from a few minor mortgage issues to deal with, the sale and purchase of every apartment was due to complete in approximately six to eight weeks. This entire development completion provided Grant with the funds he needed to get started on Bow Road and in turn, Thames Side. Things were happening in

London, things were looking good for Fisher Developments and Kat was excited to be a part of it all, helping Grant turn property into profit. Kat was feeling very relaxed when she called Grant and was expecting to hear more pleasantries, niceties and understanding but she soon got a very uncomfortable reality check from someone who wasn't so understanding. "Grant, it's Kathy. I need to mix things up a bit next week, if that's okay with you?"

"I've just got off the phone to Fabio, he's told me what I need to know and frankly, it's not okay! It's far from okay and you breaking up with T Shirt guy is now messing with my plans for next week. In case you've forgotten, I now have two new developments to focus on and the last thing I want to be thinking about is how the fuck am I going to sell them! That's your job and that's why Fabio pulled you away from Harrogate and the failing farmers. I'm speaking to Fabio in the morning and I'm sure he'll update you in due course. This is far from ideal Kathy, far from ideal. Things happen and move very quickly in London and I was half expecting you to know that by now."

"Grant, I'm sorry but I hadn't planned on breaking up with Max only 48 hours ago nor had I planned it to intentionally screw up your plans. These things happen in life, don't you get that?"

"No, not really. I make plans, I commit to them and I see them through. You however, clearly don't!"

"Come on Grant, has nothing ever gone wrong in your life, no curve balls?"

"Yes Kathy, things have gone wrong in my life and like I said, Fabio will call you tomorrow."

Kat was shocked at the way Grant had just spoken to her. She knew that he could be a bit prickly and overpowering at times but she was used to that by now. She also knew that he could be kind, charming and very considerate. But what she had just heard, immediately got her thinking about whether or not this guy was someone who she wanted to be around. Although Max never displayed the capabilities required to move mountains or achieve great things in life, she found comfort and predictability in that and as a result, 99.9% of the time she knew how Max would behave each day. The same applied to Lucy, Charlie and even Fabio, they were all comfortably predictable and that worked for her. It was now starting to appear to Kat that she may have some kind of lunatic in her life who would be Prince Charming one day and Diablo the next. That was something she'd never had to deal with previously and she immediately decided that it was something she never wanted to deal with in the future. Kat didn't want to come across as if she couldn't cope with Grants unexpected outburst and openly expose her weakness, so the thought of getting straight back on the phone to Fabio was a none starter. She also knew that she could trust Fabio and talk to him in confidence and unless Fabio had been drinking, any discussions they had would remain private and confidential. Kat gave her next move some serious thought and consideration while continuing on her journey home. Normally she would confide in Max about issues that were testing her emotions but surely the last thing Max wanted to hear and help her deal with right now was her ranting on about how rude and aggressive Grant had been to her today.

Kat would be home in twenty minutes and she really wanted to box up this issue with Grant before she had to deal with a night in with the person she would soon be leaving, so calling Fabio was her only option. "Fabio, I called Grant, you said he'd be fine with my change of plans but instead, he ripped my head off in less than two minutes. What's up with him today or is he always like this when people mess with his plans?"

"Listen honey, I'll sort things out with Grant and by the time you arrive back in London on Friday, it'll feel like nothing was ever said, trust me."

"But things were said, horrible things and he gave no consideration towards how I was feeling and coping right now, none whatsoever!"

"Kathy, listen to me and please trust me. I will deal with Grant but let me also provide you with some reassurance that I'm not just telling you what you want to hear and then I just hope for the best."

"Okay, go for it."

"Although Grant is a new client of ours, Grant and I go back a long way. In fact, I've known him for over twenty years now. I probably know him better than anyone, apart from his parents maybe. But that's debatable, it depends on who you talk to. Anyway, I know him well enough to know how he behaves when the big pressure is on and trust me, the big pressure is on. He's due to bank enough money in the next few months to retire on, easily retire on. But he's committed himself to another two developments and now, there's no exit stage left nor right. He's as we say Kat, balls deep!"

"I think I get what you're saying but if what you're saying is that Grant will sometimes blow very hot or very cold, I guess I need to either like it or lump it or go back to working full time in Harrogate?"

"You've pretty much nailed it Kat and I'm not going to say it again, leave Grant to me and you look after yourself."

Having spoken to Fabio, Kat was now feeling more relaxed about the whole Grant thing but she was left wondering why Fabio appeared to be able to call the shots with someone who was paying their bills. Whatever the reason, it worked for Kat and her transition from Yorkshire to London was almost back on track. Back on track also meant spending a Friday night in with someone who she would soon be leaving. Leaving, not because Max had done wrong, he wasn't capable of that nor had he been unfaithful. Kat hadn't found another lover nor was she looking for one. They had both shared things to look forward to, like the big explore of Corfu, but regardless of all that, Kat was leaving to start a new life for herself in London. Kat found herself sitting in her car, outside the cottage she'd shared with Max for ten wonderful years, thoughts frozen and unable to get out. She knew that Max was home and he'd finished getting everything sorted because of the white smoke which was leaving the chimney and slowly dispersing into the clear night sky. Unless it was really cold, he would only ever light the fire once he'd completed his daily rituals and was ready to sit down with a glass of wine. He also liked watching the initial flicker of fire turn into a raging but controlled inferno within the old stone fireplace. Again, it was just one of his things and something which would probably never change. Kat quickly began to feel the cold as the heat in her car slowly faded away and it prompted her to find the strength that she'd found only a day or so ago. She knew she was going to have face Max at some point this evening, so she took a deep breath, locked her car and made her way up the short path to what would soon be Max's cottage overlooking the village green.

"Max, I'm home. Where are you?"

"I'm upstairs looking for something but I won't be long. There's wine in the fridge if you fancy."

"Thanks and what are you looking for, can I help?"

"Maybe, I'm looking for my small blue backpack. You know the one, the 25 litre EuroHike pack, I last used it when we went hiking in France."

"Have you tried the box under the bed in the spare room?"

"No but I'll check now… Got it!"

Max came down the stairs wearing a slightly dusty and scrunched up rucksack and proceeded to tell Kat that he wanted this particular bag for when he went to Corfu. Had it still been the two of them going, they would have both had a similar size pack each and a larger bag or case each for the rest of their stuff. After all, four weeks away is quite a long time and even Max would require more than two T Shirts, four would have done it though. By contrast, Kat would of taken much more than she would ever need and most of her stuff wouldn't even leave the big case but would still need washing once home again and unpacked.

"It still fits you Max, that's a good thing."

"To be honest, I wasn't aware that you could outgrow a rucksack and the last time I looked, the sizing system was more to do with the carrying capacity. But thanks for the compliment all the same."

"Is that little bag going to be big enough, surely you're taking another bag with you?"

"Yes and no, I've decided to travel super light this time. I've also figured out that if I'm going to be in a different place every other day, nobody is going to know that I've been wearing the same clothes for days."

"Oh Max, what are you like?"

Kat was relieved that there was no initial tension and with a bit of careful conversation planning, the evening could go as well as was to be expected and without any fireworks. Max had prepared some dinner for the two of them, a Thai dish which just needed some chicken or duck adding, a gentle simmer and it would then be good to serve. They sat together on the sofa as they would most nights, with Max staring at the roaring flames while Kat looked at stuff on her phone. They politely confirmed each others plans for the next couple of days, which involved Lucy coming over for drinks and pizzas and Max and Charlie leaving them to it whilst drowning their sorrows in The Ted. Dialogue that evening was limited but polite and informative, just like it was on their first date as they tried to figure out each other's personalities. Maybe first dates and the final days of a perfect breakup are actually the same thing. Politely building a relationship up at the start and then politely dismantling it at the end, with some good stuff in middle. To avoid any awkwardness, Max had made up the spare room and made it evident that it was his room for the next seven nights, leaving Kat to rest easy in what was their room until she left on Friday.

"Please be careful in London Kat, it can be a dangerous place you know."

"I know and yes, I will do my best to stay safe."

"Are you sure this is what you want and please tell me again that this move has nothing to do with Grant."

"Max, if you've decided to start fighting for me now, please stop and I promise you, hand on heart, Grant is not involved. Nobody else is involved, it's just me and you and the fact that we want different things from our lives now."

"I know, I just wished it wasn't happening to us. Will you keep in touch?"

"Of course I will. Well, I will if that's what you want?"

"Absolutely! But I suppose we'll just have to take things one day at a time and see how it goes. But I guess at some point one of us may not want to keep in touch anymore."

"Maybe, but neither of us are there yet, are we? So let's just go one day at a time. Another drink?"

"Yes please and while you're getting drinks, I'll finish dinner. Chicken or duck?"

A fly on the wall would struggle to find an elephant in the room this evening and a romance novelist would soon be describing how the two lovers fell into each others arms and then into bed for a night of passionate love making. But tonight, two separate bedrooms we're waiting for Max and Kat and that's how the evening ended. Kat was the first to concede to another day, content with the fact that there had been no friction between them, whilst also planning ahead and with tomorrow in mind. She knew tomorrow evening would be a late and heavy one, what with Lucy coming over, and there would be plenty to talk about, especially with the boys being out. Max stayed up for a while and worked his way through a few more bottles of wine and a few more episodes of The Durrells. Louisa Durrell had just found out that Sven was in fact homosexual and was actually looking for a marriage of convenience and not one which would be fulled and kept alive and burning by intimate passion and lust. Although Sven promised Louisa that he would try his best to make things work for them, meaning in the bedroom, Louisa declined his proposal and told Sven that he needed to find the courage and strength to be honest with himself and proudly accept who he really was. Whilst Max was struggling to get his head around the fact that homosexuality used to be illegal, Kat was in bed, struggling to sleep and wishing that Max would join her in taking their relationship on one last lap of honour around the bedroom.

Chapter 14 ~ Four Weeks And Counting.

After a night apart under the same roof for the first time ever, Max and Kat got on with their Saturday routines. Kat had started to organise her things into some sort of order, as if she was packing for another adventure with Max. However, this time she was creating small and orderly piles of stuff which clearly weren't being taken on any sort of normal adventure. Books, magazines, a couple of old DVD's and some personal belongings, along with some of her clothes which only made an appearance on special occasions. These things were soon packed into a couple of suitcases and some cardboard boxes and then stacked neatly in the corner of what was now her bedroom. She estimated that she would only need another two large boxes to complete the task of packing her life up and having it ready to take with her to London.

Max on the other hand had chosen not to assist with nor witness the boxing up of his life with Kat and decided to go out to work for a few hours. He could make enough money this afternoon to cover the cost of his evening out with Charlie and have some left over to put aside and towards his trip to Corfu, which was now exactly four weeks away. In fact, this time in four weeks he would be making his way to Teeside Airport to enjoy a couple of pre-flight beers and an overpriced burger before flying away from all the emotional heartache and change which was currently plaguing his life. Although he was deeply saddened by the fact that Kat wouldn't be joining him, he was still excited about the trip and still looking forward to going. He saw it as an opportunity to clear his head and to use the sights and surroundings of Corfu as a way to forget about what had just happened to him. He briefly thought about how Louisa Durrell must have been feeling when she left for Corfu with her children, leaving all of her heartache and history behind in England.

Max got home around five o'clock to find that Kat had sorted everything out around the cottage and although it wasn't exactly up to his standard, he thanked her for everything she'd done and he made the most of his unexpected hour of not having to do the housework before Lucy and Charlie were due. Lucy arrived at precisely six o'clock. She'd become a Jedi Master of time keeping and diary management, quite possibly due to her having to manage more than one relationship at any one time. Being in the right place at the right time and with the right guy obviously took some doing but it clearly paid dividends. Lucy turned up with a case of Champagne, a box of expensive looking chocolates, flowers and boxed up artisan pizzas. "Oh my god Lucy, have you just won the lottery?" "No my love, better than that. This guy I'm dating, he's absolutely loaded and this little bundle of delights, apart from the pizzas obviously, arrived yesterday. So I thought I'd share them with my bestie, Champagne?" "Well, I'm not sure what we're celebrating but as you're offering, why not."

There was a knock on the door, it was Charlie. Max lent out of the bathroom window and called down to him, "The door's open Charlie, let yourself in mate." Kat welcomed Charlie in and introduced him to Lucy. They'd met briefly a couple of times before but apart from Charlie knowing a little bit about Lucy's track record and Lucy knowing that Charlie was a bit of a tech geek, that was as close as they'd got to what you would call being friends. Even though Lucy had opted for skinny jeans and a blue hoodie for her evening in with Kat, she still managed to put a look on Charlie's face which required no interpretation at all. "We're not celebrating anything Charlie but would you like a glass of Champagne?" Lucy asked of him. "Never one to turn down being offered a free drink from a lovely lady, so absolutely I would. Make mine a large one!" "There you go Charlie, bottoms up and all that." Max had finally decided which of his band T Shirts he was going to wear under his lumberjack shirt and he'd opted for the one which payed homage to his favourite band and one of his favourite songs. Shed Seven, Chasing Rainbows. Max loved that song and would sometimes play it over and over again, listening carefully to the lyrics while comparing himself to the underdog in the song, who was chasing rainbows all his life. Max finally made his grand entrance looking like he was about to go on tour or go back to university. "Charlie boy, look at you drinking Champagne with Yorkshire's finest fillies. You okay fella?"

"Never been better Max, never been better. Are you sure we're going out tonight? It's freezing out there!"

"Yes mate, we're going out. So take your eyes off the blonde one and finish your drink."

Kat heard clearly what Max had just said to his mate and it made her chuckle. She looked him up and down and put what she'd just heard with what she was seeing in front of her and thought, it could only be Max. Lucy handed Max a bottle of Champagne which had a couple of swigs left in it, Max obliged from the bottle and again prompted Charlie to drink up.

"Right ladies, we're out of here. Have a great evening, go easy on us with what you say and don't get too pissed. Come on Charlie, time to go."

Max and Charlie found a table near the jukebox, got a round of beers in and proceeded to tell each other about how their individual relationships were going, or not as was the reality for both of them now. "Who would have thought Charlie? Only a few weeks ago we were sat here talking about the collapse of your relationship and your life and now we're sat here again, both in the same sinking boat. I guess nothing's changed on your side?"

"No it hasn't. I couldn't sort the money issue out on my own, the bank are taking the house back at the end of June and redundancy is now just around the corner. We're all still in the house, pretending that we're a happy family but that's just a show for the kids' sake. When the house goes, Laura is moving back to her parents with the kids and I'm homeless. I've been trying to line up a rental place but it's proving to be impossible without a job guarantee, I'm screwed mate!"

"Look Charlie, Kat's leaving for London on Friday, you can have the spare room at my place but don't give up on life mate. Don't use this offer as a reason to do nothing about finding your feet and your own place again, promise me that."

"You're a star Max and I promise. I'll also do my best to keep the place clean and tidy. I know what you're like."

Kat and Lucy were enjoying their evening together and were talking about life, love and all things related to London, which included Kat's imminent farewell to life in Yorkshire. "I'm starting to think I've made a huge mistake. How do I reverse what I've done?" How do I stop this Lu?"

"Are you being serious Kat or are you having a wobble and want me to tell you again that everything is going to be fine?"

"Did you hear Max talking to Charlie, did you see how he looked? I know he's not your type but when I heard him and saw him standing there swigging Champagne from the bottle, my heart melted. And the silly little dick thinks I've been swept off my feet by Grant Fisher!"

"Never say never Kat."

"I'm being serious Lucy! Oh and on the subject of Grant, he ripped my head off yesterday for messing with his plans. I'm dreading speaking to him again let alone seeing him again next week and I haven't even spoken to him yet about taking on the apartment on a permanent basis. What if he says no?"

"That's a very valid point and something which you're going to need to sort out pretty quick. Have you looked at rental prices for London? Please tell me you have and you can at least afford a small room in a shared house with a communal bathroom."

"No I fucking haven't! I was assuming that when I eventually got round to asking Grant he would automatically say yes."

"And what made you think that? What made you think he'd just give you something for free which he could quite easily charge a small fortune for?"

"Because I'm stupid Lucy! I'll say it before you do."

"Kat, you beautiful thing, you're not stupid, you're learning. But at the moment, you're unfortunately learning the hard way. Sometimes however, that's the best way. Just try not to make a habit of it and learn quickly from your mistakes."

Kat knew all too well how Lucy functioned and her recent admission to being weak and insecure cemented her understanding of her best friend. But she often wondered why someone who was so damn hot and so good at their job was also as fragile as a paper lantern. What had happened to Lucy before Kat got to know her which made her so good at helping other people deal with their problems but was terrified of creating and then having to deal with her own?

Max and Charlie were now a good few beers into their evening out and Max had just bought the jukebox for the next hour or so. Next up was Shed Seven with Chasing Rainbows, "There's nothing I can do for counterparts and bleeding hearts and all the things that fall apart for you. I don't keep my secrets there, I hide them everywhere. I could deny but I'll never realise, I'm just chasing rainbows, all the time."

"Charlie, do you ever feel like we're just chasing rainbows all the time? Constantly trying to find something which is either not real or even if it is real, it's never to be found?"

"How many beers have we had Max, have we reached that stage in the night already?"

"What do mean?"

"What I'm saying Max, is have we reached that stage in the night where you start to quote song lyrics and then try to blame life's failures on the fact that nobody listens to the lyrics anymore and that's why everyone's life is a pile of shit. Nobody listened to the warning signs which were put to music and song by Bob Dylan and blah, blah, blah. But if we have reached that stage, that means you're comfortably pissed and now would be the perfect time for me to ask you if I could hit up Corfu with you. Even if it was only for the first week, what you saying Max? Come on, it'll be just like the good old days. We could even get some T Shirts made up?"

"Let me guess the design. The design would be loosely based around an England football shirt and on the back of yours would be Loser #1 and on mine, would be Loser #2? On the front, each shirt would have an arrow pointing down towards our dicks and above the arrow would be the words, this way to the good stuff. Right or wrong?"

"One hundred percent right Max, so what you saying?"

"I'm saying no to T Shirts but I'll give you coming with me some thought. Fucking hell Charlie, what have we become?"

Back at Max's cottage, Kat and Lucy were popping corks as if they were hosting a joint birthday party for George Best and Paul Gascoinge. Lucy had reassured Kat that everything was going to be fine and as a result, Kat was almost content with her decision to leave Yorkshire but couldn't stop thinking about Max. Lucy reminded Kat that her life in London urgently required some affordable accommodation and she really needed to get something sorted before she left on Friday, even if it meant sucking up to Grant. Kat took the opportunity to inform Lucy that she'd spoken to Fabio about Grant's rant and how he'd assured her that Grant would be dealt with and everything would be fine by the time she arrived in London on Friday. "It was what I wanted to hear from Fabio and I trust him when he says that he'll sort things out but this time, it was like he had some sort of hold over Grant or some bargaining power which he could use to bring Grant back in line. This guy is paying our wages, our bills, yet Fabio appeared to be one phone call away from telling him how everything was going to play out. It was very strange." "Well let's just hope that Fabio does manage to work his magic on Grant and by Friday, he's behaving reasonably again. Otherwise you my dear, will be desperately searching for a cheap hotel."

Max and Charlie thought it was only fair to let the other patrons in The Ted enjoy the jukebox, so they made their way to the Taj and challenged each other to a 'how hot can you go' competition. Max was obviously the favourite to win, having visited India and Thailand, but Charlie was well up for the challenge and fancied his chances against his mate. Charlie started with a Chicken Kohzi but Max was quick to check mate him by ordering an Andhra Chilli

120

Chicken Curry, knowing that Charlie had already peaked at a Kohzi. They ate, drank and sweated their way through the latter hours of their evening and before long, it was time to head home. Max offered Charlie the sofa at his place again, as long as Lucy hadn't bagged it first, and reminded him that it was a sofa for one, not two. He also explained how he was now in the spare room and Kat now had their bedroom until Friday. To be honest, Max had no idea whether Lucy was staying over at his place. Kat hadn't asked if it was okay for her to stay, he'd just assumed and baring in mind that Lucy had driven there and was drinking, it kind of made sense that she was. Kat checked her phone to see if it was time to stop drinking whilst hoping to find a message from Max. It was almost time to call last orders at the cottage but there was no message from Max. However, there was a message from Fabio, confirming that everything had been sorted out with Grant but she needed to check in at Fab HQ as soon as she arrived in London on Friday.

It turned out that Fabio had spent the evening with Grant in Bow Village. They'd enjoyed drinks and an evening meal at the Italian restaurant and Fabio had clearly worked his magic.

Chapter 15 ~ Strange Musical Instruments, Hats And Scarves.

Max and Charlie were half expecting to find Kat and Lucy dancing around the front room like a couple of school girls pretending to be The Spice Girls. Instead, there was no sign of them. Max checked in the kitchen before quietly making his way upstairs and Charlie got the whiskey glasses out for a customary night cap. Max was relieved to find that Lucy hadn't stolen his bedroom, meaning he wouldn't have to share the front room with Charlie and his snoring. So unless the girls had decided to go out, there was only one other place they could be, crashed out in Kat's room. And they were, both in their PJs, full of Champagne and pizza and top to tail in the bed he used to share with Kat. Max gently closed the door on the sleeping beauties and made his way downstairs to join Charlie for that night cap. Charlie handed Max a large whiskey and coke and asked him if he'd managed to find the girls.

"We've outlasted them mate, they're both asleep in what will soon be my room, so keep your voice down and no music tonight."
"What do you reckon our chances are mate, should we wake them and join them?"
"If you carry on like that, I'll change my mind about you joining me for the first week in Corfu."
"I wasn't aware that you'd made a decision, tell me more."
"Come for the first week and then be on your way. We'll be mostly around Moraitika and Messonghi, you won't know where those places are so don't even ask, but there'll be bars and if you're lucky, there might even be some girls who will at least talk to you."
"Mate, are you serious?"
"Yes Charlie, I'm serious but just for the first week. I've got plans for the other three weeks and they don't involve you, no offense mate!"

"I love you Max, this means the world to me. Do you know that?"

"It'll be fun, just behave yourself and it's still a big fat no to T Shirts and anything which resembles an England football shirt. We'll also do Captain Homer's boat trip from Messonghi down to Petriti and Notos Beach. Food and drink is included in the price of the trip and the snorkeling should be amazing."

"So what are you going to be doing with yourself once I've left?"

"When Kat dropped her bomb on our relationship and refused to use our trip to Corfu as an opportunity to get ourselves back on track, I decided to make some changes to the agenda I'd put together. It was designed for the two of us Charlie and included stuff which I knew we'd both enjoy and find interesting. But now it's just me, it's now my agenda and I've been reading all about this long distance walking path, it's called The Corfu Trail. It starts just outside Aspro Kavos and finishes at Agios Spyridonas. Basically, you walk the entire length of the island, just under a hundred miles."

"Sounds like bloody hard work to me. Are you sure you're up to it?"

"I need a challenge Charlie, something to give me reason and self belief again. I'll just take my time and go steady away, I reckon I can do it in two weeks. I've ordered a guide book which will help. It includes maps and turn by turn directions, along with suggestions on how to break up the entire route into manageable daily hikes."

"Sounds like a proper challenge to me mate but fair play to you."

By ten o'clock the following morning, Max had got some breakfast ready for everyone, which included: bacon, sausages, eggs and beans. He'd also come up with some healthier options which comprised of yogurt, fresh fruit, granola and brown toast. It wasn't long before everyone was sat at the kitchen table enjoying the food that Max had quickly but lovingly prepared. It was a strange table for four though and it could have easily been seen through the eyes of a stranger as two couples enjoying breakfast together at a small B&B. The reality however was very different, because sat at that table were people who would more than likely never see each other again after breakfast had been consumed and everything tidied away. Kat and Lucy would keep in touch for sure. Max and Kat stood half a chance at best. It was highly unlikely that Charlie would ever see Kat again and as for Max and Charlie ever seeing Lucy again, only a desperate or foolish man would bet on those odds.

Lucy was first to pay compliments to the chef, "Breakfast, or brunch, was absolutely lovely Max, thank you so much. Remind me again why you drive a van for a living and you choose not to turn your obvious passion for creating great dishes into a source of income?"

"I don't think I've ever told you why, but if you really want to know, the more people you cook for, the greater the chances are of someone not liking what you've cooked. That's why I don't want to work in a kitchen or open a restaurant."

"Fair enough, but I still think you're a wasted talent."

Kat and Charlie soon followed with their compliments and everyone played their part in getting everything tidied away and back to how Max liked his cottage to be. Neat and tidy and ready to go again but very soon, everything was about to change and that change was now only four days and a few hours away. Tomorrow would be the start of the week when Max and Kat officially went their separate ways and although it was happening for real, it still felt like they were both living in some crazy dream world. Some totally messed up version of how everything should still be between the two of them and eventually, they would both fall back down to Earth and think, what the fuck just happened there. But unless a miracle was going to ride up on a unicorn, Friday would be the day. Max and Kat were soon left alone together to figure out how best and how amicably they could get through the next few days. Kat had the last of her packing up to do and the awkward questions of asking whether or not Max wanted to keep something or whether she could take it with her to London. Technically, the cottage they shared belonged to Max, thanks again to Spike's gift of kindness, but it was their home and full of their things. Stuff that they'd collected whilst on their numerous travels around the world. Strange musical instruments they could never play. Hats and scarves they'd never worn, along with scented candles and trinkets, which when pieced together, would create a map of their adventures over the last fifteen years.

Max decided to make Kat's life easier and told her that she could take whatever she wanted, as long as she kept and looked after what she took. Maybe in his subconscious mind he was half hoping or even expecting to see those things again. But for now, it simply made their lives easier and for Max, far less painful. Max had also decided to bury his head in his van and take as many delivery routes as possible between now and when he and Charlie flew out to Corfu.

"Oh, I forgot to tell you Kat, Charlie is joining me for the first week in Corfu and I've offered him the spare room until he sorts himself out. He'll be homeless at the end of June, it was the least I could do and I wouldn't be surprised to find him here when I get in from work on Saturday."

"That's kind of you Max and I wouldn't expect anything else from you. You've always liked and looked out for Charlie, even though the two of you are like chalk and cheese."

"What time are you leaving for London on Friday?"

"I have a meeting with Fabio and Grant at 2pm so I reckon I'll head off around ten o'clock, just to be on the safe side. Apparently there's a lot to discuss and I then need to get myself settled in."

"I'm guessing Grant is allowing you to use his apartment on a permanent basis?"

"Well I'm hoping so, but as I haven't yet asked him, I'm not entirely sure. However, Fabio has assured me that there is now enough work for me in London for me to be based there permanently. So that would suggest that he's considered my living arrangements along with his work requirements, I'll have to wait and see what materialises from our meeting. If not, I'll find a cheap hotel for a few nights and go from there."

"I'm sure you know what you're doing but it all sounds a bit hit and miss to me."

"I've said this before Max, if I make a mess of everything in London, it's my mess and I'll be the one who has to clean it up."

Friday at ten o'clock very quickly arrived and Max had just finished helping Kat load her stuff into her rather small and very inappropriate car. They took a step back, dusted their hands and looked at each other in amazement at just how much they'd managed to fit into Kat's Mini Cooper. There would be no need for a courier and a van, as suggested by Max during the early days of the break up. Kat was keen to get going because she really couldn't be late for her meeting with Fabio and Grant. She was also struggling to contain her feelings and the sight of Max with tears in his eyes was emotionally destroying her, so she needed to go and go now.

"I'll message you when I get to London and I'll phone you this evening once I'm sorted, I promise."
"Take care Kat and please remember all the good times we had together, I certainly will."
"I will Max, how could I ever forget them and who knows?"
"Who knows what Kat?"
"Who knows what the future holds for us now, but I hope it's good for both of us. Take care of yourself Maxi."
"You too and please be careful."

Max was left standing there, overlooking the soggy village green, as Kat drove away from their life together and in the direction of the new life she so badly wanted. Although Max hadn't lost Kat to another man nor had he done anything wrong, he couldn't help but feel that he hadn't done enough. How could one place on a map, one stupid place down South called London, be the ultimate wedge which would drive them apart. Max had lost his girl to London, London: 1, Max: 0.

Kat arrived at Fab HQ in good time and was instructed by the young girl on reception to head straight for Fabio's office.

"Kat, good to have you back and I know it's only been a few extra days but it feels like years. Listen up my love, Grant is back in his box and for as long as you're working on his stuff, his apartment is yours. So make yourself at home this evening and thank me later. Now, I'm not going to lie to you, okay. There's shit loads to do as far as Grant Fisher is concerned. He wants to explore the option of TV advertising for Bow Road and Thames Side, you know, actors and pre written scripts and all that stuff. I'm out of my depth here, so this is your gig honey and your turn to take centre stage."

"But Fabio, I've also never dealt with TV advertising and wouldn't know where to start."

"Let's start by joining Grant in the boardroom shall we and let's tell him that we've got this."

"Fabio, You mean I've got this?"

"That's what I meant."

Fabio and Kat made their way to the boardroom whilst quickly brainstorming some ideas which would work for TV. Kat suggested using real life scenarios as a foundation upon which to build the campaign. Using herself as a prime example of someone who was just starting out in London, but that journey was made easier by the fact that she'd managed to secure herself a beautiful home and it was all because Fisher Developments made it happen, from start to finish.

"Grant, look who's back in town and full of great ideas for your desired TV campaign. So unless you really need me, I'll leave you two to carry things forward from here shall I?"

"Kathy, about the other day, you caught me at a bad time."

"Look Grant, it's fine, so let's just move on shall we. By the sounds of it, we've got a lot to do and not much time to do it."

"You're absolutely right and it's good to have you back on the front line, Fabio has been driving me crazy over the last few days. So tell me all about these great ideas you have."

Kat explained to Grant what she'd briefly suggested to Fabio, about using real people, their lives and their living requirements as the main running feature for the new campaign and how a Fisher Developments home could make their home ownership dreams come true. Grant loved the idea and gave her permission to make it happen.

"It's your baby Kathy, so own it and do what you need to do. Just keep me posted on costs and timescales. I want to move quick on this and I want to be able to see and feel something by the end of June. I don't expect the finished item, I just want the reassurance that when it is finished, it'll be amazing."

"No pressure then Grant?"

"None at all."

Kat was feeling really excited about her new advertising project and immediately started to map things out in her head. She was thinking about the type of people who would really love or benefit from a Fisher Developments home and who those people could be. She thought about the people she knew and the people in her life. What would Lucy's new home look like? What about Charlie, Laura and their kids?" What about Charlie, the soon to be bachelor and what about Max, the unique personality from Yorkshire who hates London. These individuals were fine examples of the people who Kat needed to attract. She felt empowered and alive again and these feelings were why she so desperately wanted to be in London. No more struggling farmers or failing estate agents to impress but instead, in the thick of a city where your creative decisions could potentially make people's lives better and happier. Fabio joined Grant and Kat in the boardroom and requested a very quick update on the progress made so far. Grant reassured Fabio that Kat had everything under control and as it was Friday, it was time to call it a day. Fabio agreed and invited Kat to join him and Grant for a quick drink at a bar which was just around the corner from Fab HQ. Kat was happy with that plan but was in no mood for a late one. "Just one and then I'm off. I've got a car full of my previous life to unload and unpack and only myself to do it."

"You've also got a late night ahead of you tomorrow Kathy. I hear you're joining Megan and her friends for her birthday night out?"

"I am and I'm looking forward to it. I'll call her later and confirm the plans."

"They're meeting in Hampstead at 6pm, at The Tabby Cat Lounge. You should like it, they have a DJ who plays ChillHop and LoFi beats. I have no idea what type of music that is but Megan assured me that it's pretty relaxed and I'd be down with it."

"Sounds to me like you're joining us Grant?"

"Yes I am. Megan knows but she doesn't know that I've put some money behind the bar which should keep the party going for a few hours. She's a good one and deserves a good birthday without worrying about how to pay for it. I won't be staying long though. There's another bar just up the road which is more my cup of tea."

Fabio looked across at Grant in a way which suggested he knew exactly where he was coming from and then reminded them that it was still Friday and time for drinks.

Chapter 16 ~ Sausages And Sangria, All Inclusive.

The bar which Fabio had chosen was a favorite of his and full of charismatic and creative people. The conversation was as vibrant and as lively as the clothes which were being worn by the revealers and the atmosphere was joyous and celebratory. Kat quizzed Fabio on this, "Why the celebrations, what's the deal here?"

"Life my darling, life, that's the deal here. People come here to celebrate life, not just birthdays, promotions or retirements, they're all boring compared to life. Why celebrate getting older, having less free time or too much free time, which will eventually lead to boredom, when you can quite happily celebrate being alive?"

"I see. Max used to say that about birthdays and that reminds me, I need to message him and let him know that I arrived safely. Give me a minute Fabio."

Already Kat was starting to slip on the pledges she'd made to Max only a few hours ago but that was London for you. The current was strong and impossible to fight or swim against, you just had to keep your head above water and try not to drown in the liquid energy. Kat loved it but could easily see why Max preferred the peace and quiet of Yorkshire or the mountain villages of Corfu. A place she'd left behind and a place she will more than likely never get to experience now.

Grant joined Fabio and Kat with a small tray of drinks and joined the conversation. "How's things between you and Max Kathy, are you still on talking terms?"
"We are yes, for now anyway. But I've never known of a failed relationship which turned into a beautiful or lasting friendship. That usually goes out the window when one or the other meets someone new but neither of us are at that stage yet, so we're just taking things one day at a time."
"That makes sense to me and maybe you'll both just slowly drift apart and neither of you will ever know of anyone else."
"Maybe, but I hope I see Max again at some point in the future. Even if it's just as friends, you know, I still like him. In fact, I still love him."

Kat finished her one drink and said goodbye to Grant and Fabio before making her way back to her overloaded car. She had a short drive back to her new home and used this time to call Max. "I'm all sorted here Max and before you ask, I'm safe and I've got somewhere to live, but it comes with the job."

"That's good news and I'm sure you'll soon make it your home. What are your plans for the weekend?"

"Well, tonight I'm going to unpack some essential items and then get some sleep. Tomorrow I'm going out, do you remember me telling you about Megan and her birthday? We're going for drinks in Hampstead but after that, I don't really know. Then it'll soon be Monday and back to work as usual but without the long commute to work."

"Sounds like you've got a busy and exciting few days ahead of you? Unlike me, I'm just working and mentally preparing myself for the arrival of Charlie. I'll probably do a bit of walking on Sunday, make sure my legs still work."

"That's not like you, it's been a few years since you hiked. It must have been when we were in France?"

"Yes it was and I remember it well. We walked for miles up in the mountains breathing in the fresh mountain air. I'm going to be doing a lot of hiking in Corfu once Charlie has buggered off home, I'm working on my plans now."

"That sounds like hard work but I'm sure you know what you're doing. Listen Max, I'm home now and I really need to make a start on unpacking my stuff and I'm sure you've got plenty of planning to do, so let's catch up again in a few days, okay?"

Whilst Kat was busy building herself a new nest in London, Max was busy getting his house ready for a new life with Charlie. He'd got the spare room all made up and removed any reminders of Kat. He guessed that Charlie would want to replace them with reminders of Laura and the kids but knowing Charlie of late, he could quite easily turn up with

133

pictures or posters of celebrity babes he'd like to bang. Max made the bedroom he used to share with Kat his bedroom and took advantage of the spare wardrobe and drawer space. He'd sorted out all of his hiking gear and organised it into a methodical order where specific items could be easily located to suit the weather and the terrain of any particular hiking route. However, his main aim was to ensure that he had everything he might need to hike The Corfu Trail. He had everything he needed apart from some hiking poles and a couple of bandannas and he'd easily be able to pick them up tomorrow. With that task complete, Max grabbed a glass and a bottle of wine from the fridge and settled down for another night of watching The Durrells. Louisa Durrell was desperately trying to make things work on Corfu but her children were nothing short of feral and completely oblivious to how hard it was for their mother. For Larry, Leslie, Margo and Gerry, their new life on Corfu was just one big holiday of beautiful discovery and exploration. Larry's only problem was occasional writers block. Leslie had too many girlfriends. Margo was still struggling to find the true meaning of life and Gerry was running out of places to house his creatures. Max had none of those problems, apart from a tiny slice of Margo's, but he was desperately missing Kat, and as random and as interesting as Charlie could be, he would never take the place of Kat in his cottage.

Kat was up early after a restless first night of living on her own in London. She unpacked the last of her boxes and cases and placed things where she thought they looked good or made her apartment feel like home. She put a photo frame containing a picture of herself and Max on the bedside table, adjusted it slightly to the left and then moved on to sorting out her kitchen. Back in Yorkshire, the kitchen belonged to Max. It was his place and where culinarily delights were invented and created, but this kitchen was Kat's and would either be put to good use or a place to make coffee and brown toast. Max was also up early but he was up and out delivering groceries and small packages, making money for his trip to Corfu. What Max did for a living was convenient and on a good day, he could earn decent tax free money with little or no stress at all. However, the places he had to deliver to were changing and not for the best. He'd frequently see ten year olds wandering the streets with weapons. Max had already had a couple of issues with the local wanna be Kray Twins. One day it was kids trying to steal from his van and on another occasion, a gang of three pasty looking stick insects threatened him with what looked like a screwdriver. He'd promised to himself that if anything more serious ever happened to him, that that would be his lot and it was time to move on to pastures new. Although Max had no idea where he would find the safer or greener grass, it was still his red line and his promise to himself to choose his life over convenient and tax free money.

Back in London, Kat had finalised her Saturday night plans and Megan was heading over to Kat's place for some pre drinks before going out for the real drinks in Hampstead. Megan arrived at Kat's armed with a couple of bottles of cheap Prosecco from Aldi and a few bags of crisps. Kat was buzzing at the reality of having new friends over at her new place and without delay, a plastic cork was popped and a bowl of crisps were being shared. Megan broke the ice by telling her new friend that she'd broken up with her fella, the one who favoured football over romantic weekends away and the one who fancied his chances in the boxing ring. "It was a few slaps too many Kat, emotionally and physically. I can deal with the physical slaps, I'm used to that but I couldn't cope with constantly playing second fiddle to a football club who aren't even that good anymore, you know what I mean?"

"Yes and no or no and yes Megan. I've never been in an aggressive nor a violent relationship, so I don't really know what you mean. But I do know that either way or whichever way you were hurt by this guy is unacceptable and you're better off without him in your life."

"You're probably right Kat but that means I'm single again and on my own and that's not what I want."

"Welcome to my club! I'm single and on my own and that's not what I want either, but I chose my outcome Megan. Maybe you should start choosing your outcome, take control of things and ban the same old time wasters and happy slappers from ever entering your life again."

"You're so bloody right Kat and where have you been all my life? Tonight, a new version of Megan was born!"

"You go for it girl and keep those bad boys at bay!"

Megan and Kat took a taxi across town to Hampstead to join the rest of the party group, which also included Grant. The Tabby Cat Lounge was located on Heath Street, just a short walk up the hill from Hampstead Tube Station and was a popular hang out with those who looked at life from a slightly different angle. The melodic and sometimes out of tune beats could be heard from outside and a rather large and threatening looking guy stood guard in the doorway. "Welcome ladies, just the two of you is it or are you part of Megan's birthday group?" Megan firmly replied, "I am the

136

party group, so are you going to let us in or let us freeze to death?"

"Megan, he's built like a tank. You can't speak to him like that!"

"He's nothing but a pussy cat, I've dealt with worse people than him in my life. Anyway, we're in now aren't we?"

Megan confidently led Kat towards the bar and introduced her to those who she hadn't met yet. She knew Abi and obviously knew Grant but there were another ten or twelve new faces to meet and apart from a couple of well groomed guys who were an item, the new faces all belonged to young ladies. All pretty in their individual ways, some a little rough around the edges but all very friendly and welcoming towards the new girl in town. The introductions took no time at all, Grant was getting a very expensive round of drinks in and the party was soon in full swing.

Megan and Kat were deep in conversation about life, love and London when Grant joined them. "Ladies, you're both looking lovely this evening, if you don't mind me saying so. Kat, welcome again to London and I hope you're getting yourself sorted back at the apartment?"

"Slowly getting there Grant, helped by the fact that I don't really have much stuff to sort out but I'll have everything sorted by tomorrow afternoon."

"And ready for a busy day on Monday I hope?"

"Absolutely boss and raring to go, bring it on."

Grant left the girls to their original topic of conversation and returned to his spot at the end of the bar where he resumed chatting to the bartender.

"So Kat, what do you make of Grant?"

"I haven't quite figured him out yet, I thought I had until the other day, when he lost his shit with me."

"Yeh, pretty much everyone who works for him or deals with him has been on the receiving end of one of his unpredictable outbursts."

"That makes me feel slightly better and it wasn't just me."

"Far from it Kat and don't take it personally. Anyway, do you think he's a bit of alright?"

"If you're referring to Grant, well he's not really my type but I can easily see why some girls would find him attractive. He always looks smart, he's certainly not ugly and I'm guessing he's got a few quid? In fact, I know someone who would be all over him like a rash if she was here now."

"Don't ever repeat what I'm about to tell you but some say he bats for the other side."

"He does what?"

"He prefers men over women Kat, he's gay! But that contradicts what Anne has told me and she's told me that he was married to an absolute stunner. Apparently, the marriage only lasted a year or so and that was his last serious relationship. Since the divorce, he's never been in another relationship with either a man or a woman, as far as we know but he never talks about his personal life, so it's all a big mystery."

"Well I don't care either way, as long as he continues to be kind and respectful and sticks to his side of the deal. After all Megan, if it wasn't for Grant's ever expanding business and his lovely apartment, I wouldn't be here with you now and this is wonderful. So come on, let's get some more drinks, Grant's paying."

The drinks continued to flow and Grant remained true to his word. He was done with The Tabby Cat Lounge and the strange music they were playing and after a round of goodbyes and a quick rendition of happy birthday, he made his way up the road to a little bar which was tucked away down some side street. Megan and Kat continued chatting like they'd known each other for years, filling in a lot of blanks about each other's lives and quite often astonishing each other with their admissions. Megan was amazed that Kat had only slept with Max and Kat was slightly shocked by the number of guys Megan had been with and how many of them treated her so badly. Kat felt very lucky to have only experienced the good side of love and not the constant heartache and regular beatings which Megan had become so used to. For Megan, that was normal and it was going to take some serious commitment from her and Kat if she was going to find and settle down with a guy who genuinely loved her for who she was and everything she could give.

"So Kat, now that you and Max are officially in the bin, what are your plans for the foreseeable?"
"Well that's one way of putting it but at least I know what you mean this time, unlike your cricket analogy. In answer to your question though, apart from working hard and trying to survive in London, I've not really figured my future out yet. I should have been going away in a few weeks with Max, we were going to Corfu for four weeks to explore the entire island but as you would put it, that's now in the bin."
"Why don't we go away Kat, just the two of us. We could go to one of those all inclusive places in Spain, they're

really cheap. You know, where you can have sausages and sangria for breakfast."

Chapter 17 ~ Sofrito, Philosophy And Cold White Wine.

Megan was rather tipsy by now and as a result, the stories she was telling Kat about her life were getting more and more disturbing and Kat was genuinely struggling to deal with what she was hearing. Kat suggested that they called it a night, Megan agreed and they made their way back to her apartment. Kat offered Megan the sofa for the night as there was only one bedroom but it had to be better than spending the night at the flat which Megan shared with her mum and younger brother. Megan's younger brother was a bit of a small time dealer, selling mainly to the kids and the very vulnerable who either lived on or hung out around the council flats where they lived. Megan's mum was a heavy drinker and for most of the time, incapable of doing anything and spent most of her time drinking vodka and then sleeping off the effects of her binge wherever she fell, usually on the living room floor or in the bathroom. Megan had described to Kat in great detail how her daily life in that tiny flat played out and it involved many visits from the police and Social Services, along with strangers who were looking for Boney Tony, that was Megan's brother. In the absence of a functioning mother, Megan had tried her best to keep Tony on the straight and narrow but Tony was following in his father's footsteps and thought nothing of knocking his sister about until she gave up and left him

140

alone. Although Megan did okay financially working for Grant, it was hard work and quite often stressful, especially when Grant was having one of his days. Her salary was spread very thinly between paying for them all to remain in the flat and ensuring that there was enough food and vodka in the cupboard. There was no way she could ask Tony for a contribution because she knew where that would get her and her mum's weekly benefit payments only lasted a day or two. It was easy to see why Megan had turned out to be such a tough little cookie.

"So Kat, now that you know everything about my life and my truly horrendous family, is there anything else I need to know about you and yours?"

"Nothing I can think of but I can't help feeling sorry for you. You've really been through it, haven't you?"

"I'm nowhere near through it Kat, tonight is just a break from it. Tomorrow everything will be back to normal."

"Let's do something tomorrow then, where's cool and relaxing to hang out with a hangover on a Sunday?"

"Hampstead Heath has always been my happy place Kat. From the top of Parliament Hill you can see for miles and you can see some of London's most famous buildings, including The Sharpe."

"Do you mean The Shard?"

"Yeh, same thing, I know what it looks like. It's the tall pointy looking one!"

"Oh Megan, you're such an honest and beautiful person. Can I be your adopted older sister and look after you forever?"

"If you mean a sister from another mister, then sure you can."

Kat and Megan had promised to look after each other and help each other make their lives as perfect as they could both be. Kat was going to protect Megan from the bad boys and keep her away from the day to day chaos of her normal life as much as possible. Megan was going to show Kat all the best places to visit and hang out in London whilst doing her best to keep Kat's mind off Max. She knew that Kat was still in love with her childhood sweetheart but already, Megan couldn't imagine life without her and she was her only lifeline.

Charlie wasted no time at all moving in with Max and it was now only a couple of weeks until his home was to be repossessed by the bank. Laura, in order to avoid any embarrassment on the day of repossession, had also moved out and back to her parents with the children. Laura had also told Charlie that she wanted a divorce and they'd amicably agreed to what appeared to be a simple solution moving forward. After all, there was nothing left to fight over, other than who was going to do what and when with their children. And as disappointed as Laura was with Charlie for ruining everything she wanted and had in life, she also knew deep down that he tried his hardest to keep it all together and he would always be a good father to their children, every other weekend, birthday and Christmas.

"The Corfu train is coming down the line Max and it will soon be stopping at our station. Are you ready for this, can you even handle this?"
"Charlie, have I ever told you you're a twat?"
"Yes Max, loads of times but Laura used to call me a useless 'C U Next Tuesday' for putting the white towels in

142

the drawer which was only for the grey towels. Easy mistake and I was only trying to be helpful. So to be honest, I find being called a twat a bit of a complement."

"You're unique Charlie and if you could find a way to swap some of your nerdiness for some common sense, you could quite easily be a force to be reckoned with. You also need to sort your hair out before we go to Corfu, you look like you're about to take part in University Challenge. Hello, I'm Charles and I'm reading something completely boring and equally as useless at Oxbridge."

Max and Charlie had fun spending their first Sunday together as housemates, taking the piss out of each other in a way that was only acceptable to a couple of guys who had known each other for many years. They say that time is a healer and that can be true for some and not for others. Time also provides a constantly open window of opportunity to learn new things and things about people, people you already know and people who you've just met. For Max and Charlie, they were learning to live together and they'd just learnt that they now had a lot in common. They both thought that they had their lives sorted but actually, they now both had to sort their lives out. At the top of Parliament Hill, overlooking East, South and West London, Megan and Kat were really starting to understand their lifestyle differences and were quickly becoming the very best of friends. Kat had also agreed to Megan's suggestion that the two of them should take a much needed vacation together and as she now had four weeks holiday leave to use up, it made perfect sense to use it on an overseas adventure and not just four weeks off in London. Kat told Megan to check in with Grant on Monday and sound out some suitable dates. She also pointed Megan in the direction of some alternatives to an all inclusive hotel in Spain.

Kat's first weekend in London did not disappoint and she was genuinely looking forward to getting back to work on Monday morning. She had a new friend in Megan, some exciting travel plans for the future and plenty to be getting on with in the present. She would be in and out of important meetings all day and all week. Meetings with Fabio and Grant. Meetings with script writers and casting managers. Lunches with the lovelies and dinners with the darlings and apart from not coming home at the end of each day to find Max waiting for her, her life was pretty much perfect and complete.

Max was busy picking up as many delivery routes and making as much money as he possibly could before flying off to Corfu with Charlie. He also kept reminding his mate that he should start looking for a new job, even if it did mean flipping burgers at Happy Burger, who were in fact recruiting for a new restaurant which would be opening in four or five weeks. Most evenings, Max would give Charlie a crash course in basic cookery, as if he was getting him prepared for an inevitable career change from computer programmer to burger technician.

Charlie was slowly coming round to the idea of becoming a chef, or at least starting out on his journey to becoming a chef, which could potentially start at Happy Burger and soon after his return from Corfu. He was also well on his way to leaving behind his title of self importance, which eventually cost him everything he owned and he was doing what he was naturally good at. He was programming his mind to think differently and to recognise the fact that happiness and success came in many different shapes and sizes, colours and visions. Despite losing everything, Charlie was doing okay.

Grant was more than happy with how things were progressing, both on his sites and with the new advertising campaigns and as a result, he was being very nice to everyone he met. He would occasionally take Kat out for lunch or meet her for drinks after work, in order to catch up on the important stuff, before leaving her in peace to be clever and creative. He'd also offered Megan a new sales incentive bonus which could potentially see her double her sales commission each month, if she hit the necessary sales and financial targets which he'd set for her. It would be tough but so was Megan.

Megan, with a little help from her friend from up North, was managing to stay away from the bad boys and was thinking about how she could use her extra monthly income to escape the life she currently shared with her terrible brother and drunken mother. She would have to work incredibly hard and always be on top form but if she was totally focused on her job, instead of trying to work hard whilst nursing a black eye and multiple bruises at the same time, she could make it happen for Grant and herself. Grant would make lots of money and her reward would be a place of her own to call home.

Fabio was happy because Grant was happy and leaving him alone. Kat was now doing precisely what she was brought to London to do, look after Fabio's big spender and make them both a lot of money. Grant was also happy because he didn't have to see Fabio every day and although the two of them had known each other for many years, Grant just couldn't deal with him, it just didn't work. Which was perfect, because Fabio's partner had proposed and Fabio had said yes, which meant Fabio and Patrick could spend all day and every day planning what was clearly going to be the event of the year.

Lucy was still happily but very selectively playing the field around Harrogate and York and had even received a wedding proposal of her own. She'd only been out with the guy twice when he popped the question, she hadn't even taken him for a proper test drive. Needless to say, she said no and asked him if they could just be friends for now. She was also heading to London in a few weeks to catch up with Kat and would no doubt get to meet Megan, maybe Fabio and quite possibly Mr Fisher himself. Lucy had booked herself a double room at a posh West End hotel, just in case she got lucky in London.

Back in Yorkshire, the boys were spending a normal Wednesday night in and Max had just finished showing Charlie how to make a traditional Corfiot Pork Sofrito. Max remembers having this dish at Bacchus on The Beach and over the years, he'd almost perfected the recipe but there was always that little something that wasn't quite right. It was never the same as the dish which was lovingly prepared in that tiny little kitchen at the back of the restaurant. They sat down to eat, Max took the first mouthful, Charlie looked on nervously and waited for Max's response. "You know what mate? That's pretty good for a first attempt. A little more salt and pepper and a dash more of tomato paste and you my friend can call that a wrap."

"Thanks Max! Let me try it and see if you're right about the seasoning and the tomato product. Yeh, you're right but that's bloody lovely that is! We should open a restaurant on Corfu, what do you think?"

"I think we'd be chased off the island before we even had a chance to open our doors. I know enough about Corfu to know that you don't mess with the Corfiot traditions and it's best to leave the locals to do what they do best and that's creating the dishes that they've been serving up for hundreds of years. However, if you were suggesting that we should open a burger or fried chicken place, then I reckon they'd happily leave us to it and then laugh at us when we have to shut up shop after just one season. Corfu is not Benidorm Charlie, far from it."

"How do you know all this stuff Max?"

"Because unlike you Charles, I attended The University of Life and not The University of Durham, or wherever it was. Have you finished paying off your student loan yet or is that another debt which will soon be written off?"

"Ha bloody ha Max, you think you're so smart don't you for avoiding the system and still managing to do so well for yourself?"

"I don't think I'm smart Charlie, I am smart. People boast about having what they call a really good job but the reality of that is this: they're forever burdening someone else's responsibility. They give anything between twenty and forty percent of their salary to the Government and whichever organisation it is that they work for, those slave drivers are responsible for keeping their slaves away from their family, friends and loved ones for pretty much the entirety of five, sometimes even six or seven days a week. Tell me what's good about that kind of job?"

"Well when you put it like that, I guess you're right and do you know what Max, I'm going to apply for the grill chef position at Happy Burger. Who knows, in time I might earn enough gold stars to become Restaurant Manager."

Kat's phone call temporarily interrupted Max and Charlie's night of Sofrito and philosophy, washed down with cold white wine and their usual and sometimes childish banter. Kat proceeded to update Max on life in London and informed him that her and Megan were now planning a trip of their own. Max laughed out load when she told him that Megan had suggested an all inclusive hotel in Spain. "It's funny you say that Kat, we were just talking about Benidorm."

"What makes you think we were talking about Benidorm Max, there are all inclusive hotels all over Spain you know."

"I'm aware of that but whenever anyone mentions all inclusive and Spain, you immediately think of Benidorm, don't you?"

"Anyway Max, I've suggested plenty of other places and I'm sure we'll both agree on somewhere other than the dreaded all inclusive in Benidorm. So, how are you both doing, are you coping with living together?"

Max reassured Kat that everything was fine and dandy between him and Charlie and told her that they were both looking forward to getting away. He also updated her on Charlie's pending career move from computers to burgers while doing his best to protect his housemates dignity. "He's actually a really good cook and with a little help from moi, this evening he cooked an almost perfect Pork Sofrito, you know how difficult that can be Kat? Even I can't make it taste how they cook it in the traditional tavernas."

"Good to hear you're still full of self confidence and still loving your cooking Max. I do miss your lovely cooking."

"But you don't miss me, just my cooking?"

"Of course I miss you Max but it sounds to me as if we're both moving on and getting on with our lives."

"Well I miss you terribly and right now, I should really get back to Charlie. He's in the kitchen again, my kitchen and lord only knows what he's trying his hand at now?"

"Okay Max, I'll let you go and I'm sure we'll talk again soon?"

The last thing Max wanted to do that evening was to end that call from Kat. In fact, he could of chatted to her all evening about anything at all, he just wanted to hear her beautiful voice. Hidden behind the excitement surrounding his trip to Corfu and the lads banter with Charlie, Max's heart was slowly breaking into a million pieces and he didn't know what to do to stop it from finally being irreparable.

"Charlie, I need to ask you a serious question and I need a serious answer from you."

"Go for it Max, what's up?"

"How do I get her back Charlie, how do I get her back?"

"Are you talking about your racing pigeon or Kat?"

"Charlie, since when have I owned a racing pigeon?"

Chapter 18 ~ Decisions Are Not One Way Streets You Know.

There were now less than two weeks to pass before Max and Charlie took their flight out of Teeside Airport to Corfu. Max was already packed and ready to go with everything he needed for a one week booze and baklava extravaganza with Charlie and everything he thought he needed to solo hike The Corfu Trail. Charlie had put a few items of clothing and a toothbrush in a bag for life and had asked Max whether or not that would do. "Travel like that if you want mate but don't pretend to know me at the airport and don't ask to borrow my deodorant when we get there."

"Alright, I take the hint and I'll pack my own deodorant, whatever makes you happy?"

Kat was also working to a schedule and had exactly two weeks to go before she had to present her marketing plan, including visualisation boards and content scripts to Grant and Fabio. She was on target to deliver the goods and a successful pitch meant that she could take that much needed holiday with Megan. Fabio had agreed to her amended leave request but if Grant wasn't one hundred percent happy, it would be back to the drawing board and no holiday. Grant had signed off Megan's request for two weeks leave across the first two weeks of August, unconditionally and with an additional bonus which could easily be achieved by the end of July. Grant knew that Megan would need every penny she could earn to make this holiday happen and since day one and as promised, Megan had never let him down and this would be his timely reward for that. Kat and Megan were still undecided on where to go but they had agreed to aim higher than all inclusive, regardless of where it was. Kat was leaning towards a private apartment on Santorini, Megan had no idea where Santorini was and initially thought it was a cocktail but she had however heard good things about Lloret de Mar on Spain's Costa Brava. Apparently there was a really good bar called Jimmy's and there was even a McDonald's.

Fabio had arranged a one to one with Kat or as he preferred to call them, a heart to heart. He had complete faith in his number one to keep his big spending client happy but wanted some last minute reassurance that Grant was going to be blown away. Fabio also wanted to have a separate chat with Kat, one which was officially off the records. "So my lovely, Grant buzzing or Grant raging. To holiday or not to holiday after your presentation next Friday?"

"Grant buzzing and I'm going on holiday with Megan. You guys can try and stop us if you think you're brave enough but Megan and I deserve this break and we're both working really hard. For ourselves, for you Fabio and for Grant. We will make everything happen and everyone will be happy and financially better off, if that's what this meeting is all about?"

"As far as business matters are concerned, you've just told me exactly what I wanted to hear."

"Thanks! Anything else to discuss?"

"You're an exceptional talent Kat, in a very competitive and dog eat dog world, and that's why I employed you and asked you to join us here in London. But I'm sad Kat. I'm sad because I can't stop myself from thinking that it was my selfishness, my business desires and my hunger for more success, which ultimately led to you and Max splitting up."

"Fabio, I've known you long enough now to know that you won't fire me for what I'm about to say. So please, shut the fuck up. If you're having a tough time of it, feeling guilty or sorry for yourself for whatever reason and need to offload some negative shit onto someone else, don't pick me as your trash can. If you really want to know how I'm feeling and how things are between Max and I, just ask the question and I'll happily tell you."

Fabio did ask the question and Kat replied with an honest answer. She told him that she loved London and how it had reinvented her or maybe it had just taught her things which she needed to know and experience before settling down forever with someone like Max. London was busy introducing her to new places and new people, people like Grant, Abi, Anne and Megan. People she liked and now loved and she was thrilled by that. It was a constant challenge but she embraced that and generally speaking, she was happy with her new life in London. However, Kat was also feeling sad. Sad because she knew that back in Yorkshire, Max was breaking, losing it, coming undone and it was all because of her desire to explore the greener grass. Fabio continued to listen with a caring and understanding look on his face as Kat explained everything away in great detail.

"Decisions are not one way streets you know Kat. Other than you, nobody is stopping you from doing a u-turn."
"Like I said Fabio, I'm happy in London but I'd be happier if Max was here with me."

"But he's not my love and that's the reality of your situation. So what are you going to do?"

"I don't know Fabio but before I say anything else, I'm sorry for losing my shit with you earlier. I don't know what came over me."

"It's called the London effect, I've seen it many times before. If you're not born and raised in this crazy place and slowly but surely learn how to cope and deal with things, you'll find yourself sinking one day and then believing you can take on the entire world the next. It was the same for me. Moving from Italy to London was initially very exciting but reality soon took hold and things quickly became very different indeed. The family business provided me with a comfort zone but when I left the business and ultimately my home, I had to stand on my own two feet and toughen up almost over night, that's no mean feat for a gay Italian."

"Oh Fabio! I look at you now, with your successful business and your lovely partner, or should I now say husband to be, and I stupidly assume that it was all written in the stars and with no possibility whatsoever of an unhappy ending. I've clearly still got a lot to learn, haven't I."

"We all have a lot to learn and we should all continue to learn, every single day which blesses us with life and the ability to love and forgive. I couldn't have made it in London on my own though Kat, that's why you always need a good wingman. I hear you have a new wingman or wingwoman now in Megan?"

"Yes I do and how do you know that?"

"Grant told me whilst we were out for a few drinks the other night. I wanted to tell him about Patrick and I getting married and I also wanted to reassure him that everything was going according to plan with his current campaign and he was to trust you emphatically in my absence."

"Fabio, I hope you don't mind me asking, but who was your wingman back then?"

"Oh it's a long and complicated story Kat and one for another day."

In the cottage over looking the village green, Max and Charlie were quickly becoming a polished double act. The village green was no longer looking soggy, as summer ordered the surface water to keep the trees, plants and flowers alive for another year. Charlie was cooking almost every night and he was keeping the place spotlessly clean and tidy. Charlie loved living with Max and Max was slowly getting used to the fact that Charlie was actually a useful asset and not just a useful idiot and although he would never take Kat's place in that cottage, for now he was filling a massive hole in Max's life.

"I've submitted my application Max and unless I'm pipped to the post by some spotty teenager who is also happy to work for peanuts, then Happy Burger here I come."

"Good for you mate and I'm sure you'll nail it. If you get the job but promotion doesn't follow, just take their money, learn from the experience and move on before you earn too many gold stars. I've heard that once you get four stars, you're enslaved for life and you'll need to donate an arm or leg in order to be released from the slave camp."

"Thanks for the sarcastic heads up but I need this job Max and not only for the money. It's also a new start for me and if I'm successful and I do get promoted, I can then put down some foundations upon which to start building my new life. A half decent job with some regular income means that I can continue to look after my children. Eventually I'll get a place of my own, a place where they can come and stay for the weekend. But Max, you wouldn't understand how important that is to me because the only thing which matters to you right now is Kat and you still refuse to take my advice."

Charlie had told Max that if he really wanted to get back with Kat he would have to start fighting for her again, just like he did when they were initially just friends and every other boy in town wanted to date her. Back then, Max fought hard to win the heart of the most fancied girl in town but now, it was as if he'd given up all hope of spending the rest of his life with the girl of his dreams. Charlie had also reminded him that he didn't have forever to win her back and if not now, it was only a matter of time before she was once again swept of her feet. Then he would have to fight another man in order to get her back. For now, it was a one horse race but even that didn't register with Max nor prompt him to do something about his breaking heart. However, Charlie knew his mate well enough to know how he functioned and sensed that he might be playing the waiting game, hoping that one day Kat would simply turn up out of the blue with her bags and ask to be taken back. Max would obviously say yes, Kat would tell him that it was all a big mistake and promise never to leave him again and they'd finally live happily ever after, just like in the movies. In the meantime, Max would have to apply plenty of self preservation and hope that Kat didn't keep him waiting for too long.

Max was kind of winning at playing the waiting game but through luck more than judgment, simply because Kat was far too busy for love and totally focused on her presentation, which was now just over a week away. But before her big day, Max and Charlie would finally be on their way to Corfu. It was the Friday evening before departure day and the lads were now chilling out at home. Max had finally convinced his travel companion to swap his bag for life for one of his spare rucksacks and they both checked one last time that everything was in order. Whilst Charlie was busy creating dinner for them both, Max took the opportunity to check in with Kat. It had been a few days now since she last called him and he was keen to catch up with her before they went away. "Hi Kat, it's Max. How's things and I hope I'm not disturbing you, with it being Friday evening?"

"No, you're not disturbing me and I still have you in my phone as Max. So if your call was going to disturb me, I wouldn't have answered my phone. Megan is here but she's cool and busy researching holiday destinations. How are you, looking forward to tomorrow I guess?"

"Yeh, it'll be nice to get away and Charlie's like a child on Christmas Eve. He's even had a hair cut! How's work and stuff?"

"Busy and as a result, there is isn't any other stuff! It's just work, work, work at the moment and I've got a big presentation next Friday. It's for Grant's new developments and he's spending a fortune, so it has to be spot on and before I forget, Fabio and Patrick are getting married soon. How lovely is that?"

"Yeh, that's really cool and let me guess, he's even managed to book Elton John and The Scissor Sisters?"

"I wouldn't put it past him and he is telling everyone that it will be the event of the year, so maybe you're right."

Charlie appeared with two bowls of something which looked fantastic and nodded at Max to suggest that dinner was ready. He swapped what was in each hand for a clenched fist and proceeded to act out a boxing match, signaling to Max that he needed to fight for his girl if he wanted her back. Max understood what Charlie was getting at and offered him two middle fingers in return but finally the message was starting to sink in.

"I can't keep him out of my kitchen and although I'm not entirely sure what it is he's cooked this evening, it looks and smells amazing."

"You've obviously been a great tutor Max and you should be proud of that. The last time I saw Charlie, I think he was living on ready meals and take aways. Well done you!"

"Listen Kat, I've been thinking and I know it'll be well into August now, what with Charlie and I being away and then you and Megan going away, but when we're all back, how about you and I catching up in London for a few days. We'll both have plenty of stories to tell from our travels, so there shouldn't be too many awkward silences. What do you say?"

"I would love that Max but will you cope in London?"

"If it was for anyone else, I wouldn't even consider making the journey but as it's you."

"That's very sweet of you Max and it reminds me of our second date. You really didn't want to see that film at the cinema did you but you tolerated it just for me. You were right though, the film turned out to be a right pile of shite!"

"I know right! As you do when you're lost in the jungle, you find an abandoned World War 2 plane that still works and someone in the group just so happens to know how to fly it. I think at that point we both agreed to leave and went back to your parent's place?"

"We did Max, my parents were out and I'll never forget that evening."

"Yes indeed, good times weren't they? Okay, I really don't want to go Kat but Charlie is now threatening to eat my dinner, so I better go and join him but I'll message you when we arrive in Corfu and if you like, I'll send you some photos each day?"

"Like you used to do when you were out driving your van? I'd like that a lot and please, take care and stay out of trouble out there. I know what you two can be like when once you've had a few beers and I'm guessing that's your plan?"

"Absolutely! But yes, we will stay out of trouble and good luck with your work stuff."

Max joined Charlie for dinner and complimented the chef on a great culinary creation, even though he still had no idea what it was nor what was in it. But Chef Charlie had clearly found his calling and at the rate he was going, he would be well and truly over qualified for a grill chef's job at Happy Burger. Charlie complimented Max on his phone call to Kat and asked him if he'd finally taken his advice and the fight was now officially on.

Chapter 19 ~ The Day We Caught The Plane.

Max had booked a taxi to take them to the airport and although the taxi wasn't due for another hour, Charlie was ready to go and impatiently pacing around the front room with his borrowed rucksack on his back and his passport in his hand. "You're not looking forward to this trip one little bit are you?" Max asked Charlie sarcastically.

"Are you kidding me mate, I can't wait to get out of here and with your eyes now firmly fixed on getting your girl back, that means more girls for me when we get to Corfu. You're the mate that keeps on giving, you really are."

"I don't know how you've done it Charlie? Only a few weeks ago, your life was torn apart in every aspect and now look at you."

"Because none of it was within my control Max, I couldn't save my marriage, my house nor my job. I was a casualty of other people's decisions and although it was bloody tough at the time, fighting an inevitable losing battle is just a waste of time and energy. So here I am, ready to go again but a little bit wiser from the experience. I also owe you Max, you were the only one who was there for me when I was at rock bottom."

"We've always been there for each other Charlie and here we are again and I think that might be the taxi."

It was only a twenty minute ride to Teeside Airport, which was a tiny airport compared to all the others which offered flights to Corfu. There was just one flight to Corfu per week, every Saturday afternoon and with one of those budget airlines where the cost of taking an extra bag, enjoying a small inflight bottle of wine and a bag of nuts could easily cost more than the price of the flight itself. But when they arrived at the airport, the plane was there and ready to go. No hold ups or delays and as long as the plane

159

landed safely, Max and Charlie were now only a few hours away from enjoying that first cold Alpha or Mythos Beer, traditionally served in an ice cold glass with a handle.

"Charlie, you need to fasten your seatbelt and fold away your tray table. Also, take your eyes off the young girl in the Kappa tracksuit, you're old enough to be her dad and if that's her boyfriend sitting next to her, my money's on him and not you."

"Good afternoon ladies and gentlemen, this is your Captain speaking and I'd like to take this opportunity to welcome you all aboard Flight: FR 5576 from Teeside International Airport to Kerkyra. My name is Captain Mark Anthony and this afternoon I'll be doing my very best to fly you all to the beautiful island of Corfu. Corfu is the same as Kerkyra, if for a minute you thought you were on the wrong flight. This is the first time I've flown this model of plane and the first time I've landed at Corfu Airport but I'm always up for a challenge. I've got a rough idea of how to get there but if I get stuck, I'll refer to Google Maps. Apparently the airport has a very short runway which at the end, is only a fence away from joining the main road. So please bare with me throughout the duration of the flight, spend loads of money on over priced booze, snacks and duty free and keep everything crossed for a safe and successful landing."

"Jesus Christ Max, is he for real?"

"Shut up Charlie, he's not finished yet!"

"I'm joined in the cockpit today by someone I've never met before but who really wants to be a pilot. So if I nod off, don't panic. This dude has years of experience of using Microsoft Flight Simulator and I'm only a nudge away. I'll ask you all now to listen to the cabin crew as they talk you through what to do if we get it badly wrong up here. I know that most of you won't be paying attention and you'll continue watching your devices or you'll be thinking to yourselves that you've heard this all before but don't blame me if we need to evacuate the plane and you have no idea whatsoever how to get out of this Pringle tube alive."

"Max, is it too late for me to get off the plane?"

"Yep, but you'll love it if we land safely. Everyone cheers and claps before fighting breaks out to be first off the plane."

Charlie had won the toss up to see who got the window seat and as the plane did it's customary lap of honor around the island, Max pointed out to him the sights he could see. "That's the big mountain Charlie, Mount Pantokrator but some people call it the pin cushion because of all the radio masts. There's Corfu Town, can you see the old fortress?"

"What's with the big white golf ball thing on top of that hill?"

"Well that hill is actually called Mount Agia Deka, it's five hundred and seventy six metres above sea level and the golf ball thing is there to give Captain Anthony a better chance of landing the plane safely. It's for aviation and communication purposes."

"Oh I see, you know everything don't you Max?"

"Look Charlie, there's Lake Korission! Can you see it?"

The plane continued its journey in the general direction of Kavos, Paxos and Anti Paxos before banking steeply to the left and then starting its final descent towards Corfu Town.

"Max, you can see the people on the beach and the fishing boats and everything! Are you sure we're not landing in the sea?"

"No Charlie, we're not landing in the sea! But that's where we're staying tonight, that's Messonghi and Moraitika. If you're quick, you'll be able to see the river which divides the two villages. That's the Messonghi River and where Captain Homer keeps his boat. If we get time tonight and we can find him, we can get our boat trip booked. He used to walk along the beach selling tickets a day or two before a trip was due to leave but I'm not sure what he does now. He's probably got an app or a website now and you have to book online or through the app."

After three hours and twenty five minutes of classic Ryanscair service, Captain Mark Anthony safely landed his plane on the short runway at Corfu Airport, pulling up sharply just before the nose of the plane kissed the wire fence. The passengers congratulated his success with a round of cheering, clapping and wolf whistling and Max told Charlie that he could now open his eyes and start breathing again. The fight to be first off the plane had already started, passengers were ignoring the 'Fasten Your Seatbelt' sign and frantically removing their cabin backs from the overhead lockers. Max and Charlie had both put their bets on a family of seven from Middlesbrough. Mum and dad, wearing matching Boro shirts, plus five others who could have been sons, daughters, sons and daughters of sons or daughters, the family dynamic was anyone's guess. They both waited for the riotous passengers to leave the plane before grabbing their small bags and they calmly made their way to the exit door. Max led the way, he thanked the cabin crew and Captain Anthony, who looked as if he'd just celebrated his eighteenth birthday, for a most entertaining flight and paused for a short while at the top of the stairs to breathe in the warm air of Corfu. "Smell that Charlie, that's the smell of Corfu."

"I can smell aviation fuel, if that's what you mean?"

"Partly my friend but it's mixed with the subtle hints of wild oregano, fresh lemon juice and the salty sea air which drifts in from the Straits of Corfu. Close your eyes and take a deep breath Charlie, you'll remember that smell forever."

"How much is it a bottle Max and do they sell it where we're going next?"

"No Charlie and if it were a bottle of wine, it would be priceless."

At the luggage carousel, the family from Middlesbrough were still waiting for six suitcases, three strollers, two fold up travel cots and a set of golf clubs. The boys smirked at each other as they breezed past whilst making their way to passport control and two rubber stamps later, they were outside the terminal building and looking for a taxi.

"Boys! What place are you going to, you need taxi?"

"Kalispera! Yes and Moraitika."

"Ah, English boys here for our beer and girls, yes?"

"Almost right but it's a long story. Are you free?"

Yes! I Spyro and you?"

"I'm Max and this is my friend, Charlie."

"Ah, Max as with Mad Max and Charlie Chaplin, yes? Fifty Euros to Moraitika. You pay cash? If so, forty Euros to Moraitika. Come, I take you."

The taxi journey down to Moraitika was going to make the landing at Corfu Airport feel like a child's fairground ride and Max advised Charlie that he should buckle up and have faith in Spyro to get them there in one piece. Spyro took off down the road as if he were racing against Michael Schumacher whilst chatting to someone on his phone. Occasionally he'd light a cigarette, meaning he had no free hands left to hold the steering wheel but he would then use his right and left knee accordingly, to move the steering wheel, in order to avoid a collision with an oncoming coach or sheer drop to his left.

"So boys, where from England you live?"

"In the North, near Newcastle. Do you know it?"

"Of course! All the men on Corfu know Newcastle Football Club, them the Magpies. Why the Magpies Mad Max?"

"I'm not entirely sure Spyro, I don't really follow football. Charlie, why the Magpies?"

"I have no idea Max but I am feeling slightly sick. Are we nearly there?"

"Ah, You don't like football Max? You like netball better? Where in Moraitika you stay tonight? Not the big place on the beach, you have no children with you. So where you stay?"

"We're staying at the apartments opposite The Rose Garden Restaurant. Do you know them?"

"Of course! Spyros owns them. He one of my cousins, his rooms are good."

Spyro delivered Max and Charlie safely to the village of Moraitika. Spyros met them at their apartment, checked them in and left them to relax on their first floor balcony with a couple of complimentary beers. They raised a can of Alpha each to a successful outbound journey and soaked up the evening ambiance of a beautiful place which was very different to home.

"Fucking hell Max! I feel like I've been out of the UK for months, not hours. How is that even possible mate?"

"Everyone who comes to Corfu will have a different answer for you to digest but does that really matter? Actually, I suppose it does because everyone has a different story to tell, just look at us. If it wasn't for Kat wanting to live in London, you wouldn't be sat here now drinking beer with me."

"As they say Max, everything happens for a reason and thank you Kat. On that note mate, don't forget to let her know that we've arrived safely. Come on, let's take a team photo and you can send it to her."

Max and Charlie had now finished their beers and were in need of some food. They had a quick freshen up and then made their way towards the bars and restaurants. The main road from Corfu town down to Benitses, Lefkimmi and ultimately Kavos, predominantly hugged the East coast of the island and passed through the village of Moraitika. On both sides of the road you could choose from a fine array of places to eat and drink and purchase local produce and souvenirs. Before leaving for Corfu, Max had tried to explain to Charlie the science behind a Gyros. What was in it, how it was put together and how it should be eaten but he eventually gave up when Charlie compared it to a Cornish Pasty. In theory, Charlie was right to compare it to a pasty as both were an entire meal wrapped in something but Max knew better and now had the perfect opportunity to prove his mate wrong. "Right Charlie, our first meal on Corfu is on me and I reckon we should eat here tonight. I've read that Zorbas Taverna do a fantastic Gyros, so what do you think?"

"Looks great mate and I'm starving, let's do it!"

They took a table for two which looked out across the road, ordered a litre of Retsina, some warm pitta bread to snack on and perused the traditional menu. Max warned Charlie to go easy on the Retsina and told him to drink plenty of water during the night. Failure to heed the warning would result in the mother of all hangovers the following morning. Max knew exactly what he was having for dinner that evening and that was going to be a large chicken Gyros with extra fries and a Greek Salad. Charlie quizzed Max about every dish on the menu and asked him whether or not he'd like it before copying his mate's choice. "Right Charlie, let's talk about that unique thing of culinary beauty, the Gyros. Meat, chicken, pork or mixed. Sliced tomatoes and red onion, french fries and tzatziki. Special sauce and a good sprinkling of sea salt, all wrapped up in a warm pitta bread. If the waiter or waitress asks you if you want everything, 'with everything', that's what you're going to get. Got that?"

"Crystal clear Max but if I don't want tzatziki, I just ask for no tzatziki, Right?

"You've got it in one mate and there's hope for you yet! Tomorrow, boat trip, if we can arrange it or a short hike up the hill for lunch somewhere in the hilltop village of Chlomos?"

Dinner soon arrived, Charlie was very quickly becoming addicted to chicken Gyros and Retsina and for a fleeting moment, Max found himself in a little world of his own. He was deep in thought about his life with and now without Kat and as he would sometimes do, when he had the time to drift off into a mini trance, he was thinking things through in his head. He was trying to map out his route back to complete and unspoilt happiness and he now knew that somewhere within his plan he had to find a place for both Kat and now Corfu.

"Earth calling Max, Earth calling Max! Are you okay mate? I thought you'd fallen asleep for a minute."
"Sorry! I was miles away Charlie but it was beautiful there."
"So where were you then?"
"Just up the road actually, so not that far away after all."
"What the… Is this what Retsina does to you? If so Max, can you get it on prescription out here?"
"No you can't and at three Euros for two litres in the local supermarket, it would work out more expensive on prescription. But if you still want to know where I was when I was miles away, I was sitting on Messonghi Beach with Kat. We'd just had dinner at Bacchus on The Beach and then we were enjoying a sundowner whilst listening to the sea gently kiss and caress the tiny pebbles on the sandy shoreline. When Kat got too cold, we took a short walk back to our little place on the side of the hill. The old rundown stone cottage we'd bought together and then made into our perfect home on Corfu. In return for our investment of time and love, what was now our beautiful cottage on the side of the hill, that magical place we'd created together, it paid us back every morning with sweet birdsong, the smell of the island and a perfect sunrise."

"Blimey Max! You've clearly got it all mapped out, haven't you? That's also stunningly beautiful and to be honest with you mate, I'm feeling quite emotional after hearing that. Have you ever thought about writing a novel?"

Chapter 20 ~ A Master Plan And A Cat Called Spike.

Mad Max and Charlie Chaplin, as Spyro the taxi driver had referred to them as, woke to the sound of the island's Cicadas. Max knew what was coming and it was only a matter of time before Charlie asked him what the noise was, "What's that noise Max? Sounds like crickets to me."

"They're called Cicadas and you better get used to them. They start their performance at sunrise and they don't quit until sunset. They're a superfamily, the Cicadoidea, of insects in the order Hemiptera. They're in the suborder Auchenorrhyncha, along with smaller jumping bugs such as leafhoppers and froghoppers."

"They're what... isn't it a bit early for all that knowledge Max?"

"It's never too early to learn something new Charlie and today my friend, you're going to learn whether or not your legs can walk eight miles. I thought we could walk down to the river, stop for breakfast at Maxim on the way and then hunt down Captain Homer. I really want to do his boat trip again and I know you'll love it Charlie. Also, there's bound to be a single girl or two on the boat for you."

"I hope you don't mind me asking you this but did you do Captain Homer's boat trip when you were out here with your parents and Spike?"

"Yes we did and I remember it well. The captain had an old guitar on board and invited anyone who could play it to do so. Spike knew a few chords, nothing complicated nor technical, and he just about managed to get it in tune. With the three or four chords he knew, he kept everyone mesmerized for over an hour. Everyone was singing along to Bob Dylan, Cat Stevens and Andy White but when someone asked if he knew how to play anything by Westlife, he decided to quit while he was ahead."

"Please tell me more Max."

"Spike loved that trip as much as he loved Corfu. He saw Corfu as an escape from the regime back home and although he was smart enough to know that they had rules and regulations in Greece, just like any country, he loved the way the people on Corfu expressed their angst towards the authorities. He liked the way they raised their voices and shouted at each other and frantically waved their hands around in protest. I understand how that may not entirely make a difference these days but at least they were making themselves heard and trying to make a difference. Unlike the woke British public now, who just shut up, pay up and tow the authoritarian line."

"In a lot of ways Max, you're very similar to Spike. Do you know that?"

"I hope I am Charlie and I'll take that as a compliment."

Maxim was also known as The Breakfast Place and as the name suggests, the two brothers who owned and ran Maxim with their wives, served breakfast all day, every day and it was very popular with the British tourists. After two plates of sausage, bacon, beans and toast were consumed, the day's adventure continued and in the direction of the Messonghi River. On one side of the river you would find the fishing boats and day trip boats and on the other, The Messonghi Beach Hotel, also known as the big place on the beach. The big hotel complex on the beach, still to this day, divided the locals and although it provided year round jobs for those who were prepared to do whatever needed doing, many blamed it for killing off a lot of the smaller hotels, apartment blocks and restaurants. It offered an all inclusive package which meant some families, who would have previously spent their money in the village, wouldn't leave the complex. Max hated places like that and would sometimes refer to them as prison camps, only with sunshine and if you were really lucky, slightly better food.

"I don't fucking believe it Charlie, there it is, that's Captain Homer's boat."

"What, that thing there?"

"Yes, that thing there! What were you expecting, the Titanic?"

"I'm not quite sure what I was expecting but does it still work or even float for that matter?"

"Well it's floating now you dick head, unlike the Titanic! And if that sign is up to date, the next trip leaves from here tomorrow."

Max told Charlie to shut up for a few minutes while he stood in silence next to the captain's boat, as if he were paying his respects at a close friend or family member's grave. He could see Spike sitting at the front of the boat, desperately trying to remember the elusive fourth chord which would enable him to complete another Bob Dylan song. He could see Yiani, that was Captain Homer, behind the wheel of his old but well looked after and truly loved boat and he remembered Yiani's English wife, Gail and their young son Alex, who would sometimes join them on the day trips down the East coast. It was all as clear as day but mostly in the past now, until Max was removed from his trip down memory lane by a voice he'd heard before.

"My boat leaves tomorrow at ten o'clock. Beautiful day out with swimming, then Notos Beach and Petriti Beach. Food and drink on the boat and lots of good times. You pay half now and half tomorrow before we leave. Cash or pay on the app?"

"The original Captain Homer?"

"Yes! But my son is also Captain Homer now but my beautiful wife, Gail, she never the captain. I'm getting old now boy and as much as I love this thing I do, I also need more rest and sleep now. That when Alex, my son, is captain. You've been here before haven't you, when you were young boy? I remember your cheeky face and you have brother who couldn't play the guitar very well but still make everyone feel happy. Yes?"

"Yes captain and yes, we'll be on your boat tomorrow. Charlie, give the captain fifty Euros please."

The first little piece of Max's return to a complete and unspoilt happy life had just fallen into place like a foundation brick, when joined by others, would form the support for greater and more beautiful things to be built upon. After all these years, Yiani was still Captain Homer but Alex was now his wingman and ready to take the wheel when called upon. Yiani and Gail where still happily married and were as solid as ever and still in love with what they did every day, despite the challenges of 2020 and 2021. Max had learnt from Spike to always look for the good or positive in everyone and everything and if there was nothing good nor positive to be found in a particular person or circumstance, then you should move on as quickly as possible, before you found yourself becoming a fast tracked member of the bad vibes club. However, there were no bad vibes on Corfu, only good vibes and although Yiani, Gail and Alex, along with all the other lovely people Max and Charlie had met so far, had to deal with every day stuff just like every day people, they managed to do it with smiles on their faces and a huge spring in each step they took. Max loved these people and he really loved their genuine kindness and natural willingness to help anyone. He was also incredibly touched by the fact that Captain Homer recognised him and remembered his brother after all these years. Max wasn't sure whether or not to tell the captain about Spike's passing and decided to sleep on it but if he was asked about Spike, he would reluctantly break the sad news to him. Max now knew wholeheartedly that at some point in the not too distant future, Corfu had to be his new home and he had to find a way to make it a new home with Kat.

"Max, the captain must meet thousands of people each year, so how did he remember you and Spike?"
"You'll be surprised Charlie but I think it's got something to do with the fact that the people on Corfu are genuinely interested in those who visit their island. It's more than a job to them, it's a way of life and let's be honest, Captain Homer didn't have to work too hard to take a hundred Euros off us, did he?"

"Now you mention it, it was pretty slick and on the subject of pretty, did you see the two girls behind us who were also booking for tomorrow. I think they were German and do you want to know what else I'm thinking? I'm thinking that those two beauties haven't yet realised that tomorrow could be their lucky day."

"Whatever thoughts make you happy mate, let's get going! I think you need to direct some of your excess energy towards something else instead of channeling it all in the direction of the opposite sex and yes, although one of them is not exactly my cup of tea, they're both very attractive girls."

"So where are we going now, please tell me we're not hiking up that big hill?"

"We're hiking up that big hill, to the village of Chlomos."

Max and Charlie walked slowly along the river bank and up to the road which would either take them back to Moraitika or up the hill to Chlomos. On their way up they passed The 75 Steps Taverna, which was always a firm favourite with those who were capable of climbing the seventy five steps and for the dedicated who made it, stunning views and fantastic local cuisine was their reward. The cypress trees lined the lower slopes of the hill and occasionally made way for cascading olive groves. Goats and their bells provided a sound track which was fitting to the island and sat comfortably alongside the occasional sound of barking dogs and local chit chat. Even the locals who couldn't speak English made an effort to engage and suggested with their hands that the boys were mad for walking up hill in the mid-day sun. They soon arrived at the ramshackle village of Agios Dimitrios and seized the perfect moment to enjoy the amazing views while taking a well deserved break.

"What do you think of Corfu so far then Charlie boy?"

"It's absolutely stunning mate and I can now see why you love this place so much. What would Kat have made of it, would she have loved it?"

"I reckon so and I really hope so because I want to settle down here and I want Kat to be with me. I want to grow up and grow old with her on Corfu."

"Max, you're forgetting something. You've got to win her back first and then prize her away from London. I reckon you can win her back, if you don't twat about and take too long but getting her out of London, that could be more difficult than getting a child out of Toys 'R' Us."

"Don't you worry, I've got it all worked out and by the time I get back, she'll be getting bored of London and the stress will be killing her. She'll be ready for a quieter life and that's when I'll reintroduce the idea of moving to Corfu. I just need to find that old rundown stone cottage I told you about. You know, when I was miles away but actually, just up the road."

"It makes for an epic ending to a romance novel but I think it's a risky game mate. You're not back in the UK until the 2nd of August and then Kat and Megan are going away for two weeks. That's almost six weeks, six weeks to lose your girl to another guy. Where are Kat and Megan going, have they decided yet? Maybe they're considering going on one of those singles only holidays. You know, where everyone is model material, pissed up and gagging for it!"

"Alright Charlie, I know the game you're playing but it ain't gonna work with me! I've got my plan and I'm sticking to it."

After another hour of undulating rambling and ramblings, Max and Charlie arrived at the hilltop village of Chlomos. The village was desperately quiet and beautifully calm until the church bells rang twice, signaling two o'clock and time for some food and liquid refreshment. Balis Taverna was just about open and still had a couple of choices left on the lunchtime menu. So the apprentice mountaineers ordered a couple of portions of whatever was being offered, which turned out to be meat, chips and salad, along with two cold beers and a pint of Coke to share. From where they were sitting you could see for miles and across the Straits of Corfu, you could see the mainland. Ferries and sailing boats, purposefully and for the purpose of pleasure, took advantage of the calm and protected waters and provided a gentle reminder that what appeared to be a deep blue velvet blanket, was in fact a small part of the Ionian Sea. Now well fed and watered, the boys wandered around the narrow alleyways and explored the village. There were many old buildings for sale, which interested Max but bored the hell out of Charlie, along with a beautiful little church which sat within an enclave of three and four story houses, many of which had seen better days but were still providing sufficient accommodation for the villagers of Chlomos. The church door was open so Max quietly entered, followed by Charlie and a stray cat. It was cool inside the old stone church, the walls were covered in paintings and religious artifacts and candles were burning to remember those who had passed. Max picked up a candle from the stand which was just inside the church door, he made a generous donation and then lit his candle. He stood it up in the sand which filled a large silver tray and paid his respects to

Spike. Charlie and the cat stood in silence while Max said his prayer and remembered his brother.

"Oh Charlie! After all these years, it doesn't get any easier."
"Come here mate, time for a hug and it looks like we've made a new friend. I've decided to call him Spike."

Max, Charlie and now Spike the cat continued to explore the village whilst at the same time, looking for the old donkey track which would zig zag its way down the other side of the hill and eventually, lead them back to the shoreline. Before too long they were descending through the olive groves on the old track, one which had not yet been concreted or tarmacked over and was still authentic to the island's humble past. Their new friend quickly abandoned them when it became clear that there was no food on offer and the double act of Mad Max and Charlie Chaplin continued on their journey towards the coast.

"This is what it's all about Charlie. Tell me, hand on heart, that this ain't living your best life."
"It's fabulous mate but can life be like this for ever or is just a holiday, a break from reality and the day to day rituals?"
"I guess to make it work, you have to start thinking differently. I hear so many people say 'oh, that's life and that's how it is' but it doesn't have to be like that. Why do so many people concede to a life they're genuinely not happy with? I'll tell you why Charlie, it's because they become comfortable and after years of being comfortable, they then become afraid of change. Making big changes in

one's life requires balls of steel, of which most people just don't have."

The old track started to level out as it approached the shoreline and soon Max and Charlie were standing by the side of the coast road. On the other side of the narrow road was an even narrower stretch of beach and then the sea. It was time to cool off and Charlie challenged Max to a race to see who could be first in the water. They sprinted across the quiet road, launched their bags and trainers in the direction of some old locked up sun loungers and ran into the water like a couple of big kids who were visiting the seaside for the very first time. It was fair to say that life on Corfu for Max and Charlie right now was very sweet indeed and it could get even better tomorrow on Captain Homer's boat.

Chapter 21 ~ Perfect Double D's And Cops With Guns.

Although life on the island of Corfu was playing out beautifully so far for Max and Charlic, back in London, things were about to get really messy for Megan. At exactly 4:30am on Monday the 7th of July, she was woken by loud and aggressive banging on the door of the flat she shared with her mum and brother. The door and door frame eventually gave way to the brute force which was being applied and just like that, the flat was full of armed police. "Police, police, armed police! Make yourself known and with your hands above your head!"

Megan was the only one in the flat who initially responded to the early morning wake up call, kindly provided by the Metropolitan Police, because her brother was still stoned and her mum was still under the influence of a bottle of vodka or two. Despite the chaos which was unfolding, Megan remained calm and dealt with the armed police in the only way she knew. "Morning boys! If my mum's been nicking vodka from Mr Armed's corner shop again, do you not think you're slightly overdressed and overequipped? But if you're looking for Tony, perhaps you should take your eyes off my perfectly formed double D's and try looking in his bedroom."

"We are looking for Tony and we're here to arrest him on suspicion of dealing in illegal substances and attempted murder."

"Well who would have fucking guessed? Try that door there and you big boy, you can put your tongue away now. Have you never seen a naked girl before?"

"Tony! Armed police, we're coming in, do not resist!"

A couple of hours after the police had arrested Tony and carted him off to the police station for questioning, Megan's mum reappeared looking slightly confused and clearly unable to remember the armed raid which took place at the crack of dawn. "Megs, where's Tony? He's usually asking for money or food by now."

"Mum! Are you fucking kidding me, are you on the vodka already? Tony's been arrested for dealing and trying to kill someone! Don't you remember?"

"What do you mean? Tony's a good lad, he's just like his dad. They both have their faults Megs but they're okay really."

"Neither of them are okay mum! In case you've forgotten and you probably have, dad used to beat us until we were black and blue and your precious Tony is a mirror image of him. Tony's also a drug dealer and now clearly capable of dishing out more than a few slaps. How's that anything like okay?"

Megan's mum had already started on the vodka, as she would do every morning as soon as she woke up. She drank to take away the pain. Not the physical pain, that ended years ago. Instead, the emotional pain of a very violent and traumatic past. For a few years, Megan had found herself on the same slippery slope as her mum. Although she avoided the daily drinking and occasional substance abuse, she was starting to think that a few beatings each week were just part of being in a loving relationship and if you really loved him, you took a few for the team. That was real commitment, right? But now Kat was part of her life and for as long as she was, she would never again put up with a beating simply because Spurs had lost at home. It was still early and way too early for Megan to start her journey to work, so she called up Kat and invited herself over for some breakfast. She stopped on the way and picked up some croissants, a couple of takeout coffees and arrived at Kat's place while the drinks were still piping hot and the croissants warm. Kat had introduced her to croissants and pastries and that was just one of many reasons why Megan absolutely loved Kat and loved having her in her life. Before Kat came along, breakfast would have usually been something from Greggs or a sausage, bacon and egg sandwich from the local greasy spoon.

"Kat, it's me. Can you open the door and I've got our breakfast sorted."

"The door's open babe, come on up."

"Well Kat, I've had some stories to tell in my time but this one, just you wait. It was really early and I was dreaming that I was in the arms of a really lovely guy. He wasn't particularly good looking, in fact he was a bit geeky, but he had a heart of gold and he promised to never let me down or break my heart. That's all a girl really wants, right? Anyway, we were just about to, you know, when the police kicked the door in and that part wasn't in my dream. Our flat got raided this morning by armed police who were looking for Tony and from what they could tell me, I reckon he's fucked. So, I'm stood there ain't I, totally naked and this big guy with a gun couldn't take his eyes of my tits, not surprising really, just look at em."

"Wait a minute Megan and hold the sexual fantasies for a second. What's the deal with Tony then?"

"It appears that the police have finally caught up with him and his dealings but he's also been arrested for attempted murder. Did you not see the news the other day? A guy got stabbed on our estate and they reckon that Tony could be the attacker. You know, the one with the knife and that."

"Jesus Megan! Are you sure you're okay?"

"Yeh, I'm fine! They were going to catch him sooner or later. Anyway, the big guy with the gun was slobbering like a dog with a bone and I reckon if I'd stood there for another minute or two, he would have ended up with a bone of his own."

"Megan, you're unbelievable! I'd be freaking out. What about your mum?"

"She's pissed again and still fails to see any wrong in Tony. Maybe one day she'll remain sober for long enough to see what a car crash her life and his have both become."

"Well as long as you're okay honey, I'm okay. But if I'm being honest, I'm struggling to get my head round this. So let's change the subject shall we? So, not long now until we go away. We just have to decide where we're going."

Whilst Megan and Kat ate their croissants and drank coffee which was strong enough to kick-start even the most flaccid of days, they perused a few more holiday options and after an hour of scrolling, were still undecided on where to go. Kat then showed Megan the numerous photos which Max had sent her from Corfu. A beautiful sunset, a stunning sunrise, a cat called Spike and one of Max and Charlie enjoying a beer on the balcony of their apartment in Moraitika. "Which one's Max Kat? No, let me guess! He's the one on the left, right or wrong?"

"Yes, that's Max. Look at the state of him. In almost every photo I have of him, he's wearing that same T Shirt. Shed Seven, Chasing Rainbows. His favourite band and one of his favourite songs. I guess you've never heard of them?"

"No Kat, I haven't! But look at him with his sandy coloured surfer hair, three day stubble, care free and cheeky looking smile. He's dangerous material if let loose on Corfu, without a shadow of doubt. I guess the geeky looking one in the Ralph Lauren Polo is Charlie?"

Kat momentarily dropped out of the conversation to process for the first time the possibility of Max meeting someone else. After all, he was in Corfu with Charlie, who was ready to make a move on any female who was borderline attractive, not looking for anything too serious but ready to show him a trick or two. What if Max was finally starting to get over the breakup and needed nothing more now than a little nudge from a boho surfer chick for him to completely move on and leave her behind for good. Kat let out a big sigh before replying to Megan.

"Yes, that's Charlie and you've summed him up perfectly. He's a really nice guy and boy has he been through it lately. He's just lost his wife, his house and his job but at least he still gets to see his children every other weekend. He's been friends with Max for as long as I can remember and Max looks after him like a brother."
"You know what Kat, Charlie's cute in a preppy kind of way and I bet he's a lover, not a fighter?"
"Oh Megan, you're funny and you're absolutely right, Charlie couldn't fight his way out of a wet paper bag."

Kat and Megan realised just in time that it was now time to go to work and they said their goodbyes with a hug and another promise to always be there for each other. Whilst Kat drove across town to Fab HQ, she thought about Max. More to the point, she was thinking about Max being with her replacement. Something she'd never thought about, until this morning, when Megan politely reminded her of just how drop dead gorgeous Max was. Megan also made her way to work but as if nothing unusual or traumatic had happened earlier that morning. She thought briefly about preppy Charlie and in her mind, she compared him to the guy in her dreams. Maybe her dream was actually a positive premonition and as one bad boy was being taken away from her, a good boy, a guy with a heart of gold, a lover and not a fighter, was about to take his place. At Fab HQ, everything was calm and under control and for obvious reasons, Fabio was in the best of moods. He would prance around the office building asking for feedback on how he was looking. "Jane, what do you think of this my dear? Wedding material or not? I know I'm wedding material but what about the suit I'm wearing?" Kat was very busy working on Grant's new campaigns and more than happy that Fabio was using his entire office complex as his own personal cat walk, instead of bothering her all the time. This meant that she could bury her head in her work and get on with everything she needed to do before her presentation on Friday.

At Grant's church, where miracles happened and lots of money was made, it was business as usual and as usual, Anne was keeping everything tight, running like clockwork and just how Grant liked it. As always, despite her early morning wake up call, Megan was busy moving mountains in the sales office and by lunchtime, she'd secured four more deposit payments on some apartments which where nowhere near ready yet but looked stunning in the brochure. Word was also out on the streets with regards to the Bow Road and Thames Side developments and although Megan had nothing yet to offer the 'eager to part with their cash' prospective purchasers, she was building up a pretty long list of clients who were keen to live next to a dirty old canal and even dirtier and not particularly appealing river.

During their lunch breaks, Kat and Megan briefly caught up with each other again over the phone. "How's everything going with Grant's big campaign? I guess it's so far, so good as he's very calm at the moment?"

"Yeh, everything's going according to plan. Just a few little issues to resolve but I'll have them ironed out by Wednesday at the latest. I'm sure everything will be fine on Friday and I'm guessing Grant is thinking the same because he's already booked a table for two at that fancy restaurant opposite St. Paul's. You know, the one with the three stars? Apparently he's taking me out for dinner on Saturday night as a way of saying thank you."

"That's excellent Kat! You'll have a great night and you're so clever, I wish I was as smart as you."

"Don't be daft! You're amazing at what you do and you know that. You just need to believe it's true, that's all. Anyway, are you free this Friday evening? If so, come over for dinner at seven, I need your advice."

Chapter 22 ~ Steffi And Bex. Sunsetters Or Sundowners.

It was also lunch time in Corfu and Max and Charlie were now a couple of very enjoyable and relaxing hours into Captain Homer's boat trip. His boat was due to leave at ten o'clock, but by the time everyone had eventually arrived, including the two German girls who turned up half an hour late and slightly hung over from the night before, it was almost eleven o'clock before he started the engine and carefully made his way down the Messonghi River. Steffi and Bex, the very attractive German girls, had strategically sat themselves opposite Max and Charlie and Bex wasted no time at all in questioning them on their lives back in England. Whilst the boys experienced a slightly more enjoyable and better looking version of the Spanish Inquisition, the original Captain Homer was happily steering his beloved boat along the shallow but safe waters of the East coast of Corfu. He was pointing out everything which was worth looking at, which was pretty much everything, including a lovely traditional taverna on the beach, which just so happened to belong to his brother. "Taverna Georgios, look people, there! The chef there make the very best kleftiko on Corfu island. Trust me, he my brother and I know very well my Kleftiko. He also have drinks waiting for us when we return. You call them sunsetters, yes?"

Charlie quickly raised his hand as if he were back in school and was in a race to be first to answer the teacher's question.

"Captain, we call them sundowners, not sunsetters."
"Ah, so the same thing, yes? The Sun sets, the Sun goes down. So the same thing? Max my boy. He with you? That's a shame for you, I'm sorry for you."

After Charlie was well and truly schooled by Yiani, he opted not to make a complete dick of himself again and instead, decided to cross examine Bex on her life in Germany. Bex was kind of hard or tough looking but she was still a very attractive girl. She looked as if she'd experienced life on the frontline and maybe her multiple tattoos were badges of honour or reminders of battles lost. Despite her 'I could knock you out with one punch' look, she was still beautifully feminine but in an alternative kind of way. She was assertive and overconfident but managed to get away with it and she was more than happy to answer Charlie's random and very to the point questions.

Steffi was very different to her female companion. No tattoos, no piercings and unlike Bex, whose eyebrows were painted on in an alien kind of way and whose hair was dyed a deep shade of red, her hair was naturally blonde and her face needed no temporary nor permanent alterations. She was as natural as a wild flower and as beautiful as a Corfu sunset. Although Steffi was quiet and reserved, Max had instinctively detected a mischievous side to her. He'd seen that look and experienced that persona before and although Steffi was a pretty German girl, who spoke very good English but with a delicate German accent and her hair was a different colour, she reminded him of Kat.

"So Bex, what do you do in Frankfurt for a living?"
"I'm a dancer in a club. I'm a good dancer and I make the club very busy."
"Oh, I see! Do I need to ask what type of dancing you do?"
"You don't need to do anything Charlie but if you're wondering whether or not I take my clothes off, the answer's no! I keep my clothes on and let my dancing earn the money. I'm a burlesque dancer, do you know what that means or do I need to show you?"
"Is no and yes the right answer Bex?"
"You English boys are funny, not like German boys who are always serious. I like to have fun Charlie, do you like to have fun?"

Captain Homer interrupted the cheeky banter which was quickly building between Bex and Charlie with an out of tune strum on an old guitar. It was time for a swim stop, but before everyone was allowed to jump off the boat and into the crystal clear water, he needed to address the issues of health and safety. Corfu style health and safety.

"You all here to enjoy yourself, have happy times and make good memories. So please, no to jumping at the front of my boat, unless you like anchor up your bum and no to jumping at the rear, that's where you get back on my boat. Jump only from the sides, try not to die or kill people when you jump and have wonderful swimming."

In less than a minute, the boat was twenty or so passengers lighter, Max was alone with Steffi but soon joined by Yiani, who lit up a half smoked cigarette for himself and offered full ones from a newly opened box to his remaining crew. Max and Steffi both declined the offer of a free smoke and Yiani acknowledged their decision with a shrug of his shoulders.

"You not like the water Max, what wrong with you? Everyone like the water. Pretty girl, you the same as him?"
"I don't mind the water Yiani, but I also like quiet and now it's quiet."
Steffi blushfully joined the conversation, "And I can't swim but I also like quiet. I like the space it provides to think about things."
"I confused! You think in space? We think in our heads, our brains do the thinking, yes?"
"Yiani, I think what Steffi is trying to say is that when it's quiet, she can think clearly about things and she's not actually in space thinking clearly."

"Ah, I see! Quiet moments of thought and reflection? Why did you not say that? Your English language, fucking crazy and sorry for saying the fuck word!"

Yiani left Steffi and Max to continue the conversation about space and quiet moments of thought and reflection and joined Gail downstairs in the boat's galley. Gail was busy preparing the crew's late lunch and he always liked to add the finishing touches before serving lunch on deck. Today's feast consisted of freshly caught tuna, which was roughly crumbled into a salad of sliced green peppers and red onions. The tuna mix was then doused in plenty of olive oil, freshly squeezed lemons from Gail and Yiani's garden and then finished with a generous dash of wild oregano, which grew on the hillsides all over Corfu. Gail had also baked bread that morning and bought feta cheese and local olives from the open market in Corfu Town only yesterday. Yiani made a quick but delicious Greek Salad, he pulled a dozen bottles of wine, both white and red, out of the tiny fridge and gathered up the plastic glasses. Lunch on board his boat was once again very soon to be served. After planting a kiss on Gail's lips, Yiani made his way back up the small flight of wooden stairs and picked up the old guitar again. This signaled that the food was ready and it was time to come aboard, dry off and enjoy the freshly prepared banquet.

Bex and Charlie joined their companions and immediately proceeded to tell them how lovely and warm the water was and how colourful the fish were. Max promised Charlie that he would join him for a snorkel after lunch and he offered Steffi a helping hand in the water, if she was up for it. In places near where Yiani had dropped anchor, the water was shallow enough to stand up in and from there, it was only a very short wade until the golden beach was reached. Everyone on board had a fantastic lunch and as the wine flowed generously, the entire crew very quickly became the best of friends and they all knew much more about their fellow crew mates than they did only a few hours ago. After lunch was wrapped up, another thirty minutes of swimming time was announced by Gail and once again and just as quick, the boat was abandoned by all but two of the crew.

"So, I now know that you can't swim but are you afraid of the water?"

"Yes Max, very afraid! When I was a little girl, my brother held my head under the water at a swimming pool. He was only joking but I panicked and screamed. I swallowed some water and I thought I was going to drown. So instead of being there to learn how to swim, I became afraid of the water and apart from when I take a bath or a shower, I've avoided the water ever since."

"Well I've promised Charlie to join him and it is very hot now, so why don't you join me? I used to be afraid of the dark and would only go to bed with the light on or with a torch, so I feel you Steffi. Not literally but I think you know what I mean?"

"I know exactly what you mean Max but how do I know that I can trust you? You could do the same as my brother did."

"A scout's promise, hand on heart. Hold my hands and everything will be okay."

"Okay, I trust you but please look after me and if I get near the water and change my mind, don't shout at me or try to convince me otherwise."

Max took off his T Shirt and located Charlie and Bex, who were just a short swim off the port side of the boat. Before he jumped in, he told Steffi that he would soon be waiting for her at the back of the boat and she could join him when she was ready. Max briefly joined his mate and his mate's best new female friend, who were now cuddling and kissing in the water like lovestruck teenagers, before swimming back to the boat to see if Steffi was ready to take the plunge after all these years. Steffi had stripped down to a tiny white bikini and was waiting for Max at the top of the swim ladder. She'd tied her long blonde hair up and looked beautiful and petrified at the same time. Max climbed halfway up the ladder and told Steffi to sit at the top and then make her way down towards him. He reassured her that he would catch her if she slipped and she had nothing to worry about. The water was shallow and Steffi was tall, so there was very little chance that she would find herself out of her depth but all the same, Max knew this was a very big deal for her. She finally stepped off the last rung of the short ladder, into the calm blue water and then into Max's waiting arms. Max held Steffi tight until she stopped shaking and found the confidence to take a step or two away from the safety of Max's protective hold.

"I'm in the water Max! I'm not drowning and it feels amazing! Thank you Max, thank you!"
"Hey, there's no need to thank me. You made it happen, not me. Now take a few more steps away from me and slowly lower yourself into the water, trust me and I'm here if you need me."

Steffi followed Max's calm but reassuring instructions and soon found herself shoulder deep in the beautiful water which enveloped Captain Homer's boat. Max looked on feeling quite proud of his achievement and extended his arms towards Steffi as if to suggest 'one step at a time' or 'come here for a celebratory hug'. However the suggestion was translated, Steffi carefully made her way back to Max, she grabbed hold of his hands and guided them around her waist and back in order for him to deliver a well deserved embrace.

"Come on Max, hold my hand and walk with me in the water. Let's find Bex and Charlie."

Bex and Charlie were making their way back from the beach and towards the boat when they found Max and Steffi walking hand in hand in the water. Bex was obviously surprised to see her friend in the water and Charlie was even more surprised to see Max holding another girl's hand. Yiani was strumming the guitar and Gail was waving wine bottles around, which clearly meant it was time to leave, time for some more drinks and maybe some light entertainment. Once everyone was back on board, the engine was started, the anchor was raised, drinks were poured and Notos Beach was the next destination. Downstairs in the galley, Gail was busy clearing away and tidying up from lunch whilst upstairs, Yiani was looking for someone who could play his guitar. "Max my old friend, you must know the guitar? Like your brother but better I hope."
"I'm afraid it's a no but Charlie here knows one chord. Will that do you?"
"No Max! The best songs have three chords. I from Corfu and even I knows that."

Bex gently nudged Steffi and in German, prompted her to step up and shine, "Steffi, du spielst wunderschön Gitarre. Warum spielst du nicht für uns? Bitte spiel für uns!"

Steffi was unsure about her friends request but could be tempted to perform if she had some moral support, "Ich bin nicht sicher, aber vielleicht, wenn du mit mir singst und tanzt?"

"Abgemacht! Komm, lass uns gemeinsam Entertainer sein."

Before Yiani had the chance to ask anyone else, Bex grabbed Steffi's hand and dragged her to the front of the boat where he was standing with his guitar, "We'll play for you captain! Steffi sings and plays guitar beautifully and I sing and dance for you!" Whilst Steffi tuned up the guitar, Bex danced to some traditional Greek music which Gail had put on specially to get the crew in the mood. Yiani was doing the rounds again with the chilled red and white wine and the crew were happily clapping and gently taping their feet to the sound of Zorba The Greek. Max and Charlie looked at each and as if they were identical twin brothers, connected in that unique way and silently agreed that they'd both died and gone to Heaven. By the time Bex had finished her dance, Steffi was ready to play and although she looked nervous, she'd clearly done this before and from the way she'd tuned up Yiani's old guitar, she'd obviously had some classical training. The guitar playing beauty and her flamboyant accomplice started with a perfect rendition of 'Who Knows Where The Time Goes', originally performed by Sandy Denny. Steffi knew every trick and every lick on the neck of that guitar and whilst she sang the main vocal, Bex provided subtle harmonies and sultry dance moves.

"Across the evening sky, all the birds are leaving. But how can they know, it's time for them to go?
Before the winter fire, I will still be dreaming. I have no thought of time.
For who knows where the time goes? Who knows where the time goes?"

Everyone on board sat in silence and with a drink in hand, gently moved their bodies in time to the sweet music. Earlier that day, they were all strangers but now, they found themselves connected through the power of music, voice and movement. For one elderly lady who was on her own, it all became a bit emotional and the opening performance had already reduced her to tears. Yiani sat next to her and put a strong brown arm around her shoulder. "It's okay my love, Captain Homer is here but why you cry at the beautiful music?"

"Oh captain, they weren't to know but I lost my husband last year and this was the last song which was played at his funeral. We loved Sandy Denny and especially this song. I've never played it since because I always thought it would bring back the sad memories but it hasn't, it's brought back beautiful memories of us together on Corfu. Just before he died, I promised him that I would keep coming back here every year and here I am again."

"Oh my dear lady, here have a tissue. Don't worry it's clean, trust the captain."

"Thank you captain, thank you so much!"

Steffi and Bex continued to entertain and mesmerise the crew with stunning cover versions of classic songs from some of the greatest female artists of all time. Eva Cassidy, Joan Baez, Tracy Chapman and K T Tunstall, the set list was never ending. And even when a young girl asked them if they knew any songs by Britney Spears, their reply was yes and they proceeded to make Britney sound better and more credible than she'd ever managed to achieve herself. As Yiani navigated his old wooden boat through the shallow waters and in the direction of Notos Beach, the crew took it in turn to thank the girls for their impromptu but impressive performance. Once the boat was safely tied up alongside an old rickety looking pier, everyone was free to disembark and for an hour or so, enjoy the beach and the small and peaceful village of Notos. Max and Charlie and the two girls took a short walk up the hill to check out a little chapel and enjoy the view from the Panorama Restaurant. As was typical on the island of Corfu, the chapel door was open and Max was first through it. He put his hands together and bowed his head down towards his praying gesture and paid his respects again to his late brother. Today on the boat and especially with Steffi playing the same guitar as Spike played all those years ago, only much, much better, had created a beautiful but still heart wrenching memory for Max. It was if Steffi had been sent down from up above to keep Spike's legacy and awful guitar playing well and truly alive in Max's mind. Maybe after years of cynicism surrounding fate and good luck and everything happening for a reason, perhaps angels did exist after all and Max had simply been looking in the wrong places all this time.

Max joined the others outside the church and they slowly sauntered across to the restaurant. They ordered a round of ice cold beers and cocktails and enjoyed the view out to sea. From where they were sitting, they could see the boat which was today providing them with so much fun and so many great times. Charlie and Bex were still inseparable, sat there together and as close as they could get to each other and sat opposite Max was Steffi, still looking beautiful in her white vest top and multicoloured sarong. After they'd finished their drinks and absorbed as much of the surrounding beauty as is possible in a short space of time, they walked back down to the boat and joined the other crew members. The elderly lady who broke down in tears was first to welcome Steffi back on board and thanked her again with a massive hug for bringing back so many lovely memories of her time on Corfu with her late husband. Yiani had already decided that the girls would be performing again whilst on route to Petriti Beach and then finally Taverna Georgios for sunsetters and after a very short trip back up the East coast, he dropped anchor and signalled another swin stop. Max and Charlie borrowed the free snorkeling gear, which was stowed away under the seats along with Yiani's boat stuff, and went looking for fish and octopus amongst the rocks. Bex and Steffi enjoyed a special moment together in the water and as Max reappeared with his goggles still strapped to his head, Steffi waved at him proudly with a raised arm and a wiggle of her fingers.

On the penultimate trip up the coast to Yiani's brother's taverna, Steffi and Bex took requests from the crew and nailed each and every one. Bex was a natural entertainer and there was nothing Steffi couldn't play on that guitar. "Max, Charlie! What would you like us to play and sing for you?" Charlie really didn't care as long as Bex was dancing in front of him but Max had a request or two, "Something by Pink Floyd or The Smiths?" Steffi replied, "Two of my favourite bands Max! Let me play for you the first song I learnt to play on the guitar. This is Wish You Were Here by Pink Floyd and I hope you enjoy it?"

Max quietly whispered in Charlie's ear, "If this is the first song she learnt to play, God only knows what she's capable of. Fucking hell Charlie, she's magnificent!"

At Taverna Georgios, the sunsetters were already lined up on the bar and ready to be downed by Yiani's very happy and already slightly tipsy crew. Ouzo, Limoncello and Kumquat Liqueur awaited and soon disappeared, only to be replaced just as quick. The lovely lady who lost her husband was now smiling again and telling everyone about the fantastic times she'd had on Corfu with Bill and although she missed him dearly, she was starting to feel free of guilt and ready to start a new chapter of her life. Yiani was smoking and arguing with his brother over football or politics or something else which probably wasn't worth arguing about. Gail was busy making sure that everyone was happy and still having a great time and Max and Charlie, Steffi and Bex were still making the most of their new found friendships. And everyone else, well they were happily and quickly getting completely wasted.

Chapter 23 ~ Gardiki Castle, Prasoudi Beach And Mark Twain.

After a wonderful late afternoon and early evening at Taverna Georgios, Captain Homer finally ferried his drunken sailors back to shore and safely moored his ark up on the South bank of the Messonghi River. Bex was still in the mood to party and convinced the other three, although Charlie didn't need much convincing, to hang out a bit longer and to go for more drinks. They found a little bar which was attached to a small hotel and settled in for a few more hours of good times and laughter. The bar was called Oasis Bar and was run by Billy and his partner, both originally from Albania but now residents of Corfu for nearly ten years. Billy kept a neat and tidy bar whilst his attractive partner kept the customer area spotless and the customers entertained. After a few games of cards and a grand tournament of Pass the Pigs, Max and Charlie, Bex and Steffi, said their goodbyes but not before agreeing to meet again for dinner on Thursday. Steffi suggested a place she'd seen on the beach called Bacchus, everyone was happy with her suggestion and seven thirty was agreed as the time to meet again. Bex pulled Charlie in for a goodbye embrace, she kissed him square on the lips and then set her agenda for Thursday evening, "Am Donnerstag, nach unserem Abendessen, werde ich dir die beste Zeit deines Lebens bereiten, Charlie!"

Charlie knew a little bit of German and just about got the gist of what was in store for him after dinner on Thursday. Steffi reached out for Max's hands and soon found her's in his. She happily let Max hold them tight whilst thanking him again for helping her overcome her fear of the water, "Thank you for today Max and I'm glad I trusted you. You've changed my life and I hope my singing and guitar playing today has changed yours in some way? I'll see you Thursday."

Bex and Steffi wandered off in the direction of the apartment they were renting in Messonghi, holding hands and chatting in their native tongue. Max and Charlie stood watching as they walked away and as if it were well rehearsed after months of practice, simultaneously came out with the same line, "What a fucking day!"

"Anyway, what's with you and Bex Mate? You've only just met but look at the two of you!"

"I have no idea what's going on and frankly my friend, I really don't care. All I know for now is that her body is as firm as an oak tree, she kisses like a vampire and she appears to have the hots for me. I wanted to come away with you to have fun and that's what I'm doing. If I get blown out after a couple of days, at least I'll have some fantastic memories to take home with me. So, what's with you and Steffi, you both seem to be playing it very cool?"

"A bit like you Charlie, I have no idea but is it okay to be in love with two girls?"

"Some might say that's being greedy but as long as they're both drop dead gorgeous, I think that's perfectly acceptable."

After a short stagger back to their apartment, the guys enjoyed a home from home traditional night cap and reflected on the shenanigans of the day. Whilst sat on the balcony, Max sent Kat a carefully chosen selection of photographs he'd taken, mainly of fishing boats, chapels, Greek flags rippling in the gentle breeze and stray cats and dogs. As soon as Greek and UK technology connected, Kat replied with hearts and smiley faces. Charlie was also sharing his memories but he was busy dumping over fifty photos he'd taken into his Facebook Page. Photos of him, photos of him and Max, photos of Captain Homer and his wife Gail. Photos of pretty much everything from his day out on the boat, including photos of him with Bex, photos of Max with Steffi and a team photo of the four of them, which Yiani kindly took. Charlie new that Laura would see his photos, they were still connected on Facebook, but he wasn't trying to create jealousy nor fix things between the two of them. That arrangement had checked out months ago and was no longer causing Charlie heart attack levels of stress and he genuinely hoped that Laura had moved on from locking herself in the bathroom. Instead, Charlie was simply celebrating his life. Life with Max on Corfu, his very brief love life with Bex, being homeless and jobless but now, also being immensely happy and totally care free.

"Right mate, I'm going to bed. We pick up the hire car tomorrow at ten o'clock and at this rate, I'll still be over the limit. Breakfast at Maxim and then Corfu road trip. Don't be too late tonight, the roads are pretty rough where we're going and I don't want to be stopping every five minutes so that you can throw your guts up."

"No worries Max, I'm almost done and just in case I forget to say it in the morning, thanks for everything mate. I'm having the time of my life and I hope you are too. Just one thing though, if you've got passionate thoughts going on in your head which involve Steffi, how do those thoughts figure out in your plan to win Kat back? Hash tag just saying and I'll see you in the morning."

Charlie had for once raised a fair point and one which got Max thinking seriously about his life in general, his love life and his options now as a single guy. At the end of the day, Kat had left him and although she'd not left him for someone else, she'd still played the Check Mate move.

199

Charlie had warned him only yesterday that Kat wouldn't settle for a single life in London and she was already spreading her wings and when her feelings of true love for Max finally reached a penetrable level, she would allow herself to be swept off her feet again. For all Max knew, she may even be out now on her second first date and was only a couple of drinks or future dates away from experiencing the love and touch of another man. The thought of Kat making love to anyone but him ignited a bonfire of jealousy which would make The Great Fire of London look like a few candles on a birthday cake. Max was confused and although Steffi was beautiful, she played guitar and also loved alternative bands, he thought to himself that as attractive and as wonderful as she was, his life would have remained easier and far less complicated had they not met. Max didn't even know if Steffi fancied him or not, it was surely just a crazy infatuation which would soon burn out when Steffi told him that she had a guy back in Germany but she was happy to loosely keep in touch. To keep his life simple and according to plan, Max wanted that scenario to be the outcome from their brief encounter but in his next thought, he couldn't stop thinking about having his cake and eating it or even sharing it with Steffi.

"Max, I've got a banging headache. How are you feeling?"
"Confused Charlie, that's how I'm feeling and it sounds like it's a good job I'm driving today. Have a cold shower and let's go for breakfast. You've got twenty minutes and don't forget to pack, we're moving on today!"

Max and Charlie made their way to Maxim, they enjoyed another great offering of not so traditional food and then set off to locate the hire car company.

"This looks like the place Charlie but I hope they've got more cars out the back. If they haven't, I'm guessing we've got the Suzuki Jimny. Quite possibly the worst off-road vehicle ever built and so bad, it even comes with a warning sticker on the dashboard which advises owners or drivers of the vehicle not to take it off-road."

"You Max? If yes, just in time. You taking my last and best car, the red Jimny is all yours. So, drivers license, passport, where you staying, credit card for deposit and one hundred Euros."

After a two minute admin session and a quick show round of the vehicle, which included making note of all the existing dents and scratches, the boys were on their way to Prasoudi Beach, via Gardiki Castle. Dating back to the 13th century, the Byzantine castle was the only remaining fortress on the Southern part of the island and it brought back some very special memories for Max. In a similar way to how Max and his brother Spike played in that castle all those years ago, Max and Charlie ran around and explored the ancient ruins of a bygone era. Inside the now crumbling castle walls, the grass grew naturally tall, the flowers wild and slowly but surely, nature was beautifully taking over. This provided the perfect battlefield for Max and Charlie to quickly lose each other and then scare the living crap out of each other by jumping out from behind overgrown bushes. Although there was a sign saying no climbing, it meant nothing to the road trippers who were hell bent on exploring every corner of the castle, so they went climbing and managed to find a great spot from where they could just about see the West coast of the island and what Max assumed was Prasoudi Beach.

"If you're ready Charlie, I think we should head for the beach?"

"The question is, are you ready Max? I know this place is special to you, so are we done with being Max and Spike and ready to revert back to being Max and Charlie? And I'm not being sarcastic mate, I'm just checking in on your emotions."

"Yes Charlie, I'm ready and I'm ready for a swim. We must stink after all that exploring?"

After a short but bumpy and twisty drive, the turning to Prasoudi Beach appeared in the form of a slightly rusty and not quite upright road sign. Max indicated to turn left and then joined the sandy track which would take them to the beach. On the right was a half built house which had been up for sale for years. The location was fabulous but the asking price was ridiculous and it certainly wasn't Max's idyllic old stone cottage on the side of a hill. At the end of the track was Avra Oceanos, a traditional Seafood Taverna which greeted its guests with a large glass tank full of lobster, all still alive and completely oblivious to their pending fate. Max and Charlie stood and perused the creatures with curiosity and a false display of culinary knowledge.

"So Maxi boy, which one is it going to be? That one there looks plump and ready for the plate or how about that one, he or she looks as bored as shit and ready to meet its maker."

"To be honest, I'm not a big fan of lobster and I'll tell you what, it's a good job we never came here with Spike. He'd be pulling them out of that tank with his bare hands and then gently releasing them back into the sea."

"Maybe then in Spike's memory we should avoid the lobster and order some kalimera instead?"

"I think you mean calamari Charlie but if you want to try ordering kalimera, fill your boots mate but be prepared to get schooled again."

After a very short and one word lesson in Greek, Charlie ordered the calamari and Max opted for a Gyros plate. Over lunch they chatted and tried their best to make sense of how their lives had evolved and for various reasons, ended up with the two of them both now single and sat beside the sea, listening to the waves break on the West coast of the island. Charlie had no regrets surrounding his situation and apart from wanting to see his children, he genuinely couldn't find another reason worthy of returning to the UK. Laura would never take him back and he didn't want her back. Back in the UK, the only game changer waiting for Charlie was an email or letter from Happy Burger, confirming that he'd been short listed or fast tracked to an interview. Max however was as confused as a box of frogs and really needed to find his balance pretty quickly. His mind was awash with thoughts of Kat and thoughts of Steffi. Thoughts of his life as a van driver in the North East of England and thoughts of leaving all that behind and eventually becoming accepted as a local by the true locals on Corfu. What should have been a journey of beautiful exploration around Corfu with Kat, was now turning out to be an interesting journey of exploration and discovery with Charlie. Max would sometimes quote Mark Twain when trying to educate people on life, love and the importance of travel and would often recite one of his best known works, 'Travel is fatal to prejudice, bigotry, and narrow-mindedness, and many of our people need it sorely on these accounts. Broad, wholesome, charitable views of men and things cannot be acquired by vegetating in one little corner of the earth all one's lifetime.'

"Strap yourself in Charlie because I'm about to blow your mind with my intellectual and cultural analysis on why my life is so bloody complicated right now. Are you ready?"
"Ready when you are Max but are we talking seconds, minutes or hours because I really need the bathroom?"
"Go take a piss, don't look at the lobster tank and please don't start chatting to the attractive young girl who's working the bar."

Charlie mostly followed Max's instructions, apart from 'not chatting to the attractive young girl who was working the bar', who apparently told him that he was old enough to be her father and he should go back to his friend at their table. Back at their table, Max was primed and ready to launch war on his feelings and Charlie was unfortunately the rifle range.

"I've been reflecting on the works of Mark Twain, I know mate, I've lost you already but hear me out! In one of his most famous quotes he talks about how staying in one place all the time is fatal to your development as an individual and travel is the only way to broaden your mind and evolve as a more rounded and understanding person. Well Charlie, that's Kat and I, isn't it?"

"What is Max, I'm completely lost mate and who's Mark Twain?"

"You don't know who Mark Twain is? You're unbelievable sometimes! Anyway, it was inevitable, Kat and I breaking up. It was going to happen at some point if we didn't break out of our mould or broaden our horizons and we didn't, did we? We just stayed in the same place all the time, lazily expecting everything to be amazing forever and without even working at it."

"Have you only just realised that? Not that I worried about you guys often but that was my big worry. You two knew nothing other than each other and what you had created together. At some point, one of you would get curious and it just so happened to be Kat. However, it could just as easily have been you who wanted to explore life beyond where you were and maybe without even realising it yet, Kat leaving you has just made that option well and truly open for business."

Once again, Charlie was right and it could have been Max who decided to call the relationship off. What would he have done if he was still with Kat when Steffi, or back in England someone just like Steffi, unexpectedly walked into his life and immediately prized his loving eyes away from the only girl he'd ever loved, touched, kissed and seen naked. Charlie was also spot on when he reminded Max that he was now single and if he fancied trying his luck with Steffi, he was committing no crime and that move was indeed above board and fair game now.

"Do you think I'm overthinking things Charlie?"

"Max, you always overthink things, it's in your DNA to overthink things. Your plan to win Kat back is

205

unnecessarily overthought, complicated and risky and now that Steffi has turned up, that plan may not even be a valid plan anymore. If you still want to get back with Kat, stop using your phone as a camera, call her up right now and tell her that when you get back from Corfu and she's had her holiday with Megan, you want to make things work again. As far as Kat's concerned, that's all you've got to do mate and I bet she'll want the same. But if you want a slice of Steffi, before getting back with Kat or if you now want Steffi instead of Kat, make your move on Thursday and let her know how you feel and what you want from her. Stop twatting about for once!"

"You're totally right Charlie, it really is that simple."

"I know it is mate. Now forget about your Mark Twain analogies, plug your brain back into a normal socket and sort your love life out."

"Alright mate, easy does it but thanks for that."

"So Max, what's it gonna be? Kat, Steffi or a holiday fling with Steffi and then back to Kat?"

Chapter 24 ~ Sometimes, You Just Don't Know How Lucky You Are.

After lunch and a swim in the cooler waters of the West coast of Corfu, Max and Charlie continued their road trip, heading North and aiming for Pelekas. The road they were following initially hugged the coastline but then made its way inland and in the direction of Sinarades. They stopped briefly to drop the soft top and then continued on their journey with the warm and uniquely fragranced air blowing over their faces and through their hair. Max's salty surfer hair was already looking two shades lighter and was currently tied back and away from his eyes with a red bandanna. Charlie had parked his Aviators on his head in an attempt to push back his curtains and in a failed attempt to look as cool as his very cool looking driver. They parked up in Sinarades, grabbed some cold drinks and set about exploring another beautiful place.

"I love this place Max, I could easily settle down here. If you commit to your plan for getting Kat back and all goes swimmingly and you end up together on Corfu, I could join you and we could all start again out here. Obviously once my children are older and I've done my stint at Happy Burger and I've got some money together again. What do think of that idea mate?"

"Sounds like a great idea. You could find yourself a nice Greek girl to settle down with, one who would look after you and take care of your every need. We could then all meet up in the village square with all the other locals, drink Ouzo and coffee, play cards and aimlessly chat the day away. Sounds like my kind of retirement that does."

"I know right! I'm officially the life advisor that keeps on giving. Anything else I can help you with today?"

The streets of Sinarades were quiet and mostly tourist free, perfect for wandering around and exploring. The occasional dog would appear from out of the shade and follow them for a while and the cats were being friendly for one reason only and that was because they wanted feeding. There were no annoying teenagers on stolen mopeds. No domestic situations kicking off in front gardens. No shops being robbed and as a result, no police sirens. Max thought to himself, 'surely this way of life has to be the right way and what we have slowly grown to accept back in England is actually really wrong and totally unacceptable.' Charlie had quickly checked his emails and interrupted Max's ponderings with the bad news that he'd been invited to attend an interview at Happy Burger and if successful, he would be offered an immediate start.

"But that's great news Charlie, surely you're pleased to have been given an opportunity to prove yourself and hopefully get your life going again?"

"Don't get me wrong Max, I am pleased but I'm also getting used to life on Corfu. And I know it's only been a couple of days and we're on holiday and it's warm and sunny and there's pretty girls and all that but take all that away, I'd still choose this place over what you and I currently call home."

"Yeh, I totally get you on that one. I've travelled the world but there's no place like Corfu, this place has something which is hard to explain. There's magic in the air, in the water and everywhere you go. Sometimes you can see the magic, like the people, the old buildings and the stunning scenery. Sometimes you can do no more than feel the magic on your skin, allow it to enter your subconscious mind and breathe it in whilst going about your day to day business."

"Have you been reading that Mark Twain crap again? I thought I told you to pack that stuff in."

"Charlie, I love you dearly but you're a total bell end at times. I'm trying to pay homage to the island and do it poetic justice and all you can do is take the fucking piss!"

For the first time since arriving together on Corfu, there was an air of tension between the two friends, followed by an awkward silence. The peaceful village of Sinarades fell just a little bit quieter until Charlie broke the ice.

"Max, I'm not taking the piss! But all this clever stuff you keep coming out with, it's doing my head in mate. Can't you just be happy and silly for once. Leave all the quotes and song lyrics behind for a few days. Roll them back out on Thursday when we meet up with Steffi and Bex again, girls love all that sort of intellectual and knowledgeable malarkey."

"I'm sorry mate and I'll do my best! Shall we hit the road and head for our accommodation for tonight? It could take an hour or two to get there."

"Sounds like a plan and the sooner we get there, the sooner we can get on the beers. Where are we staying tonight?"

"Old Perithia, you know, the abandoned village on the North side of Mount Pantokrator. It's going to be a unique night."

With a plan for the rest of the day sorted, the scruffy red Jimny was back on the road and heading for Palaiokastritsa. They passed through Pelekas, the village of Kokkini, Liapades and then motored up the final hill to enjoy the stunning views down into Palaiokstritsa Bay. The water was cyan blue and the shoreline was littered with charming little fishing vessels and trendy looking speedboats. Traditional dwellings and purposeful looking hotels clung to the hillside like a herd of ibex and down in the bay you could just about make out the sound of carefree laughter. Max and Charlie snapped away with their phones before setting of again and on the final leg of their journey. Charlie was following the route on a paper map he'd bought in Moraitika and had now ticked off the villages of Doukades and Troumpettas. He would soon tick off Agia Paraskevi and if his tourist map was even slightly accurate, they would soon arrive in Roda. They had no desire to stop in Roda and both were by now craving an ice cold beer and a basket of warm pitta bread, so they pushed on along the coast road until they saw a sign for the village of Loutses. Charlie ticked off three more villages before they reached Loutses, here they decided to stop briefly. The small village was almost completed destroyed by the wildfires which ripped through the valley the previous year. The evidence of the damage caused was still clear to see but nature was very quickly coming back to life all around and any reparations which were being carried out by the local builders were struggling badly to keep up with nature's will to return to the wild beauty which was there before the fires came along. The bumpy tarmac road continued to climb, twist and turn and eventually gave way to a part concrete and part rubble road, they had finally arrived safely at the abandoned village of Old Perithia or as many referred to it, the ghost village.

"Here we are mate, possibly the most unique place on the Island, Old Perithia."

"Okay Max! I have three questions for you: One, where are we staying? Two, where do we get food and beer? Three, do people actually live here?"

"We're staying at The Merchant's House, I've heard Taverna Foros is excellent and finally, only a handful of people live here and aren't they lucky. Look at this place Charlie, it's beautiful."

"That's one way of describing it, that place hasn't even got a roof on it and that one looks like it's about to fall down."

"Come on, let's get checked in and then do some exploring before it gets too dark."

Max walked away from Jimny and in the direction of a recently renovated building. Charlie followed with their bags in his right hand and his paper map still in his left one. They were soon met by David and Marieka and their two very cute sausage dogs. David and Marieka were the very proud owners of the only accommodation option in the village and they far from took advantage of the lack of competition and instead, presented a unique guest experience which could easily suggest that there were multiple places to stay and choose from. The whole place was beautifully appointed and the fixtures and fittings were in keeping with the history of the building and the village. In each room, the newly welcomed guests would find locally sourced and complimentary bathroom items along with a fridge full of drinks, sweets on the bedside tables and a book explaining how the village became what it was today. David led them to their room, which was on the ground floor of the two storey building and had immediate access to the West facing terrace, before offering them a complimentary drink from the newly constructed, outside gin bar. Needless to say, Max and Charlie accepted David's offer and the three of them enjoyed their drinks whilst watching the last of the day visitors leave the village. David set his guests free to explore his village and off they went, both mesmerised by what they were seeing.

And it wasn't long before they met Thomas Siriotis, the owner of Taverna Foros, standing outside his restaurant, looking for the last remaining daytime visitors.

"Hello my friends, please, come join us. What you like to drink?"

Charlie immediately replied, "Two beers please and some warm pitta bread."

"Yes, please sit. Anywhere you like, it's quiet now. It's nice here now."

"Well Max, this certainly ain't Happy Burger! Look at this place, it's absolutely beautiful."

Taverna Foros was located in the heart of the village and at the foot of a well polished sequence of old cobblestones, polished by the footfall of the daily visitors and certainly not the residents. According to David, the number of residents now being six at most. Half a dozen tables sat beneath a canopy of natural foliage and inside, another four tables, most of which were covered in menus, newspapers, cases of Mythos and colouring books. This was a family run business and the family made no attempt whatsoever to hide that fact.

"Here my friends! Beers, pitta bread, garlic bread and wine on the house. Please, enjoy."

"Cheers Max and here's to us and good times ahead!"

"Indeed my friend and isn't this just great? I'll say it now, before we have too much to drink and you'll think I'm just pissed again and don't actually mean it. Anyway, I know I can be a pain in the arse and I know I overthink stuff but it's just the way I am mate and I genuinely wish I could be more like you. I wish I could just take everything in my stride and as you requested of me earlier, just be happy and silly for once. Also Charlie, I'm really proud of you mate and please don't ever change who you are."

Thomas returned to their table, pulled out a chair and joined them for a further introduction. He told them all about the wildfires last year and how he nearly lost his restaurant and his home and it was only down to the bravery of his daughter and her partner, who managed to keep the fire just one meter away from his house in Loutses. Whilst the fire was burning through the village and continuing on its path of destruction, they used buckets and water from the well in his garden to keep the flames at bay. Thomas also told them how he had to set his goats and his chickens free, it was the only chance they had of possibly surviving the incoming inferno and he became very emotional when he explained how they all returned safely after the fires were eventually extinguished.

"So my new friends, I see you here for dinner tonight. Same table?"

"Absolutely Thomas! What do you reckon Max, eight o'clock?"

"Perfect."

With the thoughts and images of what their newfound friend had just told them still fresh in their minds, the lads continued to explore the unique and charming surroundings of a most wonderful and magical old place. Max was snapping away and taking arty shots, which he would later send to Kat and Charlie was content with taking selfies and the occasional picture of himself with his reluctant friend. Whilst Charlie was reading an information board all about the history of the village, Max quietly walked up to him from behind and then stood alongside his old pal. He put his left arm around Charlie's shoulder and let out a long sigh before quoting exactly what was on his mind, "We're so bloody lucky mate, do you know that?"

Chapter 25 ~ Jimny, Aurora And Megan Accepted.

Whilst Max and Charlie were feeling totally relaxed and heavenly blessed in Corfu, Megan's life in London was still as dysfunctional as ever and Kat was pretty sure that she was now only a handful of days away from having a nervous breakdown.

Megan was sat at the kitchen table opposite her mum, pointlessly stirring her coffee whilst reading a letter from the lawyer who was trying to keep Tony out of prison. "Do you want to know what the lawyer has to say or will I be wasting my time reading it to you?"

"Of course I want to know, it's my Tony. Will he be okay?"

"Not really Mum! The lawyer has advised him to plead guilty to both charges. According to the police, there's sufficient evidence, including eyewitnesses and CCTV footage which proves that Tony was dealing drugs to the kids that night and he was the one who stabbed the guy. If he pleads guilty and the judge accepts his plea, he would be sentenced immediately and the lawyer reckons he'll get between five and ten years. Apparently that's his best option."

"Five to Ten years, there must be a mistake, surely?"

"Read the bloody letter yourself if you don't believe me! Alternatively, go and get pissed again and pretend that everything is gonna to be okay! I'm going to work, some of us have a life to live and bills to pay."

Bony Tony's outcome, now in the hands of the law, appeared inevitable and as hard as Megan had tried her best with him, she couldn't help a looser who didn't want to be helped and she somehow knew this day would eventually rock up. She still loved Tony but only because he was her brother and if he were a work colleague, she'd tell him exactly how she felt about him and would avoid him like a bad smell. But already Megan had selfishly started thinking about how much easier and less complicated her life was going to be once Tony was banged up behind bars. No more unannounced visits from sickly looking kids who desperately needed their next fix of Tony's good stuff. No tip toeing around the flat as not to disturb her sometimes violent brother and no more early morning raids from sex starved cops with guns. Her biggest worry now was her mum and when, or if, reality finally caught up with her, she knew that her mum would finally bury herself in self pity and cheap or stolen vodka from Mr Armed's convenience store.

Kat was up super early and already working from her flat on the last minute alterations which Grant had requested to his big bucks advertising campaign. The pressure was really on now, she was definitely feeling it and was running out of time and options to find an affordable actress who looked like Judy Dench and an available actor who had the same mannerisms as Bill Nighy. She was now starting to regret suggesting 'The Best Exotic Marigold Hotel Hotel' when

215

Grant asked her for a film recommendation which was suitable for a cozy and feel good night in. Grant loved the characters Judy and Bill played and pictured them perfectly as elderly singles who would initially meet as strangers, having just bought a Thames Side apartment or bungalow each. After a short while, they would become friendly neighbours, then companions and eventually, move into a place together which they would both call their perfect dream home. In Grant's mind, they were just one of the Thames Side success stories he was keen to portray and he was far from letting up on this idea. Kat was now waiting for a call back from a small casting agency who said they may be able to help but couldn't guarantee anything. Failing that, she would have to hit the streets of London in search of a couple of looky likeys who fancied taking a punt on a new acting or TV career.

On her way to work, Megan called up Kat to see how she was coping with her overload of stress, "How's it going my love, are you getting there with those characters you need? I wish I could help you but my mum looks nothing like Judy Dench and even if she did, she'd never remember her lines."

"Well I've not drawn a blank yet but I'm pretty close! Anyway, how are you and is there any news on your brother?"

"Yeh, a letter arrived this morning from the lawyer and he reckons five to ten years. Have you heard from Max lately and what about Charlie, his cute and geeky mate, is he okay? I've found him on Facebook you know and I've friend requested him but he's not accepted yet. I guess he doesn't even know who I am or how I know him?"

"You've done what! You've been social stalking Charlie? Megan, what are you like! Have you got a crush on him or something?"

"I might have and what's wrong with that anyway? He's not my usual type but look where my usual type got me. I just want to be loved by a nice guy who's going to treat me right and from what you've told me and what I've seen, Charlie looks and sounds like that type of guy. So, what about Max?"

"Max is good I guess. He's been keeping in touch and sending me some lovely pictures from Corfu and I'm not lying Megs, it's looks absolutely stunning. I wish I'd gone with him now, even if it was just as friends. But hey, I had my chance and I said no so I've only got myself to blame for missing out."

"There's nothing stopping us from going to Corfu Kat, if you like the look of the place that much. I just want to get out of here as soon as. Let's talk about it on Friday when I'm over at yours for dinner and you can show me the photos Max has sent you, any of Charlie?"

Not long after Kat and Megan had finished their catch up call, Kat's phone rang again. It was the casting company, "Morning, is that Kathy from Fab Success?"

"Yes it is."

"Hi Kathy, it's Sue from Connect Casting. Do you want the good news or the bad news first?"

"I'll take any good news at the moment Sue."

"Okay. I've found you two candidates, that's the good news. The bad news is they're not coming cheap at such short notice but they can commit to your time schedule, give or take a couple of days either side. The lady who's interested looks a bit like Judy Dench but she's prepared to cut her hair a tad shorter and lighten her colour. She'll add that cost to her expenses. The guy I've found loves Bill Nighy, in fact, he's his favourite actor. He does a pretty good impression and I genuinely think that will take the viewers mind off the fact that he doesn't look anything like Mr Nighy. That's the best I can do for you Kathy and I'm afraid I need an immediate yes or no and a payment advance to secure their commitment."

"Go for it Sue and thank you so much for pulling out the stops. This means I can now go on holiday with Megan."

"I don't get what your saying Kathy and who's Megan?"

"Oh, it doesn't matter! Just send me your invoice and I'll get it paid straight away."

After a fabulous evening at Taverna Foros, where Max and Charlie ate and drank the night away with Thomas and his family, they enjoyed an equally wonderful breakfast on the terrace at The Merchant's House. Marieka had prepared fresh fruit and fruit juice, homemade grenola and bread, served with yogurt, honey from the village bees and crushed walnuts. For just one morning only, the boys were treating their bodies like temples and maybe it was all psychological, but their hangovers were quickly being cleansed from their battered brains and livers and they both felt born again. After saying goodbye to their lovely hosts and one last look around their new favourite place on the island, Max pointed Jimny in the direction of Kassiopi. Kassiopi was where they were staying tonight, before taking the scenic route back to Moraitika for their dinner dates with Steffi and Bex. Max had decided to take Jimny off-road, possibly for the first time ever, and take a descending mountain track he'd found on Google Maps which would eventually lead them out on to the Kassiopi road. At the very tight hairpin left, they continued straight and immediately joined the old mountain pass. Coming the other way, a group of hikers stepped aside to make way for Colin McRae and his trusty co-driver as they gingerly made their way along the bumpy and somewhat overgrown track.

"Are you sure this is a good idea Max? If we have to turn back, so far, I've seen nowhere wide enough to turn this thing around and to be honest with you, the thought of having to reverse all the way back up to the road slightly worries me."

"Happy and silly Charlie, happy and silly! Isn't that what you said? I'm happy and now you're being silly."

"Alright mate, fair comment but take it easy and please get us to where we're going next in one piece. Where are we going next?"

"Kassiopi Charlie, that's where we're going and unless things go badly wrong or Jimny gives up on us, we'll soon be enjoying cocktails at Limani Bar."

After almost three miles of off-road descending, Max fancied a break and decided to pull up next to a bench which had been thoughtfully placed in order to capture some more stunning views. Looking slightly North/West, they could see the beaches of Kalamaki and Apraos and to the East of where they were now sitting, they could see Kassiopi. Across the calm blue Ionian Sea, hosting ferries and sailing boats, was the coastline of Albania and the popular resort of Sarandë.

"Here's something interesting for you to take on board Charlie…"

"Hold that thought Max! It better not be Mark bloody Twain again!"

"No, a brief history lesson for you instead. Just across the pond, over there in Albania, Fascist Italy invaded and occupied. April the 7th, 1939 is the precise date and just for the records. The Italians eventually surrendered to Nazi Germany in 1943 and Germany then occupied until 1944. Later that year, November I believe, Albania was liberated by the Allies. Corfu was also occupied by both Italy and Germany, 1941 and 1943 respectively."

"Thanks for that mate, but I learnt all that stuff at school. Remember, I went to a private school, where they taught us proper history, languages and principles. It cost my parents a small fortune and I remember them having to remortgage the house to pay for the last set of school fees. Anyway, where did you learn all the World War Two stuff?"

"Google Charlie, that's where and it cost me nowt!"

"It must have been terrible, war is terrible Max, end of and please tell me you agree."

"I agree with you totally but things are hotting up in Europe now with Ukraine, NATO and Russia. It could get really messy and very quickly."

"I know mate and if it does all kick off, I think we should all head for Corfu. We'll bug out in one of those old abandoned houses and wait for it all to blow over. How's that for a slice of fried gold?"

"And have a nice cold pint and all that? You've watched Shaun of the Dead too many times Charlie. I think we should make tracks now, are you ready to go?"

Jimny just about handled the last two miles of off-road exploration but nevertheless, delivered his passengers safely and in one piece to the beautiful fishing village of Kassiopi. Now parked up on a narrow side street, wing mirrors tucked in and soft top back on, the little red and slightly battered hero of the day was treated to a well deserved rest. Max and Charlie had found and checked into their apartment for the night, a small but clean and tidy studio which was only a minute away from the harbour, and were now enjoying celebratory cocktails at Limani Bar. Whilst not so elegantly chugging their fancy drinks and snacking on a complimentary bowl of mixed nuts and other rabbit treats, they watched on as a sailor was attempting to moor up his yacht on the short and crowded pontoon. The Harbour Master had finally arrived on her bike and was now assisting the sailor by telling him to go back out and reverse back in again but with more anchor chain let out. The whole process looked very stressful but Max and Charlie still looked on whilst laughing at the sailing shenanigans.

"Can it really be that difficult to park a boat Max, surely it's just the same as reverse parking a car but with some ropes and an anchor thing?"

"I have no idea mate but it does make for great entertainment. Parking one of them aside, they're lovely aren't they? I mean boats with sails and not the two girls on the thing at the back. Look at how it sits in the water, do you reckon they're out for the day or do you think they live on that thing? It's certainly big enough."

"Why don't we go and check it out then, take a closer look?"

"The boat or the girls Charlie?"

"Both! Come on, drink up!"

Charlie had made a fair point and although he may have been more interested in the bikini clad girls who were prancing around on the thing at the back, Max was eager to get closer to what he was now assuming to be some sort of floating caravan, and which was now successfully parked up in Kassiopi Harbour. According to the decals on both rear sides of the boat, it was either called or perhaps made by Hanse and some numerals suggested that it was number forty five for some reason. It was all new to Max and he was intrigued and fascinated by what he saw in front of him. Whilst he was trying to figure out how the black ropes at the back and the chain at the front were holding the boat still and preventing it from floating away, he was greeted by a tall, slim and very tanned gentleman.

"Bonjourno my friend! You're from England I think?"
Max thought to himself, how did he know that, before replying, "Yes, how did you know that?"
"Your T Shirt, The Smiths. The miserable band from Manchester in England but a good band and a band I like. Please, step on board if you want a tour of my yacht."

Max had now learnt that the floating caravan thing was actually called a yacht and from what he could initially see, was basically a floating caravan but with one big sail in the middle and another smaller one at the front. Once on board, Max quickly caught Charlie's eye and affirmatively shook his head to confirm with him that the two young girls were off limits and he was to be on his best behaviour.

"I'm Marco and here are my lovely daughters, Adriana and Emilia. This is our yacht, she's a Hanse 45 and she's called Aurora. That was my wife's name, she was beautiful, like my girls and our yacht, simply beautiful. But sadly, Aurora was taken from us last year, she'd just celebrated her fortieth birthday. She was still so young and adventurous."

"I'm sorry to hear that Marco. I'm Max and this is my best friend, Charlie."

"You guys like a beer, Peroni okay? But first, let me show you around Aurora."

After Marco had finished the tour of his beloved yacht, he grabbed three bottle of beer from the fridge and whilst gathered around the on deck table, proceeded to tell Max and Charlie the story of Aurora. "We bought the boat when my wife was still alive and we'd made plans to sail around the Greek Islands but Aurora had been feeling unwell and she was always tired. Anyway, she eventually went to see a doctor and it wasn't good news. Just three months later, she was gone. But her spirit lives on in this beautiful yacht and therefore she still travels with us when we sail her."

"That's a lovely story Marco and you're incredibly brave and obviously an amazing father to your daughters. I also have children but I'm not sure I would have coped with that heartbreak in the way you did."

"Life has to go on boys. Losing Aurora made us realise that our lives can be incredibly short and bitterly cruel sometimes. I asked my daughters what they wanted to do next and they told me straight. They wanted to sail around the Greek Islands in the sunshine and have fun and here we are. So my friends, salute to sunshine, fun times and happiness always!"

Max had swapped phone numbers with Marco and Charlie had now become friends with him on Facebook. They all agreed to keep in touch and meet up again somewhere on their travels. Marco had even invited them both to join him and his daughters on a sail out for a few days. Max was really keen on that idea, Charlie was also up for it and Marco, Adriana and Emilia were more than happy to show both of them the ropes and teach them the basics of sailing.

"Well Max, another fantastic day so far and Marco, what a guy. A true inspiration to all who have to face and deal with tough times."

"Absolutely! Also, imagine just sailing around in your floating home, going where the wind and waves take you. I love that idea Charlie, surely that's ultimate freedom?"

"Well, never say never Max and if anyone can pull off that lifestyle, I reckon you're the man. You've just got to learn how to sail first and as we've learnt today, it's quite clearly not that simple."

For the newly inspired friends and now lovers of all things to do with sailing yachts, Taverna Levanda was the restaurant of choice in Kassiopi that evening. Located a short stroll away from the harbour and offering a wide range of traditional cuisine, Levanda provided the perfect ending to another brilliant day on Corfu. Max ordered the Stifado, tender beef cooked slowly in a rich and aromatic tomato sauce, made with red wine, cinnamon and shallots. Charlie opted for the chicken Gyros plate, a mountain of succulent meat served on two warm pitta breads, with thinly sliced red onions, tzatziki and salted fries. Two litres of cold white wine complemented each dish perfectly and just like that, they both found themselves in culinary heaven. Max picked up his phone and sent Kat some photos from today's adventures, including some of the wonderful Sailing Yacht Aurora. Charlie downed another glass of wine and then joined the daily update session by uploading some more random photos to his Facebook Page.

"You know what Max, Facebook's a funny thing really, don't you think?"

"I think you're asking the wrong person mate. As you know, I don't go anywhere near it nor does Kat. But anyway, what makes you say that?"

"I hardly ever get friend requests, and yes I know and it's got something to do with actually having some friends, but when I do, OMG! I have no idea who she is but her name's Megan and apparently she lives in London. Do you think it could be one of those fake profiles?"

"No idea mate, let's have a look. She's cute though!"

"You're right there Max, drop dead cute! Hey, what could possibly go wrong, what I have got to lose? Megan accepted!"

Chapter 26 ~ Cold Ginger Ale With Lemon And Rooster Pastitsada.

Before leaving Kassiopi and heading South, the guys took a leisurely walk back down to the harbour. Max wanted to see Aurora one last time and Charlie badly needed some more deodorant and some razors before their date night in

Messonghi with Steffi and Bex. To Max's disappointment, SV Aurora had already left and was enroute to another location somewhere in the Ionian Sea. Charlie picked up everything he needed from the shop which appeared to sell everything from deodorant to garden spades and they made their way back to Jimny.

"Where to next Max and just in case you've forgotten, it's date night tonight at Bacchus on The Beach. Have you got any clean T Shirts left or do you need to buy a 'I Love Corfu' one from somewhere? I can always lend you one of my Ralph Lauren Polos if you're struggling or want to look smart for once."

"I'll have you know Charlie, this shirt was clean on yesterday and still remains clean today and as you try your best to make me look like a complete idiot. So thanks, but no thanks pal. As to where we're going next, the answer is Kalami. It featured in The Durrells and I really want to check out some of the film locations. I reckon we'll get some lunch there as well."

"Great! After Kalami, anywhere else before we get to where we're staying tonight?"

"A couple of other places, yes. And just in case you've forgotten, you're leaving on Saturday but I'm staying here. Remember, I'm then going to hike that Corfu Trail route. So there's this little village I want to visit before I set off, it's called Dafnata and I reckon it's about a third of the way along the trail. There's a taverna and accommodation in the village which is owned and run by a guy called Kostas, I'm hoping he'll have a room for me. If not, I'll have to find somewhere to stay In Benitses."

"Thanks for that reminder, I've been trying really hard not to think about Saturday."

Jimny had picked up another scratch and a little dent in the rear bumper whilst parked up on the narrow side street but started first time and sounded ready to go again. Before setting off this time, the soft top came off, the shades were on and they were soon on their way to Kalami. Max was really excited about visiting this place and although the White House wasn't the house which featured in the TV series, it was the actual house which Lawrence Durrell lived in with Nancy, Nancy being his wife. The house which featured in The Durrells was located just a little further down the coast and was also on Max's list of location check-ins. As they exited Kassiopi, the words spoken between Max and Charlie were unusually few and far between but far from in a bad way. Max would occasionally look across at his mate, who was clearly captivated by the beauty of this magical island, and raise his eyebrows and gently nod his head in a way which suggested he knew exactly what Charlie was thinking. Charlie would silently point out stuff to Max, lost for words for once but also knowing that his friend would approve of what he was pointing at and the target needed no explanation nor commentary.

"Hold on tight Charlie! We're about to drop down the steep hill and into Kalami Bay but don't panic, we're staying on the road this time."
"I trust you Max. I've sometimes doubted you but I've always trusted you to do the right thing when it matters."
"That's cute Charlie and I love you too but for some reason, the breaks on this thing are starting to feel a bit squishy!"
"Tell me you're joking, please tell me you're joking."

227

Max confirmed that he was only joking by bringing Jimny to a sharp and sudden stop in a small gravel car park which was located at the foot of the hill. Charlie opened his eyes to the reality that he was still alive and he would get to see Bex again that evening.

Once Charlie had stopped shaking, he had something to say to Max, "How we've remained friends for so long is beyond me and even my private education can't figure that one out. What is it with us mate?"

"Stop overthinking things dude, we're here to have fun, right or wrong?"

"One hundred percent right but seriously mate, you and I, we should hate each other?"

"Shut up twat face! You're Charlie and I'm Max, that's how it's always been. You're you and I'm me, chalk and cheese. The perfect combination, built to last."

Never in the sixteen odd years that they had now known each other had Max and Charlie felt so close, so connected and so happy to have each other in their lives. Max was bang on the money when he described their chalk and cheese relationship but Corfu appeared to be sprinkling its magic on them and helping them on their way to a bond which was clearly getting stronger by the day.

"I'm going to miss this place Max and I'm going to miss you when I leave on Saturday."

"I'll miss you too mate but we'll soon be back together. Remember, we live together now. Back in England, where it's cold and grey and raining most of the time. By the way, when's your interview at the burger place?"

"The Monday after I get back, so I better muster up some enthusiasm because if they're looking to employ people on their attitude, I'm screwed!"

"Just think of the money Charlie, take the money. You can then start paying me some rent and buying your share of the food."

"I know you're right mate but it sucks back home. But hey, next weekend I get to see the children and I can tell them all about our trip."

Max and Charlie walked along the shoreline in the direction of The White House whilst listening to the waves gently land on the beach. The tall trees were reaching up into the clear blue sky and the Cicadas were now in full swing while native birds caught the thermals and hovered gracefully overhead. The brightly coloured fishing boats were bobbing and bouncing around in the waist deep water and slowly, one table and one chair, one sunlounger and one umbrella at a time, Kalami Bay was coming alive, waking up and effortlessly painting another picture of pure and unspoilt paradise.

"Look Max! Out there, beyond the boats which are anchored. That's Aurora, I'm sure of it."

"I think you're right Charlie, it's flying an Italian flag. Let me call Marco and see if that's them."

"Max! Already, you're ready to come sailing with us. Where are You?"

"I was just about to ask you the same question but sadly, we can't come sailing with you just yet. Charlie and I think we can see you, so where are you now?"

"Ah, I see. Do you understand coordinates Max or would it be easier if I told you that we were just outside of Kalami Bay?"

"So it is you? Look towards the beach Marco and hopefully you'll be able to see us."

Max and Charlie jumped up and down whilst frantically waving their arms in the air, as if they were doing some kind of over energetic beach workout...

"Hey, I can see you on the beach and remember, anytime you fancy trying your hands at sailing, just call me. I mean that guys."

"We will Marco, trust us on that. Anyway, where are you heading for now?"

"We're on our way to Paxos, that's why we left early. It gets busy there, so you have to arrive early if you want to get a good spot to drop anchor."

"I understand what you're saying Marco and I think at this point, Charlie and I now say 'safe sailing'."

"Indeed my friends and remember, 'fun times and happiness always'."

As Aurora vanished behind the headland, the boys waved their final goodbye to Marco, Adriana and Emilia, whilst genuinely hoping to see them again in the near future and take Marco up on his offer of a sail out.

Charlie looked at Max and came straight out with it, "I want to be Marco, the guy's a fucking legend!"

Max laughed at Charlie and pointed him in the direction of a white building which was further down the beach. As they walked barefooted in the shallows of Kalami Bay they talked briefly about sailing boats and the prospect of actually going sailing one day with Marco and his daughters. Max was still fascinated by the whole idea of living on a yacht and like a tortoise, only on water and not on land, being able to take your home with you whenever you got bored of looking at the same things for too long.

"Do you reckon they're expensive mate, one of them sailing boats, like Marco's?"

"I've no idea Charlie but I'm totally gonna find out. That way of living would suit me down to the ground, I kid you not."

"What's happened to the stone cottage on the side of the hill, is that plan now dead in the water? No joke intended."

"I'm just keeping my options open, that's all. Like you said the other day mate, I'm a free agent now and maybe it's time I started thinking and acting like one."

"Keeping your options open, like with Kat and Steffi?"

"That's a bit rich coming from you mate, like with Bex and now Megan?"

"Touché Maximilian, touché! However, there's a difference between you and I here. I have lustful feelings towards Bex and if she remains true to her promise tonight, I will more than likely be well and truly out of my depth, but I'm also more than happy to drown in an ocean of bizarre love making. As far as Megan is concerned, I don't even know if she's actually a real person yet. But if she is, I most certainly would, maybe even twice or thrice. What I'm saying Max, is I'm not in love, it's a lust thing only."

"Have you quite finished…"

"No, I haven't! However, you my friend, it's all about falling in love. You jump off the tallest building you can find and into a pool of love hearts, red roses, Winnie the Pooh balloons and eternal rainbows. Name your cliché Max but I've already seen it and that's how you won Kat's heart all those years ago. All the other lads back then, including me, don't forget, were either too lazy to fight for her or too self deserving."

"Finished now…"

"Almost! Synopsis, do you know what that means Max? Thought so, education or Google? So here you go, you're still in love with Kat, only your pride is slightly dented because she left you, dented like Jimny's bumper. You've never stopped being in love with that girl mate, even when everything was kicking off big time and you were adamant that she was screwing Grant Fisher. As for Steffi, the seeds of love have now been planted. She's stunningly beautiful and I've seen the way she looks at you and that certainly isn't a look which hints at being just good friends. You know that Max and that's what you like and with a bit of this and a slice of that, you could easily have her eating out of the palm of your hand. You're dangerous Max, fucking dangerous and you need to figure your shit out before tonight. If it weren't for Kat, people would be following you on your journey of exploration around the world by downloading your map of broken hearts. Don't start on that project now mate, you're better than that, just stick to your plan."

"I'm not quite sure what I'm supposed to say next Charlie?"

"Say nothing, take your arty pictures of some random white house near a beach and let's hit the road!"

After Max had paid homage to the former home of Lawrence and Nancy Durrell, some food was ordered and quickly devoured at a place called Callao and immediately after lunch, they were on their way to the village of Dafnata. Jimny made its way back up the steep hill, mostly in first gear but occasionally in second, before reaching the coast road which would take them to Benitses. From there they would snake their way up another hill until they reached their next stop of the day. A place which was often remembered by those who had visited the village for its slightly out of place, but typically British and very retro, red telephone box. The village of Dafnata was limited in terms of what it had to offer its visitors but it had what most visitors wanted. A place to eat and a place to get drinks. A place to sleep, if you needed or wanted to stay the night and if you were just passing through, a place from which to enjoy the most amazing views. Kostas claimed that the views from his village were the best views available, if you wanted to look North and up the East coast of Corfu. Kostas wasn't wrong and the views were as splendid as his taverna and the upstairs rooms he offered.

"Kalispera! You need rooms for tonight, food, cold beer or ginger ale with lemon? If you need rooms, sorry, we full tonight, tomorrow night and the night after the night. Food and drink, no problems. I'm Kostas, please and welcome to my place.

Kostas put forward a strong looking hand and welcomed Max and Charlie to Cafe Snack Bar Kostas. The boys took a table in the shade and accepted the recommendation of a cold ginger ale with lemon. Max had really bad memories of ginger ale or ginger beer, as it was most commonly know back in the UK, but this version was indeed something else. Sweet and sharp at the same time and as refreshing as a cold swim on a hot day.

"Take a swig of that Charlie, I've not tasted anything like it."

"Wow! That's totally lush and with a measure of vodka or two, and if I had any, I'd happily drown my sorrows in that all day long."

Kostas joined the boys at their table and was keen to find out why they had decided to visit Dafnata, "Why you come to my village today? Apart from my place, the telephone box and the view, there's nothing here for you. You not walkers, so why?"

"You're right Kostas, we're not walkers today but I'm attempting to be a walker next week and I was hoping you may have a room available for Tuesday evening?"

"Ah, you walk our beautiful trail, The Corfu Trail, yes?"

"Well that's my plan. Is it easy, do you think I can do it?"

"I don't know you, so how do I bloody know if you can do it! But if you keep putting feet in front of feet for long enough, you get somewhere in the end. Advice from Kostas, if you love Corfu, you will do it. It's hard my friend and it hot now, so go slow and drink lots. Water, not beer or Ouzo!"

"Thanks for the advice and do you have a room for me when I reach Dafnata on Tuesday?"

"Yes, of course and on Tuesday my cook is making Pastitsada with rooster. Not chicken, rooster, man chicken. You understand me?"

"Absolutely Kostas and I will definitely see you on Tuesday. By the way, I'm Max and this is Charlie but he goes back to England on Saturday, so it'll only be me staying for rooster Pastitsada."

"Okay Max and you enjoy my cook's food for perhaps the last time. She finish at my place soon, to spend more time doing nothing with her time. You English call it retired? I say 'bat shit crazy' and it a problem for me, then no cook at my place!"

Charlie immediately looked at Max and raised his eyebrows in a way which may have suggested that he was interested in the upcoming vacancy at Kostas Place or alternatively, it could be a great opportunity for Max to add another valid reason to his list of reasons as to why a life on Corfu was better and maybe soon, even a viable way of life.

Chapter 27 ~ Bacchus On The Beach And Early Evening Skinny Dipping.

Max and Charlie both said goodbye to Kostas with a firm handshake and a manly embrace. Kostas wished Charlie all the best back in England and reminded Max to take it easy on the trail and to drink plenty of water. Max carefully steered Jimny back down the hill and once safely on the coast road, pointed him in the direction of Moraitika and Messonghi. Charlie had managed to connect his phone to the newly upgraded stereo system and was now the enroute

DJ, dropping cringe worthy tunes like hot cakes and causing Max to continuously shake his head in disapproval and disbelief.

"Pack it up, pack it in, let me begin. I came to win, battle me, that's a sin. I won't ever slack up, punk, ya better back up. Try and play the role and yo, the whole crew'll act up. Get up, stand up (c'mon) c'mon, throw your hands up. If ya got the feelin', jump up towards the ceilin' I came to get down, I came to get down. So get out your seat and jump around."

"Love this tune Max! No idea what it's about but it just puts you in the mood to do crazy shit. I'm ready for some crazy shit Max, ready for some crazy shit with Bex!"

"I'm the cream of the crop, I rise to the top. I never eat a pig 'cause a pig is a cop. Or better yet a Terminator, like Arnold Schwarzenegger. Tryin' to play me out like as if my name was Sega."

"Charlie, you've changed since coming out to Corfu. Do you see or feel the changes in you or is it just my imagination and you're still Charlie the geeky computer programmer?"
"Well Max, I'm certainly not a programmer anymore but do we ever really change or are we just temporarily distracted or sidetracked from who we really are and will ultimately always be?"
"Dude, say that again but without the essence of Mark Twain."

"I've clearly spent too much time around you Max. What I mean mate is this, I'm not trying to be different nor someone I'm genuinely not, I'm just going with the flow. Life with Laura and behind a desk all day clearly suppressed my flow. So I guess what you're seeing now is just a new version of me, happy and free again."

"I hear you mate and we did have fun as kids, didn't we? We were always up to something. Do you remember jumping over shopping trolleys on our BMX bikes? I remember how everyone laughed when you clipped the last trolley and then went over the handlebars."

"Left here Max and our apartment should be on the right. The Mayflower Apartments and Studios, there we go fella. Now, let's get some beers in and get dressed to impress."

Whilst Max checked in at reception, Charlie went to the supermarket to get some cold beers and some pre-dinner snacks. He also bought Max a thank you present in the form of a 'I Love Corfu' T Shirt, knowing full well that he wouldn't wear it, but thinking it was funny all the same.

"Close your eyes Max, I've got you a present. It's even got your name on the back."

"Thanks mate, it's truly awful! Sorry, I meant awesome but you know I won't wear it, right?"

"I know that but put it in your bag, take it with you tonight and we'll get Bex and Steffi to sign it. It'll make a great souvenir and it'll always remind us of our time together on Corfu."

"Bless you Charlie, come here mate."

After a few cold beers, a sharing bag of BBQ Ruffles and two very cold showers, Max and Charlie were dressed up and ready to meet up with Steffi and Bex again. Charlie had activated 'Full Oxbridge Mode" and was dressed from head to toe in his very best RL Polo Collection. He'd chosen a baby pink shirt which sat untucked above a pair of navy blue shorts and beige loofahs with tassels. Max had opted for his favourite Quicksilver surfing shorts, the ones with a small rip near the left pocket, and a Pink Floyd band T Shirt. These two items, combined with his very old FatFace flip flops and hair band, made him look as if he'd just stepped off a beach in Australia, he should be no friend of Charlie's and he certainly wasn't going out for dinner with two very attractive German girls. They decided to walk through the big hotel on the beach and take the water taxi to the other side of the river. The water taxi was basically an old rowing boat which belonged to an old lady or man, who appeared to turn up out of nowhere when somebody needed to cross the river. They parted with a couple of Euros each and proceeded along the beach to Bacchus on The Beach, where Steffi and Bex were already drinking and waiting for their dates.

Bex was the first to spot them approaching and was immediately out of her chair and running down the beach to meet her date for the night, "Charlie, look at you all dressed up and just for me. Oh Charlie, you're still my favourite boy on Corfu and we're going to have so much fun tonight."

Max couldn't stop himself from laughing and had a funny feeling that Bex was going to absolutely destroy his best mate tonight. Whilst briefly walking behind Bex, Charlie gave Max a double thumbs up to confirm that he gave no fucks whatsoever towards what Bex had just said and he was one hundred percent ready for what may be coming his way.

In complete contrast to her extravagant friend, Steffi sat patiently and elegantly at the table and waited for her surfer boy to arrive, "Max, Pink Floyd, one of our favourite bands I believe?"
"I believe so Steffi and you look lovely tonight."

Charlie looked across at Max and gave him a mouth closed smile and a subtle nod of his head. To a complete stranger, this could have meant anything but Max knew exactly where Charlie was coming from and what was expected from him this evening. Charlie was expecting Max to do the right thing and that meant no breaking hearts. Stick to the original plan or ditch the plan completely and move on with Steffi as Kat's replacement. Max and Charlie sat opposite their dates and waited for the owner of Bacchus to take their order. Charlie and Bex were again holding hands, giggling and occasionally leaning across the table to join lips. Steffi was lovingly listening to Max as he told her where they'd been since first meeting on the boat trip and was now keen to visit Old Perithia and Kassiopi for herself. Occasionally the girls would converse in German, leaving Max completely lost and Charlie not far behind and then regroup in English again. A table full of food and drink was ordered and between mouthfuls of devine cuisine and cold white and red wine, the conversations continued to flow seamlessly and as the sun went down on Corfu, a fantastic evening was being had by all.

"Come on Charlie, let's go swimming. The water looks beautiful and if it's cold, we will soon warm each other up."

"But Bex, the shorts I'm wearing are the only ones I have with me tonight, they're cotton and really expensive."

"Then take them off big boy, let me see what you're made of."

Bex gave Charlie no other option but to join her in the silky dark water and with both hands, she dragged him across the narrow beach and into the sea. Max and Steffi briefly looked on in amusement before continuing their conversation, which was centered around which one of Pink Floyd's albums was their most complete piece of work. Steffi also told Max that her love of proper music, not the computer generated rubbish which now filled the charts, came from her parents, who were both music teachers at a music academy in Frankfurt. She had to choose between playing the piano or the guitar and obviously chose the guitar. She'd hoped one day to be in a band but her parents had other ideas for their daughter and now Steffi was doing a job she hated and one which had nothing to do with playing the instrument she'd spent years learning to play.

"My friend is crazy Max, she's lovely but she's crazy. She does what she wants, when she wants and just doesn't care about what other people might think of her. We're very different, I think you've established that already though?"

"Very different! That's an understatement for sure but then Charlie and I are very different. Just look at him and look at me."

"I guess you're right Max and I suppose that's what helps people connect. There's no way I'd go swimming naked in

240

the sea, that's for sure! What about you Max, would you take all your clothes off in front of me?"

Before Max had a chance to reply to Steffi's question about skinny dipping, Bex and Charlie had returned and informed the non naked swimmers that they were going back to the apartment where Bex and Steffi were staying to get dry and to warm up under the covers.

"You don't have to hurry back Steffi, take your time and get to know Max a bit better. I'll message you later, okay? Max, look after my girl won't you, treat her like a princess."

Bex and Charlie ran off down the beach and then disappeared down a side street and in the direction of their love nest, leaving Steffi and Max alone to enjoy the peace and quiet of Messonghi Beach. Just up the beach and in the direction of the river was a small wooden pontoon, precariously extending itself out into the calm ocean and the mysterious darkness which had now fallen all over Corfu. Max pulled out his credit card and picked up everyone's bill and the evening at Bacchus was concluded by the offering of complimentary cake and a round of shots. The owner of this wonderful taverna had no idea that Bex and Charlie had gone for the night and had brought enough cake and alcohol for four. Not wanting to offend the owner, Max and Steffi enjoyed double portions of lemon cake, washed down with two shots each.

"Come on Steffi, let's take a walk up the beach. We can sit at the end of the old pontoon and listen to the sound of the waves."

"Sounds like a perfect ending to the evening Max but no naked swimming, got that?"

They sat on the pontoon listening to the sound of the waves and other noises which were inexplicable. Possibly strange insects, trees rustling in the gentle breeze or maybe even fish, darting around in the water below the salty wooden uprights and tired planks of wood. Occasionally the waves would reach their feet, which were now bare and dangling over the edge, and Steffi would instinctively pull her feet up as if she still had a chance of keeping them dry. Steffi was starting to feel the chill of the night, so Max pulled his gift from Charlie out of his bag and offered it to his date.

"You don't have to wear it if you don't want to, just put it over your shoulders. It might help keep you warm."
"Thank you Max, you're very kind. Let's walk along the beach a bit further and see what we can find, maybe go for a quiet drink somewhere, just you and I."
"That sounds great to me Steffi. Here, let me hold your hand while we're on the pontoon."

Still hand in hand, they walked along the now deserted beach until they reached the mouth of the river. They decided to trace their steps back until they got to Booca Beach Bar and here they stayed for the next two hours, sipping cocktails and getting to know each other better. Charlie had just messaged Max and told him that it was more than likely going to be a long night and asked him if it was okay for them to regroup in the morning. Max had no problem with Charlie's plan but his immediate thoughts were more to do with Steffi and where she was going to stay that night. After all, she clearly wasn't the sort of girl who would happily look away, whilst in the small apartment they'd been sharing together, her crazy friend entertained her latest lover. Steffi had also received a message from Bex, asking her how well she was getting to know Max and for one reason or another, could they trade apartments for the evening. Steffi was getting to know Max better and she trusted him but she was slightly unsure about her friend's suggestion, which meant spending the night with Max at The Mayflower, even if it was to be in two separate beds.

"Please don't take this the wrong way Max but I don't really have any other options and I'm not sleeping on the beach. Look, I like you, I like you a lot but I'm not Bex. I never have been and I never will be. Anyway, I hear you kind of have a girl back in England? If you're already wondering, Bex told me, so I'm guessing Charlie must have told her."

"Yeh, well it's kind of complicated, but to be honest with you Steffi, I don't even now what the deal is at the moment. We're apart now but really we shouldn't be. She should be here now and I shouldn't be here drinking with you and Charlie shouldn't be here either, now having sex with Bex. Like I said, it's all a bit complicated."

"It's not complicated Max, you just need to decide what you want and who you want to be with. I'll tell you now Max, I'm not a 'try before you buy' kind of girl. If you like me in the same way as I like you, you need to commit to me and love me unconditionally. Nobody else Max, nor feelings for anybody else, it really is that simple."

Steffi had clearly set her stall out and Max knew exactly where he stood, it was either her or Kat. No passionate holiday romance with Steffi, but if he did choose her over Kat, his life would be starting all over again and heading off into the unknown with a girl he'd only just met. That thought terrified Max but it also excited him because he genuinely had feelings for this beautiful German girl and he now knew the feelings were reciprocal. He would also have to learn how to deal with the thoughts of Kat being with another man and he already knew that wouldn't be easy. Max needed another drink or two, pretty quickly and he needed to speak to Charlie, but he knew that that wasn't going to happen now until tomorrow morning.

Chapter 28 ~ Sugar Coated Doughnuts And One Last Blast.

This particular Thursday evening was going to be remembered by this group of old and newly acquainted friends, lovers and work associates as the mother of all sleepness nights and it was now performing at two venues. In Corfu, staring Max, Charlie, Steffi and Bex. Also in London, with Fabio, Kat and Megan, all jostling for center stage.

Fabio had called an emergency meeting with Kat for Friday morning at eight o'clock sharp, the same day she was due to present her marketing strategy to Grant and now the production team, who were going to take over the management of the TV side of the campaign. Fabio's urgent meeting had nothing to do with Grant and his high income account and he had every faith in what Kat had managed to pull together in a very short space of time. Fabio also knew that Grant would love what she had done and be happy to sign off the campaign just like that. However, what Fabio had to discuss with Kat so urgently was not going to sit well with his number one girl and this worry was keeping him awake all night.

Kat was struggling to sleep because she was stressed, over worked and drinking too much as a result. She knew she'd done everything she could in order to present an amazing and captivating campaign to Grant but she still needed big dog's signature. Grant's squiggle on the dotted line meant a very healthy bonus at the end of July and a much needed holiday with Megan. To add to her already off the scale stress levels, she now had an urgent meeting with Fabio to attend and still had no idea why she was being summoned. Fabio had insisted on them discussing things face to face, not by email nor over the phone.

Although Megan's brother, the delightful Bony Tony, was still being held by the police and as a result, her flat was no longer a hornet's nest of chaos and criminality, she still had her alcoholic mother to look out for. That was no easy task for a young girl who was getting very tired of having to act like a forty or fifty year old, when all she wanted to do was have fun and fall in love with a nice guy like Charlie. Megan had been thinking a lot about Charlie but she'd also spent a lot of time looking at his photos on Facebook and as a result, she was starting to think that her cute but geeky nice guy was already a non starter. She also had to tell her mum the outcome of Tony's court hearing and it wasn't good news, unless Tony's lucky number was eight.

Back in Corfu however, Charlie was the only one so far who was being kept awake all night for positive and not negative reasons. He was on a one way highway to sexual nirvana and was loving every minute and seductive movement of it. He knew it was a mutual holiday fling between him and Bex, she'd made that clear now on a number of occasions. There was no lovey dovey future waiting for them in the morning and that made saying goodbye on Friday or Saturday a very easy task to handle. The next chapter of Charlie's life was almost ready to begin back in England, with a new job and a weekend spent with his lovely children. For Bex, it was another island or another man and then back to Frankfurt to dance and perform in front of lots of other men.

Max couldn't get to sleep either but on this occasion, it had nothing to do with stress, chaos, crazy love nor the love confusion which had been clouding his usually clear thinking mind lately. Whilst listening to Brian Kennedy and Passenger, on the two single beds which they had agreed to push together, Steffi had finally fallen asleep with her head resting on Max's shoulder and one of her bronze arms draped across his chest. Every time Max tried to move her arm, she would stir and then naturally reposition herself on him before effortlessly drifting off to sleep again. In the end, Max gave up on the two of them being separated in sleep and as the Sun started to rise again on Corfu, he eventually gave in to his tiredness and fell into a blissful slumber with Steffi now sleeping peacefully in his arms.

Fabio and Kat were the first to face the Friday after the night of sleepless nights and both were in Fabis private office bright and early, both looking exhausted and both with a strong coffee in front of them. Fabio reluctantly started the urgent meeting with a swig of black coffee and an apology, "I'm sorry Kat and I know you're not going to like what I'm about to say but hear me out. Also, it has nothing to do with your presentation this afternoon, that's in the bag and I've already signed off your bonus for it. Your getting paid very well for that project, trust me."

"Fabio! Will you just get on with it, I'm tired and I'm about to cry."

"Look Kat, I need you back in the Harrogate office, okay? It's a fucking clown show up there at the moment and the current set up is bleeding money. At the rate they're going, I'll have to shut that branch before Christmas or alternatively, fund it with the profits we're making here. But unless something changes up there, they'll bleed us dry too."

"But Fabio, my life is in London now! I've got nothing in Yorkshire, not even a place to live anymore. What the fuck Fabio!"

"Kat, I'm sorry but you came to London to work and then chose to make it your home. I've always guaranteed you the best gigs but I never promised you a happy ever after in the capital city."

"I'm not sure what to say but I'm thinking screw you Fabio!"

"I need you up there on the 21st, that's a week on Monday. I'll meet you there and we'll start shaking things up immediately. Unless of course, you've got other ideas?"

Megan sat her mum down at the kitchen table and put a mug of tea in front of her before breaking the news she'd recently received, "Eight years mum, Tony's been given eight years. He's in Wandsworth Prison for now but he might be moved in a few weeks."

"Oh, I see. So when's he coming home, back to us at the flat?"

"I'm not sure mum, let me have a look at the calendar and find out what the date will be in eight years time."

"Who's gonna look after us now Megs, now Tony's not around for a while?"

"Don't you worry yourself mum, you keep doing what you do and I'm sure we'll figure something out."

Kat's call to Megan conveniently interrupted the pointless conversation she was having with her mum and she immediately took the incoming call.

"Fabio wants me, actually, let me rephrase that Megan, Fabio is giving me no other alternative but to return to the Harrogate office. A week on Monday apparently and together, we're going to sort his shit show out!"

"No Kat! That can't happen, that really can't happen. I need you here with me, in London. You're my only chance babe and without you, everything I have will crumble. I know I sound selfish but no, just no!"

"It's okay though because everything is going to be fine this afternoon in the boardroom and I'm getting paid handsomely at the end of the month. Fucking perfect that is!"

"Look Kat, try and get through the day and I'll see you tonight at you're place for dinner. You haven't forgotten that have you? Remember, we were going to talk about our holiday plans and you wanted my advice on something."

"No, I haven't forgotten but thanks for reminding me."

It was now ten o'clock in London, mid day in Corfu and while Max and Steffi were still sleeping, Bex and Charlie were up and about and enjoying a quiet walk along the beach. Charlie stopped briefly to look out across the calm blue sea and whilst doing so, he noticed Captain Homer's boat. It appeared to be heading in the direction of the swim spot where Bex first planted her ruby red lips on his and where they then played like carefree children in a paddling pool. Bex nudged Charlie and reminded him that she wanted a coffee and a cake from the bakery and it was time to stop boat watching and time to go cake and coffee shopping.

"You're leaving Corfu on Saturday, that's a shame Charlie. Steffi and I are here for two more weeks. We love it here, it's an escape from our lives in Germany. This place genuinely feels like home to us, unlike Frankfurt, where everything feels fake and staged. Every inch of Corfu is real Charlie and it's where I met you, still my favourite, even though you snore like a pig."

"Yes, today is my last full day, unfortunately. Max is taking me to the airport in Jimny, one last trip together in our little red jeep thing. I think we're leaving at 10am? Anyway, Max knows what he's doing, I trust him."

"And then your life back in England starts again, hopefully with a new job at Mr Burger and with your children."

"It's Happy Burger, not Mr Burger but it's still a pile of crap. I'm only doing it for the money, it means I can support myself and my kids. I'm really looking forward to seeing them Bex but I'm gonna miss this place, really miss this place."

"Most people do things they don't enjoy for the money but that's life Charlie. You're also doing it for the right reason, for your children. You're a good person Charlie, don't you ever forget that. You're also an amazing lover, gentle, thoughtful and passionate. Unlike German boys, who are rough, selfish and would rather be drinking beer and watching football."

Finding a bakery in the village of Messonghi was as easy as falling in love with the island of Corfu and the smell of freshly baked bread, cakes and pastries was just one of many reasons why visitors found themselves helplessly but happily falling. Another reason, it was perfectly acceptable to eat doughnuts the size of dinner plates for breakfast on Corfu and that's exactly what Bex and Charlie were going to do. Having purchased four sugar coated doughnuts and two take out coffees, they wandered back to the beach and sat at the end of the same pontoon where Max and Steffi had sat the previous evening.

"The mainland almost looks close enough to swim to, what do you reckon Bex, do you think we could swim it?"
"I think it's further than you realise Charlie, maybe take a boat instead and make it there alive."
"Yeh, that sounds like a better plan. A boat like Marco's, one of them sailing boat things."
"Who's Marco? You've not mentioned him before, should I know him?"
"Max and I met Marco and his daughters in Kassiopi a few days ago. They had this lovely sailing boat called Aurora, named after Marco's wife. Aurora sadly passed away last year but the girls, Adriana and Emilia, still wanted to to sail around the Greek Islands with their dad and that's exactly

what they're doing now. When we last saw them, they were on their way to Paxos."

"Oh Charlie, that sounds heavenly. Maybe one day, what do you reckon? When we're both finished with all the silly and serious stuff, we'll sail off into the sunset."

"Don't tempt me Bex, don't tempt me. Anyway, we should go and find Max and Steffi, see what they're doing now."

Shortly after 1pm, Max finally woke up to find Steffi sitting on the balcony of the apartment they'd shared the night before. She was still wearing his Pink Floyd T Shirt and had prepared some coffee for them both. Max flicked the switch on the kettle and while the water was boiling, he joined Steffi on the balcony in the spot which was now starting to catch the early afternoon sun.

"Good morning sleepy head, or should I say good afternoon?"

"How long have you been awake and sat out here? I didn't even feel or hear you move."

"About an hour and you were sleeping like a baby Max. Let me know when you want your shirt back and I'll go get changed. Have you heard anything from Charlie or Bex?"

"I'll go and check my phone now. Nope, nothing yet"

Not long after they'd both checked their phones, Bex and Charlie appeared in the shady courtyard below the balcony where Max and Steffi were now enjoying their coffee. Charlie looked up at them and shouted, "We've brought you some breakfast! Doughnuts the size of dinner plates and covered in sugar, we're on our way up. Are you both decent?"

Max grabbed another shirt from his bag and Steffi tied a bath towel around her waist, just before Charlie let himself in and presented them with their sugar charged breakfast.

"These sugary treats are amazing and they go perfectly with a strong coffee. Try eating one without licking your lips, it's impossible mate. Try it and I'll bet you my last Euros you won't last two bites before caving in to the excess sugar which ends up around your chops."

"Someone's in a good mood this morning, did you have a good night Charlie?"

"Max, I can't even begin to explain and I certainly can't tell you in front of Steffi. What about you guys, are you both okay, anything I need to know?"

"Nothing which can't wait until later and changing the subject, what's the plan for today? It's your last day Charlie, so you decide what we do. We've got Jimny until 1pm tomorrow, so if you want to hit the road again, that's fine by me."

"Hey Bex, fancy a drive out today? Steffi, what about you? We've got the red thing for one more day, it'll be a shame not to make the most of it. We can all go and check out some new beaches and stuff. Max is driving, so us three can get on it early. Sundowners on the West coast somewhere, who's up for it?"

Four hands were raised in support of one last blast in Jimny and like clockwork, everyone was doing what they needed to do to get everything together for a great afternoon out. Bex and Steffi quickly returned to their apartment to get changed and to pick up a cool bag, some towels and their swim stuff, whilst Max and Charlie got supplies from the supermarket and then waited in Jimny for the girls to return.

Chapter 29 ~ Mirtiotisa Beach And The Golf Ball Thing.

Max had decided to kick off his private tour of Corfu by taking his party to Mount Agia Deka, via Agios Mathaios, Vouniatades, a few more villages which everyone other than Max was struggling to pronounce and the village of Agios Deka itself. Steffi was riding up front with the driver and Bex and Charlie were snuggled up in the back, enjoying their last day together on Corfu. Occasionally and helped by the uneven road surfaces, Steffi would rest her head on Max's right shoulder, leaving it there long after Jimny had stabilised himself again. Max would turn his head slightly to acknowledge Steffi's presence, Steffi would then smile at him and sit herself back up, until the next tight bend or patch of uneven road pushed her back in Max's direction.

As they approached the summit of Mount Agia Deka, Bex curiously asked, "What's with the big white bollock thing up there? The thing that looks like a golf ball?"
"Don't take your eyes off the road Max, I've got this. Well Bex, it's to help the planes land and stuff. It's for aviation and communication purposes."
"My clever Charlie, looks clever and is clever. How do you know that?"

"Well, you know, some people know this sort of stuff and some don't. I guess I'm just one of those who know."

Max was just about to bust his best friend by telling Bex that it was in fact he who told Charlie all about the golf ball thing but instead, he decided to let Charlie impress his crazy, tattooed, pierced and now bright pink haired beauty, one more time. After all, it was Charlie's last day on Corfu and after everything he'd been through, prior to his unexpected trip with Max, he surely deserved to leave his favourite place and girl on a high. Max parked Jimny in the shade of a tiny chapel, which was the only building to be found in this particular location, at five hundred and seventy six metres above sea level. Charlie and Bex jumped out of the back of the little red island explorer, no doors needed, whilst Steffi and Max sat for a while and watched their friends peruse the terracotta roofed place of worship. The views from where they were now all stood were nothing short of breathtaking and as they all looked directly West, South/West and then North/West, words could not replace the sights, sounds and smells of what was continuously being painted in front of them. Charlie spotted a way marker for The Corfu Trail and subtly brought to Max's attention that the trail he would soon be hiking, climbed up and over the mountain which they had just driven up in first gear only.

"That's one steep hill to climb up. Are you sure you're going to be up to it Max? And, it's getting hotter next week."
"Guys! I think it's time to hit the road and find a beach on the West coast somewhere. Everyone happy with Mirtiotisa? It's considered by many to be the best small

beach on Corfu. Charlie, do you remember what Kostas said? One foot in front of another and all that."

Charlie, Steffi and Bex shrugged their shoulders politely in agreement but also in a way which indicated that none of them had heard of Max's suggested sunset location. Either way, Mirtiotisa was confirmed as the perfect place to end another wonderful day on Corfu. Now back in Jimny and on the move again, the far from perfect foursome we're about to witness their last Corfu sunset together. The following morning, Charlie would fly home to his children and another weekend of being an every other weekend dad and his job interview on Monday. Max would take his pal to the airport, before heading down to Aspro Kavos and then getting some much needed rest before his big hike started on Sunday. As for Bex and Steffi, they still had almost two weeks left on Corfu and it would be a safe bet to place that Bex would still be going for it large but also thinking of her favourite boy, her Charlie. Steffi would continue to turn heads wherever she was going next and would obviously be thinking of Max as he hiked his way from the South to the North of the island. The island where both of their lives harmoniously collided and where Steffi had set out clearly the rules of engagement. Steffi's rules now meant that Max knew exactly what he had to do next and all he had to do now was trust his heart.

Whilst the sun was setting again on Corfu and at the same time turning the evening temperature down a notch or two, back in London, Kat was almost ready to wrap up her boardroom presentation. She'd spent the last four hours going through every inch and aspect of her advertising campaigns for Grant's latest developments, Bow Road and

Thames Side. Grant was now just a signature away from spending a record breaking amount of money with Fab Success and if his ink did hit the paper, Fabio and Kat were in for a treat at the end of July and over the course of the next two to three years, Grant would net an eye watering amount of money whilst at the same time, making many more home ownership dreams come true.

Kat moved on to her last slide, titled 'Any Questions', before addressing her audience, "So, Grant, Fabio and of course our lovely guests today from Make It Happen TV and Media, any questions, comments, input or feedback and dare I say it, concerns?"

Fabio was first to speak, "Bravo, bravo my dear and where do I sign to secure one of those Bow Road conversions? The former paint brush factory, if I've got that right? After the wedding, Patrick and I will soon be looking for a new home to call our own and that place looks perfect."

Grant was next, "You'll need to speak to my sales team about that Fabio but I'm not offering mates rates, even to you. Kathy, I think what you've put together is fantastic and it hits the spot perfectly. As long as our TV and Media guys can deliver the vision, we're on to a winner. Thank you and I'm more than happy to hit the start button."

Gareth, one of the media guys, was last to comment and had one concern, "I hope you've got a generous budget behind you because this isn't going to be cheap, that's my only concern?"

"Gareth, don't you worry about the money. Just make it happen and make it amazing. Fabio knows I'm good for the money and if needs be, we can prove it and make a healthy advance payment, if that helps and calms your concerns?"

"Well my lovelies, are we all happy and can we conclude that today is a success? If so, let's wrap things up and get out of here. After all, it's Friday and we all know what that means."

Everyone in the boardroom was now happy and Fabio insisted on a quick round of celebratory drinks at his favourite bar. The bar where everyday was party day and where people celebrated life and love. Kat had no choice but to join the party but stayed for just one drink, before heading home and getting ready for Megan's arrival at seven o'clock. By the time Kat got back to her borrowed apartment, Megan was already waiting for her, patiently sitting in her car clutching a carrier bag full of wine and snacks.

"Hey babe! What's in the bag? Please tell me it's alcohol and crisps. That's all I need in life right now, and you, obviously."
"Four bottles of wine and two bags of Chilli Heatwave Doritos. Will that do you?"
"Perfect and what a fucking day! But hey, Grant's signed off on my campaign proposals, so that's a huge weight off my shoulders and a pretty awesome looking pay slip at the end of the month. How are you doing Megs, are you okay?"
"I'm good but I'm also really concerned about my mum. I called her at lunchtime today to see how she was and she was already so pissed she didn't even know who I was. Christ only knows what sort of state she's in now. I tried calling her again while I was waiting for you but there was no answer. She's probably fallen asleep somewhere in the flat. The last time she did that, I found her asleep on the toilet and it wasn't a pretty sight, take my word for it."

Kat had now showered and found comfort in her PJs while Megan had changed into her favourite Stüssy hoodie and a pair of Superdry cargo shorts. Kat told Megan all about her presentation and hinted at how much her bonus was going to be. Off the back of that, she assured her that their vacation was definitely on and the only thing left to do now was to decide where to go. She also spoke briefly about having to return to Harrogate but moved on from that topic pretty quickly. Kat already knew Megan's thoughts on that move and as she had no alternative plan yet, continuing with that conversation would only stress Megan out. She also reminded her that she had a dinner date with Grant tomorrow evening and at some point, before they both got too tipsy to be of any help to each other, she needed Megan's advice on both life and love.

"Right Megs! I reckon we order some pizzas, chips and wings and while we're waiting for the food to arrive, I'll show you the photos which Max has been sending me from Corfu. How does that sound?"

"Sounds great and it also sounds like you're mind's made up on where we should go but hey, I'm down with that Kat and more than happy to go to Corfu. Come on then, let's see these photos and after that, I'll show you some of the photos which Charlie has been posting on his Facebook Page."

Kat had saved all of Max's photos in an album she'd created which was called Corfu 2025. And with Megan now sat only an inch away from her on the snug two seater, both with a large glass of wine in their hands, they scrolled through Kat's collection of arty shots which Max had lovingly taken, edited and then sent. Max's photos were nothing short of stunning and each picture he'd taken had been thoughtfully cropped, toned and tinted to create an image which could easily give any picture in a holiday brochure or travel guide a bloody good run for its money. He had clearly managed to capture the feel and essence of a place he loved so dearly and unbeknown to him, he'd just secured Corfu two more eager visitors.

"Okay Kat, I'm sold! Corfu it is and let's look at flight prices from Luton. The cheaper the better for me, even if it's a budget airline. All I want now is a seat on a plane to Corfu with a small suitcase full of bikinis."

"Are you totally sure? Do you not want to look at any other places?"

"Nope, totally sold and can't wait. Can we go tomorrow?"

"If only Megs but don't worry, it'll soon come round. Right, more wine and then let's see Charlie's photos from Corfu."

Kat grabbed another bottle of wine from the fridge and joined Megan back on the sofa. Megan pulled her iPad out of her bag, tapped the blue and white icon and proceeded to find Charlie's profile. The first few photos were of the boys at Teeside Aiport, then on the plane and then shortly after they'd arrived in Corfu. There was a picture of them both with Spyro the taxi driver and one of them sat on their balcony with a can of Alpha each. Charlie had included a couple of customary pictures of food and these were taken at Zorbas Taverna, whilst enjoying their first traditional meal together. Half a dozen photos of them both hiking up the hill to Chlomos bridged the gap between land and sea and it was now boat trip day. This kicked off with a photo of Max with Captain Homer and a photo which the captain had taken of Max and Charlie. So far, Kat and Megan had laughed and humorously commented their way through Charlie's photos, but everything was about to change and get slightly more serious. Not so much for Megan, she'd been keeping a close eye on Charlie's photographic journey of discovery and had already got her head around the fact that her dream boy was now spoken for. However, Kat was in for a short, sharp shock and was about to witness the other side of Max's time spent on Corfu. No more artistic photos of fishing boats and sleeping dogs in doorways. No eclectic but beautifully painted doors and window shutters and no more photos of the stunning East and West coast of Corfu. Instead, a whole bunch of pictures of Max with Steffi, Charlie with Bex, all four of them together on board Captain Homer's boat and just to top it off, a team photo from Bacchus on The Beach.

Megan downed the last of her wine and broke the awkward silence, "Just boys being boys on holiday. Typical isn't it? And there I was, thinking that Charlie and I could one day be together. My kind and gentle lover, who would look after me and love me for who I was. I mean, look at the girl he's with. Red hair, covered in tattoos and from what I can see, she's got more holes in her body than a tea bag. She's nothing like me, Charlie wouldn't look twice at me. Kat, are you okay? You look like you're about to cry."

"Forget the one with the red hair! Sorry Megan, just look at the girl holding Max's hand. She's absolutely stunning and you were right. You told me he'd be dangerous if let loose on Corfu and there's the evidence to back it up. Fucking bollocks! Shit, fuck, bollocks!"

The pizza delivery guy had just arrived and put a timely stop to Kat's swearing. She buzzed him in and waited for his arrival at her open door, "You okay my love? I thought the arrival of our delicious pizzas again would put a smile on your face. Everything okay?"

"Not really but I guess I should have expected it."

"I'm not being rude sister, but I have no idea what you're going on about. You'll be pleased to know though, there's no cheese on the pepperoni and chicken pizza, if that's you're problem?"

"It's not you nor your pizzas. It's a long story but it has something to do with a stunning girl who has golden blonde hair and piercing blue eyes."

"Well my love, that doesn't sound like a problem to me but I'll leave you to figure things out and I hope you enjoy your pizzas."

"Thanks and I'm sure everything will be fine after a few more bottles of wine."

Megan joined Kat in the kitchen and before helping her sort the food out, she put her arm around her and did her best to comfort and calm her down. Megan knew that Kat had been under pressure recently and she knew that she'd been drinking more than usual. Kat's drinking concerned Megan and it was a problem which was too close to home to be ignored or swept under the carpet.

"You won't find the answers to life and love at the bottom of an empty wine bottle. You do know that? Have I just given you the advice you needed or do we still need to talk?"

Chapter 30 ~ Saying Goodbye And Hubble Bubble Pipes.

The act of saying goodbye is never easy and made even more difficult when you genuinely don't want to say goodbye to someone. Sadly though, saying goodbye to someone was just another one of life's realities. Up there with Lucy's theory that true love always ends in tears. Someone either leaves or someone dies.

Whilst Kat was having a meltdown in London, on the island of Corfu, Charlie, Bex, Max and Steffi were enjoying their last round of drinks together. They'd decided to visit Oasis Bar one last time before heading off in different directions the following morning. Bex and Steffi had decided to visit the North of the island, as they were now keen to check out Old Perithia and Kassiopi. They would jump on a bus early in the morning and make their way up the East coast, stopping at Kalami Bay on the way for an early lunch and a refreshing swim. Max and Charlie were leaving for Corfu Airport at ten o'clock sharp, in order for Charlie to catch his early afternoon flight back to Teeside Airport. Charlie called one last round of drinks before their last evening on Corfu as a foursome was officially called a wrap.

"Right, you beautiful people. One cocktail and one shot each. What's it gonna be? Bex?"
"I'll go for a Porn Star Martini and an Ouzo please. And you Charlie?"
"A Moscow Mule and a Limoncello. Max, Steffi?"

"I reckon two Cosmopolitans and two Kumquat Liquors. Steffi, are you okay with my choice?"

"As always, your choice is perfect Max."

Billy soon delivered the drinks and a toast was raised to life, love, fun times and happiness always. It took no time at all for the drinks to be downed and the empty glasses returned to the table. Now it was time to say goodbye.

"Goodbye Charlie, my lovely boy from England and still my favourite boy. You behave yourself now and keep doing the right things. Love your children, make time for yourself and good luck with your interview at Mr Burger."

"Thanks Bex! You made what was always going to be an amazing trip a truly awesome one. Please look after yourself and don't forget what you said. When we're finished with all the silly and serious stuff, we'll sail off into the sunset."

"So Max, now it's our turn. I still have your Pink Floyd T Shirt, do you want me to go and get it?"

"Keep hold of it for now. You might want to wear it again, even though it's a bit big on you."

"Thank you. I'll look after it, I promise. And thank you for everything Max, especially when we were on the boat. Please be careful on your walk and keep me updated when you can. You have my number and you know where to find me."

Steffi and Bex made their way back to their apartment and started packing up in readiness for tomorrow's journey. Steffi neatly folded Max's favorite T Shirt and placed it carefully and lovingly in her bag before letting out a big sigh. Bex heard Steffi and gave her an understanding smile and some comforting advice, "Don't be sad, please. I know how much you like Max but for now, you have to let him go and have faith in your feelings for each other."

"I know, you're right but I already miss him like crazy."

Max and Charlie headed in the direction of their apartment but thought it would be rude not to have one last drink, just the two of them. They found a bar on the main street called Time Out and both agreed that it looked pretty cool. As well as beers, wine and cocktails, Time Out also offered Shisha, sometimes referred to as Hookah. "Look Max, they have those hubble bubble pipes. You know, it's kind of like smoking but with water in a fancy bottle and bubbles and stuff."

"I've never been a smoker Charlie, as you know, but it does look fun. Maybe we should try one, just for the craic. What do you think?"

"Nothing to lose now mate, other than our minds! Come on then, a couple of beers and a bubble pipe thing."

Max and Charlie drank, coughed and spluttered their way through the next few hours until they were reminded by the bar tender that it was nearly closing time and they should now be drinking up and finishing their last pipe.

"I don't know about you Max, but I feel a bit light headed. How are you feeling?"

"I'm not totally sure but I think I need to go to bed. My head's all over the place, like I'm on the Magic Roundabout."

"So while you're off your tits on bubble pipe fumes, I'll ask you again about your night with Steffi. What happened mate? Just between you and me, come on dude, spill the beans."

"Who's Steffi? What are you going on about Charlie? Look mate, I've had too much to drink and too much Shisha. Can we just go now and go to bed? Please!"

"Alright lightweight, let's get you to bed before you pass out."

Charlie helped Max across the street and up the stairs to their apartment, where he fell onto his bed and immediately to sleep. Charlie positioned the lightweight on his side, just as a precautionary measure, put a pillow under his spinning head and wished his out of it pal a peaceful night's sleep. Charlie took a couple of photos of Max, just for old times sake, grabbed a bottle of water from the fridge and spent some time alone on the balcony updating his Facebook page. Whilst Max was presumably still on his Magic Roundabout ride, Charlie was nostalgically looking back over his uploads from his week on Corfu with his best friend. The pictures he was looking at certainly told a story and very few would be able to guess that only a few weeks ago, Charlie was at rock bottom and with nowhere attractive, positive nor hopeful to aim for. But it was Charlie who told Max that when you've got nothing, you've also got nothing left to lose and Charlie was now definitely living by his own meaningful quote. He was bouncing back. One step at a time, one day at a time, one relationship at a time. All he needed now was a new job and a steady income again and he'd soon be back in the game. He was walking, talking, living proof that you can be down but never entirely out.

Someone who could do with taking a page out of Charlie's book was Kat. Now she was down. Completely and helplessly, down and out. It didn't matter how much money she was going to be paid at the end of the month nor how much wine she drank, neither of those quick but always temporary fixes were going to help her fix her troubles.

"Megan, everything's a pile of shit right now and I don't know how to make things better. Please help me."

"Okay honey. Finally you break your silence. It only took two and half bottles. Do you really want my advice?"

"Yes, yes I do."

"Okay. Start by drinking less and thinking clearly again, just like you used to. When you were able to help me and give me advice. You've lost yourself Kat. All you do now is work and occasionally find some time to have fun. From what you've told me, that's not how it used to be. Okay, we're going away soon but after that, what next? Back to work? Back to making other people more money, so they can then buy more temporary happiness? That's screwed up babe."

"What do mean Megan? That's just life, right or wrong?"

"Wrong Kat! It's a way of life, a way of life which people like you and I have chosen because we're told that's how it works. We work our tits off to make life easier and better for the likes of Fabio and Grant. You and I would both be replaced tomorrow if we decided to quit our jobs. Let's not kid ourselves here."

"Are you saying we should quit our jobs?"

"No, I'm just trying to be honest with you Kat and if you want me to help you, we have to be honest with each other, we both have to put our cards on the table. Look at my life now, what have I got to look forward to? A holiday with you, back to work and back to looking after my piss head of a mum. You're not the only one who's feeling it right now Kat, mark my word."

Megan and Kat spent a good hour trading words, woes, realities and alternative scenarios but Kat had not yet heard the answers she was hoping to hear. That probably had something to do with the fact that she hadn't yet asked Megan the all important question.

"Okay Megs! Now we've put the world to rights and kind of figured out an alternative future for ourselves, can I have your advice on Max and I?"

"Of course you can, fire away babe."

"It may not be relevant now, what with the photos I've just seen of Max and his new girl, but before Max left for Corfu, he was keen for us both to meet up in London. He hates London but the fact that he was prepared to do that, made me feel that we could sort things out between the two of us. You know, make things work again. Start dating again and then see how things go from there. What do you think?"

"Cut to the chase Kat, you want to get back with Max, don't you? But is that really what you've waited all week to ask me or have the photos of Max with another girl made you jealous?"

"Well, a bit I suppose but I was really looking forward to him coming to London to see me. I was hoping that he might start to like the place but now that idea is over before it even began. As you know Megs, I've got to go back to Yorkshire a week on Monday and I've currently got nowhere to live, now that Charlie has moved in with Max. I really don't want to go, I want to stay here with you and I want Max here with me. You see, everything's a mess right now and I've created it."

"I know and together, we'll find a way to make everything better, I promise you. Anyway, Max certainly isn't with anyone new tonight. Look at the picture which Charlie has just posted, he looks absolutely out of it."

Having spent a few hours in the company of Megan, Kat was starting to feel a little more relaxed about her life and love troubles. She had every faith in Megan when she told her that together they would fix things and everything would be okay. Megan was still upset at the thought of Kat having to leave London but was also wise enough to know that sometimes in life, things don't always go according to plan. Their friendship was strong enough now to cope with their separation and as long as they both remained committed to helping each other through the constant twists and turns of life, they would remain the best of friends forever. Kat had made a promise to drink less, relax more and make time for herself and tomorrow, before Kat went out for dinner with Grant, the girls would spend some quality down time together on Hampstead Heath. They'd also planned to hop over to Primrose Hill for a spot of lunch before heading back to Kat's place. Megan had asked Kat if she could stay for another night and hang out there while she was out with Grant and Kat had no problem with her request. In fact, she loved the idea of having someone waiting for her when she got home. Had it been Max waiting for her, she would of undoubtedly been made up but hopefully, that was for another day. Kat also had to catch up with Lucy over the next few days and ask her very nicely if she could stay at hers for a short while, just whilst she got her head around being back in the North of England.

As punctual as ever, Grant arrived at exactly six o'clock to take Kat out for dinner, his way of saying thank you for all the effort and hard work she'd put in over the last few weeks. Grant knew the entry code for the apartment block and made his way up the stairs to the second floor landing. He knocked gently on the door and waited for Kat to answer and let him in. Despite Kat's promise to drink less, she'd already had a couple of drinks with Megan and was in a pretty relaxed and jovial mood already, "Good evening Mr Fisher, we've been expecting you. Please, come and join us."

"Us? You have company? Megan! Have you moved in or are you just visiting?"

"Don't worry boss, just staying the night. Leaving in the morning. It's lovely here though, much nicer than our shit tip of a flat!"

"Stay as long as you like Megan, as long as that's okay with Kathy?"

"Don't worry Grant, we've got everything figured out. Haven't we Megs?"

"Okay Kathy, shall we go?

Grant had hired a driver again for tonight's dinner date and he joined Kat in the back of a very large and expensive looking Mercedes. The driver had clearly been given his rendezvous instructions before picking up his passengers as there was no 'where to mate' nor 'you'll never guess who I picked up the other night' banter, just polite acknowledgement, followed by careful driving and silence from the driver.

"Looking lovely as always Kathy. How's things with you?"

"Thank you Grant. New jacket or one from a vast collection of jackets?"

"It's a new jacket and how are things with you?"

"Things are okay. Could be better, could be worse but I guess that could be said for everyone. Right?"

"You're probably right Kathy but let's not get too deep tonight. Let's just kick back and take a break from all that stuff. I'm very aware of the fact that the workload of late has been taking its toll on you. You've more than pulled out the stops but trust me, things will be calmer and more relaxed now."

"You're obviously aware of the fact that I'm leaving London on the 21st? Apparently Fabio 'needs' me back up North. Together we're going to turn the Harrogate office around and start making profit again, instead of it bleeding him dry."

"I've told Fabio to cut his losses and close that office but he won't listen to me. Times are changing Kathy and they're changing quicker than many businesses can cope with. Your boss should consolidate everything into his London office and be done with Harrogate. Between you and I, consider Fabio's demands or requests seriously before making your move back up North. If you really wanted to, you could hold your own in London without Fabio and Fab Success."

"Thanks for the heads up Grant and I'll bare that in mind. I've got lots to think about right now but what you've just said makes sense to me and it may make one of my pending decisions easier to make."

"I'll leave the decision making to you and trust you'll do the right thing but we're at the restaurant now and I have a request."

"What's that?"

"Turn off work and worry mode!"

Chapter 31 ~ Blondes, Brunettes And A Beautiful Admission.

Grant had chosen a restaurant which overlooked The River Thames and offered spectacular views of Tower Bridge, The Tower of London and St. Katharine Docks and Marina. Grant was obviously a regular, or the staff were very well rehearsed, as the smartly dressed young man who opened the door for them referred to Mr Fisher as Grant, whilst welcoming him back with a genuine smile and polite tone of voice.

"Grant, lovely to see you again and you'll be delighted to know that we have your favourite table reserved for you and your guest this evening. On that note, who is the lovely lady on your arm this evening?"

"James, this is Kathy but I'm hoping one day I'll be able to call her Kat. Kathy, are we there yet?"

"Yes Grant, Kat is fine. James, nice to meet you and this place looks amazing."

"Thank you. Please, follow me and I'll escort you to your table."

It was pretty easy to see why Grant's favourite table was in fact his favourite. A large table for two with beautifully crafted woodwork and matching chairs which were dressed in purple velvet. James pulled out the heavy chairs and assisted Grant and Kat in getting comfortable for the evening ahead. James asked Grant if he wanted to see the wine list or was it a bottle of the usual. Grant knew by now that Kat liked her wine, so it was indeed a bottle of the usual. A bottle of Stopbanks, a Marlborough Sauvignon Blanc from 2018, was soon on its way. Whilst Grant was enjoying the views from their table, Kat found herself thinking about Grant and his mysterious life. Everyone knew him or of him. Every posh restaurant in London welcomed him back with open arms. He preferred quiet little bars over busy bars which played ChillHop or LoFi beats. Grant never went on holiday nor travelled outside of London. He obviously had a close connection to Fabio but was also happy to call Fabio out over his business decisions and apparently, there was no Mrs Fisher. Kat was intrigued by all of this and as she knew she may soon be leaving London and Grant behind, she had decided to dig a little deeper and uncover a little more of the elusive Mr Fisher.

"This is very kind of you Grant. It's nice to be out in London on such a beautiful evening but it saddens me to think that this may be my last time. Still, if it is, then what a way to leave town. Just look at the views across the river."
"It's my pleasure Kat and the least I can do to say thank you. I also appreciate what you've done for Megan. She's always worried me that girl but lately, she's like a different

person and I know you mean the world to her. I'm sure you know that already but please bare that in mind when you finally decide what you're going to do about leaving town and heading back up North. Megan will be devastated."

"That dilemma is top of my list of dilemmas but I'll have figured out what I'm going to do in the next few days. I need to speak to my friend Lucy tomorrow. She may be able to accommodate me for a week or so but if not, I'm not sure what I'll do. I can't move back in with Max, for obvious reasons, but he's also got a lodger now. It's his friend Charlie, who went to Corfu with him for the first week. He's home now but Max is still out there for another three weeks. Lucky bugger!"

"Have you and Megan decided where to go yet? It's not long now."

"Funny you mention that Grant. We've also decided to go to Corfu and we'll be flying out the day before Max flies back. I think we fly on the 1st of August, from Luton with one of those budget airlines. I've left Megan in charge of sorting the flights out and I'm dealing with our accommodation. We're really looking forward it."

"What about you? Any plans to get away this year?"

Over pre-dinner drinks and fancy starters, Grant and Kat exchanged general and lighthcartcd conversation. Touching loosely on holiday destinations, brief plans for the future and experiences from the past but nothing was revealed which was breaking news nor which may have come as a bit of a shock to each other. Kat was trying her best to gently chip away at Grant's armour but he was very good at swerving questions which he may have thought were deliberately aimed at opening him up. He was turning out to be a very secretive guy and that intrigued Kat further still.

273

James made sure that there was always a bottle of Stopbanks chilling in the ice bucket and it appeared that Kat was doing the lion's share of the drinking, despite her promise to Megan that she would real it in a bit. After all, it was Saturday night and possibly her last night out in the place she'd grown to love so much but also the place which was the root cause of all her problems right now. After downing a bottle and a half of wine, Kat was starting to feel the effects of drinking on a pretty empty stomach. Although the food at Grant's venue of choice was beautifully presented and delicious on the palate, Kat was left feeling hungry and craving something hearty. Max's Thai or Indian creations always hit the spot with Kat and from thinking about Max creating culinary works of art in their kitchen, Kat found herself thinking about Max and his new girl. The mysterious girl with golden blonde hair and piercing blue eyes, known to Max as Steffi. Maybe another glass or two would make her forget about her love rival. Maybe another glass or two would change the topic of conversation completely.

"So Grant or Mr Fisher. The mysterious Mr Fisher. Now I've let you in and you can finally call me Kat instead of boring old Kathy and you now know a lot about me and my life. What do I need to know about you and yours? I've trusted you over the last few months but apart from knowing that you fix up old buildings and you've known Fabio for years, I know nothing about you nor your life."
"I'm not entirely sure what else you need to know about me. Maybe it's time to get you home?"
"Maybe it's time for me to get things started? Okay Grant! Blondes or brunettes? Which do you prefer? You see I'm a brunette and you always tell me how nice I look. My Max

only ever loved a brunette but according to Facebook, he now loves blondes. So what's it to be blondes or brunettes?"

"Look Kat, I find this really awkward and do you really need another glass of wine? Let's not spoil tonight. It was supposed to be a thank you, a celebration of our successes but it's now turning into an episode of The Jeremy Kyle Show. James, can we have the bill please?"

"You prefer blondes, don't you Grant? You're just too nice to tell me that you don't find brunettes attractive. I get that, that's cool. My Max doesn't fancy brunettes anymore, he prefers blondes now. Maybe you and Max do have something in common after all. You both prefer blondes and how bloody typical. Maybe I should die my hair blonde? That'll fix everything. What do you reckon Grant, should I go blonde?"

"I think we should leave now. Let's go somewhere a little less public, have a break from the wine and drink some water."

Whilst James was preparing the bill, Grant called his driver and requested a change of plan. Instead of dropping Kat off and then disappearing to wherever he lived, Grant had decided to take Kat to his favourite little bar. The same place he went to after he'd heard enough ChillHop and LoFi being played at The Tabby Cat Lounge, the evening of Megan's birthday celebrations in Hampstead. The journey across London gave Kat a chance to sober up a bit and apologise to Grant for her behaviour in the restaurant.

"I'm really sorry Grant, really sorry. I've been drinking way too much lately and I'm well aware of what that does to people. Megan reminded me of that. A therapist would probably tell me that I'm coming undone or having some kind of breakdown and they wouldn't be wrong. I am coming undone and my life is a bit of a mess right now."

"Look Kat, it's fine and Megan has every right to warn you of the consequences which come with drinking too much. Just try your best to act on the advice which the people around you are giving you. If you take nobody else's advice, please take Megan's."

"I will and thank you for your advice."

Grant offered Kat a comforting hand to hold and although it wasn't Max's hand she found herself holding, she still felt comforted and protected. Kat knew that she had to sort her life out. She wanted to be back with Max and she also wanted Megan in her life. She knew that she'd neglected Lucy and might now need a big favour from someone who she hadn't spoken to for weeks. She loved Fabio but hated his idea of redeploying her back to the Harrogate office. She'd made a fool of herself in front of Grant and was now desperate to have blonde hair, just like Steffi. She definitely had a lot of life to sort out. Grant politely instructed his driver to park up somewhere near The Mount and from there, they had only a short walk to the bar. Grant continued to hold Kat's hand and reassured her as they made their way down the quiet and narrow side street. He'd also requested firmly that she went easy on the wine and asked her how she was feeling now. Kat had learnt her lesson and without hesitation, she told Grant that she was ready for an orange juice and she was now feeling slightly less under the influence. Grant pointed in the direction of an old Edwardian pub, which was sandwiched between two houses, and then made his way through the narrow double doors with Kat in tow. Once inside and seated next to the original fireplace, he reassured her once again before ordering some drinks.

"So, this is my favourite bar in London. What do you think Kat?"

"It looks really old but it's lovely in here. It's very calm and peaceful. You wouldn't know it was here if you weren't specifically looking for it."

"That's why I like it. Calm, quiet and private. You won't find Sky Sports or Karaoke in here. People come here to relax and have a quiet drink. Everyone's friendly and you can talk to other people if you want but if you want to be left alone, that's absolutely fine. Apart from it looking really old and lovely, do you notice anything else about this place?"

"I'm not sure what I'm supposed to be looking for Grant, are we now playing eye spy? Give me a clue."

Kat was baffled by Grant's question but continued to look around for something which he may have spotted, noticed or knew to be worth mentioning. Then the penny dropped and she thought she had her correct answer, "I might be completely wrong but there doesn't appear to be many women in here. In fact, I'm the only one in here. Is that what you're getting at Grant?"

"Well done Kat and well spotted. You wanted to know about my life? Well, I thought about what you asked of me in the restaurant and I think it's only fair you do know. But before I go any further, forget about my preference towards blondes or brunettes, neither particularly float my boat. In fact, I prefer a closely shaven head. Maybe even a bald one, if he's tanned and got the right shaped face. Another orange juice?"

"Can I please have a large glass of wine?"

Kat was slightly taken aback by Grant's out of the blue admission. It had nothing to do with what he had just told her but more to do with the fact that he'd gone from being the mysterious Mr Fisher to now being Kat's second gay friend, Fabio being the first. Fabio had been open with Kat about his sexuality since the very first day they met and he was comfortable talking about his life in London as a gay man. Kat thought back to the time when Fabio told her about his decision to leave the family restaurant business and the start of his new life in advertising. Exposed, vulnerable, naive and nervous but happy with who he was and focused on what he wanted from his life. He also explained to Kat the importance of having a good wingman. That special person who will always be there to catch you when you fall and say the right words for you when you can't think of anything to say. Fabio never revealed to Kat who his wingman was all those years ago but she had a sneaky suspicion that it may have been Grant. Kat wanted to check in with Megan and asked Grant if she could have a minute or two outside. Instead of Kat having to face the now much cooler London evening, he took himself off to the bar to chat to a guy who he'd clearly met before.

"Hey Megs! Are you okay my lovely?"
"Yeh, I'm good thanks. How's your evening with Grant going? Anything juicy to report?"
"Where do I start? I'll tell you everything when I get in this evening but it's been interesting to say the least. What are you up to?"
"I'm just watching television. I've found this series called The Durrells and it's all about Corfu and a family from

England who move there. It looks lovely but apparently there's no electricity on Corfu and only one taxi driver. A handsome guy called Spiros. He's a bit of alright though and I'm not kidding you Kat, I would."

"Oh The Durrells! Max would watch The Durrells until the cows came home. Have you eaten? Have you spoken to your mum?"

"Yes and kind of. I've finished some left over pizza and I tried to have a conversation with mum but she wasn't quite sure who I was and despite that, she kept asking me when Tony was coming home. I can't help her anymore Kat. She doesn't want to help herself, so what can I do?"

"Alright honey. Look, I won't be long, okay."

Grant had noticed that Kat had now ended her call to Megan. So he said goodbye to the guy at the bar by gently placing his hand on his friend's shoulder and made his way back to the table where Kat was seated, still curiously looking around at what was to her, a very unusual environment. Grant was just about to say something but Kat got there first with a question for him, "Why did you bring me here to tell me you're gay? You could have told me at the restaurant?"

"I feel comfortable here, that's why. The people in here know more about my sexuality and less about my business dealings and I like that. Old buildings and money making conversations are left at the door. Look around you Kat, show me someone who looks stressed out."

"You're so right Grant. Everyone appears to be very relaxed and at ease with each other. I really appreciate you being honest with me and for bringing me here."

"You're a sweet girl Kat and before tonight is over, I need to tell you a true story. One which may help you sort yourself out. But you have to promise me something."
"Of course Grant, what's that?"
"You keep it to yourself."

Chapter 32 ~ The Durrells And A Pizza To Share.

Megan had found herself instantly addicted to The Durrells and was rapidly laughing and crying her way through Series 1. The storyline confused her slightly but she didn't really care much about the story. She was more interested in the stunning scenery and was keeping herself amused by trying to match the characters in the series to the real people she knew. She'd paired Sven up with Grant and Larry was Charlie. Angry Leslie could be any one of her previous boyfriends and Louisa was Kat, desperately trying to keep everything together. Gerry was the kind and loving brother she never had and Spiros was simply gorgeous and out of her league. As for Margo, Megan saw a lot of herself in her. Just a young girl who was desperately trying to find the right guy. Megan paused watching The Durrells to call her mum again but got no reply. It was getting late now and judging by the state she was in earlier, Megan assumed that she'd finally drunk herself to sleep. After all, that was the usual drill most evenings. She hit play to continue watching her new favorite series and waited for Kat's return. She was desperate to hear about her evening out with her boss, so she propped herself up and turned the volume up a notch in order to stay awake.

In the old Edwardian pub, Grant had ordered another round of drinks and a pizza to share. It clearly wasn't just Kat who was still hungry after dinner at the fancy restaurant. Whilst they waited for their pizza to arrive, they joked about the tiny but delicious portions. Grant sipped on his whiskey and Kat went slowly on another glass of wine. It was the first time she'd seen him drinking whiskey, maybe this was another one of his secret pleasures. One which was reserved especially for his favourite bar.

"So Kat, as we appear to be leaving no stone unturned this evening, what's the deal with you and Max at the moment? From what you were saying earlier, it sounds to me like your Max has moved on and is now with a blonde girl."

"Well that's what it looks like. It's a little complicated but let me explain. Megan and Charlie are now friends on Facebook, Max and I don't do Facebook. Anyway, Charlie had been uploading photos from Corfu, photos which Megan could now see. There were quite a few photos of Max with this girl, obviously not your type, all beautiful and blonde and with the bluest eyes I've ever seen. She was like a catwalk model. They were holding hands in the water and at the dinner table. They were having dinner at the place where Max and I should have been going to but she'd obviously taken my place at the table."

"Max and this girl holding hands could mean nothing more than a close friendship. You and I were holding hands earlier and we clearly weren't going to end up in bed together."

Kat and Grant laughed at what they'd just said as if it was a way of life they'd both known about for years. Grant was a different man now and perhaps it was due to him being honest with Kat about his sexuality which was now allowing him to feel at ease and talk more openly. Kat now felt like she'd known him for years and not months.

"Before I tell you my story, tell me what you want Kat. What's going to make you happy again?"

"I want to be with Max again. I want Megan in my life, we're great together and I want to see Lucy again. We used to be so close. There's things I know about that girl which would genuinely blow your mind. She'd be all over you if you weren't, you know."

"Your route back to happiness doesn't sound that complicated to me. You've just got to prioritise the things which are important to you. Pick up your phone now and tell Max how you feel. Make plans which include Megan and then commit to rebuilding your friendship with Lucy. Your future happiness is in your hands now and it's down to you to make it happen. Let me tell you my story and remember what I said, this is between you and I."

Grant started by going way back to when he was a young boy growing up in the tough and not so trendy East End of London. He told Kat how his mum worked in a supermarket on Roman Road and his dad worked at Tilbury Docks. Mum kept the house neat and tidy and dad kept order around the house. Grant's mum was everyone's friend and his dad was a proper man's man. Short in stature, broad across the shoulders and with a handshake the Bionic Man would be proud of. In his early teens, Grant had little or no interest in girls and spent most of his time trying to help his mum and please his dad. Mum loved him for who he was, regardless, and as far as she was concerned, her youngest son could do no wrong. By contrast, Grant was a disappointment to his dad. He hated football and rugby even more. He refused to go with his dad to watch the boxing at the local club and he had absolutely no intention whatsoever of following in his father's footsteps by taking a manual job at the docks. Grant wanted to be an entrepreneur and when he left school with barely enough qualifications to catch a bus, that's exactly what he became. His journey started with a stall on Roman Road Market, selling fake Lacoste, Sergio Tacchini and Fila sports wear. However, after a couple of close shaves with the law, he decided it was time to make some clean and honest money. Before the East End became yuppie central, you could pick up a one or two bed flat or house for almost next to nothing. He used his slightly dodgy profits to raise some further capital and bought an old run down terrace on Zealand Road. After six months of hard and costly renovations, the old house was now hot property and netted him a very tidy return when he sold it. The rest, you could say, is history.

"By my early twenties, I knew I wasn't like all the other lads who had girlfriends. To be honest with you Kat, I found the handsome boys who had pretty girlfriends more attractive than their girls. That was when I started exploring the gay scene. I'd take myself off somewhere on a Saturday night, having told my mum and dad that I'd got a hot date with a girl up West, and I'd go looking for gay bars and clubs. I'd heard through the grapevine about this place in Hampstead, this actual place, and that's when everything started to make sense. That's when I met my first gay lover."

Grant paused for a minute as if he was either trying to remember what came next or he was reflecting on a period of his life which was still pure bliss or perhaps lost and now just captured in memories. "Is everything okay Grant? Please, don't stop now."

"Sorry Kat! I was miles away down memory lane for a while. Where was I? Oh yes, my first boyfriend. We were good together and we helped each other out in different ways. He was starting up his first business and I gave him some advice, not that I knew everything about running a business but I was already making my own money and had some experience. He'd already told his friends and family that he was gay, so there were no secrets but it was very different for me. I think my mum knew but dad either had no idea or he chose to believe the opposite. You know? No son of mine could possibly be gay and all that."

"It must have been difficult for you?"

"It wasn't easy, that's for sure but it was horrendous when I finally told my family. My mum was as understanding as ever but dad was having none of it and he gave me an ultimatum. He told me to sort my life, meaning get over the boys and get with the girls, or accept that I would never be a part of his family ever again."

"How could he do that? That's awful."

"I know. I wasn't expecting a celebration but nor was I expecting him to disown me for having a boyfriend."

"So what did you do?"

"I made the biggest mistake of my life Kat, that's what I did. After a wonderful year of being the happiest I'd ever been in my life, I ended the relationship. By then, I didn't care about my dad but the thought of not being able to see my mum, my brothers and my younger sister, that was unimaginable. About six months later I hooked up with a girl, it was all fake, all for show and I probably did it to validate my place back in the family. We married but it only lasted a year and a half. I'm surprised it lasted that long to be honest. She wanted to start a family but as you can imagine, that department really wasn't my forte."

Over another glass of whiskey and his share of a margarita pizza, Grant continued to tell Kat his story of true love, love lost and what he'd hoped would be love found. "Around the time of my divorce, my family, like many modern families, were now all over the place. Divided in their opinions, beliefs and what they each thought was acceptable. Dad and I never made up and he erased me from his life by telling everyone that he only had two sons and a daughter instead of three sons and a daughter. I would meet up with my mum at the weekend and we'd go for a walk around Victoria Park and then do lunch together. My brothers and my sister soon got used to who I really was and it was actually my sister who convinced me to look up my former lover. I soon found him. In fact, I found him again in here but by then, it was too late. He'd met someone else and they were officially a couple. Not married but going steady and very much in love."

"No way Grant! Listening to you is like reading a love story. I'm sorry, that must have sounded awful and your story is incredibly touching but I think you know what I mean?"

"Kat, please, you don't have to apologise. I know what you mean. A story of true love, love lost and the happy ending would have been love found. For me, that ending wasn't to be and this is why I've told you my story. Don't make the same mistake I made but if you do or you already have, don't wait too long before you try to correct things or make things better."

"Grant, you've never once mentioned his name. What was your lover's name?"

Grant paused for a moment before replying, "His name? His name was Fabio. I believe you know him?"

Kat joined Grant on his side of the table and gave him the sort of hug which was normally reserved for Max. She thanked him for telling her his story and because of that, everything now made sense to her and Grant was now officially the second most amazing guy in her life. All she had to do now was find her way back to her favourite guy, her Maxi, who was currently somewhere on Corfu.

Kat eventually arrived home just before midnight and found Megan fast asleep on the sofa. She said goodbye to The Durrells, dimmed the lights and took herself off to bed. Instead of counting sheep, she mapped out in her head her route back to happiness. The journey would start in the morning with a phone call to Lucy. With regards to Fabio's proposal, She'd pretty much made her mind up but needed to speak to Lucy first. Maybe Lucy would be in need of a break and fancy joining her and Megan on their trip to Corfu. She would need to speak to Megan about it and that would also happen in the morning. She would reply to the messages Max had sent her, the messages she'd previously chosen to ignore because of her anger, sadness and jealousy. She would get her excessive drinking under control and refrain from making a fool of herself in public. Kat would also love Grant forever, stay true to her promise and come what may, she would get back with Max.

Chapter 33 ~ Feet In Front Of Feet And The Corfu Trail.

Whilst Kat and Megan were still fast asleep, back on the beautiful island of Corfu, Max was up and on it and getting himself ready to tackle his first leg of The Corfu Trail. On this bright and sunny Sunday morning, he would leave Aspro Kavos and steadily make his way to Agios Georgios. This particular AG was located on the West coast of the island, South of Lake Korission and North of Santa Barbara Beach. Famous for its long and golden sandy shoreline and wonderful sunsets, AG South was a popular holiday destination with the British and the Germans. Max had booked a cheap room for the night and was hoping to arrive there no later than 3pm. To achieve this, he would have to leave Aspro Kavos at 8:30am but this schedule would allow him enough time to take a break and have some lunch in Lefkimmi. Following the advice which Kostas from Dafnata gave him, he put feet in front of feet and made his way out of Aspro Kavos and to the start of the trail. Max was now looking for a sign which gave directions to The Monastery of Arcoudilas but if he was lucky, he may even find an official sign for the trail. A small yellow metal square with the letters C and T, along with a directional arrow printed on it.

The trail started off on a scraggly concrete road which soon became a dusty sandy track. By ten o'clock it was already warming up and Max quickly found himself working up a sweat. The tall and gently swaying trees occasionally offered some relief from the early morning sun and after a few more twists and turns, ascents and descents, he found himself at the site of the ruins of the signposted monastery. His attention was immediately drawn towards the crumbling but still beautiful old building but when he turned around and walked towards the edge of the steep cliff, through a small clearing in the bushes, he was presented with the stunning views out to sea. He could see for miles and miles and could just about make out a couple of sailing boats which were gracefully making way through the calm blue water. Max stood for a few minutes just looking out to sea and all around. Everything was calm, everything was natural, there was no artificial noise and he felt incredibly privileged to be the only person who was enjoying this special moment in time. He took some photos of the monastery, a perfectly framed photo looking out to sea and then made his way down a narrow and slightly overgrown path. Blissfully unaware that back in London, Kat and Megan were also up and about now and busy crafting and creating their perfect future moments.

"Megs, before I tell you about last night and how I made a complete fool of myself, can I ask you something?"

"Come on Kat! You know me, you can ask me anything. What do you want to know?"

"How would you feel about my friend Lucy joining us on our holiday to Corfu? I haven't said anything to her yet because I wanted to speak to you first but she's cracking good fun and a genuinely lovely girl."

"Is Lucy the blonde one you were telling me about? If so, crack on and invite her. One blonde, one brunette and whatever colour my hair is. We might even get mistaken for Bananarama and net ourselves a few free drinks."

"Thanks Megs, you're an absolute treasure. She might not be able to nor want to come but I need to speak to her anyway about work and stuff so I'll give her a call now."

Megan was now in the kitchen knocking up two healthy breakfasts, she was in charge of making sure that they were both bikini ready in time for Corfu, while Kat was now on the phone to Lucy. "Hey gorgeous girl, I hope I'm not disturbing you and I know it's been too long but I really need to speak to you. I want to pick your beautiful brains, I might need a big favour and then tell me that you fancy a much needed holiday."

"Kat! Good morning and please tell me that you've called for a catch up and not because London is bankrupting you and you need to borrow some money. You know I would if I could but business ain't great up here at the moment. On both accounts and by that I mean the advertising game and rich men worth dating."

"Lucy, I think I know what you mean but it's Sunday and it's still quite early. Please explain in a way which is slightly easier for a mildly hungover thirty year old to understand."

"Sounds like my bestie has been out on the town again. Anyway, tell me about that later. New enquiries have dropped off the edge of a cliff. I haven't signed up a new client for nearly four weeks. I've now resorted to reaching out to lost business and if things carry on like this, I'll very quickly have to get used to living off my basic salary."

"And what about all the rich and handsome men who keep you well dressed, well fed and shower you with all the luxuries?"

"Well, the fact that I'm taking your call so early on a Sunday morning is a clue to how that's going at the moment. Last night, I was all dressed up, looking my best and ready to go on a second date with this lovely guy I met a few weeks ago and then my phone pinged. He cancelled on me by text at the last minute. Apparently he got called into work and that took priority over spending an awesome evening with me. I was really looking forward to seeing him again. He was a really nice guy and for the first time in a very long time, I thought that maybe this time around, things could be different. You know, make it work and have a proper relationship."

"You were about to break your rule Lucy. What's going on up there? What do I need to know?"

"I'm tired of all this playing the field. I'm thirty two now Kat and behaving like I'm in my late teens or early twenties. What will I be doing and where will I be in five years time? Washed up and punching above my weight, that's where I'll be. And on the subject of girls in their twenties, have you seen these chicks lately? Kat, I'm being replaced by younger models. Quite literally."

"Don't be stupid! You'll still be a catch when you're in your fifties and sixties. But if you are genuinely getting tired of the dating game and not just licking your wounds from last night, set your heart free. Let someone in and let someone love you. I know you're afraid of having it broken but it's not a physical break, it's an emotional thing and you know I'll always be there for you."

"I know you would but what do I do about work? The company won't keep me if I'm not making them money. I've already had my first performance review. You know how it works Kat, three strikes and you're out. It's not just me who's having a tough time of it though, apparently it's a regional problem. Businesses up here which are doing really well are not spending their profits on advertising and those which are struggling have already or will very soon run out of money. It's carnage and there doesn't appear to be any light at the end of the tunnel. I've got to find twenty five new contacts from somewhere tomorrow but as things stand, I reckon the best I can come up with is ten. I'll be lucky if I get a signature out of just ten contacts."

"Look Lu, don't get all stressed out over something which by the sounds of it is not your fault. I'm sure you'll work your magic and swing things around. Have you heard any gossip surrounding Fab Success."

"Oh yes sister! Where do I start?"

Lucy told Kat everything she knew about the problems and the goings on at Fab Success and she was shocked to hear that there had already been redundancies and staff who had chosen to leave before they were managed out of the business. She was even more shocked to hear that there were rumors going around that the Harrogate office was going to close and if you wanted to keep your job you would have to relocate or travel to London. Kat proceeded to tell Lucy all about Fabio's plans to redeploy her back into Harrogate in order to turn things around but from what Lucy had just told her, it sounded like her redeployment was going to be too little, too late. Kat had by now made her mind up and had decided that she wasn't going to run with Fabio's plan but she wasn't quite sure yet exactly what she was going to do if he still offered her no alternative. Megan tapped her on the shoulder to indicate that breakfast was ready so Kat told Lucy that she would call her back in half an hour and they both tucked into bowls of granola, fresh fruit and yogurt.

"So, is Lucy coming with us or not?"

"We didn't get that far but I'm not going back up North Megan, that's for sure. Lucy told me that there's big problems up there and if I'm being honest, I don't want to be a part of it."

"That's sweet music to my ears but what will you do if there's no other option?"

"I'm not entirely sure yet."

After breakfast, Megan tried calling her mum again but still couldn't get hold of her so she told Kat that she would have to head home and check that everything was okay. Kat called Lucy back and spoke to her about their upcoming trip to Corfu and asked her if she fancied joining them. Lucy jumped at the chance of taking a much needed break but had to clear it with her manager first but at the rate she was going, she might not even have a job to request leave from. Kat tidied up after breakfast and around her apartment and made herself another strong black coffee. She then set about replying to Max's messages. By now there was a bit of a backlog as she'd stopped replying days ago. She was kind of surprised but also delighted to see that the messages were still coming through on a regular basis. Every message which Max sent her included a photo or a few photos from his current whereabouts and a brief description of what she was looking at. The last photo he'd sent was from Aspro Kavos and it was taken early that morning as the sun was rising over Corfu. Roughly two hours before he was about to set off on his solo journey from the South to the North of his favourite island.

As Megan made her way back to the council estate which she hated so much, built in the late sixties as the ideal housing solution but now a den of crime and dysfunctional behaviour, Kat was falling in love with Corfu, one message and one picture at a time. She was now desperate to see Max again and she grilled herself hard on why she chose her career and London over the guy who meant so much to her. The boy who fought so hard to win her heart all those years ago. The same one who loved and adored her perfect imperfections and the lover she may now have lost forever. After Kat had finished viewing and then saving all the new photos to her Corfu folder she sent Max a message wishing him all the best on his hike. She finished her message with 'hope to see you soon' and would now have to wait patiently and on tenterhooks for the kind of reply she so desperately wanted to read.

Kat now had the day to herself and as it was a lovely warm day in London she decided to go for a walk around Hampstead Heath. She knew the place well now and could easily find all the best places to enjoy the very best views across the London skyline. The top of Parliament Hill being her favourite spot, the place where Megan first took her not long after they'd first met. However, before she even had a chance to make the short journey across town, her phone rang and it was Megan, "Kat! Kat! It's my mum, she's on the floor in the kitchen and I can't wake her up. What the fuck do I do Kat?"

"Call 999 straight away and tell them everything you know. Let me have your address and I'll be over there as quickly as I can. Do it now Megan, call 999 now!"

Chapter 34 ~ A Chance Encounter With Lara Croft And Ionna Triantafyllidou.

Kat was now racing across London and picking up points on her license like a bank robbery getaway driver. She was pretty sure that she'd been zapped twice for speeding and had jumped two red lights but she really didn't care. She needed to get to Megan's place as soon as possible but was terrified of what she might find when she got there. Megan had sent her the address of the flat where she lived but upon entering the concrete jungle which was home to some of the most unsavoury people you hope you never have to meet, the finer and final details of the journey were unnecessary. Kat first spotted an ambulance then an open door on the second floor balcony. She thought to herself, unless this is a regular occurrence around here, that must be Megan's flat. She ran up the stairs pushing a couple of skinny and pasty looking lads out of the way, confirmed the address, took a deep breath and then entered the tatty looking flat.

"Megan! It's Kat, where are you?"

"Are you Kathy? Megan told us that a friend was on her way. I'm Simon, one of the paramedics. My colleague is currently looking after Megan, she's in shock and needs some time and space to get herself together. Don't worry though, she'll be fine and we'll stay for as long as we need to. We also need to wait for the police to arrive but they won't be long now."

"What do you mean? Why the police? What's up?"

"We would have done everything we could but on this occasion, there was nothing we could do. I'm really sorry."

It turned out that Megan's mum had once again been drinking all day and then took some prescribed painkillers. The combination was just too much for her tired and fragile heart to deal with and her troubled life eventually came to an end. Another tragedy and another victim of unfortunate circumstances. Megan was now alone and had only Kat and a couple of other friends to rely on. Once Megan was stable and able to function again, Kat was allowed to join her in the living room. She scooped her up in her arms and told her to pack whatever she needed so that she never had to return to the place where so many bad memories were forged. Megan packed her clothes into a couple of old suitcases and put a few personal belongings into a bag for life. Trembling in Kat's arms, she waited with the paramedics for the police to arrive and do whatever it is they have to do under these circumstances and she thought briefly about the task of telling Tony.

Shortly after the police had done their bit, a white unmarked ambulance turned up to take the body to the hospital morgue. The police then left with Simon and his colleague, leaving Megan and Kat to have a quick tidy around, pack the last of Megan's stuff, lock up and never come back. Kat messaged Grant to let him know what had happened and he immediately replied with his deepest sympathies and told Megan to take as much time off as she needed. They drove slowly back across town to Kat's apartment and did their best to try and figure out what they both had to do next.

"I've never had to deal with anything like this before but don't worry Megs, together we'll sort everything out. How are you feeling now? You've got some colour back in your face, that's always a good sign."

"I knew this day would come and it would be just like this. I've been trying to prepare myself for it but nothing prepares you for the moment when you find your mum dead on the kitchen floor. I knew she'd gone and was now at peace but a part of me wanted her to wake up and realise that her life was still worth living and she would sort herself out. I tried Kat, I tried fucking hard to fix her but she was having none of it."

"I know you did everything you could Megs. I saw it every day and you couldn't have done any more. Let's get you settled at my place and if you fancy it, let's go and get some fresh air and clear our minds. I was heading for the heath when you called, I know you like it there."

"A walk on the heath sounds like a good idea to me."

"You and I have got a lot of stuff to figure out and get done now and we don't have much time to do it. I don't know about you babe, but I'm ready to get the crap out of this place and that doesn't mean that I've changed my mind about going back up North."

"What do you mean then?"

"Grant was right in what he said about London. He told me that this city will either make or break you and at the moment, I feel like the city is winning and we're losing. We need to go somewhere where life moves at a different pace, where the people are genuinely kind and caring and not pretending to be kind just because they want something from you."

"Do you mean Corfu? But we're already going to Corfu, in a few weeks. Kat, I'm confused."

"I know we're going to Corfu in a few weeks but I'm ready to go now. I'm also ready to rip up everything I know and start again. You and I are both good people and we deserve to be happy, not miserable and stressed out the whole time."

"Some happiness would be great and some sunshine. But what about work and we've got to deal with my mum's funeral."

"Like I said, we'll figure all that out and from what I've already read, it can take weeks to arrange a funeral."

"I'm glad you know what you're doing Kat because I don't know where to start. So what do we do now?"

"Megan, are you ready to rip everything up and start again? Will you come with me? We'll go in search of happiness together and we'll bloody well find it."

"Well I've got nothing left around here anymore, other than you and my job and I guess it's only a job. So why not."

The life which Kat was now craving was exactly the life which Max was now living and although in reality it wasn't ever happening, the clocks on Corfu appeared to tick slower than the clocks in London and even in Yorkshire. The people of Corfu were singing off a completely different hymn sheet compared to those living in England. In England it was all bigger, better, faster, more. On Corfu, they were happy with their small house and an old car. A moped was fine as long as it seated two and it was capable of carrying the daily shopping on the handlebars and what was the point of wanting more when you already had enough. Life on Corfu is different, it's not for everyone but for Max, it was perfect. Having spent the last hour wandering through quaint little villages and then in the shade of the olive groves, Max would soon cross the main road which led to the ferry port. Then he would arrive in Lefkimmi, known for its canal, Venetian architecture and traditional laid back atmosphere, and here he would rest his tired legs, get some air to his already blistered feet and consume as many calories as possible.

Before crossing the bridge which straddled the Potami, Max took a right turn and started looking for somewhere to enjoy a much needed lunch. He chose a little place called Agali. A cafe and restaurant which was located on the South bank of the river and right where all the fishing boats were tied up. He was instantly met by a pretty girl with long dark hair whose name turned out to be Kostantina and he seized the opportunity to impress her by practicing his Greek, "Kalimera, yassas."

"Kalimera, you speak Greek very well but I think you are English. I am right?"

"Yes, you're right. I'm Max and can I get some lunch here?"

"Of course, please, this way. I have a table which looks over the river, just here. Do you have any other Greek words for me or am I talking only in English now?"

"I know two more but I'll save them for when I leave. I already know what I want to eat, the beef Stifado with chips and rice and can I also get a Coke and a large bottle of water please."

"Of course, you must be hungry Max? I think also that you are walking the trail. By yourself, why by yourself Max?"

"Yes, by myself. My friend has now gone back to England and I'm currently single. It's a long story but I hope to get my girl and find my happy ending when I finish my walk."

"You are a romantic person Max and I like that. So, to get your girl, you will have to walk a long way and work very hard. The Corfu Trail is not easy and more harder when you find the big mountains."

"You mean Agia Deka and Pantokrator, the biggest mountain?"

"Yes, it is very high and the path is bad and very steep."

"You know a lot about The Corfu Trail."

"Yes, I do the trail last year with my boyfriend. But we do in April, when it is cooler. Not July, when it is what you English call roasting. You are crazy Max and must be careful in the sun. Please, drink lots of water and no beer until you end each day. Then you have beer and celebrate your win."

Kostantina fetched a map from behind the bar and whilst Max tucked into his generous portions of protein and carbs, she pointed out to him some places of interest which were dotted along the trail. Tough hills to climb, tricky descents to tackle, places where it was easy to take a wrong turning or get lost and local shops and tavernas where he could get food and water along the way. Max had told her that he liked photography so she also made him aware of the best places to take arty photographs of his beloved chapels, fishing boats, brightly painted doors and window shutters, stray cats and lazy dogs. The last thing Max needed in his life right now was further complications which were associated with the women in his life but he found himself instantly attracted to and in ore of Kostantina. Her shiny long black hair, perfect pillar box red nails and slender figure gave no clues away whatsoever to what she was quite clearly capable of achieving with a rucksack on her back and a pair of hiking poles. Max thought to himself that her boyfriend was one very lucky guy to be with a girl who appeared to model herself on a hybrid of Lara Croft and Ioanna Triantafyllidou. He also thought that it was time to practice his Greek again and say goodbye to Kostantina, "Efcharistó Kostantina, my lunch was fantastic and thanks for your help and advice. I need to get going now so can I please have the bill and I believe I should now say Ta leme Kostantina."

"Almost right Max, unless we are going to see each other later. If so, your Greek is splendid but I don't think we will be seeing each other tonight. You will be resting in Agios Georgios and I will be in Kavos having fun with my boyfriend. Let me get the bill for you. Cash or Card?"

Max settled his bil at Agali, hoisted his rucksack onto his back, waved goodbye to his action girl and started picking his way through the narrow streets of Lefkimmi. Venetian villas towered over the traditional single story buildings which could be found all over the island of Corfu and the eclectic mix of architecture was like nothing Max had ever seen before.

The Venetians had clearly stamped their mark on the island when they occupied in the 15th Century but it was also clear to see that the Greeks were not willing to be entirely influenced by their presence. No two buildings were the same size, height nor width and Max was intrigued to find out why and when the building of homes became so boring and uninspiring. This place was unique. It was magical and it was easy to see why the stray cats and dogs were so reluctant to leave town. Max had now crossed the road which led to the ferry port again but at a crossing which was slightly further North up the road and in the opposite direction to when he was heading for Lefkimmi. He soon found an official sign for the trail, backed up by a splodge of yellow paint on a fence post, he followed the directions and started a gradual climb on a sandy track which was heading in the direction of the West coast. At one point Max thought that the sun and the heat were finally taking their toll on him and he was starting to lose the plot. Instead, he soon figured out that The Corfu Trail did not follow a straight line, far from it. The trail appeared to be going round in circles and occasionally it would double back on itself before again, heading in the direction he wanted to go. After a brief rest in the shade of an old olive tree, Max found the strength to complete the last mile or so of his walk. Hot and tired and in need of a shower, he quickly located his accommodation for the night, dumped his heavy rucksack on the bed and made a beeline for a little bar he'd spotted which was near the beach. Max would now celebrate his first day win with a cold Mythos and a plate of salty chips.

Chapter 35 ~ Flipping Burgers Is Not For Everyone And Charlie's New Idea.

After Max had declared victory over his first day on The Corfu Trail, he took his much needed shower, stretched a few more cramps out of his tight and tired legs and counter balanced his beer consumption with equal measures of bottled water. Later that evening he would catch up with Charlie before his all important interview with Happy Burger, send Kat some photos of Lefkimmi and reply to the message she'd sent him that morning. Then it would be time for a hearty evening meal and a good night's sleep before tackling what appeared to be a slightly easier day two. Tomorrow's hike would start with a nice easy stroll along the beach before passing Lake Korission and Prasoudi Beach. The place where Max and Charlie had lunch and curiously eyed up the lobsters as if they were pretty girls and they were a pair of virgins in a nightclub for the first time. The destination for tomorrow was Paramonas but now it was time to call Charlie, "Max! How you doing, are you still alive?"

"Charlie boy! I'm alive but it was a tough today, I'm not gonna lie to you mate. At one point I thought I'd lost it, I felt like I was going round in circles but it's all good. I'm now in Agios Georgios, a little sore but in one piece."

"Well done you mate. You did good and keep it going. What's the latest with Kat and Steffi? Anything your Uncle Charlie needs to know about?"

"Nothing you need to know about fella. I've got this, I've got my plan and I'm going to get my girl. Anyway mate, I've called to say good luck for tomorrow. I know it's not your dream job but give it everything you've got. Make some money, treat your children and then start paying me some rent. And, keep the place tidy and no parties while I'm away."

"Anything else I need to do while you're on a roll?"

"I don't think so but I'll let you know if I think of anything. How are the kids?"

"They're good thanks mate. I'm not totally convinced that they really know what's going on but as long as they're happy, I'm happy. I'm sure things will get slightly more complicated when Laura and I have to make things formal but for now, I'm just going with the flow."

"It's all you can do Charlie. Anyway, I'll love and leave you and again, good luck tomorrow."

"Thanks Max! And remember what I said, don't over complicate things, keep it simple and happy hiking."

Max now got on with editing the photos he took around Lefkimmi in readiness to send to Kat. He picked his favourite five and sent each one with a description or note of interest. He also read the last message she'd sent him and replied after spending a minute or two carefully considering his response. There was also a message from Steffi, asking him how his first day went and reassuring him that she was still looking after his favourite Pink Floyd T Shirt and just to prove it, she'd sent him a picture of herself wearing it again. Max laughed to himself at the picture of her striking a beautiful pose whilst she appeared to be blowing him a kiss. Max was now all caught up with the people who were the closest to him and ready for some dinner and then bed.

Kat and Megan were now making their way back from Hampstead Heath having spent a good three hours strolling around the park whilst trying to come up with some genuinely workable plans for their future happiness. Kat had emailed Fabio requesting a meeting with him first thing in the morning in order to discuss his proposal. She was still adamant about not going back up North and wanted to inform her boss of this as soon as possible. The outcome of the meeting could be anyone's guess but by the time the meeting was over, either Fabio would have come up with another option or she would be out of a job. Megan had regained enough composure by now to call Grant personally and tell him exactly what had happened and Kat was not surprised at all to find that Grant was genuinely upset by the news. He told Megan not to rush back to work and he reassured her that she would not miss out on any of her bonuses. He also offered his assistance should she need any help with arranging her mum's funeral.

"You know what Megs, I had my doubts about Grant when I came to London and met him for the first time but the more I get to know him, the more I understand him and like him. He's actually a really nice guy. Kind, caring and considerate."

"Well he couldn't have been any nicer to me just then. At least four weeks off and no money worries. That makes my life slightly less complicated. I think that was your phone Kat, I'm guessing it'll be Fabio or Max."

Kat pulled her phone out of her bag to see whether it was Fabio, who didn't want to wait until the morning, or Max, who was also hoping to see her soon.

"It's Max, he's sent me some more photos. He's been to a place called Lefkimmi today and he's now in Agios Georgios. Both places look lovely and the weather looks fabulous."

"Has he just sent you more photos with the usual notes or did he say anything else?"

"Yes, he said that we have to talk but not over the phone. When we are both free, he wants to see me and talk about us."

"What, me and you? No Megan, Max and I!"

"Oh, I see. I've got you now. Okay, well at least he wants to see you. That's a good thing isn't it?"

"It could be but what if he wants to see me face to face to say goodbye. You know, one last moment together after all those years and before he gets on with his new life with her, the pretty blonde one."

"I think you're overthinking things Kat. I've never known a guy to choose that option. Surely if he was moving on with a new girl he'd choose the easy option and just send a text message or something. Sometimes I didn't even get a text, I'd just get ghosted and then see them out with another girl."

"Perhaps you're right Megan and I do hope so. I reckon we should get a couple of bottles of wine and watch a good romcom tonight. Do you have any favourites?"

"I know it's not Christmas but how about Love Actually? I love that film."

"Me too, it's one of my favourites but I'll warn you now Megan, I'll be crying my eyes out from start to finish."

That evening, Max slept like a baby with a belly full of food, beer and water. Kat and Megan laughed and cried their way through Love Actually and raised a glass to the plans which they had both agreed on. Charlie dropped his children off at Laura's parent's house before making his way back to Max's cottage on the green. He now had to muster up something to wear which would be suitable for his interview in the morning. Did he go all in with a suit and tie combo? What about smart casual or should he stick to what he does best? Oxbridge prep, courtesy of Ralph Lauren.

The following morning, Max set off along the beach of Agios Georgios, wearing his flip flops and in the direction of Lake Korission. His first successful milestone of the day would be a small bridge which allowed visitors and walkers to cross the salt water inlet to the lake. Kat made sure that Megan was okay and sorted for the day before heading across town for her meeting with Fabio. Charlie had opted for smart casual and was now trying to come up with some enthusiastic replies to the questions he'd figured he would be asked. He was cringing to himself at the thought of all the false pretense which came with finding and maybe securing a job he didn't even want but he knew Max was right and he needed to earn some money if he was going to be able to support himself and look after his children.

Max had found his all important bridge and was now pushing on to Prasoudi Beach. Kat was now waiting for Fabio to arrive at Fab HQ and Charlie was sitting in a holding room full of uninterested teenagers looking slightly overdressed in his smart casual attire. A lady wearing a trouser suit which had clearly been cut from a sheet of corporate bullshit cloth opened the door to the pen and called in the next candidate, "Charles Smyth-Buchanan, you're up next."

"It's okay to call me Charlie, everyone calls me Charlie. My best friend Max calls me all sorts of other names but I wouldn't repeat them in front of a stranger. Not that we're strangers, I guess if we're here, we're all friends now. You know, all wanting to be part of your organisation and make great things happen together."

"Charles, can you start by telling me a little bit about yourself. Let me give you some ideas: what are you currently doing for work at the moment. Without going into too many personal details, tell me about your family life. Do you have any children to care for. What are your hobbies or how do you like to spend your free time. And something which is very important to us, where do you see yourself in two to five years time?"

"Okay, I used to be a computer programmer but I lost my job to a robot, so I'm currently unemployed. My wife has just left me and taken our two children with her. Our house was repossessed by the bank because on my own I couldn't make the family ends meet. There's a high probability that I'll be declared bankrupt. In my spare time, but also as an essential to staying well fed and alive, I love cooking and make an almost perfect Sofrito, that's according to my friend Max. I've just returned from a trip to Corfu with Max and to be honest with you, I'd rather be back out there than sat here now telling you what you want to hear. I think my reply fits your script but please let me know if I've missed anything."

"I appreciate your honesty Charles and unlike many of the other candidates who are here today, you're obviously intelligent, you know how to have a conversation and form a sentence. Those qualities are important to our business but we are looking for people who can follow instructions. There's no improvisation nor making it up as you go along with us. You have to comply with the way things are done at Happy Burger. Every restaurant we have operates in exactly the same way. It's part of our model for success."

"It's Charlie, not Charles! My mother doesn't even call me Charles anymore. In fact, she hated the name but my father insisted on it. Look, whatever your name is. Do you realise you haven't even told me your name? I think we're wasting each other's time here and I guess I'll wait to hear from you. Or maybe not if your organisation rejects candidates by not writing to them and instead, prefers to leave them guessing for weeks on end as to whether or not they were successful."

"Well Charlie, there's never a dull day in the recruitment department and please don't take this personally but I think you're applying for the wrong job. We have positions available in the IT and Systems department which would suit your skills and personal characteristics better. I can get my colleague from that department to contact you if you want."

"Can I have some time think about things because I'm not entirely sure I want to work with computers again. I currently have a bit of a personal grudge towards them, one which I need to deal with and put to bed first. It's a personal thing, I'm sure you understand?"

"When you're ready Charlie. Like I said, we need people like you in our business, just not in our restaurants."

"Thanks for being honest with me and I'll consider your offer, just don't hold your breath. What did you say your name was?"

Charlie wasn't quite sure what had come over him but he knew one thing was for sure, his next job would not be at Happy Burger flipping beef patties like a robot and then wrapping them up in a piece of paper which had the correct folding instructions on it. He equally hated the idea of working with computers again, whether it was at Happy Burger's head office or any other organisation where technology was slowly but surely taking over. Charlie now had to come up with a new plan and he had to figure out what he was going to tell Max. After all, he didn't exactly sell himself nor did he give it everything he'd got. Before heading home for the day, Charlie decided to change back some left over currency he had and treat himself to a spot of lunch. It wasn't much but just enough to afford a freshly made sandwich and a coffee at one of his favourite little cafes. He'd been visiting this place for many years now and it was where him and Laura would sometimes meet up when they were together and their lives were happy, simple and affordable. Now their lives were apart, complicated and far from financially stable but Charlie's visit to Bella's Cafe had given him an idea. He just had to find a way and the money to make his idea work.

Chapter 36 ~ Bella's Cafe, A P45 And A Girls Holiday.

Fabio had now arrived for his meeting with Kat and she wasn't surprised at all to see that he was hungover. He also looked like he'd been dragged through a hedge backwards and could do with a short stint in rehab. The usually dapper and flamboyant Fabio looked like a businessman who was really under pressure and about to crack. She thought back over what Lucy had told her surrounding the state of affairs at Fab Success and focused on the rumours which were circulating. Maybe the rumours were true and not just malicious dirt which was being concocted and stirred up by the competition.

"Kat, good morning. Let's make this quick and to the point because I need to curl up and die somewhere for a few hours. I've then got a meeting with the finance team this afternoon. By then I need to be in a position to concentrate and make some important decisions. So what's the deal with this meeting you've called?"

"I don't want to go back up North Fabio. That's the deal with this meeting."

"Look my love, it's not about what you want. It's about what the business needs and my business needs you back up North. Harrogate is a sinking ship and you're the only one who can save it. Think of it as a opportunity to really make a name for yourself. You've made a name for yourself in London now with Grant so go back to Harrogate and do the same. You know, be the Angel of The North."

"Okay, I'm flattered but I'm done with making a name for myself. Let me put it another way Fabio, I'm not going back up North. It's not happening. Not for you, not for your business nor anyone else's."

"Then I'm sorry it has to be this way Kat and in light of your decision, the best I can offer you is a week's notice and a glowing reference."

"Thanks Fabio, thanks for everything! After how many years, this is how you treat me. Coming to London for you has cost me everything I had and everything I was happy with. I'm now out of a job, I've got nowhere to live and I've lost Max. Thanks a fucking bunch, thanks for nothing Fabio."

"Kat, I'm sorry but I can't carry your salary here anymore. Grant has spent a small fortune with us recently but he's not spending anymore for at least a year or two now. For once, he's playing it safe and watching his money very carefully."

"Save it Fabio! My last day will be the 21st and I wish you all the best with keeping your ship afloat."

Kat left Fabio to recover from his hangover and took herself for a walk along the banks of The River Thames. She was now just one week away from having no job, nowhere to live and from what she could establish from Max's last message, her time with him in her life, as a friend or a lover, had also run out. Just like Charlie, she had everything. She'd lost everything and was now having to start all over again from scratch. Kat was now close to tears and totally lost in London with only Megan for company. She would once again have to speak to Grant nicely and ask a huge favour of him but on this occasion, she would have to ask him if it was possible for both her and Megan to hang out at his apartment for a short while. At least while they both got themselves straight and in a position to start work on their plan, their journey back to true happiness.

Kat mustered up some strength from deep within and decided to break the news to Megan, "Hey honey! Are you okay?"

"I'm good thanks. I'm just watching The Durrells again and trying to write some nice words to say at mum's funeral. I've figured out that I'm going to have to tell a few white lies. I want to say that she was a fantastic mother to Tony and I but was she? She adored Tony, with all his faults and behaviours which mirrored my dad and she'd do anything for him but she was never there for me Kat. Yet I was the only one who was there for her, right to the very end. That's the reality of it but I can't say that, can I?"

"Maybe you could say that if things were different in her life, she'd have loved you and looked after you until the end and I'm sure she would have. Every mother wants to love and look after their children until the end but sometimes things get in the way and make it a bit more challenging."

311

"Yeh, that's spot on that is. That's what I'll say. Anyway, do you still have a job or are you now free to do what you want, when you want?"

Kat told Megan how her meeting with Fabio went and how her last day at Fab Success was Monday the 21st of July. She also told her that she was going to speak to Grant about her apartment arrangement and was hoping that he would understand and let them both stay for a while. Megan was obviously worried about Kat's pending situation but she had every faith in her friend that she would sort things out. She knew that Kat both wanted and needed some space and time to find herself and feel free again but Megan hadn't banked on her being prepared to quit her job in order to do so. When Kat told Megan that she was ready to rip everything up and start again, she genuinely meant it and was wholeheartedly prepared to see her plans through 'til the end.

According to Max's schedule, he was now a little over an hour away from Paramonas and happily flip flopping his way along a track which was protected from the early afternoon sun by cypress and olive trees. Apart from an old guy who was asleep under a tree with his dog, he hadn't seen anyone all day. He would occasionally talk to the goats and the sheep as if they knew what he was saying and he would whistle and sing to himself without a care in the world, "How I wish, how I wish you were here. We're just two lost souls swimming in a fish bowl, year after year. Running over the same old ground, what have you found? The same old fears, wish you were here." Singing this song by Pink Floyd got Max thinking about Kat and the wonderful times they had together before the breakup and he thought about how much he missed her when she would go away, which wasn't very often until she introduced London to their relationship. He was also thinking about Steffi and how she left him mesmerised with her performance of this heartfelt song whilst on Captain Homer's boat. Max stopped for a few minutes and rested his legs by sitting on the edge of an old stone well. He picked up a couple of stones and dropped one into the well to see if there was any water at the bottom. After a couple of seconds he heard a slight splash and his curiosity was satisfied. He downed the last of his water, demolished a couple of cereal bars and set about covering the last mile or so of his second day on The Corfu Trail. Max arrived at his accommodation for the night with plenty of time spare to enjoy a well deserved couple of hours by the pool. He sent Kat some more photos, replied to another message from Steffi and then called Charlie to see whether or not he would soon be in a position to start paying his way.

"So Ronald McDonald, for the sake of your children and my bank balance, did they offer you the job?"

"Not exactly Max. Over qualified is what I think she said in a roundabout kind of way but hear me out. Apparently I could easily land myself a job in the IT and Systems department at Happy Burger's head office."

"That's awesome mate and I'm guessing you'll take them up on their offer. When do you reckon you'll start?"

"With a bit of luck, never. I'm done with computers Max and ready to try my hand at something new. I went for lunch at Bella's Cafe after my interview and that gave me an idea. I'm going to open my own cafe or bistro and it's going to be called Charlie's."

"Am I hearing you straight? Have you been on the hubble bubble pipes again? Charlie, you haven't got a pot to piss in and you're thinking of starting up your own business. Where are you going to get the money from?"

"I've spoken to my parents and they're prepared to gift me some inheritance. It's not a lottery win but it will tide me over and get me started. I just need to find a suitable premises with the right usage and affordable rent. I'll need to fit a catering kitchen and deck it all out nicely. I was thinking about a Greek kind of theme, similar to Bacchus on The Beach. I'll also have to come up with an awesome menu and I was hoping you could help me out with that. I need to apply for an alcohol license, get the right insurance policies and I'll need to find some staff. I think that's about it? Easy peasy, right?"

"Charlie, I love you loads mate and you know I'll always have your back but on this occasion, I think you're insane and completely delusional."

"Excellent! So you've not said no to helping me create the menu, that's brilliant mate! You help me with the menu and leave the rest to me."

"For once you've left me speechless Charlie."

"Thanks Max and I love you too."

After Max had finished trying to figure out whether his best pal had either completely lost the plot or whether he'd created an unstoppable force of nature by helping him to cook, travel and see life from a different perspective, he went for dinner at Restaurant Sunset. Here he tucked into Charlie's favourite Greek dish, a chicken Gyros portion, with an extra tomato, cucumber and red onion salad on the side. He washed his food down with a couple of ice cold beers and then ordered a small bottle of Retsina, which went down perfectly with the setting sun. He thought briefly again about Charlie's plans to open his own bistro and came to the conclusion that his ambitious idea should actually be admired and he pledged to himself that he would do everything he could to help Charlie become successful in his new business. After all, that's what best mates do. They help and support each other, right?

Back in London, Kat and Megan were helping and supporting each other to get through some pretty dark and uncertain times. The reality of losing her mum was starting to catch up with Megan and she was constantly blaming herself for not being with her on that fateful Saturday evening. Kat kept reassuring her that she had done everything she could and the people who actually let her mum down were Tony and their father. Kat was playing it relatively cool, bearing in mind she would soon receive her final salary payment and a P45 from Fabio. However, she would occasionally have little panic attacks and come close to picking up the phone to Fabio and asking him if her job was still available. At that point, Megan would step up and tell her that everything was going to be fine as long as they both stuck to their guns. The two girls could really do with some good news on this Monday evening and it soon came in the form of a phone call from Lucy, "Kat my darling! When are you girls planning on going to Corfu?"
"Lucy! Well I'm free after the 21st and hopefully I'll stay free for the rest of my life. I've decided to leave Fab Success and currently have no idea what I'm going to do next other than find happiness again. Megan is on compassionate leave, I'll tell you about that another time, so she is free now and will be for the next four weeks. Please tell me you can join us."

"Yes, yes, yes you beautiful thing! I can take two weeks holiday after the 25th of July so let's see if we can fly on the 26th, if that works for you two?"

"Megan, it's Lucy. She can come to Corfu with us. How are the flight prices and availability looking at the moment?"

"Teeside is still the cheapest but we can only fly on a Saturday. Luton is not far behind though and there are more flight options."

"Right Megs, find us the best deal you can for Saturday the 26th and let's get out of here. The girls are going to Corfu!"

Chapter 37 ~ Grant To The Rescue And Max's New Family.

Megan spent the next hour exploring various flight options and concluded that it would be cheaper and easier for the three of them to fly from Teeside. Kat could drive and they could pick Lucy up on the way to the airport. Parking at Teeside was cheap by comparison to other airports and the return flights were currently showing at just under two hundred pounds each. They could fly out on Saturday the 26th of July and return on Saturday the 9th of August. Megan checked with Kat, who then checked with Lucy, that her suggestion worked for all of them and after a very positive nod from Kat, she booked their flights to Corfu. Kat and Lucy got on with the task of finding some nice places to stay, with a little help from Max's photos and notes, and quickly put together a two week schedule which would allow them to explore and enjoy the best parts of the island. The girls were absolutely buzzing now at the thought of jetting off to the sunshine island together and for two weeks, they could kick back, have fun and forget about their individual troubles, sorrows and dilemmas.

With no intention of extinguishing the excitement of going away, Megan raised a fair and valid point with Kat, "Unless he's changed his plans, you do realise that Max will still be there, somewhere on Corfu. Are you going to tell him that we'll also be out there?"

"Good point Megs. If I don't let him know and we happen to bump into each other, he'll think I'm stalking him or hunting him down like a crazy and jealous ex. I'll message him and let him know a bit later. It's only fair."

"Yeh, I think you should and you never know, he might want to meet up with you."

"Maybe, but I don't want to meet up in Corfu if it's to say goodbye for the last time. I want our trip to be remembered for all the good times we had and not a final goodbye from Max. I'll save that for when we're all back in England."

It was now the morning of Tuesday the 15th and according to his guide book, Max had almost five hours of hiking ahead of him before he would once again meet Kostas in Dafnata and hopefully enjoy a hearty Pastitsada cooked with man chicken and served with spaghetti. He made his way back up the steep hill until he joined the main road which continued to lead away from Prasoudi Beach. He was now looking for a steep concrete path which would carry him through the shady olive terraces, vegetable plots, old farmers huts and traditional dwellings. His book described a pretty little square and a huge lime tree which he should see just before he entered the village of Ano Pavliana. He reached the square and rested for five or ten

317

minutes in the shade of the mentioned tree. He hydrated his already thirsty body, munched on a breakfast bar and then continued along the winding trail towards Kato Pavliana. He would then pass through the beautiful villages of Vouniatades and Strongili before reaching a white monastery and then the final climb of the day to Dafnata.

Whilst Max was blissfully zigzagging his way from the West coast of Corfu to very nearly the East coast of the island, Kat was trying her very hardest to do as little work as possible for Fabio. He'd given her the task of chasing up some lost business, basically these were potential clients who'd chosen to take their business elsewhere, it was a thankless task and not for someone who was now less than a week away from leaving. It was usually a job which was reserved for the new starters who had a point to prove and could boast about how they managed to close the client when the sales executives failed. A successful call could last an hour or more and every objection from the lost client would be met with but, what if, if we can, are you sure and what if we can save you some money or generate you more business. Kat's calls were lasting no more than ten or fifteen minutes and for most of that time, she would be talking about the weather and her upcoming girls holiday to Corfu.

Megan was keeping her mind off her recent loss by watching back to back episodes of The Durrells and was now getting started on Series 4. The Durrell's rented family home was now open for business as a guest house. Gerry had just announced that he would soon be opening his own zoo and Margo was realising that making a career change and starting her own beauty business wasn't going to be as easy as she'd first thought.

Charlie was busy creating some sort of clever spreadsheet which would enable him to track and log his progress as he worked his way through the extensive list of things he would need to source, buy, create, register for and do before he could finally call himself a restaurateur. But Charlie was like a dog with a new bone and was determined to make his idea a reality and now he'd got a small budget to work with, some money to spend and a point to prove, nothing was going to hold him back.

Whilst Max took a short break before tackling the last climb of the day, Kat took a break from chasing lost business to call Grant, who was quick to answer her call, "The answer's yes Kat. That is if you're calling to ask whether or not you and Megan can use my apartment for a few weeks after the 21st. If you're calling to propose to me, then the answer's no. I'm now spoken for."

"I'm guessing you've spoken to Fabio?"

"Yes I have and I called him an idiot for letting you go. He's losing it Kat and if he's not careful and quick with some important decision making, he'll loose everything he's worked so hard for. You're better off out of there but what are you going to do now?"

"I'm not sure Grant but at the moment I don't really care. Megan and I and my friend Lucy are heading for Corfu on the 26th and that's all I can think about right now. Anyway, what do you mean you're spoken for. Grant, tell me more."

"Well Kat, it's early days but I've started seeing the guy I was talking to when you and I were out in Hampstead. You know, the one at the bar."

"That's amazing Grant and I hope everything works out for you guys. Maybe you'll start relaxing a bit more and who knows, do some travelling together."

"If it's going to work between us, I'll have to get used to travelling. A bit like you and Max, he's already visited dozens of countries and wants to visit more. He has this bucket list plan of travelling around the world and to be honest with you Kat, I kind of like the idea too. Do it before I'm too old and have to be pushed around the world in a wheelchair."

"You should Grant, just get on and do it, before it's too late. Remember what you told me?"

"I remember. On that note, what's the latest with you and Max?"

"I want him back, badly but it may be too late. He messaged me and asked if we could meet up. I'm guessing he wants to say goodbye for the last time."

"I think you should stop guessing and get to the point. Call him up and talk over the phone, you're good at that, it's part of your job. Close your man like you would close a business deal."

"Max doesn't want to talk over the phone, so it'll have to wait for now."

"Okay, just don't wait too long. Remember what I said."

"Thanks Grant, thanks for everything you've done."

"We're friends Kat, that's how it works now."

Having spoken to Grant about her apartment arrangements and other stuff in general, Kat was now feeling better about her life and the guy who she once compared to Diavlo himself, was now turning out to be her Guardian Angel. Always saying the right things at the right time. Listening carefully when she had nobody else to talk to. Providing advice and guidance when it really mattered and now, offering her and Megan some free accommodation in a city where renting a garage could easily cost you two grand a month. Kat had also noticed a slight shift in Grant's attitude or approach to life and for the first time since she met him at Fab HQ on her first day in London, she heard him talk openly about a relationship and the possibility of travelling or taking a holiday. Maybe Kat's story of comfortable security to short lived success and now emotional sorrow had triggered something in Grant which had made him realise that there was in fact more to life than working and making money all the time. She didn't want to take any credit for Grant's new persona but the thought of maybe having done so made her feel even better about herself.

Kat broke the good news to Megan and reassured her that they could stay on at Grant's apartment, but not forever or not for free, if they were looking at staying indefinitely. Megan let out a sigh of relief as one more life problem became one more problem fixed, at least for now. As much as Kat didn't want to go back up North, she was also done with London and although she had no firm ideas in her mind as to where she would like to settle next, it had to be warm, sunny and calm. Under no circumstances was Megan going to return to the flat where Tony was arrested and her mum took her final breath but similar to Kat, she hadn't yet thought that hard about where her next place to call home could be, feel or look like. Having said that, it had to be a safe and happy place and if at all possible, as far away from the troubles she'd had to live with for so many years. If a genuinely kind and nice guy like Charlie shared that new life with her, well of course, it would be about as perfect as perfect could possibly be.

Max had now reached the hilltop village of Dafnata and successfully completed his third day on The Corfu Trail. As he made his way through the quiet whitewashed village, where beautifully coloured and scented flowers provided a perfect and natural contrast and an abundance of photo opportunities, he felt an overwhelming sense of achievement. It had been many years now since Max had done some serious and proper hiking but he remembered it very well. It was in France and with Kat. Hiking was never really Kat's thing but because Max loved it, she dutifully followed her beau along every mountain pass and woodland path until they arrived at another sunset destination. Kat was always reluctant to lead a hike and instead, preferred to follow. Max would tell people that she chose that option so that she could constantly look at his perfectly formed backside and sprinter's calves. This silly little story would always raise a laugh or two and always a cute little blush from Kat. Max wasn't wrong though, Kat would enjoy that few more than the surroundings sometimes and it was of many reasons why she adored him so much. In her eyes, he was perfect, even though he would drive her crazy sometimes with his quirky habits and odd rituals.

Kostas was standing outside his place chatting to a fellow villager when Max came crawling up the road. He instantly recognised the now very weary solo hiker and put in a couple of meters for the team by meeting Max just up the road from his cafe. "It's Max, my boy! You say you be here at Tuesday and you are here. Well done my friend! You take my advice and you put feet in front of feet, yes? Of course yes, you here now. Ginger ale with lemon?"

"Kostas! Yes please and then a cold Mythos. I see from the blackboard that you have Pastitsada on the menu."

"The board is old dated but yes, Pastitsada tonight but with rooster, not chicken. The proper way and only for special family. You now in the family Max."

"It's been a very long day Kostas and I'm so glad to be here now. It's so quiet and peaceful up here. I'll sleep well tonight, that's for sure."

"Yes, I have your room ready. Your Charlie is back in England now? Sorry for him Max and he hopes to be here not there?"

"Probably. He loved Corfu and he had such a great time. Don't worry Kostas, he'll be back, I'm sure of that."

Max, Kostas and some very friendly people from the village all spent a wonderful evening eating, drinking and telling stories. Kostas challenged anyone to beat him at pool, but nobody did. Max tried his best to explain to everyone how he'd broken up with Kat, but nobody really got the story. As for the people from the village, they could have been saying anything, it was all Greek to Max, but he genuinely felt accepted and was more than happy to be a member of what Kostas called the family.

Chapter 38 ~ Kostas Has A Problem And So Does Max.

Max joined Kostas for breakfast at nine o'clock and while Kostas covered the table with toast, honey and jam, bowls of fresh fruit and yogurt, pots of coffee and glasses of orange juice. Max flicked through his guide book in order to get a feel for the day ahead. Either which way he looked at it, the hike from Dafnata to Pelekas was going to be a rollercoaster of a journey with many ascents and descents. Gillian, the author of the guide book which Max was relying on, recommended that hikers should allow at least five and a half hours and be prepared for a strenuous but rewarding day. Kostas told Max to take it easy at the start and to go steady on the climb up to the summit of Mount Agia Deka, as the climb could take even an experienced hiker well over an hour. Over breakfast they chatted about their lives in England and on Corfu. Max told Kostas all about his future plans and wishes and how he was going to make everything work and hopefully, live happily ever after. Kostas told Max that his cook was finishing on Friday and should he return, he should expect pizza or salads and not Sofrito or Pastitsada with rooster. Kostas excused himself from the table and proceeded to stick a small hand written poster in the window and another beside the bar. Max assumed that the posters had something to do with the upcoming job vacancy at Kostas Place but decided to ask the question anyway.

"Hey Kostas! What are the posters for?"

"I told you Max! My cook finishes Friday, to spend more time doing nothing. She also help with the rooms and cleaning. So after Friday, I screwed, as you say in England."

"And you honestly can't find anyone who wants the job up here, nobody from the village or from Strongili?"

"Nope! All the girls now want to do hair or nails, not cooking and cleaning. And the boys, well, this is not a man job. They want to play football but if crap, they drive a taxi or work a bar in busy towns."

"I'm not sure about making up the rooms and doing the cleaning but I know someone who would love that job."

"Who Max? Can she start Saturday?"

"I'm afraid not Kostas and it's not a girl or a woman. I'm talking about my friend Charlie. He's hoping to open his own cafe back in England but I reckon he'd jump at the chance to work in your kitchen, even if it was just until the end of the busy season. It could work well for both of you."

"If he come Max, I pay his flights and he stay here. He good cook?"

"He's very good and cooks an almost perfect Sofrito from scratch, even the sauce. But he also has two children and he has them every other weekend. It wouldn't work Kostas and I shouldn't have mentioned it."

"Tell Charlie bring the children. They can do rooms and cleaning. How it was on Corfu before modern times."

Max and Kostas laughed at each other, having talked a lot about his problem but without actually achieving anything, and Max then finished his daily routine of updating Charlie, Kat and Steffi. Kostas set about clearing the tables after breakfast, with a little help from Max, who was quickly figuring out where everything went, and then it would soon be time for the two of them to say goodbye. Max's phone already needed some extra charging and as he had a long day ahead of him, he plugged it into a charger which was on the bar while he squared up his bill with Kostas. Kostas couldn't remember what Max had last night but settled for twenty Euros and his help that morning after breakfast.

Max returned to his room to pack the last of his kit and was soon ready to head off again along The Corfu Trail. Kostas found Max in his room and gave him two bottles of water for the start of his journey and wished him all the best, "You good egg Max and welcome anytime at my place, welcome more if you happy to work. I joke with you Max. Follow a heart and I think you say, live a dream, yes?"

"Almost Kostas. We say, follow your heart and live your dreams and yes my friend, I most certainly will."

"Take care Max and be safe along the trail. You promise Kostas?"

"I promise and I promise to come back here with my girl."

"Good boy! Now go, before it gets hot."

Kostas helped Max ruck up for his long day of hiking and just about managed to squeeze the two bottles of water into his side net pockets. After one last very firm handshake, Max left Dafnata and made his way down the hill towards the village of Stavros and then Makrata. Here he would cross the Corfu Town to Strongili road and start the climb to the summit of Mount Agia Deka. The path on the lower slopes of the climb weaved its way through some long forgotten olive groves and the dry stone walls which made up the terraces were decorated in various shades of green moss. Needle sharp cypress trees had punched their way through the thick canopy and continued to reach for the sky, while wispy ferns were content with their life in the lower and cooler echelons of what could easily be compared to a film location from Jurassic Park. Instead of trying to flee from flesh hungry dinosaurs, Max enjoyed watching the graceful butterflies dance around like flying ballerinas and marveled at the way the tiny geckos would make themselves visible and then, as if by magic, disappear without a trace.

Whilst Max was happily lost in Corfu's very own Jurassic Park but still safely on The Corfu Trail, Charlie was scratching his head and trying his best to figure out why his clever spreadsheet continued to report a net loss and practically a zero chance of him lasting more than three months in business. He'd found a suitable premises but it was small and would only accommodate twenty covers at any one time. If he made a move on that place, he would have to up his pricing strategy or employ less staff. He changed some numbers on the sheet and instantly things looked better. Not much better but at least he would be making a small profit instead of a large loss. Higher prices or less staff, those were his only two options. As keen as Charlie was to open his new business and really start living again, he was terrified of finding himself high and dry once again and back on the bottom rung of the ladder. He would have to give this dilemma some serious thought and consideration before moving on but for now, he decided to take a break from the number crunching to catch up on the messages which Max had sent him last night and this morning.

Charlie smiled to himself at the photos of his best pal with Kostas and laughed out load at the fact that even after six games, Max was still unable to beat him at pool. The message which Max had sent Charlie this morning included a picture of Mount Agia Deka and the golf ball was clearly visible on the summit. His words read 'It's going to be the mother of all days today, so wish me luck and I'll call you when I arrive in Pelekas. Hopefully no later than 5pm. Take care fella, Max'. Although Charlie had no desire whatsoever to join Max on his solo hike of the island, he would have acted on the drop of a hat if Max messaged or called him up and asked him to join him again on Corfu.

Kat, Megan and Lucy also had a dilemma which involved some number crunching but it had nothing to do with creating a workable and profitable business model. Instead, it was more to do with how many bikinis, vest tops, sarongs and pairs of flip flops to pack, along with a collection or two of outfits which would be suitable to impress of an evening. Kat had never had to think about packing for this type of holiday as she'd only ever been away with Max and in typical Max style, it involved travelling light, washing clothes in the shower or even wearing them inside out if they were getting a bit grubby.

At Kat's apartment, Megan had started to unpack the stuff she'd crammed into the old suitcases which were last used for the purpose of happy holidaying when her dad was still around. One of them still had an outbound flight tag on which told a story of a pretty normal family doing pretty normal stuff during the long summer holiday of 2010. Megan thought long and hard before sharing the moment with Kat, "I would have been fourteen or fifteen when this case was last packed with my stuff and Tony would have been eleven or twelve. Without even looking at the tag I could tell you where we were going, it was Majorca. I remember Tony and I being really close back then and playing happily together while mum and dad tried their best to play happy man and wife."

"Could things have been different Megan? With your dad and your mum?"

328

"I doubt it. Even when we were in Majorca, dad was pissed by lunchtime and looking to fight someone. He'd even invite Tony to join him and when mum tried to calm things down, well, you already know what would happen next. I knew it was all wrong but didn't know what to do. Mum was afraid of my dad and then afraid of Tony and I witnessed it all. In all its messed up, screwed up and fucked up glory. Another normal family hitting the wall because of too much alcohol and too much attitude."

Kat left Megan to unpack her case and the memories of her last family holiday and got on with sorting her own stuff out. She'd arranged her chosen holiday attire into neat and folded piles which were colour coded and cleverly sorted in a way which would make a small selection of holiday clothing look like an entire fashion range. As she had always managed to do, Kat could pull off a miss matched bikini combo and pair it with a colourful wrap or sarong and still look as if she were about to glide down a Paris catwalk. After she was happy with her final selection, she made some coffee for them both, ignored a call from Fabio, closed her laptop and sat down to enjoy Max's latest updates. He'd also sent Kat some photos from Dafnata and these included one of the amazing view looking North with Mount Pantokrator in the distance. He'd added a note to this one which said 'I'll be hiking up and down this mountain in a few days time, I've got this Kat'. There were numerous shots of the beautiful flora which surrounded the village and a picture of some random salvage art which had been created by using a knackered old moped and a bicycle frame. He finished his message with a smiley face and a single kiss.

Back on The Corfu Trail, Max was now tackling the toughest and steepest section of the climb before reaching the summit of Mount Agia Deka. At this point he was glad he'd bought some hiking poles and was using them to both steady himself on the very rugged and uneven trail as well as using them to push himself up, what was in places, an almost vertical elevation. Up ahead of him he could see the bright blue sky, framed within a break in the thick canopy, and he focused on this as he pushed, puffed and panted his way up the final few metres. Finally he'd arrived at the summit and instantly spotted the small white chapel which he'd visited once before but with Charlie, Steffi and Bex. As was often the case along The Corfu Trail, Max found himself alone and enjoying the splendid views without any unnecessary noise nor interruption. With nobody else to talk to or to congratulate him on his epic achievement, Max congratulated himself, "Five hundred and seventy six metres up Maxi boy. You've officially earnt yourself the title of 'awesome dude' and now it's time to hydrate, get some snacks in the shade and then take some pictures. Well done, chap! Bloody well done!"

Max pulled out the bottles of water which Kostas had given him, he unwrapped some cereal bars and then sat in the shade of the old chapel whilst he got his breath back. After he'd cooled down a bit and his arms and legs had finally stopped shaking, he rummaged around in his rucksack for his phone. He checked his pockets and he checked in his rucksack again and again. He even emptied the entire contents of his pack and still couldn't find his phone. Then he remembered where he last had his phone…

"Bollocks! Fucking bollocks! Max, you total bell end, you've left it on the bar at Kostas Place!"

Chapter 39 ~ A Life Without Tech And Nina's Motivational Advice.

Max now had a dilemma of his own to deal with and this one would require some serious self-negotiation skills. Did he return to Dafnata to pick up his phone, a round trip which could easily take two to three hours and as a result, run the risk of not making it to Pelekas and his accommodation for the night. His accommodation was already booked and payed for and he knew where in the village it was located, so he didn't need his phone for that. Max always carried a small digital camera with him just in case anything happened to his phone, so he didn't need his phone in order to continue taking pictures along the way. He'd got his guide book, which was so far proving to be a life saver, so he didn't even need his phone for maps and directions. Max also had plenty of cash and a credit card on him, so he wouldn't need to access his banking app for at least five or six days. But what about Charlie, Kat and Steffi? He'd updated them all this morning on his progress and plans for the next couple of days ahead but after those days were up, how would they know that he'd successfully and safely made it to another location along the trail. Charlie would initially think that Max was having such a good time, he'd simply forgotten or found himself too busy to update him. Kat would more than like think that Max had once again met up with the blonde one and again, had little or no reason to keep in touch and Steffi would probably be thinking that Max had fallen or had an accident and was somewhere along The Corfu Trail and in serious trouble.

"Okay Max, you've got to make a decision on this or toss a coin and hope for the best. Heads you return to Dafnata, tails you push on without your phone and hope that your friends find your story mildly funny in five days time."

Max pulled a two Euro coin out of his pocket and tossed it high in the air before letting it land in the sand and gravel which surrounded his feet. He looked down at the coin and was instantly told that it was time to push on without his phone. Max packed up his rucksack, downed the last of his water and finished the last few crumbs of his cereal bars before setting off again in a round about way but generally in the direction of Sinarades. He quickly found himself descending on a wide but loose rubble track before taking a narrow and very hazardous old path which would finish at the Agia Deka road. Max would now be looking for a yellow mansion, where he would turn right and then locate a pretty paved square, and then, after a few more miles of pleasant ups and downs, twist and turns, he would be looking for the church tower at Sinarades. Here he would top up his water supplies, treat himself to the Greek version of a Double Chocolate Caramel Magnum, politely acknowledge a couple of old guys who were busy doing nothing and then continue on his way to Pelekas.

Back in London, Kat was still ignoring Fabio and was now refusing to make anymore lost business calls. Although things didn't end well for her at Fab Success, Fabio had at least confirmed by email that she would be well paid at the end of the month and there would also be what he called an additional 'thanks for everything' bonus. Kat now knew that she could survive for a month or two without working and that thought very much put her mind at rest. For the first time in a long time, Kat was starting to feel free again and she could feel the build up of stress and tension slowly but surely leaving her body. She quickly caught up with Lucy, made sure that Megan was still okay and then replied to Max's message and told him to be careful in the mountains. She ended her message with 'I know you've got this and I've never doubted you Max' and a cheeky face blowing a kiss. Just when Kat thought that she was all caught up with everything, Megan asked her whether or not she'd remembered to let Max know that they would also be on Corfu for a few days whilst he was there.

"Good shout and well remembered Megan, I'd completely forgotten and I'll do it now before I forget again."
"We're pretty good together you and I, what say you Kat?"
"We sure are babe but I think we're just getting started and some amazing times are ahead of us now. It's funny isn't it? How things sometimes have to go badly wrong before life gets better. Almost like a test or exam to see if you're ready or worthy of the better stuff."
"When you put it like that, totally. We just need to sort our love lives out, find somewhere beautiful to live and then win the lottery. It's really not too much to ask for."
"Maybe we should start buying some tickets each week then, in it to win it and all that."
"Or maybe we should just wait and see what happens when we're in Corfu."

Max was now just an hour away from Pelekas and the end of today's route could not come quick enough. His legs were tired, he'd got blisters on both feet, he'd finished the last of his water and was also out of food. Alone on the trail again and in the shade of the trees, he heard footsteps coming up behind him. He stopped briefly to see who or what it might be and was surprised to see a fresh faced young girl hiking towards him at a pace which could suggest that she'd only just set off for the day. The young girl stopped briefly to say hello but soon noticed that Max was struggling and hung around a while longer to make sure that he was okay, "You okay mate? You look like you're done for the day. Anything you need?"

"I don't suppose you've got some water which you can spare and a new pair of legs."

"Plenty of fluids dude but these legs are mine and that's the way it's gonna stay. Where you heading?"

"Pelekas, all being well. About an hour away I reckon."

"Yeh, a little under an hour now and it's pretty flat going from here but when your legs are tired, which I'm guessing yours are, it'll feel like you're climbing a mountain. Here, get this down you. It's got electrolytes in and it'll help you make it to Pelekas. I'll tell you what, let's walk together. I could do with slowing my pace down a bit. I'm Nina by the way and you?"

"Max, I'm Max and thanks for the drink with electros in. Is it meant to taste like that?"

"Like what? It's designed to help regulate your fluid balance and ph levels. It also helps your nerve and muscle functionality. You don't drink it for the taste, you drink it to perform at the highest possible level your body is capable off. You're new to this game aren't you?"

"You could say that. This is the first long distance, back to back hike I've done. Prior to this, I've walked around a few supermarkets and to the pub and back with my mate Charlie. He's back in England now."

"Okay! Well you're not doing too bad for a beginner. That is if you left Aspro Kavos four days ago and avoided the temptation to jump on a bus or hail a taxi."

"Hey! I may be a beginner but I'm not a quitter and yes, I left Aspro Kavos four days ago and I've been walking every day."

"Good lad. Start taking hiking and yourself seriously and who knows, you might be as good as me one day."

"You obviously do a lot of hiking then?"

"You bet I do and last year I solo hiked The Sentiero Italia. It took me eight months in total. You should try it, it's an epic hike and takes in some truly stunning surroundings."

"Sounds cool but let me make it to Pelekas first and then the end of The Corfu Trail in five days time."

Max and Nina hiked the last stretch of the trail to Pelekas together and whilst doing so, Nina told him all about the trails she'd hiked. She'd hiked around Italy, Spain and France. Australia, New Zealand and Thailand. Nina was only in her mid twenties but already had a wealth of experience under her belt and really knew how to explore off the beaten track. When they finally arrived in Pelekas, Max offered to treat Nina to a meal, "Look, it's the least I can do to pay you back for the drink and company. What do you say?"

"That's really kind of you Max but I'm not stopping at Pelekas. I'm cracking on until dusk and then I'll find somewhere to set up camp for the night and cook something up on my stove. You get yourself something decent to eat tonight, hydrate your body properly and by the morning you'll be raring to go again. Trust me, I know what I'm talking about."

"Well you take care, thanks for everything and happy hiking. Who knows, our paths may cross again."

"You never know Max and remember what I said. Start taking yourself seriously."

After Max had checked into his room for the night, washed himself and his kit in the shower and put on some clean clothes, he found a quiet little bar and ordered a beer and a large bottle of water. Max was still blown away by the stories which Nina had told him and just how much she'd achieved in her relatively short life. He compared what she had achieved so far to where he was right now with his life and although he had a pretty good life, he hadn't really done nor achieved anything which could form part of some motivational story or speech. Maybe Nina was right, maybe he needed to start taking himself seriously and actually get on and achieve or do something outstanding, instead of casually drifting his way through life. His chance meeting with Nina today made him even more committed to finishing The Corfu Trail and he felt fired up and ready to write some serious history.

It was now nine o'clock in Pelekas, seven o'clock in England and Charlie had still not heard from Max, who told him that he should be finished for the day by 5pm at the latest. Charlie had already sent Max a couple of messages checking that everything was okay and was now just one more unanswered message away from making the call. Charlie didn't want Max to think that he was treating him like a child who was allowed out after dark for the first time but he was genuinely getting a bit concerned. There were no photos sent during the day, something which Max would usually do and still no reply to his messages, which hadn't even been read.

"Come on Max you tosser! Where are you? Max, it's Charlie. I hope everything's okay mate and you've arrived safely somewhere, I think you said Pelekas today. Anyway mate, give me a call back or send me a message when you pick this up and hopefully I'll hear from you soon."

Kat had also been checking her phone and although she wasn't as concerned as Charlie was as to Max's whereabouts, she was a little bit disappointed that he hadn't replied to her cheeky face blowing a kiss. For now she would just have to wait and hopefully receive Max's daily dose of arty photos.

As for Steffi, we'll, she'd messaged and tried calling Max not long after he'd left Dafnata and needed a response from him pretty quickly. What Steffi had to tell him could potentially put a huge spanner in the works of Max's best laid plans and just as Nina had advised, Max may soon have to start taking himself and life very seriously.

Chapter 40 ~ Would He Think And Behave Like Bear Grylls, Probably Not.

It was now Thursday the 17th of July and having taken Nina's advice, Max had that decent meal she told him to have, he consumed a few beers less than normal, drank plenty of water instead and even managed to find some drinks at the local super market which had electrolytes in. One was bright red, the other was bright blue and both looked like a chemical you'd pour into a high performance racing car and not the neglected and generally unhealthy body of a thirty year old guy. Having said that, Nina was not wrong when she told him that he'd done well so far for someone who'd not trained for the event nor taken it entirely seriously. So, with Nina's advice still fresh in his mind, two bottles of wonder juice in his pack and a body which genuinely felt healthier and happier as a result of his new evening ritual, he set off once again along The Corfu Trail.

Today Max was heading for Liapades Beach. Located on the West coast of the island, just South of Paleokastritsa and incredibly popular with those who wanted to experience the rugged coastline and crystal clear blue waters of the Ionian Sea. In the late 70's and early 80's, both Liapades and Paleokastritsa were playgrounds for the rich and famous and were often frequented by members of royalty and those from the Hollywood collective. Nowadays, you were more likely to find rich Germans and Italians parading around in their tiny trunks and even skimpier bikinis. Max's stay would be slightly more grounded and he'd booked himself a small room above a supermarket which was located on the Corfu Town to Paleokastritsa road and a short walk from Taverna Spiros. His trusty guide book quoted six hours for today's leg, so

Max had decided to leave bright and early, shortly after 7:30am, in order to get some miles in before it got too hot.

Back in England and whilst Charlie, Kat, Megan and Lucy were still fast asleep and more than likely dreaming of Corfu, Max was living his dream and would soon be visiting Mirtiotisa Beach again, 'Perhaps the loveliest beach in the world', according to Lawrence Durrell. He would then descend into the Ropa Valley and pass the golf course before climbing up to the town of Giannades. He'd decided to take a short break here and grab some lunch from a small cafe before pushing on to Liapades. Although today was a long day on the trail, Max felt surprisingly good and was hiking along with a new found spring in his step. Perhaps it was down to his newly discovered drinks, maybe he was just getting fitter and stronger each day or could it be that he was focusing more on his challenging hike and less on his phone and it's constant distractions. That said and although he certainly wasn't missing the distractions, he was thinking about his friends back in England and how they might be coping with him now being officially lost in action.

Charlie was the first to rise and check to see whether or not there was any word from Max. Charlie's concern for him was just turned up another notch when he discovered that there were no missed calls and his messages still hadn't been read. Whilst he was making some coffee and fixing up some breakfast, Charlie racked his brains and tried to figure out what might be going on with Max in Corfu.

"Right Charlie, try and think clearly now! You haven't said anything nor done anything to upset him, check. What if

Kat's met someone else and wasted no time in telling him and now he's sulking and doesn't want to talk to anyone, it's a possibility and the sort of thing he'd do. What if he'd decided on a life with Steffi but she turned him down or it was only to be on her terms, doesn't bear thinking about. But what if he's had an accident, broken or can't get to his phone and is now stuck somewhere and quickly running out of food and water. Would he think and behave like Bear Grylls, probably not."

Having considered the various scenarios carefully, Charlie decided to call Max but once again, he got no answer and could only leave him another message, "Look Max, it's Charlie again by the way, I genuinely hope everything's okay mate and you're not in trouble but if your sudden absence has got anything to do with Kat or Steffi, stop being a cockwomble and start answering your phone or at least reply to your messages. If I don't hear from you soon, I'll have no option but to, well I'm not sure what to do next but please get in touch Max, please!"

Kat and Megan were now up and about and Kat was also checking her phone to see if there'd been any messages from Max. There were no messages nor daily photo dumps and as a result, a little piece of her heart just broke away and she found herself fighting back a little tear. Megan noticed her sadness immediately and sat next to her in a bid to comfort her and make things better, "Look Kat, I'm sure there's a genuine or plausible reason why Max hasn't been in touch. Maybe he's damaged his phone or something. He might even have lost it somewhere, we just don't know at this stage. Let's give it another day or so and see where we are then."

"I'm tired of living in limbo Megan and I either want to know where I stand or I want things to be back to how they they were. You know, Max and I back together and happy again. I can't wait any longer for an answer, it's just not fair."

"I know babe but give it a couple more days, please!"

"Are you still friends with Charlie on Facebook?"

"Unless he's cancelled me, then yes. Why?"

"Will you send him a message to see if he's heard anything from Max?"

"Of course, I'll do it now."

Megan spent a minute or two trying to figure out how best to introduce herself as a friend of Kat's and not just some random stalker who would then be deleted from Charlie's friends list. She'd always hoped that one day she would get to chat to or even meet Charlie but she hadn't banked on it being like this and felt a little awkward about the whole situation. But this wasn't about chatting up Charlie, this was all about her friend and trying to figure out what was going on with Max in Corfu.

"Hi Charlie! We're obviously friends on Facebook. I found your profile, sent you a friend request and you accepted. But I'm also a good friend of Kat's, you know, Max and Kat. Well, I'm currently living with Kat in London and she was wondering if you'd heard anything from Max? He seems to have disappeared and although it's only been a day, Kat says it's very unlike him and she's getting a little concerned. Please get back to me with whatever you know and I'll pass it on to Kat. Thanks, Megan. X"

"Hey Megan! I was wondering who you were and now it all makes sense. I'm glad I'm not the only one who was getting concerned about his whereabouts and you're right, it's only been a day but Max is a creature of habit and something is not right. The last time I heard from Max was on Wednesday, just before he left Dafnata. He said he was heading for a place called Pelekas. From what you've just said, I'm guessing that Kat hasn't said anything to him or told him anything which would upset him? Anyway, let's keep in touch and hopefully we'll hear from him soon. Take care, Charlie. X"

Charlie and Megan continued to trade messages for a while longer. Charlie promised her that he would let her know as soon as he heard anything from Max and Megan reassured him that she would keep Kat in the loop. She also told him that Kat was desperate to see and get back with Max and although she was trying her best to be calm about everything, she was just about keeping that part of her life together. Charlie didn't really know what to say or how to reply to that because for some reason, Max was keeping his cards very close to his chest, at least as far as the women in his life were concerned.

"Well Kat, I don't know if this makes things better or worse for you but Charlie's just told me that he hasn't heard anything from Max since the morning of the 16th, that's Wednesday. What are you thinking babe?"
"Oh shit! That's what I'm thinking now. What do you think we should do?"
"Charlie's promised to keep in touch and he said he'll let me know as soon as he hears from Max. We should

obviously do the same and like I said, let's give it another day or two before sounding the alarm."

"What do you mean sound the alarm? That sounds serious!"

"I don't know how we would go about sounding the alarm but I've heard that's what you do if someone is unexpectedly missing. I guess if it comes to that we would call on Charlie to help us out."

"Christ Megan! This is getting worse and sounding more like a suspense movie by the hour."

Max was completely oblivious to the mini drama which was slowly unfolding back home between his existing and newly connected friends and was now well on his way to Liapades Beach. Soon he would be making his way through the narrow streets of the village, past pretty little dwellings with beautifully painted doors and then arrive at the Cricketer Taverna and Liapades Beach Hotel. From here he would briefly start tomorrow's stage with a short boulder climb and then a climb up an old wooden ladder with a rope before joining the path and then arriving at his accommodation for the evening. Being the creature of habit which Charlie had described him as to Megan, Max washed his dusty and salty kit out in readiness for tomorrow's stage. A relatively short one by comparison but another stunning one which would take him to Agios Georgios in the North. He visited the supermarket which was attached to the rooms where he was staying and stocked up on his new favourite and brightly coloured drinks and then got his pack ready for another wonderful day on The Corfu Trail. After he was happy that everything was ready for another early departure in the morning, Max took a gentle stroll down the road and enjoyed a wonderful evening meal at Taverna Spiros. Mixed meat Souvlaki, chips and rice and a side salad of tomatos, red onions and cucumber all served with the customary dusting of dried oregano, a generous shake of salt and a good splash of olive oil. Just two cold beers and a large bottle of water washed it all down. Nina would have been proud of his preparation and performance today and after one more bottle of water to keep himself hydrated, it was time for Max to hit the sack again.

Whilst Max was peacefully getting in his much needed recovery sleep, Charlie was pacing around the cottage still trying to figure out what might have happened to or still be going on with Max. After almost wearing a hole in the carpet from pacing around, Charlie made a decision. If he'd not heard from Max by the 19th, he would contact the police on Corfu and also fly out in order to assist them with any enquiries or searches which may need to take place. Hopefully this would not be necessary and Max would just appear as quickly as he disappeared and he'll also have some random story to tell about how a goat ate his phone and how he had to hang around for a few days until the goat relieved himself. And while he was waiting, he could hear his phone ringing but obviously he couldn't answer it and it was all very funny if you were there but not if you were the goat.

"I've just had another message from Charlie. He's going to wait until the 19th and if he still hasn't heard anything from Max, he's going to contact the police on Corfu and fly out to assist them. Sounds like he has a plan Kat and I just hope it's all a false alarm but at least Charlie is taking this seriously now and we're not having to deal with this on our own."

"I'm frightened Megan, really frightened now! He shouldn't be out there, up in the mountains on his own. He should be with me and we should be exploring the island together. Just like we'd planned to do all those months ago. If anything's happened to him Megan, it'll be my fault, again!"

Chapter 41 ~ A Rusty Torpedo And Mission Impossible.

With still no word from Max, Kat spent most of her evening tossing and turning and trying to get some much needed sleep. But every time she managed to drift off, she would imagine she'd heard her phone and hoped it was a message or a call from Max. Charlie had set an alarm to go off on the hour, every hour and was also hoping to find a message or call from his missing pal but as another morning in London and in Yorkshire opened its doors, Max was still assumed missing somewhere along The Corfu Trail. With Kat and Megan's agreement, Charlie created a post with an up to date photo of Max and posted it in some of the Corfu Facebook Groups. 'Last seen in Dafnata at Kostas Place, now assumed to be somewhere between Dafnata and Pelekas but could now be as far up the West coast as Liapades Beach. Any information or possible sightings of Max greatly appreciated'. But by lunchtime, the only comments received were from what appeared to be a desperate looking woman in her fifties who wanted to know if he was single and another from a total moron who thought he knew everything about jungle survival.

Whilst Charlie, Kat and Megan were desperately trying to find out where Max could be, Max knew exactly where he was. He was now away from Liapades Beach and at the top of the first hill looking down on Paleokastritsa Bay. The view was mind blowing and although he was now starting to think that choosing to leave his phone behind in Dafnata may have been a stupid idea, his current location reminded him that after today's hike, he'd only got three days left on The Corfu Trail before he could then return to Dafnata, reunite with his phone and tell his story to Charlie, Kat and Steffi.

"Okay Maxi boy! Let's get going, tick off the village of Krini and then start the decent down the Kalderimi to another Agios Georgios. Another day soon in the bag and avoiding any total cock ups, this trail should soon be well and truly called a wrap."

The Kalderimi is an old mule track which pretty much connects the village of Krini to the coastal town of Agios Georgios and it's start, at the highest point, sees the track pass through a gap in the rocks which would have been cut out by hand many years ago. Once through the gap, Max would get to experience the most amazing views of the bay whilst descending gradually down through the olive groves until he reached the golden shoreline. Once again and in keeping with his budget, Max had booked a cheap room for the night at a small apartment block which was located just behind the Butterfly Bar. Here they served a limited selection of traditional cuisine but were known for their amazing pizzas and cocktails. As Max had set off bright and early and the route for today took just over three hours, it wasn't even mid afternoon yet in AG North, so he decided to take a wander around and then spend a few hours relaxing on the wonderful beach. He found this particular AG to be a rather odd place and lacking in the usual charm and character which he'd previously experienced along the trail and had grown to love so much. Personal opinion aside, there was still a fantastic range of bars and restaurants and he spotted one which looked suitable for a great evening meal whilst watching the sun set. Max had chosen a place called Athina and he wasn't disappointed at all with the food, the service nor the price.

Max's time spent in Agios Georgios turned out to be purposeful rather than enjoyable but after a great night's sleep on a full stomach and well hydrated body, he was ready for another tough day. Ahead of him he had almost six hours of trail hiking to cover before he would arrive at the mountain village of Sokraki. He'd purchased his usual supplies for the day from a small supermarket while on route and began an almost immediate climb up and away from the road which led back into AG North.

"Right fella, get to the villages of Prinilas then Pagi and then you should be able to tick off your first hour. Steady away Max, steady away and after today you'll be one day closer and only two days away from officially being a solo hiking legend. You've got this Max. Kalimera my friend, Kalimera!"

Whilst Max was happily greeting everyone he met with his best Greek accent, Charlie was now trying to decide at what point during the day he should sound the alarm and contact the police on Corfu. After all, it had now been four days without a peep from Max and today was the 19th, the day Charlie said he would act. Via Messenger, he decided to give Megan a call to see if they'd heard anything from Max, "Megan, it's Charlie! I hope you don't mind me calling you but I think we need to talk today and agree on a plan of action. Is Kat there? Have you heard anything from Max?"

"No Charlie, not a sausage from him and yes she's here. Let me call her. Kat! Charlie's on the phone and he needs to talk to you about Max."

"Oh dear God! Is it bad news?"

"Not entirely but there's no real good news either. Max is still missing somewhere and Charlie thinks we should now do something in order to find him."

"Charlie, it's Kat. Please do whatever needs to be done to find Max. I'm in pieces down here and it's all my fault."

"Kat, it's hardly your fault and I'm sure the daft bugger has just lost his phone or something. Look, leave it with me. I'm going to contact the police and check out some flight options to Corfu. I think I can fly from Newcastle late this afternoon and if we've not heard anything from Max by lunchtime, I'll be on that flight. Don't worry and let's keep in touch."

"Thanks Charlie! You're our hero and Kat will feel much better knowing that someone is now trying to find her Max."

It was now lunchtime on Corfu and Max had now reached the hilltop settlement of Agios Athanasios. Here he would need to locate an old rusting torpedo which was either placed there strategically as a reminder from the war or it had completely missed its target and almost hit the hilltop monastery. Max found the weapon of mass confusion and proceeded down a flight of steps in time with the monastery bells. His next checkpoints were the villages of Rekini and then Valanio. He rested and replenished his supplies at a tiny store in the village of Valanio and spent a calm and relaxing ten or fifteen minutes exploring the beautiful village with its cute little houses, chapels and abundance of colour and charm. He left the village on a narrow path which skirted around the left flank of the village cemetery and soon found himself in a vast forest of olive and cypress trees. After just under an hour of level hiking, Max would soon start the steady climb up to the village of Sokraki, his finish line for the day. Once he'd arrived in the village, he quickly located a small cafe called Emily's, where he grabbed a cold drink and a freshly baked pastry, before heading gently downhill to the Agallis Corfu Residence. Max had really spoilt himself with his choice of accommodation here because this place even had its own pool which offered stunning views of Mount Pantokrator. A great view indeed but also a solid reminder of what was in store for him the following day, his penultimate day on The Corfu Trail.

Lunchtime in England had also passed and Charlie was now in a taxi and on his way to Newcastle Airport. Carrying with him just a few basic items and enough clothes to last a week, he dashed across the busy car park, cleared through customs and made his way to the departure lounge. The plane was due to leave on schedule and he had just enough time to try Max one last time before take off, "Max, it's Charlie! You better have a good excuse mate because I'm about to board a plane to Corfu. We're all going to pot back here while you're gallivanting around Corfu on your magical mystery tour. Look mate, if something serious has happened, I'll take that back but anyway. When I land, I'm heading for Dafnata and I'll see if Kostas can help. Love you Max, you fucking idiot!"

Before putting his phone on Flight Mode, Charlie quickly messaged Megan with a brief rundown of his plan and where he would be heading for as soon as he'd landed in Corfu. The last thing everyone needed right now was more uncertainty and one more missing person. Soon he was in the air and on his Mission Impossible to hopefully find Max and reinstall some normality back into everyone's lives. Megan had by now read his message and updated Kat on what was happening and she referred to Charlie as her Tom Cruise, on a mission to find the missing asset. For the next three hours or so, Charlie occasionally slept while Megan and Kat waited patiently for further updates from there superhero. Charlie's flight touched down bang on time and he wasted no time at all in hailing a taxi to take him to Dafnata.

"Kalispera my friend! Are you free?"
"Yes, I free and you been here before? You Charlie, yes?"
"Yes I am and it's Spyro, isn't it?"
"Yes but where Mad Max, he not with you?"
"Spyro, it's a long and complicated story and I never thought I would say this but as quickly as you can, Dafnata please."
"You stay with Kostas, right? I know Kostas, we do school together but lots of years ago."
"Why doesn't that surprise me Spyro? Now, fill your boots and let's get going."

"What you mean Charlie, fill boots? I wear Adidas Gazelle ."

On the way to Dafnata, Charlie kept his mind off the terrifying journey by explaining to Spyro what had happened or what he thought may have happened to Max. Spyro offered to help by calling on his friends and family to organise a search party and Charlie kept his business card just in case that was necessary. Soon Spyro was racing up the hill from Benitses and in the direction of Dafnata. It was like a scene from Mario Karts or The Italian Job and he was genuinely enjoying the fact that for once he had a real good reason to drive like a maniac.

"Just here Spyro and thank you for everything. I've got your number just in case I need any help."

"Yes Charlie, here, Kostas Place. On the right. Good wishes Charlie and call me if you have problems with Max."

"I've had problems with Max all my life but that's a story for another day. Take care Spyro."

The village of Dafnata was as quiet as usual and the only place where the lights appeared to be on were at Kostas Place. Charlie quietly approached and softly called out to see if anyone was around, "Kostas, are you here? Anyone about?"

"Charlie! Yes, Kostas here and I think Max sent you for my job here. Please tell me yes, you here to work at my kitchen and make my rooms nice."

"Not quite Kostas. I'm here looking for Max. Can you help me?"

"You come late Charlie! He here on Tuesday, I say four day ago and you should also."

"I know he was here on Tuesday Kostas but we haven't heard from him since then and yes, that's four days ago now."

"Okay Charlie, that a problem and in the morning we must start looking for Max and when we find him, we give him this and tell him to be better careful in future. This Max's phone, yes? It need charging now."

"Yes Kostas! That's his phone."

That evening, Charlie and Kostas cobbled together some food and set about drawing up a plan. Over a few beers and then a couple of bottles of Retsina, they studied an old copy of the guide book and established that if Max was strictly following the route he should be in Sokraki and in the morning he would start his hike to Old Perithia. Kostas explained to Charlie that unless you had a helicopter, it was almost impossible to find someone along The Corfu Trail and even if you did, you still wouldn't find a missing person who was in trouble and amongst the thick canopy of the many forests and olive groves.

"Kostas has a plan Charlie. In morning we drive to Sokraki and ask if people see him. It be a small village with not many places to eat. If Max has been, the villagers will know. You have new photo of Max, yes?"

"Yes Kostas, I have dozens. Take your pick."

"Charlie, this could be serious and many people have problem with our trail. So please, serious now. If Max in Sokraki now but leave in the morning, we drive to Perithia, the old village and we wait there. Now, tell your people in

England what happening and then bed. We may have long day tomorrow."

Charlie called Megan and Kat and told them that he'd now got Max's phone, which had been left on the bar at Kostas Place and in the morning they would start their search for him. At last there was some good news surrounding Max's disappearance but for now, they all had to hope and keep everything crossed that he'd not had any problems along the way and he was still safe and well and following the guide book to the very word and by every mile.

Chapter 42 ~ The Story Of Mr Siriotis, David And Goliath.

Kostas owned a VW Mk 1 Golf which used to be Rosso Corsa or Racing Red but after years of exposure to the sun, it now looked as if it had been washed with bleach every week and then dried with wire wool. Kostas assured Charlie that his old car was still good for at least another hundred thousand miles and would easily make it up and over Mount Pantokrator if they had to drive to Old Perithia in order to find Max. They grabbed a few bags of crisps and some oranges from behind the bar and set off early in the direction of Sokraki. It wasn't a straight forward journey and the road they were on took many twists and turns and Kostas would be stopping all the time to chat to people as they passed through each village. It was if everyone on the island of Corfu knew Kostas and everyone had the time to stop and chat to him. Charlie asked him if he was asking whether or not they'd seen Max and Kostas replied with, "No Charlie, we talk about the football and crazy politicians. We look for Max when we at Sokraki. That is the plan."

After what felt like a two hour roller coaster ride, they pulled up just outside the centre of the village and then on foot, looked for some signs of life and maybe even Max. The village was quiet and only a small shop and Emily's Cafe were open. Kostas told Charlie to go to Emily's, because she spoke perfect English, while he checked in the shop for any clues.

"Kalimera Emily, I'm wondering if you can help me."

"Well I'm not Emily but if I can help you, of course I will. What can I do for you?"

"I'm Charlie and I'm looking for my friend, he's called Max and here's a recent photo of him. Have you seen him lately?"

"Yes, of course Charlie! He was in here yesterday. He bought a bottle of our ginger ale and a cake. He's a handsome boy your friend."

"At the moment, he's a bloody pain in the arse but that's fantastic news."

"Have you seen him since yesterday?"

"Yes, he was here about an hour ago, maybe a little more. He bought another drink and a spinach pie to go. He said he was leaving the village early because he had to climb the big mountain. You know, Pantokrator. I asked him where he was going after he'd climbed the mountain and I'm sure he said Old Perithia. You know, the old village."

"I'm so sorry! I didn't ask your name."

"That's okay Charlie. I'm Sophia but my friends call me Sophy."

"Sophy, you have just made me the happiest man alive and if I had the time, I'd tell you how your news is about to make a friend of mine the happiest girl in the world. But seriously, my friend Kostas and I need to get to Old Perithia as soon as possible. I love you Sophia and have a great day!"

Charlie found Kostas outside the shop chatting to someone else he knew or someone who just wanted to talk about football and politics but there was no time for chit chat today and with a positive and unquestionable sighting of Max now chalked up on the dashboard, it was time to hit the road again, "Kostas! Max has been here and he's heading for the old village. We must go now! Come on Kostas, football and politics can wait."

"This great news Charlie and I told you my plan will work."

"I don't remember you telling me that your plan would work Kostas but yes, it's great news. How far or how long until we get to Old Perithia?"

"The way to the old village is not a simple way Charlie. The new road up starts the other side of Pantokrator, on Kassiopi Road but there is the old mountain road. We take that track, we break my car or maybe die. So we go a long way but the safe way."

Kostas pointed his trusty VW in the direction of Ipsos and took off down the road with Charlie clinging on to the dashboard for dear life. Once through Ipsos, they would join the coast road up to Kassiopi and then continue along the North coast of the island before taking a sharp left, passing through the village of Magarika and then Loutses before hopefully arriving safely in Old Perithia. Charlie remembered the drive up to the old village from when he did the very same trip with Max in Jimny. Back then, it was all a little bit more leisurely and laid back and there certainly wasn't any urgency involved. But this time, Charlie and Kostas were on a mission. Not exactly on a mission from God, like Jake and Elwood Blues, but instead, a mission which was way more important than putting a band back together. This way all about bringing people back together and putting smiles back on people's faces. Whatever happened after that was in the hands of Cupid and for Max, it was all about doing the right thing for once. As for Charlie, well he had no expectations nor hopes which extended any further than seeing his stupid mate again but he did kind of like the idea of meeting up with Megan once all the drama was over.

"Megan, it's Charlie. Are you free to talk for a few minutes? I've got some good news and hopefully the news is about to get even better."

"Sure Charlie! What's the latest news? Please tell us that you've found Max and he's okay."

"We've not found him yet but he was in Sokraki last night and this morning. A girl in a cafe recognised him and she thinks he's on his way to where Kostas and I are now waiting. It's an abandoned village called Old Perithia and Max and I came here when we were out here together. We've just got to wait now and hope he turns up."

"Fuck me Charlie! You're the man and I honestly don't know what Kat and I would have done without you."

"You'll need to thank Kostas as well. He came up with the plan and got us here, hopefully before we've lost Max again."

"Kat and I will pay him a visit when we come out to Corfu, that's on the 26th, it's a Saturday."

"What do you mean 'when you come out to Corfu'? I didn't know that you and Kat were coming out here."

"Yeh and Lucy is coming with us as well. We fell in love with the place after we'd seen Max's photos. Kat sent him a message to let him know but I guess he wouldn't have seen it and therefore, he wouldn't have told you. How long are you staying out there for?"

"I've no idea Megan and because of that I'd only booked a one way flight but let's find Max first and then go from there."

"Sounds like a good plan Charlie, please keep in touch and maybe we'll get to meet up at last."

Kostas and Charlie took up a table at Taverna Foros and over lunch, kept a watchful eye for their missing person. Charlie started to tell Kostas the story about Thomas and how his family saved his home from the wild fires but Kostas was already there, "Mr Siriotis and the family are heroes here Charlie. They fight the fire with buckets and bare hands. They like Dave and the giant."

"You mean David and Goliath?"

"Yes Charlie! The small wins over the big guy. It the same with Mr Siriotis. They win over the terrible fire, a big fucking fire Charlie but they win with buckets full of water and hands."

"It's a miracle Kostas, a bloody miracle."

"It not a miracle! It what you do if you want to save someone or something."

Charlie thought for a while about what Kostas had just said to him and he was so right. If you really want someone or something. If you desperately want to achieve something or make a positive change to your life or that of someone else's, you have to fight to make it happen and sometimes with your hands. Thomas delivered two bowls of his signature salad and a basket full of freshly toasted garlic bread to their table. Charlie thanked Thomas for the food and Kostas got ready to bless him like a famous footballer who had just scored the winning goal in a cup final, "We must bless Mr Siriotis Charlie, he his a man which looks like everything good, and his family. His beautiful family are good family."

They both closed their eyes for a minute to say a blessing and whilst doing so, Charlie felt a wave of emotion flood over him. It was a feeling he'd felt before whilst sitting on the balcony with Max on their first night in Corfu together. It was what Max had described as the magic of the island. Sometimes you could see it and taste it. Other times, you just knew it was there and this time, sat at a table outside Taverna Foros with Kostas, the magic of Corfu was there and all around them.

"Charlie! Wake up now! Look, look up there!"
"What am I looking for Kostas?"
"Look, there be a person coming down the hill on the trail. I think Max?"

Charlie used his phone to zoom in on what Kostas had seen and lo and behold, there he was. It was Max, looking as fresh as a daisy, as tanned as a pro cyclist and as happy as a pig in muck, gingerly making his way down the steep hill towards the village.

"I don't know whether to hug him or put him on his back Kostas. What would you do?"

"Love your friend Charlie. He done good on the trail and tomorrow is easy peasy day for him. I think you could do tomorrow, it that easy."

"Thanks Kostas for the advice and the compliment but this boy has created chaos for his friends and it's time he grew up and started acting like an adult."

"Yes Charlie but give time. We learn in different ways and maybe this is his school."

Max had now disappeared behind the old buildings and would soon reappear and be greeted, along with somewhat surprised, by Kostas and his old pal. Charlie ordered in another salad and a beer in readiness for his arrival and sat patiently waiting for Max to rock up. Soon, Max turned the corner into the square which played host to Taverna Foros and caught his first glimpse of Charlie since dropping him off at Corfu Airport, just over a week ago.

"Charlie, Kostas! What are you doing here?"

"Max, have you forgotten something?"

"Oh yeh, sorry! Nice to see you guys and what a lovely surprise but I finish The Corfu Trail tomorrow, in Agios Spyridonas. Not here in Old Perithia."

"Your phone Max! Are you missing your phone?"

"Funny you say that. I think I left it on the bar at Kostas Place."

"You did Max and it be a big problem for your friends. They worried for you and that why we here now. You boys need to talk. I come back soon."

Although Charlie was over the moon to see Max and delighted to hear that he had so far been having a fantastic time exploring Corfu on foot, he was still livid with his friend for being so inconsiderate towards other people's feelings.

"Max, you've got to start taking life seriously and start thinking about other people. We've been worried sick since Tuesday and as happy as I am to be back out on Corfu, I really wish it wasn't like this. I fucking love you mate but please, sort your life out and find some real purpose. Set about doing something amazing and think seriously about making someone's life magical again and you know who I'm talking about."

"I get it Charlie and I guess you're talking about Kat, right?"

"Yes Max, I'm talking about Kat. A lot has changed back in England while you've been away. Start by checking your messages and voicemails, that would be a good idea."

Over lunch at Taverna Foros, Max and Charlie caught up on all the going's on back home and Max told Charlie some of his tales from the trail. He told him how he tossed a coin at the summit of Mount Agia Deka and therefore it was the coin's fault and not his. He told him about Kostantina from Lefkimmi and Nina, the pro hiker who he'd met on the way

360

to Pelekas. He described every gut wrenching climb in accurate detail and helped Charlie picture every stunning view, beautiful sunrise and wonderful sunset. Charlie explained how they managed to track him down and if it wasn't for Megan's friend request, Kat would have had no idea what was going on and how things would eventually end up being just about okay. Kostas had now arrived back at the table and once again had a winning plan which would involve Max and Charlie hiking the final leg of The Corfu Trail together. He would then pick them up outside the yellow church of Spyridonas and taxi them back to his place in Dafnata. There they could both spend a few days getting everything straight whilst helping him out around his taverna as a way of saying thank you.

"So boys, you like my plan?"
"Yes Kostas, we love your plan and we'll see you again tomorrow."

Chapter 43 ~ It's All Work And No Play At Kostas Place.

After Kostas had left for his place and lunch at Foros was over, the boys took a short walk up the hill to The Merchant's House. Max had chosen to spoil himself on his last night along the trail and had booked a luxury double room which he was planning on enjoying all to himself. However, with Charlie now in tow, it was now a luxury room for two after David and Marieka, the delightful owners of the establishment, kindly let Charlie stay for the night in Max's room. That evening, whilst sat on the terrace outside their room, they continued to swap stories from their week apart and tried to figure out just how everything had changed so much but in a strange kind of way, everything seamed to be getting back to normal pretty quickly. Charlie spent a good hour on a video call to Megan and from what Max could hear, they appeared to be getting on like two peas in a pod. Max continued working his way through all the missed calls, voicemails and messages which were waiting for him before taking a short break to call Kat.

"Hey you! It's me and before we go any further Kat, I owe you an apology. I'm not sure what I was thinking but it's been brought to my attention that I was only thinking about myself and that's going to change from now on."

"Max, it's so nice to hear your voice again. I was so worried, we all were. We had no idea where you were or whether you were safe or not but thanks to Charlie and Kostas, now we know. Megan has been keeping me in the loop and she told me about their plan to find you. Have you picked up my messages yet? Do you now that Megan, Lucy and I are flying out to Corfu on Saturday the 26th?"

"Yes Kat, Charlie mentioned it briefly and apparently it's my fault because I sent you all the lovely photos I'd taken and you girls had then fallen in love with the island. With or without my photos, it's easy to do and you'll soon see for yourself just how beautiful it is here."

"So, with Charlie being there again, what are your plans now? Another lads holiday on the beer and babes?"

"No, far from it. Tomorrow, Charlie and I are going to finish The Corfu Trail together and then we're going back to Dafnata to spend a few days at Kostas Place. He's picking us up from the yellow church, that's the official end of the trail. Apparently we're helping him out around his taverna as a way of saying thank you for his help. It'll be fun and the least we can do to pay him back. You never know Kat, I might get used to working at his place and it is a beautiful village."

"What are you like Max? You've been missing for almost a week but already, I can't keep up with your crazy plans and ideas."

"Hey! There's nothing crazy about wanting to work at Kostas Place and it's surely got to be better than working at a Wetherspoons or a Premier Inn."

"When you put it like that, I can't really disagree with you Max. Anyway, I hope you don't mind but we're going to drop by Dafnata on the Sunday after we arrive and say thank you to Kostas. Will you guys still be there?"

"Yeh, I reckon so but if anything changes, I'll let you know. It'll be good to catch up with you Kat and by the sounds of it, we've both got a lot of catching up and talking to do."

That evening, Max and Charlie spent another wonderful evening in the company of Thomas and his family at their beautiful taverna. The drinks were flowing, stories were being told and everyone was having a great evening but something was on Max's mind and Charlie could spot it a mile off, "What's up fella? Is normal life starting to become a reality again now all the fun and excitement is almost over? Is the thought of driving a van for a living again getting you down? If so, I don't blame you mate. I know how much you love this place and to be honest with you Max, I'm not far behind you there. Come on mate, what's up?"

"I've had a few missed calls and messages from Steffi and apparently she needs to see me before her and Bex leave on the 26th. She said we need to talk and it's really important."

"Then meet her somewhere and listen to what she's got to say."

"I've already arranged it Charlie and we're meeting up in Benitses on the 25th at seven o'clock but it's just the two of us. Bex won't be there, before you get any crazy ideas."

"Well, there you go. All sorted and like I said Max, listen to what she has to say and then do what you need to do. Just don't do anything stupid. Right, it's time for some more beers and then let's get on the Ouzo shots."

Slightly hung over from the night before and one too many shots, Max and Charlie finished another fantastic breakfast at The Merchant's House and were soon on their way along the final leg of The Corfu Trail. The relatively short and mostly descending route shouldn't take them any longer than three hours and was perfect for a beginner like Charlie. For Max, today's hike would be a walk in the park by comparison but it would also be a special day for him. After nine days alone and with only the occasional stranger or donkey for company, Max would finally complete The Corfu Trail and he would cross the finish line with Charlie by his side. Once again and like it has been on so many occasions before, the two of them together until the very end. Through thick and thin, the ups and downs and the break ups and make ups of life. Both of them still had their share of dilemmas and difficulties to deal with up the road but for as long as they stuck by each other, everything would continue to be okay in the end.

Before starting a gradual descent through a thick and ancient olive forest and then crossing the dry river bed of the Parigori River, they stopped briefly to take in the views looking North and in the direction of the golden coastline which they would soon be walking along. No words were needed nor spoken as the sound of the gentle sea breeze and the native birds collaborated with the scent of wild oregano and flora to create an experience which no poet could match. Now in the shade of the forest and following a gently undulating path, Max and Charlie both found themselves bouncing along like spring lambs. Soon they would join a quiet lane which would eventually met the Kassiopi road. Once crossed, they would walk along a back road to Almiros Beach and then follow the coast until they crossed a bridge at Lake Andiniotissa. Having left the bridge behind them, they would soon spot the yellow church and all being well, Kostas and his Mk 1 Golf waiting for them to arrive.

"Boys! My boys! You complete The Corfu Trail. Good on you both!"

"I'm not going to lie Kostas, today was a killer and I couldn't have done it without Max by my side. He's a legend!"

"Right, we go now. I have more guests at my place and they hungry, they are walkers doing the trail and want proper grub, not pizza and salad."

"Ready when you are Kostas and Charlie and I are ready to work for our keep. We won't let you down, will we Charlie?"

Back at Kostas Place in Dafnata, a group of hungry and tired looking walkers were waiting under the canopy and in the shade it provided. It was a very hot and very still day on the island of Corfu and everyone appeared to be doing everything they could possibly do in order to do as little as possible. Kostas welcomed his new guests with a round of complimentary drinks. Max hurried around doing exactly what he did best and that was tidying and straightening everything up so that the place looked as neat and as organised as a show home and Charlie had made a beeline for the small kitchen and was quickly rummaging through the store cupboards to see what he could knock up for lunch.

"Kostas, how about stuffed peppers with green beans and pan fried artichokes? Served with a traditional salad and warm pitta bread."

"Charlie, you must stay and work with Kostas. Tonight you cook Sofrito? Max tell me your Sofrito is best. Let me tell our guests. People, for lunch: stuffed peppers, green beans, artichokes from the pan and our special salad with pitta bread. For dinner: Sofrito with French chips and rice. Lots of beer and then Ouzo. Everyone happy?"

The announcement was met with a round of applause and while Charlie quickly got on with making lunch for everyone, Max was busy clearing tables, fetching more drinks and keeping everything neat and tidy. As for Kostas, well he was stood outside his place chatting to some people from the village, more than likely about football or politics. Although it was hot and hard work, both Max and Charlie we're happily having the time of their lives and never had work been so much fun and so rewarding.

"Hey Charlie! Are you still keen on the idea of opening your own cafe or do you now fancy the idea of staying for a while and working for Kostas?"

"You know I can't stay Max, I've got my children back home in England. Anyway, it looks like you've found your calling and an alternative to driving a van. What are you going to do?"

"I love it Charlie, absolutely love it but like you said yesterday, I've got to sort myself out and stop playing at living and my love life still hangs in the balance. Remember that small technicality?"

After the lunchtime service was cleared away and the kitchen cleaned down and ready to go again, Kostas, Max and Charlie enjoyed a few games of pool. Kostas remained unbeaten, a round or two of beers were consumed and it was soon time to enjoy some down time before the guests wanted feeding again. That evening, Max did a marvelous job of making everything look cosy and inviting for the group of walkers, Charlie was busy in the kitchen preparing his Sofrito and Kostas was happily watching his favourite football team win their first game of the season. The evening service went without a glitch. The walkers had been well fed and had no idea that the Sofrito had been lovingly cooked by Charlie, who had never cooked for a group before nor worked in a catering kitchen, and while Kostas held front of house, Max shared his story and his tales from The Corfu Trail. It was almost as if the village of Dafnata was totally immune from anything going wrong, any chaos or drama and with a little bit of luck and improvisation, great times were always guaranteed.

The group of walkers had now retired to their rooms, Kostas had also decided to call it a day and had left Max and Charlie to do the last of the cleaning down and then lock up once they'd finished the beers and a small bottle of Ouzo which formed part of their salary for the day. The two lads were relaxing and chilling outside as if they owned the place when a smart looking car pulled up, driven by a very handsome looking man.

"Good evening boys. Kostas told me he had found some help, are you the help?"

"I guess that's what we're called. I'm Max, this is Charlie. Are you here to see Kostas? If so, he's called it a day after a busy one and we're now holding fort. Can we get you a drink?"

"Yes please Max and I'll have a small red wine. Chilled though, try looking on the bottom shelf in the drinks fridge."

"You speak excellent English. Have you spent much time in England?"

"Yes Charlie and it's where I met Kostas. We both worked at the same hotel in London. Kostas was working to pay for his travels and I wanted the experience of working for a large hotel chain. Kostas soon returned to Corfu to open this place but I stayed a few years longer. When I returned to the island, I opened my first hotel and as you say, the rest is history my friend."

"Here you go sir, chilled red wine from the bottom shelf of the drinks fridge."

"Max my friend, this is Corfu and my name is Vasilis. Vasilis Panayiotou and it's an absolute pleasure to meet anyone who is a genuine friend of my dear friend Kostas."

"Thank you Vasilis and although we've only known Kostas for a handful of weeks, we already feel as if we are part of his family."

"You are part of his family and our family my friends. On Corfu, we are one big family and that's the way it should always be. Anyway, please tell Kostas that I dropped by and remind him that we are doing dinner together in Benitses on Sunday. Seven o'clock at Vana's Family Taverna. Hopefully you two can join us, that is if you're not holding fort?"

Chapter 44 ~ Vasilis Panayiotou, Writing Chapters Together And Yamas.

Max and Charlie finished their beers, downed a shot of Ouzo each, locked up for the night and went to bed. It had been another crazy and surreal but fabulous few days on the island of Corfu for the boys. Max had gone from being on Corfu's most wanted list to being head bar tender at Kostas Place and Charlie was still lapping up the attention which came from being Corfu's very own Tom Cruise. Kostas was clearly head of operations and controlling every move from behind his bar whilst watching television and occasionally shouting at people down the phone. The following morning, the group of hikers were up early and ready to tackle their very own journey from Dafnata to Pelekas. Charlie had anticipated an early start and was already bossing the kitchen while Max ran backwards and forwards with plates of eggs, bacon, beans and toast. There was also fresh fruit, picked from the trees that morning, bowls of yogurt with honey and endless pots of coffee and jugs of freshly squeezed orange juice. The boys were poetry in motion and hadn't even realised that Kostas had already left for Corfu Town to get the items required for the lunch and evening services. The group of walkers left a generous tip and then left Dafnata to enjoy another wonderful day along The Corfu Trail.

Kostas had now returned with bags and boxes of fresh produce from the open market and just in time to have missed the morning clean down. The boys quickly got on with sorting the now vacant rooms out and were then released from their duties to enjoy a quiet and relaxing walk around the village.

"Max my friend, did you ever imagine anything like this? I know what you're capable of and you never shy away from a new challenge but come on dude, what the fuck has happened here?"

"I've no idea Charlie but whatever is happening, it works for me mate and I really don't want to give it up."

"You're seriously thinking about staying aren't you? Look mate, it's okay with me, honestly. And if my situation was different or the children were older, I'd be thinking the same."

"This place feels more like home by the day and the thought of returning to England to drive a van around some of the shittiest places you can imagine makes my stomach turn."

"Come on Max, let's go this way and check out the view."

After a short climb which started at the red telephone box, Max and Charlie reached the famous Dafnata view point. From here they could see Mount Pantokrator and the fortresses at Corfu Town. Benitses looked as pretty as a picture from up there and again, Kostas wasn't wrong when he said that his village offered the best views of his beloved island. They wandered back down the hill and spent some time with Kostas planning the day ahead before jumping on the bus to Benitses. Max and Charlie had a couple of hours to kill before they were required back at the taverna and decided to check out the yachts in Benitses Marina. Max was still fascinated by these floating beauties but for now, he was more than happy with his life on Corfu and maybe owning one would be something he'd look at if he ever got bored of life on the island.

Having served breakfast at Kostas Place but not having had the time to feed themselves, Charlie suggested that they grab some food from one of the many cafes which made up the vast selection of places to visit along the strip, "This place looks smart Max, how about here?"

"Looks great Charlie and I could eat a horse. It's hard work in hospitality but really rewarding when the guests leave with smiles on their faces, like the walkers this morning."

"They were a good bunch mate and no spring chickens either. Still going for it in their golden years, fair play to them."

"Absolutely and their tip from this morning will easily cover the cost of our breakfast."

"So where are you meeting Steffi on Friday? Have you got that far yet?"

"Yes mate, we're meeting at Sunshine Bar and it's just up the road from here."

"What do reckon she's got to say?"

"I've no idea mate!"

Kostas drove down the hill to Benitses to pick up his staff and ferried them back to work. He advised the boys that another group of walkers would soon be arriving and they were expecting a traditional Greek lunch. Between the three of them, they put on a spread which was fit for Greek Royalty and took care of the groups every need and request. Kostas Place was now running like a well oiled machine, the warm and sunny days were flying by and soon, another Friday on the island of Corfu very quickly came around. Kostas gave Max a lift into Benitses and told him to call him when he needed picking up. Max was unusually quiet in the car and Kostas had picked up on this, "You quiet this evening Max, you okay?

"I'm okay Kostas, I've just got a big decision to make and although I think I know what I want, a little part of me is telling me otherwise."

"Women Max, bloody women! They complicate and mess with our heads but you Max, you must follow your heart and hope the woman follow you."

"That's the plan Kostas but what if she doesn't follow me and I end up on my own."

"Then you fucked Max and you start again or leave the girls alone."

Kostas dropped Max just a short walk away from Sunshine Bar and he then nervously made his way up the road to meet up with Steffi. Steffi had already arrived and was sat at a table for two looking as beautiful as ever but also with a deadly serious look on her face. She took a sip of her orange juice and stood up to greet Max as he approached her. She stretched out her tanned and slender arms and welcomed Max with a gentle embrace. For some strange reason, Max found the atmosphere between the two of them tense and unusually awkward but decided to break the ice with a well deserved compliment, "Steffi, you're looking as beautiful as ever and it's great to see you again. How's your time on Corfu been?"

"It's been wonderful Max. Bex and I have been everywhere, all the places you told us to go. Even the old village in the mountains. How was your hike? And I guess I should say congratulations."

"It was fabulous Steffi! I made a few cock ups along the way and stressed a few people out by not thinking straight but that's in the past now and it's time to move on."

"I've missed you Max and I never stopped thinking about you whilst you were on your walk."

"Look Steffi, I've also been doing a lot of thinking and I was wondering if you and I could..."

"Please Max! Let me stop you there. Max, I'm pregnant and I must return to Germany to have my baby. My life will continue in Germany and if you get your way, your life will continue here, on Corfu. It's what you've always dreamt of Max and I can't be the one who shatters your dreams. I love you too much to do that to you."

"But Steffi, I don't understand. How? What? I'm really confused now."

"Max my beautiful Max, I will always love you and remember you but we have to say goodbye now."

"I'm sorry Steffi but I have to ask you this. Do you know who the father is?"

"Yes Max, I do and I must go now. Please, look after yourself Max."

Max was now left looking into the bottom of an empty beer glass and wasn't totally sure as to what had just happened to him. Just when he thought that all the confusion and uncertainty in his life was about to come to an end, a brand new and even more dramatic chapter had just been written by a girl who he would never forget. Steffi wasn't wrong though. Max had no desire to live in Germany and why should he assume that Steffi would want to settle down and raise a family on Corfu. Max sank another beer and a couple of shots and asked Kostas to come and pick him up. Max needed to take his mind off what Steffi had just told him and the best way to do that was to get back to work with Charlie at Kostas Place.

Charlie was rushed off his feet at the taverna but still found the time to check with his mate that everything was okay and he was in the right frame of mind to get back to work, "So Max, everything okay? Anything I need to know?"
"Well it wasn't exactly what I was expecting but apart from one little mystery, everything is fine Charlie and you'll be pleased to know that I'm very soon going to get my girl."
"Bravo Max! These plates are for table six, table four want the bill and table five are waiting for two more beers."

After another successful evening service was declared a wrap, Max and Charlie sat in their usual spot outside the taverna and chatted over a couple of well deserved beers. Max told Charlie what he needed to know about him and Steffi and how it was actually Steffi who decided on their future and not him. Again, Charlie told Max to embrace his

374

love of Corfu and his evident desire to at least stay a while longer or maybe even indefinitely. Max gave Charlie credit where it was due and assured him that he would nail it as a restaurateur if only he could sort his finances and staffing issues out. The following day, another plane would leave Teeside Airport and on this particular flight would be Kat, Megan and Lucy. The loose plan the girls had made to visit Kostas and the boys at his place on Sunday was now a firm plan and a time of four o'clock had been agreed.

As the girls stepped off the plane and into another warm Corfu evening, Max and Charlie were serving the remaining guests before clearing down yet again. With fun, sunshine and Charlie on her mind Megan was the first to comment on how bizarre life could be and how good things can happen when you're least expecting it, "Do you not think it's crazy? I'm really excited about meeting someone I've never met before and as for you Kat, you were expecting to see Max again back in London. What about you Lucy?"

"Well Megan, I'm just glad to be away with you two and not flogging advertising to failing businessman. That'll do me nicely thank you very much."

"I reckon we'll have just enough time for a round or two of cocktails before bed. Lucy, Megan are you in?"

"Absolutely Kat!"

Tomorrow, Max would be reunited with Kat after many weeks apart and Charlie would get to meet Megan for the first time. Lucy would obviously be catwalk ready and looking as stunning as usual, despite the fact that she'd finally given up on men and looking for love. But before this beautiful and truly awesome bunch of individuals can each start writing their own happy endings, Max and Charlie had one more breakfast and lunch service to prepare for and the girls would need to endure a typical Corfu taxi experience.

Kostas had no guests staying Sunday evening. So after lunch was finished and everything tidied away, he'd decided to close his taverna to the public so that Max and Charlie, Kat, Megan and Lucy could all enjoy their time together without waiting on tables and cooking food in the kitchen. A few friends from the village were also allowed to join the party but that was it. This was a very special gathering of people who Kostas had got to know incredibly well and a few who he was about to meet for the first time. Shortly after four o'clock, a spotlessly clean Mercedes taxi pulled up outside the taverna as if it were dropping off celebrities at the end of a red carpet. Lucy had been riding up front with the taxi driver and certainly wasn't waiting for him to open her door. She was first out the taxi, closely followed by Kat and Megan and soon they were met by Kostas.

"Beautiful ladies! Welcome to Kostas Place and welcome to Dafnata, our beautiful village. You looking for boys, yes?"

"Hello Kostas, I'm Lucy. I'm not looking for boys but I do know two girls who are."

"Come Lucy, come girls, boys and drinks are inside and other friends from the village join us soon."

"Max, Max! Spare the stories and get yourself over here, right now!"

"Kat, it's been too long, way too long. Look at you, all dressed up and ready for long hot days in the sunshine."

"You must be Charlie, my superhero?"

"Well I've never been called a superhero before but I'll take that all day long. You must be Megan?"

"That's right but you can call me Megs. Let's gets some drinks in, I'm gasping!"

"Max! You're needed behind the bar, Megan's gasping for a drink."

Despite Kostas giving Max and Charlie the afternoon and evening off, he just couldn't stop them from doing what they now loved to do and it was as if they wanted to prove to the girls that guys can and will happily wait tables and run a catering kitchen. Max made sure that everyone had a drink in hand and every table was immediately cleared and cleaned. Charlie knocked up a meza of Greek and Mediterranean delights and ordered Max and Kostas to present it perfectly on the long table at the end of the bar.

"You look like you're enjoying yourself Max?"

"I love it Kat and I love it here!"

"Can I see what you're doing in the kitchen Charlie?"

"Sure, but remember, this is my kitchen now. So no touching!"

Kostas interrupted the gathering to let everyone know that in an hour they would all be leaving for Benitses to enjoy Sunday dinner at Vana's Family Taverna and his rooms were open if anyone wanted to take a shower or get changed. Charlie took a break from working in his kitchen and led Megan by the hand and up the short hill to enjoy the magnificent views together. Max and Kat wandered off in the opposite direction to explore the village together and while doing so, Max would show her where The Corfu Trail entered Dafnata and he would tell her just how tired he was at that point. Kat told Max all about Fabio's plan to send her back up North and how her refusing to agree led to her being let go. Max reminded Kat that it was only a job and used himself as a fine example to prove to her that there were new opportunities everywhere, all you had to do was open your eyes and look for them. Megan told Charlie about her mum, her brother and her troubled past and Charlie listened to her like a child would listen to their favourite story being read.

"So Max, how are you going to write the next chapter of your life? Does it include Corfu and do I feature in it?"

"This is what we need to talk about Kat. What do you want to happen in the next chapter?"

"I want us to be the happy ending Max and I want us to feature in the follow up."

"Do you think you could find your happy ending here, on Corfu?"

"I'm willing to give it a go but what would we do for work?"

"There'll be a vacancy or two at the taverna soon."

"So Charlie, now you've completed your Mission Impossible and safely returned the asset to his girl, what next?"

"I'm not totally sure Megan but I was working on opening my own cafe or bistro back in England but I'm struggling to make the numbers stack up at the moment. The cost of hiring staff is ridiculous."

"I can be cheap Charlie. Not cheap as in easy but cheap to hire, you know what I mean."

"Really, are you being serious about this Megan?"

"Why not? I think we'd be good together, in business that is but never say never."

"What about your job at Fisher Developments? Won't you miss it?"

"It's just a job and it's certainly not something I'm in love with."

By the time Max and Kat, Charlie and Megan and everyone else who was part of this exclusive gathering were all back in the bar and ready to go, a small fleet of taxis were already waiting to ferry the revellers down the steep hill to Benitses. Lucy had spent most of her time talking to Kostas about her love life, or complete lack of it, and Kostas kept telling her that she needed to find herself a real man, a Greek man. One who would treat her like a goddess and not a trophy to be displayed around town after a winning match day. Lucy listened on hopefully while Kostas continued to sell the features and benefits of Greek men and the importance of having the time to spend with your loved one.

Shortly after seven o'clock, everyone was seated at a long table which had been specially prepared by the owners of the taverna. Kostas took the seat at the head of the table while the other guests grouped together in pairs or by some sort of family connection. Lucy was sat opposite Kat and next to an unoccupied chair which would soon be taken by a guest who was running a few minutes late, "Kostas, who are we waiting for?"

"My friend, he running late again. He busy man Lucy but a good man."

"Okay! Is he sitting next to me?"

"Yes and he here now. Lucy, this is my dear friend Vasilis."

"Lucy, Vasilis Panayiatou and its lovely to meet you."

With the guests all now present and seated at the grand table, the nonstop conveyor belt of food and drink began. Starters from around the island and main dishes which had been cooked in exactly the same way for generations. This very special table offered a truly exceptional array of tastes and smells and according to Vasilis, this was one of the best restaurants on the island and he clearly knew what he was talking about.

"So Vasilis, tell me what you do on Corfu."

"I own hotels Lucy. The best hotels on the island and in all the best locations. Paleokastritsa, Liapades Beach, Kassiopi and in Corfu Town."

"Wow! How amazing. I don't think we've staying at any of them."

"That's a shame but if you like and your friends are happy to lose you for a day or two, I'll give you a tour of my hotels and our beautiful island."

"I'd love that Vasilis and anyway, I think my friends are going to be busy with the boys for a while."

"Wonderful! We can take my boat, it's here in Benitses Marina."

After a fantastic evening in Benitses and in the company of some truly wonderful people, everyone was ready to retire to their rooms, hotels or village houses. Kostas, his staff and his guests returned to his taverna with Kat and Megan now in tow. Lucy had decided to go for after dinner drinks with Vasilis and after a quick drink at Kostas Place, his friends from the village made their way home. Kostas was now curious as to everyone's intentions but was also concerned that he may be about to lose his helpers.

"So boys, now you have your girls, what next for you?"

"I've had an amazing time Kostas and as much as I'd love to stay, I have to consider my children. They're still young and they need me around. So I'll be leaving shortly but I'm definitely going to open my own cafe now and it looks like I've found some cheap staff or maybe even a partner. You know, business partner."

"That is wonderful Charlie and I think your partner is Megan, yes?"

"Yes Kostas, I think Charlie and I will be good for each other."

Kat looked across at Megan knowing all too well where this story was going and how it was going to end. She gave her a smile and a look which was full of encouragement and she knew it wouldn't be long before Charlie was asking Max if it was okay for Megan to move in.

"Max, missing Max and Charlie's pain in the arse, what do you do now?"

Well Kostas, if Charlie's leaving soon, I'm guessing there's a job or two going at your place?"

"But what about your girl Max? You just got her back and now you lose her again? You fucking crazy Max!"

381

"No Kostas, Max is not the crazy one, that'll be me. Max and I have talked things through and as long as we can find some work and a place to live, we're now going to write some chapters together, here on Corfu."

"You work here with me, you both work here and I have a house for you. It was our family house, old and need some fixing up but it doable. Is on the hill near Makrata village and it has a bloody lovely view over Benitses and to the sea."

Charlie nodded at Max in approval and raised his glass to toast and celebrate an evening where new chapters were about to be written and all with happy endings. As for Lucy, well she'd just messaged Kat with the words 'I think I'm in love with Vasilis and if it's okay with you, I'll see you in the morning'.

The island of Corfu had once again worked its magic and now there was only one thing left to say…

Yamas!

Made in the USA
Monee, IL
21 July 2025

21192551R00225